# CODE PINK!

## Also by Charles Clark

Trails to Dos Encinos

Return to Dos Encinos

Suit Up in Scrubs

Dark Side Hospital

# CODE PINK!

**A Novel by
Charles Clark**

iUniverse, Inc.
New York  Lincoln  Shanghai

# CODE PINK!

Copyright © 2007 by Charles Clark

All rights reserved. No part of this book may be used or reproduced by any means, graphic, electronic, or mechanical, including photocopying, recording, taping or by any information storage retrieval system without the written permission of the publisher except in the case of brief quotations embodied in critical articles and reviews.

iUniverse books may be ordered through booksellers or by contacting:

iUniverse
2021 Pine Lake Road, Suite 100
Lincoln, NE 68512
www.iuniverse.com
1-800-Authors (1-800-288-4677)

This is a work of fiction. All of the characters, names, incidents, organizations, and dialogue in this novel are either the products of the author's imagination or are used fictitiously.

ISBN-13: 978-0-595-41553-3 (pbk)
ISBN-13: 978-0-595-67918-8 (cloth)
ISBN-13: 978-0-595-85900-9 (ebk)
ISBN-10: 0-595-41553-9 (pbk)
ISBN-10: 0-595-67918-8 (cloth)
ISBN-10: 0-595-85900-3 (ebk)

Printed in the United States of America

To my wife, Joyce

# Acknowledgements

My sincere thanks to the following for their invaluable assistance:

Janis Graham Jack, United States District Judge

Ben F. McDonald, Jr., Esq., Attorney

Jeanene Anthony, Associate Administrator Corpus Christi Medical Center

Beth Barham and her friends at the Dallas Police Department

Jack Peterson, Consultant, Peterson and Associates

Kay Clark, graphic artist

Danny Clark Photography

# 1

## Dallas, Texas

Leanne Joberst slowly opened one eye and stared at the clock on the bedside table. At this late hour, Anthony had probably already left for his office. Good. She wouldn't have to face him this morning. She closed her eyes again and concentrated on harnessing the memory neurons in the higher centers of her brain, trying to reconstruct the events of the night before. She and Anthony had gone to the art museum fund raiser—a dinner and dance attended by elite Highland Park socialites. She recalled that she had bid on something and won—what was it? Then she remembered: a Ming Dynasty vase. The bidding had started at five thousand and she had kept bidding, determined to win, until the auctioneer dropped his gavel at fifteen thousand—her winning bid.

She climbed out of bed and stood still for a moment to gain enough sense of equilibrium to walk without falling. The same nausea she'd experienced every morning lately sent her stumbling into the bathroom, where once again she heaved from an empty stomach. Until now she'd thought that her stomach was upset due to the stress of her unhappy marriage. She had read about stress causing ulcers.

"God knows I have a stressful marriage," she said aloud. "Maybe this time it is from the alcohol." She had had far too much to drink—wine before and with dinner, and then several vodka on the rocks at the nightclub that she, Anthony, and several other couples had visited after the event.

Her head pounded as she crawled back into her bed. She lay on her back and stared at the ceiling while thoughts whirled through her mind. As the fog cleared from her sensorium she remembered more about the night. She and Mark Marchesa had danced almost every dance, both at the gala and later at the club. It was there that the pulp media photographers had followed their every move and had taken picture after picture in spite of their protests.

She had wondered why Anthony hadn't stepped in. Mark finally had to offer the photographers a couple of hundred-dollar bills each so they would leave. As usual, Anthony—oblivious to all else—had gathered with a group of his cronies at a corner table for conversation and drinks. As far as she knew, he had never even once noticed her dancing with Mark. When rock music played they flailed arms, legs, and torsos to the beat of the rhythm. Then when slow music played they held each other close, their bodies melded into one, and glided across the dance floor. Thoughts of dancing with Mark brought back memories of their fabulous month together in Monaco—hardly two months earlier.

They had decided to end the affair after returning to Dallas; last night had been their first time together since. Being with Mark had rekindled her feelings for him. She cared deeply for Mark and was miserable to be married to someone whom she despised. Why had she ever married Anthony? He was older than she, they had no common interests, and they certainly subscribed to different values. He was the most cruel, insensitive person she had ever known. The fragments of Anthony's conversations with his business acquaintances were enough to tell her that he could be ruthless with anyone who crossed him.

Their relationship had been sexless from the very first, due to a total lack of libido on Anthony's part. Leanne even suspected some sort of sexual aberrancy between Anthony and some of his associates, but she couldn't define it. He frequently made unexplained, extended "business" trips, quite often with his attorney, Richard Weatherford.

But Richard Weatherford was an icon in the Dallas social world. He was considered an exemplary husband and father of his two daughters. Tall, masculine, athletic build—there was never anything about Richard that would lead to a doubt of his sexuality.

Leanne couldn't complain about Anthony's frequent out of town trips, however, since they gave her free time to be with Mark. Ever since they had decided not to see each other, her life had been empty. Considering the evening before, she was now ready to rescind their agreement to stay apart. She hoped Mark felt the same way.

She blamed her father for encouraging her to marry Anthony. On the surface, her father's only interest had appeared to be his daughter's welfare and social status. Being the wife of Judge Anthony Joberst would keep her in the social circle in which she belonged and sustain the prestigious lifestyle to which she had become accustomed. But from the comments Leanne had heard, she now knew that her father had seen the marriage of his daughter with Judge Joberst as a healthy move for his own interests. A federal judge in the family! What could be better for business?

But Leanne couldn't blame anyone but herself for her unhappy existence. She could have refused to marry Anthony, but she had watched so many of her friends marry—with elaborate weddings and receptions—and she had reached an age when she had to make a move toward marriage if she ever intended to. She laughed at her earlier fears that she would be labeled an "old maid." She knew now that she just had wanted a wedding, not a marriage—an elaborate affair that would dwarf anything that any of her friends had planned. How stupid she had been. Every day that passed since the wedding, she grew more certain that she had made a mistake. She should never have married Anthony. And worse was the realization that there didn't seem to be any way out without scorching embarrassment or the risk of serious consequences.

She and Mark had discussed her leaving to spend her life with him, but they were reluctant to take that step too soon. Anthony would seek retribution against Mark—probably against his hospital corporation. As a federal judge, he would find a way to harm Mark. She knew how ruthless he could be; he would kill to protect his image. Being with Mark again—feeling her passion enflame—reinforced her belief that she and Mark belonged together, whatever the risk. However, they would have to wait for the opportune time.

Leanne rolled over on her stomach, but the move seemed to trigger more nausea and an even more severe headache. It would be impossible to go back to sleep, so she again pulled herself from the bed and stood. Her head seemed much clearer as she walked around the room and gazed out the large floor-to-ceiling windows. She remembered how, as a child, she would sit for hours watching the wind-driven cumulous clouds—puffs much like those she was watching now—take the shapes of animals and other identifiable objects. She wished she felt more like enjoying the fabulous view from their twenty-third-story luxury condominium. She had to face it: she felt horrible.

She had learned from experience that she could tolerate frequent small meals of toast, ginger ale, and dry cereal without becoming nauseous, so she targeted the kitchen pantry and refrigerator for relief. Although she felt better after eating, she still postponed her daily five-mile jog on the winding path through the wooded grounds around the condo.

Back in the bathroom, she stepped on the scales. Her weight flashed on the digital screen: 108 pounds—another pound added to her usual 104. She looked at the mirrored walls and assessed her figure. Beyond question, she was putting on weight. Maybe she needed to watch her diet more carefully. Her clothes felt tight and uncomfortable and now she was sure that she could see swelling in her thighs and abdomen. The sensation was much like the one she felt a few days before a menstrual period. She stopped and thought for a moment: a menstrual period! My God! She couldn't remember when she had menstruated last. It was not unusual for her to be irregular, however. Her gynecologist had told her that it was normal for women who exercised vigorously to miss periods. Sure ... that explained it. Running the track every day was her stress outlet since she had married Anthony. She used the time to think and to plan. Maybe she had overdone the exercise.

She dressed in her gym clothes, headed for the terrace floor of the condo, and entered the elaborate salon. A few minutes in the sauna and a body massage might make her feel better—and she would treat herself to a manicure and pedicure while she was there. Dripping wet, she stepped out of the sauna cabinet, dried, donned a loose-fitting robe, and sat at the juice and vitamin bar to wait her turn with the masseuse. She picked up a copy of *Woman's World* and scanned the index of articles. Her hands shook and her heart pounded. The cover story headline jumped off the page and glared at her: *Don't Let Morning Sickness Cripple You*. The recommendation was ginger ale with dry toast and frequent small meals.

"Oh, no!" she cried out. She jumped to her feet, belted her robe, bolted out of the salon, and took the express elevator to her floor. Once home, she curled up in her favorite chair and waited until her breathing and heart rate calmed.

*My God! How could I have been so dense?*

She closed her eyes and tried to collect her thoughts. How could it have happened? She had been so careful, had taken her pills every day.

*Monaco.*

When they went to Monaco, she had accidentally left her OC pack at home. She remembered laughing when she told Mark that she hoped Anthony found them while she was gone. But Mark knew she was not protected. "I'll take care of it," he had said.

Now what? She and Mark had agreed not see each other again for a while. Being together last evening had changed all of that as far as she was concerned. Should she tell Mark what she suspected? His responsibility with the hospital was a heavy enough burden without adding this unexpected discovery. She would seek an abortion; that was the only answer. But what would Mark say? Was there any chance that they could raise their child together?

Anthony would be furious when he found out and would use every means possible to block her being with Mark. There was no question about the identity of the father; she and Anthony had never shared the same bed.

She reminisced about her wedding to Anthony. He wanted a wealthy trophy wife and she wanted a wedding. They both got what they wanted. She had not wanted a pregnancy, however, certainly not while Anthony was her husband.

She paced around the room, picked up the phone a couple of times, and then re-cradled it without dialing Mark's number. Mark deserved to know—she had to tell him—although she had no idea what his reaction would be. There was only one way to find out, she finally decided. She dialed his cell phone, still not sure if she wanted him to answer it. After only two rings, she heard his voice.

"Mark Marchesa here."

"Mark, it's me," she said. "I need to talk with you."

"Hi," he said. "I was just thinking about you. I'm in a meeting next door. Can it wait?"

"No, it can't," she replied, struggling to keep her voice from cracking.

"Something's happened," said Mark. "Where are you?"

"I'll be in the parking lot at the country club."

"I'll be right there."

\* \* \* \*

Leanne arrived first and parked as far away from the entrance as possible. Mark soon joined her.

"What is it?" he said when he saw her swollen face, wet from tears. "Has he hurt you?"

"No, it's not that," she said, sobbing as she grasped his hand and held it to her chest. "I don't know how to tell you." She stared out the window for a few silent seconds and then turned back. "Mark, promise me you'll be honest with me."

"Of course I will," he said. He stroked her cheeks to wipe away the tears. "I love you. I will always be honest with you."

"We have a decision to make."

"What's happened?" he asked. "Look, there's nothing we can't whip together."

Leanne was quiet. How to begin?

"Mark, I think I might be pregnant."

Mark didn't wince, as Leanne had feared. His dark eyes became misty, his face blossomed into an affectionate smile, and he pulled her close for a kiss.

"Are you sure?" he asked.

"I have every symptom. How could it have happened, Mark? We have been so cautious."

Mark kept smiling. "Except once," he said. "Do you remember the night that we went skinny-dipping at midnight at the beach house pool?"

Leanne jolted to attention. "Yes ... yes I do," she said. She wiped her cheeks and chuckled. "Contraception was not on our minds that night."

"We do have some planning to do," said Mark, grinning gleefully. "Accelerated planning."

"Mark ..." She gazed firmly into his eyes as she spoke. "Do you want me to have an abortion?"

"Do you want to have an abortion?" he replied, the sparkle gone from his eyes.

"I want to have your baby, Mark," she said, "even if you don't want me to. I could never bring myself to do otherwise. I don't want to embarrass you or do anything to harm your company ... but ... no ... I don't want to lose this baby."

"Then we agree. My life with you and our baby is the most important thing in the world to me—far more important that anything else."

"I have no idea what Anthony will do when he finds out," she said. "One thing's for sure: he will not want the world to know that the baby isn't his."

"Then we wait to make our move—unless he does something to harm you or the baby."

"Don't underestimate his power, Mark."

"We'll tread cautiously," he said. "The first thing we need to do is confirm that you are pregnant." Mark laughed and added, "And if you are not, maybe we had better start seeing to it that you are."

Leanne laughed. "The first laugh I've had today. I'll pick up a home-testing kit."

"We'll do the test together," said Mark.

*    *    *    *

With sober faces that reflected their mounting tension they carefully unwrapped the kit and read the directions. No sooner had the drop of urine hit the testing strip than the bright blue color appeared—a positive result. They both remained silent for a few moments, staring at the strip, and then looked into each other's eyes even longer. Their faces became radiant with the realization that their lives would change and that they were committed to each other regardless of any peril that lay ahead.

# 2

*Dallas ... seven months later*

Andrew M. Goldeyer held the envelope up to the light hoping to see the word "accepted" or "congratulations" instead of the dreaded "We regret to inform you ..."

How many times would he have to go through this agony? Most of the applications had required a full middle name. For some reason, the rejections all seemed to be the ones where he'd entered "Mordecai." Maybe he just imagined it.

Three more months of classroom curriculum and study and he would be eligible to receive his master's degree in Hospital Administration from Southern Methodist University in Dallas. But first he had to serve a one-year residency in an accredited hospital. Fortunately, during his tour of duty in the hospital, he would be gainfully employed for the first time since he'd begun his career in healthcare management.

So far, all of his applications to hospitals in the state had been rejected. In spite of his excellent scholastic record, no hospital seemed interested in accepting him for a position as an administrative resident. Even more frustrating, most of his classmates had already found openings.

Maybe this reply would be different. Trinitus Medical Center Westlake had an opening for an administrative intern. He had excellent referrals from the school, and this position would fit his plan to finish his training by working in a non-profit hospital. He had heard horrendous accounts of unscrupulous dealings by for-profit hospitals and had decided early on that he wanted no part of any entity that profited from the health care of a community's ill and injured.

What would he tell Barbara if he was turned down this time? She had been working as a pool nurse, pulling night duty in any hospital in Dallas that might need her, to support them while he had been in school. He fumbled with the letter opener, dropped it once, and then with tremulous hands and pounding heart carefully opened the envelope. His eyes dropped below the salutation to the body of the letter. His face exploded in a grin, and like a victorious athlete, he threw both arms into the air and let out a whoop.

"I made it!" he screamed. "Barbara, come here! I made it! Trinitus Medical Center Westlake accepted me!"

Interrupted from dressing for work, Barbara ran into the room partially clad. "I never doubted that you would get this one," she said as she tousled his dark, wavy locks of hair and threw her arms around him. "Now I need to see what nursing positions might be available in Westlake next year. Wouldn't it be great if we both could work in the Trinitus system there?"

"Yeah, maybe you can find a job in the nursery," he replied.

"I should be able to get some references from the Trinitus hospital here. I've worked there off and on during the last two years. Maybe I can get assigned to a neonate intensive care unit! I hope they have a training program at Trinitus Westlake. Then I can get certified as a NICU nurse. It's so exciting, Andy!"

"You haven't mentioned one advantage if I get a paying job." He laughed, grabbed Barbara's petite frame around the waist, and lifted her from the floor. He twirled her around the room as her feet dangled in air. "We can start planning a nursery of our own."

"Andy, don't think I haven't thought of that." She gave him a sloppy kiss and slid out of his arms. "Right now I've got to hurry to work. Still a lot of heavy traffic out there with people rushing home at the end of the day."

"The first thing I want you to do is give up these night shifts."

"I promise," she replied. "We have so much planning to do—look for housing, think about packing and moving. We need to start putting money away for the move. And I know you will want to go visit the hospital in Westlake. The weeks pass so fast, you know—"

"I know, I know: *We can't wait 'til the last minute.*"

"Okay, so I'm obsessive-compulsive. Could be worse," she said. She waved him off and laughed, scurrying back to the bedroom in their small apartment to finish dressing. "I'm not sure I'm ready for this change—I've gotten so used to you being a 'house husband.' By the way, you need to help me change the sheets and turn the mattress in the morning—and if you have time, please vacuum the carpet and clean the bathrooms."

"Right now I have time for anything, but I just vacuumed yesterday," he retorted.

"But I saw some crumbs in front of the TV," she said as she climbed into her clean, pressed white pants and donned a colorful scrub top.

"I'll be more careful."

He laughed, wondering if taking care of newborns all day made her so obsessed with cleanliness. They would have a super-sterile environment for a baby, if they ever had one. He grinned at the thought. As Barbara said, "could be worse."

Barbara finished cleaning and whitening her shoes, grabbed her make-up kit, headed for the door (which Andy held open for her), gave him one last kiss, and ran.

Moments later, she crashed back through the door and swept a pink identification badge off the counter.

"Forget my ID."

"Be careful in the parking lot. It's already dark at seven."

"You worry too much. Love you!" she yelled as she hurried back out the door.

\* \* \* \*

Barbara Goldeyer drove her fourteen-year-old VW Bug into the parking area. She found an empty spot close to the employee entrance to the four-story Women's Pavilion—a part of the gigantic Trinitus Medical Center Dallas—and parked, hoping her faithful "chariot" would start again the next morning. If the well-seasoned VW held together for a while longer, maybe they could afford a new car.

With her ID card in hand, she made her way through the packed parking lot toward the security check-in station. The same beat-up-looking gray van—parked in the fifteen-minute zone every evening lately—blocked her way, forcing her to detour. The van always appeared driverless, but each time she passed it she had a weird feeling that someone was watching her. Certainly nothing to worry about that close to the security guardhouse.

She swiped in and glanced at the clock—6:50 PM. A few minutes early, but within allowable range. Five minutes earlier and the hospital would have to pay her for a fraction of an hour, and then the nursery supervisor, Wilda (the Witch) Witcher, would admonish her and write-up a report that would go in her folder. She wondered if all Trinitus hospitals were as stern with policy. Probably it was not the hospital, just the "Witch."

Barbara could never understand why Wilda didn't like her. As far as she knew she had never done anything to offend Wilda. Occasionally she had joined the others in the break room when they all made joking comments about Wilda's dumpy physique and waddling gait. But surely Wilda had not heard the remarks, so they couldn't be grounds for the treatment she dished out.

Barbara welcomed Andy's news that they would be moving to Westlake soon. She would get away, finally, from Wilda's beady-eyed surveillance every time she worked at Trinitus. Wilda watched over her every move, always finding fault with her work, usually over trivial issues. She never seemed to reprove the other nurses—not as often, anyway.

If she could just complete her training in neonatal intensive care, she could become a certified NICU nurse and receive exempt status. Then she wouldn't have to swipe in. She would be salaried and treated like a trained health professional instead of a nursemaid who did nothing more than change diapers, hold bottles, and transport newborns to their mothers. Such a waste of her talent!

She changed into a clean nursery-pink gown, donned shoe covers and a hair net, and entered the restricted sanitary report room to find that she had arrived ahead of everyone else. One by one, the others drifted in. The day shift could be identified easily by their weary appearance, wrinkled clothing, their tousled hair caused by wearing a hair net for twelve hours.

Each with a note pad, the nurses gathered around an oblong table to review each newborn's chart for any status variances from normal. Was the baby alert? Were the temperature, respiration, heart rate, skin color, muscle tone, and nursing reflex within normal range? As always, a few not-so-complimentary remarks about the attending pediatricians were tossed about, usually triggering a roar of laughter.

Within the report given by the day-duty nurses to the oncoming nursing staff were notations regarding time of last bedside feeding by the mothers. The exact location of each infant, right at the time of the report, had to be confirmed by both exiting nursing staff and the incoming night-duty nurses. All the babies should have been tucked in their cribs at that time, none of them out with mothers. As always, many were asking with loud cries to be taken out again.

"Oh, Barbara, I forgot to tell you," said day-duty nurse Jodie Abrams after report was finished and everyone was readying to leave the room, "we have a VIP baby in your assigned nursery unit. Born this morning. The mama is the wife of Federal Judge Anthony Joberst. Big-time publicity—TV station reporters and photographers all over the place.

"Is that the older judge who married the twenty-eight-year-old heir to some fortune?"

"Yeah, that's him. She's one of two heirs to the Blanton fortune. You remember the hype—*People* magazine and the tabloids raising questions about the fatherhood. Seems Mrs. Joberst had an affair going with some guy about the time she got pregnant. The lab has already done a DNA on the baby today, at the judge's request, to squelch the rumors. Front-page stuff! Wish I could stay around and watch."

"You're welcome to pull my shift," said Barbara. Looking at Jodie's disheveled appearance, she knew what the answer would be.

"No thanks! I couldn't stand a shift with the Witch hanging over me every minute, like she does you."

"So, you've noticed it too. It's not just my imagination then, is it?"

"No, it's pretty obvious. I think it's because you're pretty and she's so bug-ugly. She's envious."

"She makes me so nervous. I'm in constant fear of making a mistake."

"Oh, I almost forgot to tell you," said Jodie. "The Joberst mama is a bitch. Don't let her get to you."

"What do you mean?"

"She's haughty, demanding, ungrateful, orders you around like a maid-servant."

"Is she nursing the baby?"

"Nah. Says she's gonna try, but you can tell right off she's not going to. Already complaining about the discomfort, won't do anything you tell her to do. She had a Cesarean. You'd think she had major brain surgery. Rumor has it she demanded the Cesarean so she wouldn't have to go through labor and she didn't want her twat torn up by vaginal delivery."

"Sounds like this is going to be a challenging night."

"You can handle it," said Jodie. "Also, don't be alarmed about the armed guard outside her room."

"What's that all about?"

"The judge says it's for security—since he is a federal judge. But everyone says it's to keep her boyfriend away. They even have the telephones blocked. No incoming or outgoing calls."

"The poor girl is a prisoner!"

"Virtually, yes."

"Does she have any family?"

"The record shows only a sister as next of kin. She lives in California. The sisters have feuded ever since the parents died—about money of course. As far as we know she has had no visitors. No family or friends, not even her husband."

"How sad," said Barbara. "She must be terribly lonely. Even with her money she has no one to share her happiness with. I would give anything to have a baby, Jodie. I guess that's why I enjoy working in a nursery."

"Why don't you have one? Or just take one of these." Jodie laughed and then frowned. "Some mothers would like to give 'em away."

"As soon as Andy gets a job, we plan to start a family."

"Not for me. I see enough of these little bastards right here. Hope all goes well tonight," she called out as she left the report room, shelling out of her sterile garb as she exited. Before the door completely closed, she re-entered. "Oh, I forgot to tell you. The babies have no electronic ankle tags. Administration says stop using them, probably because they are too expensive. Don't think they're necessary anyway. Nobody's gonna take a baby and go down the elevator."

# 3

After gloving, Barbara checked each of the six babies under her care. All but two or three were asleep, and those awake were squirming around in their bassinets purposelessly, waving their tiny clinched fists in the air, their eyes wide open and roving as if looking for a familiar face. She checked each bar-coded name bracelet and greeted each awake baby in a cooing voice.

Remembering what Jodie said about the judge's wife being demanding, she picked up the Joberst baby first and placed it on the padded treatment table to make it presentable for its mother. She could tell from the overflowing soiled linen cart parked near the exit door that the table covering had been left clean, but she hated seeing the cart left in the nursery with dirty linen. Surely the night shift housekeeping person would be by soon to drag the cart to the laundry room.

Barbara undressed the Joberst baby, cleansed its skin of some of the remaining white gummy substance from the birth, inspected the umbilical cord for bleeding, and changed its diaper. In the baby's chart, she noted the presence of a dime-size port-wine birthmark on the neck, behind his left ear—certainly nothing to worry about. A beautiful baby boy! What a shame that there was no proud father, grandparent, or friend standing outside the nursery gazing through the view windows.

She carefully cleaned the infant's scalp and then, using a soft bristle brush, combed his fine-textured, silky black hair into a part. By the time she tied a tiny blue bow in his hair, "Mr. Joberst" let the world know he was ready to be fed. She cuddled him for a few moments until he stopped crying, all the while gazing lovingly at the tiny child. Out of the corner of her eye, she noticed the "Witch" watching through the window from the adjacent nursery unit.

Barbara carefully replaced the infant, once again asleep, in the mobile bassinet and wheeled the crib through the exit door and into the corridor toward the mother's suite in the VIP wing. A short distance down the hall, she could see the unsmiling guard standing stiffly by the door. He took one look at the sleeping baby and nodded. She checked the identification card in the slot on the door. It read, "Leanne Blanton Joberst." Barbara first tapped lightly and then slowly opened the door.

The drawn curtains and closed blinds darkened the room completely. In the center of the room, Barbara barely could see the figure of the mother lying on her side in the hospital bed, facing away from the door. In the semi-darkness, she could make out the jerking motion of Mrs. Joberst's non-stop sobbing. She made no effort to turn and face Barbara. After waiting a few moments, wondering what to do next, Barbara broke the silence.

"Good evening, Mrs. Joberst! I have a hungry young man here who wants to see his mother," she said cheerily.

A full minute dragged by with no response from the mother. Barbara wheeled the bassinet close to the bed and scurried about, waiting for some recognition. She first opened the curtains and blinds to allow light from the many rooftop fixtures outside to brighten the room a bit and then began picking up magazines and newspapers that had dropped to the floor.

While straightening up the room, Barbara noticed a *People* magazine that had been dropped on the floor beside the bed. On the cover appeared a picture of the judge and his young wife, both smiling. Underneath the larger photo was a smaller shot of Leanne dancing with a handsome, bronze-skinned young man with curly coal-black hair that almost reached his shoulders. A bright diamond stud shone in his ear. Bold text lettering across the cover alluded to Leanne's pregnancy and father-identity of the child to be born.

"Would you like me to come back later, Mrs. Joberst?"

Still no reply from the distraught mother, only muffled crying. Surely she wanted to see and hold her baby. Barbara waited a few moments before speaking again. Thankfully the baby continued to sleep. Finally, Barbara seated herself in a chair close to the side of the bed, reached out, and took Leanne's hand in hers.

"Is there anything I can do for you, Mrs. Joberst? I have the time. I hate to see you so sad."

Leanne, her face contorted from trying to suppress sobbing, gripped Barbara's hand tightly and with swollen, tearful eyes looked up at her.

"Thank you. I know I'm being a pest—a spoiled brat. Isn't that what everyone is saying?"

"You're upset, Mrs. Joberst. You are not a pest. If you need to cry, it's okay," Barbara said while stroking the top of Leanne's hand. "I'll take this beautiful young man back and we'll return later—when you feel better."

"No, no ... I'm all right. Stay with me for a while, will you?" she pleaded.

"Sure," she replied. "Let me take a couple of other babies to their mothers and I'll be right back."

"Fine, thanks. What is your name?"

"I'm Barbara, Mrs. Joberst. Barbara Goldeyer."

"You've been so kind, Barbara. Please call me Leanne," she said as she sat up in bed and dried her eyes with tissue. She glanced at the baby. "He *is* a beautiful child, isn't he, Barbara?"

"He is," she answered as she placed the infant in Leanne's arms. "And he's so alert and strong. Place your finger in is hand. See how strong he grips?"

"He'll be strong like his father," she said. Then her mouth dropped and her eyes widened. She glanced at Barbara as though she had made a terrible mistake. Barbara pretended not to notice.

"Have you decided on a name?"

"Not yet," she said abruptly, signaling she didn't want to discuss it further.

Leanne cradled the baby in her arms and with one hand tenderly fingered every feature of the child's face. With an awe-struck expression, never taking her eyes off the infant, she held him close to her chest while Barbara assisted her in her preparation to nurse the baby.

"I want to name him Victor," she said finally. "After his grandfather." She looked at Barbara squarely in the eye, as if trying to determine the other woman's reaction to the name.

"I'll be back in a little while," said Barbara.

Barbara pushed the bassinet aside and turned to leave. Why had she told her who the baby would be named after? Unquestionably, Mrs. Joberst needed a friend. Something was messed up in this girl's life. Regardless of what Jodie had said, Mrs. Joberst was not demanding or rude. She was disturbed.

# 4

Barbara informed her co-worker in the nursery unit that she would be away for a few minutes and then hurried back to Leanne's suite. She was sure the Witch would be on her case when she found out what she was doing. So what! Whatever other obligations she had been assigned, she was still a dedicated nurse-caregiver, and this patient needed help.

The security guard stopped her at the door and studied her ID badge for a moment before allowing her to enter. Leanne was out of bed and in a chair, her back to the door. She was rocking the baby in her arms and singing softly, her eyes glued to the infant. Barbara had no doubt that Leanne would be a good mother. It was so sad. In spite her wealth and luxuries, there seemed to be so much emptiness in Leanne's life. It seemed as though she were crying out for help.

"Oh ... hi, Barbara," she said. "I didn't hear you come in."

Barbara grinned. "I believe you are preoccupied."

"He nursed for a while and then fell asleep," said Leanne. "Is that normal?"

"It's okay. Newborns tire easily. He'll catch on quickly," Barbara replied. "How are you feeling?"

"I'm fine now. I think I was in a self-pity mode for a while. You were so kind to me. Do you have children, Barbara?"

"Not yet. Andy and I plan to start our family soon—maybe next year."

"What is your husband like?"

"He's the most wonderful person ever," said Barbara, beaming. "He's still in school—hospital administration. In two months we will move to Westlake. He has a job there in the Trinitus Westlake Hospital."

Leanne turned toward the window and gazed wistfully outside for a few seconds. Her face sagged into a downtrodden portrait.

"I am truly happy for you, Barbara," she said as tears formed in her eyes. "Crazy way to show it, isn't it? I guess I'm going into another slump. I'm envious! You really care for your husband, don't you?"

"With all my heart!"

"I wish I could say that."

"I'm not going to ask you why you can't," said Barbara while she straightened Leanne's bed and fluffed her pillows. "I know you're disturbed about something—that's pretty obvious."

"I can't stand to be around Anthony another minute," she said bluntly. She stared straight at Barbara with fire in her eyes. "I can't take my baby home, Barbara. I refuse to take him home." She began sobbing and handed the baby to Barbara. "What can I do?"

"You can leave your husband."

"I wish I could. I'm a prisoner! He watches my every move or hires some pea-eyed detective to follow me. I can't even go to the restroom without some woman he hires following me."

"Won't the baby make a difference?"

"Come on, Barbara!" she said. "Read *People* magazine. The whole world knows the baby is not his. They don't need a DNA test. I will tell anyone who asks who the father is. He's the most gentle, wonderful man I have ever known. And he can't even get in here to see his baby."

Barbara listened empathetically, wondering why Leanne was telling her these stories. What could anyone do to help this poor lady? She had a husband that she despised, had no family support, was under guard every minute of her life, and was hopelessly in love with the father of her baby. How lonely she had to feel. Barbara wondered what she could possibly do.

"That is so sad, Leanne. I wish I could help in some way. I'm not a counselor. I'll probably get in trouble with my supervisor for being here so long, but I'm not going to worry about that. But you have to get out of this trap somehow."

"You have no idea how powerful Anthony Joberst is ... how dangerous he is." Her brow furrowed. "I even fear for Mark's life. Anthony is ruthless."

"Who is Mark?"

"Mark Marchesa. I had one glorious month-long fling with Mark nine months ago. There is no question that he's the father of this child, Barbara. Anthony Joberst and I have not shared the same bed since we married."

"You must care for Mark a lot."

"I do. And he cares for me." She cuddled the baby close to her chest and gazed at the child silently for a few seconds. "We should be together right now, sharing the beauty of this miracle that we have created."

"How did you get to know Mark?"

"Actually, we grew up together in Highland Park as snot-nosed rich kids. We went to the same schools but never were serious about each other. During college Mark stayed in Dallas and went to SMU and I went away to Vassar in New York. We'd see each other only on occasion, at social affairs. Our families were close. My father helped Mr. Marchesa when he started the hospital corporation."

"A hospital company?"

"Yeah, CareCompHealth. It started with only two or three hospitals. Now it's the largest healthcare system in the nation. Mark is one of the Dallas division executive officers. He has done very well, much to the surprise of everyone. In college he was a playboy. No one thought he would ever be anything else. He's ready now to take the reins of the company whenever his father steps down."

"What a shame you couldn't have gotten together earlier. How did you and the judge become acquainted?"

"Are you sure you want to hear all these sordid details?" she asked as she handed the baby, now sleeping soundly, to Barbara to be replaced in the bassinet.

"I think it makes you feel better to talk about these things, even though I'm sure they stir up some unpleasant memories."

Leanne grinned. "You say you are not a counselor, but you are so wise and you are a good listener. Get ready to hear an ugly story of political influence and greed: Anthony was an attorney for CareCompHealth in the early years of its existence. He specialized in healthcare law and successfully defended the company in some rather sticky allegations of Medicare fraud.

"Mark's older brother, Stephen, had no interest in a position with the company. He graduated from medical school and became a successful surgeon in Dallas. With encouragement from the medical associations, he drifted into politics and managed to get elected a U.S. senator from Texas. He has served for the last two terms of office. He is now the Senate majority leader, and he wields strong influence in Washington. Maybe you've heard of him?"

"I do remember the name, but I didn't put it all together." Barbara laughed. "My lifestyle right now doesn't stimulate much interest in politics."

"So, with Anthony's previous connection with CompCareHealth, and with the backing of the Marchesa family and my father, he managed to get an appointment to a Federal Judgeship in Dallas. With Stephen being a senator, his confirmation went through easily. With his reputation for handling healthcare litigation for CareCompHealth, his court became a favorite with attorneys for cases involving all healthcare systems—non-profit as well as for-profit."

"Has he been a fair judge?"

"He's for sale, Barbara!"

"What do you mean?"

"He has been able to docket select healthcare provider cases in his court and then rule for whoever comes up with the most favorable kickback. He's accumulated a fortune—stock options, offshore account deposits, political favors for his friends, who in turn pay a price for his favoritism. It's about as dirty as you can imagine."

"How does he keep from getting caught?"

"It's all part of the scheme. It's not widely known, but Anthony brags to me about how he has manipulated people and how he has been able to damage individuals who have crossed him. He has built an unbelievable network of thieves."

"Is Mark's brother a part of the network?"

"Mark says he's not. Now that Anthony knows about Mark and me, there's no predicting what might evolve. One thing is certain: Anthony will seek vengeance. He'll attack Mark's hospital corporation in some way, even though Mark's family, including his brother, helped get him appointed as a federal judge."

"Why did you ever marry him?" she said as she tucked a blanket around the baby and prepared the bassinet for the trip down the cold corridors. "That's an unfair question ... I'm sorry."

"That's all right," Leanne said. She bent over and gave the baby a final kiss on the forehead. "It's all part of the story. Sometimes I feel like I was the sacrificial lamb. I suspected ulterior motives when my father encouraged me to develop some sort of relationship with Anthony. I was nearing thirty, unmarried, and traipsing all over the world trying to find a place for myself. Of course, he wanted me to settle down, but he also saw the advantage of his daughter being married to a man with so much power."

"So you really didn't know what you were getting into."

"I was just what Anthony wanted, a wealthy trophy-wife. Our wedding—the ceremony, the reception, the parties—was the major social event of the year in Dallas. It really *was* fabulous, just like a fairy tale on the surface, but it quickly turned into a nightmare. I'll tell you about it sometime. I know you need to get back to work."

"You were never happy with him?"

"No, never! He began manipulating me from the first, and he was unbelievably jealous, psychopathically so. That's what worries me now about Mark—and about my baby."

"Why does he want the baby to have a DNA test? He must know that it's not his."

"I can tell you this right now: The DNA test that's reported to the media will confirm that Anthony is the father."

"How can that happen?"

"He has a way, Barbara. He'll probably have the results sent to the CEO of Trinitus. The CEO will direct his laboratory director to report the DNA results just the way he wants them. Anthony would never want it known that he was incapable of impregnating his young wife. Image is the most important aspect of his career."

"When he found out about you and Mark, what did he do?"

"He didn't find out for a long time. I'm sure he was suspicious. He had me followed by a detective who could hardly follow a Boy Scout trail." Leanne chuckled. "I would play tricks on him—like go to the airport and actually board a plane for one destination, and then, while he was scurrying about trying to board the same plane, I would slip around him and take another plane for somewhere else, like Monaco or Paris. That was one trick I used to meet Mark sometimes."

"You would like for Mark to see the baby, wouldn't you?"

"More than anything! At least let him know about the baby—and that I love him." Tears again seeped from her reddened eyes. "It's not fair, Barbara. I can't even let him know what the baby looks like or discuss a name with him. I'm sure he's seen the newspapers and the tabloids. He can't call in—even my cell phone has been deactivated."

"If it would make you feel better, I can—"

Before she finished, there was a knock and the door opened slightly. Without looking up, Barbara knew it was Wilda, ready to strike out because she had been away from the nursery unit so long.

"Nurse Goldeyer!" said Wilda in a stern, guttural voice. "Come to the door please."

"She will not!" snapped Leanne. "She's helping me and she's not finished. Close the door please and leave."

Barbara could not constrain a faint chuckle. Wilda was likely in shock, but she quickly closed the door without a sound.

"That must have been your supervisor."

"That was Wilda Witcher. We call her the 'Witch.'"

"I can see why. Rather rude, I'd say."

"I'll probably be in for a tongue lashing, but I really don't care. I feel like you need some help. It just tears my heart out to see you so miserable."

"I'm sorry if I got you in trouble, but you have been a godsend. Just blame everything on me. I don't think anyone will admonish you for giving me extra care. I really don't deserve it, but I do appreciate it."

"Sure you do. Whatever anyone says, you are an abused spouse."

"Thank you again, Barbara. Some mystical force sent you just in time. Please come back."

"I'll see you a couple more times during the night. If you need me, ask the floor nurse to call me in the nursery."

"You were going to offer to call Mark for me, weren't you?"

"Or bring my cell phone in for you."

Leanne's brow furrowed. "Don't get in trouble because of me, Barbara. If Anthony found out, I don't know what he would do. He is vicious, Barbara."

"Before I go off duty in the morning, give me Mark's cell phone number. Or tell me how to find him. I'm serious. You don't have to put up with this cruel treatment."

Leanne's eyes welled with tears again. She dropped her head for a moment, reached for a tissue, and then looked up at Barbara, her face wet. "Would you just give me a hug, Barbara," she said, childlike.

"Sure," Barbara replied. "I'll be here for you. Now dry those eyes! You have a lot of planning to do."

\* \* \* \*

Barbara tightly clutched the piece of note paper in her hand as she climbed into her car to start for home. Leanne said the best time to reach Mark would be about this time of day, before he started meetings at the office. The breaking dawn showered the employee parking lot with subdued light, just enough to trigger the off switch for the pole lights in the lot. The only activity was the scattering of night-shift employees searching for their cars. The day-shift group had already entered the hospital to start their day.

Barbara's hands trembled as she dialed her cell phone. What should she say? More important, what would he say? After four or five rings, a soft-toned voice answered.

"Mark Marchesa, here."

"Mr. Marchesa, my name is Barbara Goldeyer. I am a nurse at Trinitus Women's Services Unit. Leanne Joberst is a patient of mine."

There was a long pause. Barbara could hear voices in the background.

"I'm sorry, Miss. You must have the wrong number."

"I'm terribly sorry, sir."

What a shock! Barbara checked her cell phone. There was no mistake. She had dialed the number Leanne had given her. Was Leanne acting out some sort of fantasy scene—a tryst with someone whom she claimed to have fathered her baby, the saga of a cruel husband who would even falsify a DNA test to preserve image, the loneliness of a poor little rich girl? Barbara felt violated, as though she had fallen prey to a ridiculous scam.

She backed out of the parking lot and pointed her VW toward home, never remembering being more exhausted. She needed sleep badly, and she had to put the events of the night out of her mind. Still, something in the back of her mind told her that Leanne's story held some truth. Even though she didn't have years of experience judging people's behavior, she had a serendipitous feeling that she had a role in helping this poor girl—that Leanne had been sincere in describing her plight.

The freeway was more crowded at this time, the result of leaving just a few minutes later, and her trip home lasted over an hour. She looked forward to waking Andy with a kiss and then crawling in bed alongside him to get at least three hours of much-needed sleep. She decided to wait until later in the day to tell Andy about the incident.

She rounded the corner of the side street to her apartment complex and turned into the driveway leading to her parking slot. In the visitors' parking area, she noticed a dark-blue BMW 550i—an unusual site in this part of town. No one who lived there had a car with this sort of price tag, and it was unlikely their visitors did either. She parked and exited her car and headed toward the steps to her apartment. Most of the vehicles in the tenants parking slots had gone, carrying their owners to their various nine-to-five jobs.

Holding on to the handrail, she began ascending the stairs when she became aware of someone behind her. She started for a second and took a couple of steps up the stairs when a voice called out to her.

"Miss Goldeyer?"

Barbara turned to face the person behind her, not knowing whether she was about to be attacked. She wondered, of course, how this stranger knew her name. When she saw the handsome, deeply tanned thirty-something man of athletic build, with curly black hair and a diamond ear stud, she knew who it was. His eyes cast a wistful, melancholic look in spite of their sparkle. Barbara knew immediately it was Mark Marchesa.

"Yes," she answered, now relaxed.

"My name is Mark Marchesa. I apologize for this intrusion. I was in a meeting when you called—a meeting which I cancelled immediately—and I couldn't respond to your message. I looked up your address on the Internet. So here I am. Again, I apologize; I had no intention of frightening you."

"Not at all, sir," said Barbara. "I'm just glad to know that I hadn't made a mistake in the number that Leanne gave me."

"Is she all right?" he asked. His brow creased and his chin and lower lip quivered.

"She's fine, Mr. Marchesa. And she has a beautiful, healthy baby boy at her side. She wanted you to know."

"Thank you, Miss Goldeyer. She must have told you the whole story for you to contact me, for her to give you this number. She lives in constant fear," he said. "As you must know, this was the only way for her to contact me."

"What are you going to do, Mr. Marchesa? Leanne needs you," Barbara said, her tone sincere.

"I have a plan. All I can tell you now is that I am going to do something. My company probably is already in jeopardy because of Judge Joberst. Did Leanne tell you anything about her husband?"

"She painted a pretty ugly picture."

"That's putting it mildly."

"Why does she stay with him?"

"Out of fear, Miss Goldeyer. We thought that when he found out she was pregnant he would kick her out of the house, but we should have known. That would have been too damaging to his image."

"What can you do?"

"I really can't reveal my plan yet. I feel like I can trust you. Leanne would never have given you my private cell phone number if she didn't think that also. But I don't want to get you involved in something that could place your safety in jeopardy."

"I guess I really shouldn't be talking to you now."

"You are probably right," he said, a stern, determined tone to his voice. He looked straight at Barbara with sad, misty eyes. "But I want you to carry a message to her: I love her very much and she is not going to have to go through this torture much longer."

"I believe you mean it."

"You are right!" he answered as he gazed past her into the distance. "I probably won't see you again, so I want to thank you now, from the bottom of my heart, for what you have done for us. We won't forget it."

"She could really use a friend," said Barbara. "I feel like I have to help her in some way. I think I'll go back right now and tell her we've talked."

"No, no!" he said, "If you do that they will suspect something."

"You mean the guard will report visitors?"

"Joberst has her guarded every minute, day and night. Sometimes I even suspect that I am being followed."

"I guess I'll wait until tonight."

"You have been an invaluable friend, Miss Goldeyer. Please do one more thing to help us: Don't tell anyone about our encounter."

"I tell my husband everything," she responded.

"But no one else, please."

"I promise. And good luck, Mr. Marchesa."

## 5

John "Gator" Dunbar poured another generous portion of Seagram's Select into his glass, took a big swig, and let out a loud, expiratory sigh while he wiped his unkempt beard with his shirt sleeve. This time he hadn't added ice or 7 Up, diluting its punch. Between swigs he occasionally glanced through the blind-covered window of the old house-trailer. Squint should have been back by now, unless he ran into some kind of trouble.

Then he heard a rumble and caught a glimpse of the beat-up old gray van as it chugged to a halt. How much longer would that dilapidated wreck hold together? If they pulled this job off, they would have enough money to buy a new van. He and Squint had to have a van. Like every other time they had been evicted, it served as a place to sleep until they could rake up enough money to pay the first month's rent somewhere.

Gator hoped Squint had gotten some better pictures this time. They didn't have much time left before they had to put the plan into action. For one thing, he couldn't rely on Becky staying clean for very long at a time. So far he had convinced her to stay on the methadone. What was he going to do with her afterward? He had to decide soon. He surely couldn't leave her free to be questioned.

Squint Cameron signaled his arrival by slamming the van door as hard as he could, which always made the loose rear bumper rattle. As he grabbed the handrail and pulled his overweight torso onto the rickety makeshift porch, a disturbed possum bolted out from underneath and scampered under the house trailer.

Squint struggled to get the stubborn aluminum door open, uttered a few profane words, and then climbed into the trailer without knocking. Squint's weight and clumsiness rocked the trailer, rattling the few pieces of glassware in the kitchen cabinets.

"Why don't you fix the goddamn door, Gator?" said Squint as he plopped his three hundred pounds of blubber into one of the table chairs. "If you ever had a fire in here, you'd fry before you could get out."

"Quit your bitching," he replied. "Pour yourself a drink and tell me what you got."

"I think I've got enough pictures this time. Won't take much to make Becky look like her identical twin. *Look* like her, but a far cry from making Becky *act* like her."

"Let me see the pictures. Lay 'em out on the table," he said while he poured Squint a drink about two fingers deep.

Gator studied each picture closely and compared them with the current photos of Becky.

"These look good, Squint," said Gator. "Show me the movie clips. We're gonna have to concentrate on teaching Becky this girl's body movements. We've got to keep Becky sober enough to practice."

"That ain't gonna be easy," said Squint as he tossed down the drink with one swallow and held his glass to be refilled.

"We're getting closer, partner," said Gator. "Did you get good pictures of the ID card? Squint! Wake up, goddamn it! I'm talking to you."

"I'm not asleep, Gator. Just resting my eyes."

"Then open your fuckin' eyes, Squint!"

"They're open, dammit!"

"Can you get an ID card made from these close-ups?"

"Piece of cake, Gator. Same guy that made those passports for us last year."

"Did you get good detail of the barcode?"

"Couldn't be better," he replied, reaching for the bourbon bottle again. "We're about to run out, Gator."

"Then stop at the store and get another. Better get two this time," said Gator. "Now, get that card made as soon as possible. We don't have much time—need to test it at the employees' security entrance gate. We can't have any fuckin slip-ups, Squint."

"Just trust me!"

"I'd feel better if you'd stop squinting your goddamn eyes."

"I can't help it. My eyelids get heavy."

"When we finish this job, you need to get that fixed. Go to a plastic surgeon."

"I'd rather keep the money," he said. "How much is Tate going to pay us, Gator? And when?"

"Plenty—after we deliver the goods," said Gator. "Let me handle it. Also, when Becky gets here you need to take her shopping. Buy scrubs identical to the ones this girl in the pictures is wearing. Don't forget to match the shoes. Becky needs to start wearing them now."

"What about her hair? Becky is gonna freak when she has to have her hair cut."

"Take her to a stylist. Take the pictures and show him or her how we want it to look. Do you have enough cash to handle all this?"

"Yeah, I think so."

"Then get moving, Squint!"

"How are we going to know when to go into action?"

"Tate will tell us when. He said real soon the last time I talked to him. But we need to be ready at any time he gives the word. He said it will be within the next two weeks. We have a lot to do yet."

"Gator, I ain't going in that hospital. Everyone will remember me."

"You won't have to, Squint. I'll take care—"

A screeching sound of a car coming to a halt interrupted him. Next came the sound of a slamming car door, followed by the sound of wheels spinning in acceleration.

"Must be Becky."

Becky struggled to get the sagging aluminum door open and stepped inside. She glared at Gator.

"Don't send me out with that freak again! And why don't you fix that fuckin' door."

"Settle down, Becky. How much did you get?"

"Here's your half," she said as she tossed a fifty-dollar bill on the table. "He should have been hit for more, knowing what he wanted me to do. Why in the shit do I need you, Gator? Hell, I could turn tricks on the street and come out better off and be safer than I was with that creep."

"Forget it, Becky. We have work to do. Now sit down and listen!"

"Is this the deal where I play nurse?"

"It ain't play, goddamn it!" said Gator. "Now either you listen and learn or we're gonna turn your sweet ass in to the cops. And make sure you don't miss any of your methadone treatment sessions."

"Fuck you, Gator!" she retorted. "You ain't gonna turn me in—be like turning yourself in."

"Get serious, Becky. Tate is paying us well to pull this off, and you're the key. Look at these pictures and at the video that Squint made. This is the way you will have to look and act. Now study them close."

"Cut my hair?" she cried. "Shit no, Gator. Get somebody else."

"Fine," said Gator. "We just have to know. You don't want to be cut in on the take, fine. Now, just haul your ass out of here. Hit the street! We've got work to do."

Becky sat in the corner of the small so-called kitchen area and sulked without saying a word. She pulled a mirror from her bag and stared at herself for a few seconds and then stared at the pictures that Squint had taken of the nurse. Gator and Squint sat by silently. Gator poured another drink for himself and Squint and then poured a half-glass for Becky. She looked up at him, smiled, and took a big swig.

"I'd look pretty good as a nurse, wouldn't I, Gator?"

"Sure you would, Becky."

"How much will I get?"

"We'll split three ways. Should be enough for you to turn your life around, Becky."

"Think so?"

"Yeah, I do, but you have to want to."

"I want to, Gator, Squint. I really want to. I might even become a real nurse."

"You can do it, Becky."

"Sure, I can do it! Count me in, Gator."

# 6

Even in this, the shabbiest trailer park just outside East Dallas, the cheap, dilapidated house trailer stood out like an ugly pustule on a pretty girl's face. Outside, in the midst of littered trash and knee-high weeds, stood a crossed-out "For Rent" sign alongside an unwashed, unpolished gray vintage van. In the middle of the afternoon, the temperature hotter than usual, the place was eerily quiet except for the grinding sound of the small window air conditioner in the trailer.

Inside, Gator played solitaire on the kitchen table while Squint, ensconced in the one overstuffed armchair—his eyes open as far as possible for him—watched afternoon soaps on the eleven-inch TV. In spite of the window unit, he repeatedly swiped a small towel across his forehead to blot the beads of sweat. Across the table from Gator, Becky filed her fingernails.

"Damn it, Gator, why do I have to keep my fingernails so fuckin' short?" Becky whined. "It's taken me months to get 'em long."

"And I've worked weeks getting you ready for this job," he replied. "I don't want you to blow it by walking in that hospital looking like you live in a brothel."

"What's a brothel?" she said without looking up, still filing away at her nails.

"A whorehouse, damn it!" said Gator. "And that's where you're going if you screw up this job. Now go back there and practice your act again. We should be getting the call any day."

Squint came alive hearing those words. "I hope it comes pretty soon. I'm getting tired of all this waiting shit."

"Do you have everything ready, Squint?"

"Yeah ... I'm ready."

"Once again: Becky's ID ready? Been tested? You made arrangements to get me a quick hospital census of newborns and new mothers?"

"Yes, to everything, Gator. And before you ask, the van is filled with gasoline," he answered as he reached for a glass and the bottle of bourbon on the side table. Gator reached out and blocked his hand.

"Leave off the booze, both of you!" said Gator. "We can't go into that hospital reeking of liquor."

"I ain't going into that hospital," said Squint.

"You might get pulled over by a cop."

"I'll be glad when this is over," he replied as he redirected his narrow-eyed gaze at the TV. "If I ever get any money, I'm gonna buy me one of them big-screen televisions."

"If you opened your eyes, you'd see more of the picture." Gator laughed.

"Fuck you, Gator!"

"I'm gonna take my money and go to college," said Becky, holding her head high with a look of pride on her face.

"Becky, you've got to get your GED first," said Gator. "Then you can go to college. A good idea. You can do it."

"What are you going to do, Gator?" asked Squint.

"Don't know," he said. "Might travel some. Gettin' sorta tired of this place."

"Quit dreaming, Gator," said Squint. "You know as well as I do. You're gonna do what Tate asks you to do."

"Hell, we can't afford not to be ready for the next job he asks us to do."

"Who the hell is Tate? Do you know, Gator?"

"Why should you care as long as he—?"

Before he finished, his cell phone simultaneously vibrated and played an electronic tune. Gator grabbed the phone and struggled to raise the flap. He heard only two words.

"It's time."

It was the two-word code they had been waiting and preparing for. All three scrambled to their feet and began to get ready.

Gator jumped up and raced to the bathroom ahead of the other two. He splashed cold water on his face, shaved his beard, brushed his teeth, dabbed a bit of weak cologne on his body, and quickly dressed in his best—suit, tie, clean shirt. He looked in the mirror once more to reassure himself that he looked like a grandfather about to go to the hospital to gloat over his new grandchild.

"When do you think it happened?" asked Squint as he stood up, stretched his leg muscles, and struggled to pull on his overalls over his portly torso.

"Probably sometime yesterday."

"Why've we waited so long?"

"Damn it, Squint! We don't go in until after twenty-four hours! We've rehearsed this a dozen times. And we'll go over it again on the way to the hospital. There's no room for slipups. We have to be there when they change shifts. Now does everyone remember their parts?"

"We're ready, Gator," said Becky, now dressed in her pink scrubs, a mask hanging from her neck and a hairnet in hand. "You know, I'm not even nervous."

"Good. Okay, let's get started," replied Gator as he double-checked his bag, looked in the mirror, and sprayed one last fog of hair spray on his head.

\* \* \* \*

With Gator and Becky well hidden, Squint parked the gray van in the fifteen-minute parking zone in the front of the hospital. At Squint's signal, Becky hopped out the rear door. As soon as he was sure that no one from the oncoming shift was watching, Squint waved to Gator to do the same. So far so good!

Squint next eased the gray van into the street that coursed along the backside of the medical center campus. He went past the sign that said, "Emergency Room Entrance" until he reached the service entry area. He then parked in a space that gave him a full view of the rear stairwell door to the women's pavilion. Fortunately there were no ambulances or delivery trucks arriving or leaving. He parked beneath a sign that said, "Loading Zone—No Parking."

\* \* \* \*

Becky took a deep breath as she stood before the swipe-in slot on the door to the Women's Services Unit. Squint said not to worry, that it would work. Sure enough, she heard a click, and the "Enter" light flashed. Once inside, she did just what Gator had told her: put on the hairnet, placed the mask on her face, and walked through the corridors at a brisk pace. No one she passed even glanced at her, let alone spoke to her. Everything was going according to Gator's briefing, but that didn't quiet the pounding in her chest.

She located the laundry room and the adjacent exit to the rear staircase. Looking behind her, she saw that she had a good view of the visitor waiting room at the end of the long corridor. Gator would be easily visible when he gave her his hand signals. Just as Gator had said, a uniformed guard was seated in a chair at the door to one of the patient rooms. He seemed absorbed in a magazine, but his half-closed eyes and the repeated dropping of his head showed that he was ready to be relieved of duty.

Nothing to do now but wait. Gator was set to appear soon and would go through with his "grandfather" act. Then he would take a seat in the waiting room and signal her when it was time for her to enter the mother's room. No one had challenged her yet. She did what Gator had told her to do: walk briskly in the hall and stay out of sight as much as possible at the end of the corridor while she watched for his signal.

*Seems like it is taking a long time,* she thought. *Maybe I'm just getting nervous.*

\* \* \* \*

Gator hit the ground behind the van and pulled his wheeled carry-on bag with him as he headed for the hospital entrance. He looked around. No one had noticed him as far as he could tell. The lobby area was mostly empty, with only an occasional janitor pushing a floor polisher or a vacuum cleaner. From the map Squint had given him, he knew the exact locations of the restrooms, the security station, and the elevators.

His first stop was the restroom. Behind a stall door, he checked the nursery census Squint had acquired from the day before in order to find a recent admission. Baby Boy Lawson had been admitted to regular nursery yesterday. A search through the list of admissions to the post-partum floor showed the mother to be Sandra Lawson, in Room 416. He tore the census into shreds and flushed it down the toilet. Next, he pulled on the thin latex glove with the fake fingerprints embossed on the surface.

The information desk was unattended, as he had expected. He walked straight to the visitors' entrance pulling the bag behind him and approached the security check station. A stern-faced guard came forward and stopped him. Now was the time to start his performance.

"Good … here you are. I need some help, sir."

"You're too early for visiting hours, mister. Come back at eight."

"You're Mr. Benedict—I see from your name tag. Mr. Benedict, I just arrived from Los Angeles. I came straight from the airport. My daughter had a baby yesterday. A baby boy! My first grandchild! I'm on my way to Washington and only have a few minutes. I understand the need for visitor hours, sir, but this is a special occasion. I can't stay long, but this is my only chance to let her know I'm here and perhaps get a glimpse of my grandson."

"What's your daughter's name?" the guard asked as he thumbed through the hospital census pages.

"Lawson, Sandra Lawson." Gator gave an affected chuckle. "Guess the boy doesn't have a name yet. Just born yesterday."

"She's in Room 416. I'll call the floor. If it's all right, you can sneak in for a couple of minutes. The baby is in Nursery II."

"Thank you, sir. Thank you very much!"

"Just step through here and place your index finger on the detector so I can issue you a pass."

"Of course, can't be too careful. Thank you again, Mr. Benedict. When I get to Washington, I'm going to write a commendation letter to the hospital administration about your kindness."

The stone-faced guard responded flatly, "The elevators to the fourth floor are down the corridor. You'll need your pass to access the floor."

Gator followed the routine and headed for the elevators. As he walked away, the guard called out, "Congratulations!"

*Couldn't have been easier,* Gator thought. *He didn't even check my bag after all I went through to get it in here.*

## 7

Barbara checked her watch while she walked from the employee parking to the employee entrance. She was almost late again, so the Witch probably would be on her case her all night. The beat-up gray van was parked in the same place as usual, but this time she could identify someone seated in the driver's seat. When she got closer, she could make out his features—a beardless, beefy head with eyes so narrowed she wondered how he could see even large objects.

He seemed so preoccupied with either surveying the area or looking in his rear-view mirror that he didn't notice her. She momentarily toyed with the idea of writing down the license number, but she was already close to being late. After she passed the van, she heard a car door slam and soon afterward the engine started and the van moved away. Strange! She hadn't noticed anyone else seated in front. Should she notify security, or was she just being overly suspicious?

Barbara hurried to the entrance security check station and entered her ID card. A "no-entry" light flashed, followed by instructions to log out.

*What's going on here? The monitor is telling me I'm already here. I must have forgotten to swipe out this morning. The Witch is really going to come down on me when she finds out.* She logged out, re-entered her card, and heard the door click open.

*I'm sure I logged out this morning. The equipment must be faulty,* she thought as she stepped off the elevator on the Women's Services Unit. She inserted her ID card into the receptacle by the door to the nursery and found it to work normally. *I guess I did forget to log out when I left this morning.*

Now she would have to face the Witch. She needed to spend some time with Leanne to report on her visit with Mark and didn't want to get cornered for a long-winded scolding. After she had awakened in the afternoon, she had debated whether to visit Leanne during the day. She knew that Leanne would be anxious to hear her news. Mark had warned her not to be seen visiting Leanne except when she was on duty. She wasn't sure why but had decided to follow his advice and wait until after she had started her shift to talk to Leanne. She would contact her briefly right after report, before taking the babies out, to let her know she had seen Mark. Such a sad situation. Mark said he had a plan but wasn't specific about what he intended to do. What could he do?

\* \* \* \*

Once on the fourth floor, Gator found the waiting room and looked down the corridor toward the stairway exit door. No Becky in sight at first, but then she rounded the corner in a fast walk, just as instructed. She turned, nodded slightly, and took her position near the stairwell door, in clear view of the waiting room. Gator positioned his bag where she could see it. He then approached the nursery view-windows and gazed at the babies inside.

He spotted the nurse that Squint had targeted. What an unbelievable resemblance! As long as Becky wore the facemask, the two girls looked identical. The names of the babies were written on the bassinets in a code: "Boy" or "Girl," followed by the last four letters of the family name. The nurse inside the nursery was holding in her arms an infant that she had just taken from the crib marked "Boyerst." That would be baby boy, Joberst. At first, Barbara hadn't noticed Gator looking through the glass viewing window. After a few seconds, Gator decided he needed to ask about his "grandson."

"Miss," he called out through the speaker tube in the window.

Barbara started when she realized he was there, and then smiled. "Oh ... I forgot. You must be here to see the Lawson baby. Security called to say you'd be coming up."

She replaced the Joberst baby and pulled another bassinet with the Lawson baby close to the viewing window.

"Is he all right, miss?" Gator asked, his eyes fixed on his "grandson."

"Yes, sir, he's a fine baby. Too bad you can't stay and hold him when I take him out. The guard said you had to leave."

"I just wanted one quick look. I'll be back in a couple of days. He's a good looking boy, don't you think?"

"Absolutely!" Barbara grinned. "The best looking baby in the nursery."

"I bet you tell that to all the grandfathers." Gator laughed. He noticed her name on her ID. "Thanks for showing me, Miss Goldeyer. You're taking the other baby out now?"

"He's all clean and ready to go to his mother. When I get back, I'll take your grandson out. If you are still here, maybe you can come into Mrs. Lawson's room."

"I'll watch for you. I wish I had more time," he said, checking his watch. "I'll sit in the waiting room as long as I can before I have to leave. Thank you for your kindness."

"I'll look to see if you are still here."

"Thank you, Miss Goldeyer."

\* \* \* \*

Becky sauntered down the corridor, pausing at times to put her cell phone to her ear and gaze out one of the windows, pretending to be carrying on a conversation. The waiting room was still empty, except for a janitor running a carpet cleaner. Occasionally a worker or a nurse wandered by, but they hardly noticed her.

*Where is Gator?* she wondered. Surely he'd find some way to notify her if anything went wrong. His bag was still where he'd left it, so he wouldn't be gone long.

She walked back to her strategic lookout spot by the stairwell door and stood behind a column, out of sight of anyone in the hall but still with a clear view of Gator's bag. Finally Gator appeared at the waiting room, seated himself close to his luggage, and nodded to Becky that all was well. Becky had no sooner relaxed a bit than the next signal came from Gator for her to be alert. The bassinet with the Joberst baby was being wheeled by Barbara into the mother's room. Gator signaled her to be ready for the next move. Becky and Gator stayed motionless, waiting for the time when their plan would be put to the crucial test.

\* \* \* \*

Barbara stood close to the guard so her ID badge would be visible. Without even looking up or speaking, he motioned for her to enter and dove back into his *Sports Illustrated* magazine. She guided the crib into Leanne's room.

Leanne, standing with her back to the door, was gazing out the window. As soon as she realized Barbara was there with the baby, she turned to face her. She must have anticipated Barbara's arrival—face made up, hair combed, and wearing a beautiful silk robe with monogrammed embroidered initials. The cosmetics couldn't conceal, however, the apprehension on her face. Her tear-filled red eyes betrayed her despondency.

"Barbara! You're here ... finally," said Leanne, dabbing at her face with a tissue. "I have been frantic, worrying about you—and your call to Mark."

"It went fine, Leanne," said Barbara. "Sit for a few moments, and while you feed this handsome guy I'll tell you about Mark. We had a very pleasant visit early this morning."

Barbara lifted the baby from the bassinet and placed him in Leanne's arms. Within seconds, he found his mother's breast and began vigorous nursing. Barbara described in detail the story of her encounter with Mark.

"I wanted to come right back this morning to tell you, but Mark advised against it."

"I'm not surprised," she replied. "He knows how treacherous Anthony can be—probably has detectives following Mark's every move. Mark wouldn't want you to be placed in danger."

"Leanne, he said more than once that he had a plan and said you wouldn't have to put up with this torture much longer."

Leanne became pensive. She kept her eyes glued to the baby without speaking. She looked up, her mascara smudged from the tears. "I'm so worried, Barbara. What do you think he meant?"

"I have no idea, but there was a tone of determination in his voice that was scary."

"Barbara, promise me you won't contact Mark again. I would just die if anything happened to you because of me."

"If you say so, but I'll stay in touch with you as often as possible today. I'll probably have trouble finding much free time today. I'm sure the Witch is coming after me after I had trouble swiping in."

"What happened?"

"For some reason, the security check-in monitor showed that I had failed to check out this morning. I guess I just forgot. The Witch will be furious when she finds out."

"You were probably nervous about calling Mark."

"Maybe so. Guess I'd better get on back to the nursery and take my licks."

"Good luck! Barbara, you don't have to put up with that woman, you know. Let me know if you need me."

"Thanks, Leanne." Barbara moved the bassinet close to Leanne, patted her shoulder, and prepared to leave. "I can handle it. Right now you just need to concentrate on what you're doing."

Barbara exited Leanne's suite and turned toward the nursery. The guard, his face buried in the magazine, never looked up. Gator waited ten seconds after Barbara was out of sight before he signaled Becky to move toward Leanne's room. At the same time, he started casually walking toward Becky's "hideout," pulling his wheeled luggage behind him. He nodded slightly as he passed Becky in the corridor and then positioned himself so he could witness the next phase of the scheme. He watched closely as Becky held up her ID badge for the guard and was waved through.

\* \* \* \*

Once inside the door, now facing the mother and baby, Becky hesitated before going farther. In spite of the many times they had rehearsed this scene, her first reaction was to bolt and run. With her heart pounding in her chest, she took a deep breath and told herself to stay calm. Leanne looked up briefly.

"You're back so soon, Barbara," said Leanne, her eyes fixed on the baby. "He's really going after it tonight."

"His doctor is here and needs to examine him," said Becky as she slipped on her gloves and wheeled the bassinet closer. "I'll bring him right back,"

"You're wearing a mask," said Leanne. She handed the baby to Becky. "Do you have a cold?"

"Just beginning," she answered. "It's probably just an allergy, but I don't want to take any chances."

"I guess that's why you sound so hoarse."

"I'm sure it is—I don't feel bad."

"Take care of yourself, Barbara."

"I'll do that. Get some rest while we're gone."

\* \* \* \*

Becky pushed the crib out the door and past the guard, who showed no interest in her leaving. She headed down the hall as if she were going into the nursery. She had taken only a few steps when she saw the chubby nurse waddle toward her and stop right in front of the bassinet. Again, her heart skipped a beat and her throat tightened. This was it! They were caught for sure this time. In her mind she, gauged how long it would take her to reach the stair door in a run.

"Nurse Goldeyer! Report to my office as soon as you return that baby to the nursery. And do something about those filthy shoes! Where are your shoe covers? You look disgraceful."

"Yes, ma'am," said Becky in a weak voice as she moved past Wilda Witcher.

*Shoe Covers! What the shit? Nobody said anything about shoe covers.*

In the meantime, Gator had opened the stairwell door and held it while Becky wheeled the crib through. No alarm sounded. He looked behind her. No one had seen their exit. He quickly unzipped the bag and pulled out the small oxygen canister and the tiny mask hidden beneath the false bottom. He then extracted a heavily insulated bag and held it open while Becky placed the baby inside the make-shift cocoon. Gator placed the infant oxygen face mask next to the baby's head, turned the valve to the appropriate setting, swaddled the baby in the crib blanket, and zipped the bag shut.

"Go Becky! Down those stairs, fast. An alarm might sound when you exit at the ground floor but don't pay any attention to it. Just climb in the van with Squint. I'll be at the front entrance."

\* \* \* \*

Not a sound came from the bag. Gator walked at a leisurely pace to the elevator and punched the down button, meeting only an occasional person on the way to the ground floor. He took off his visitor sticker and, as instructed by the security guard, initialed the back side with the pen that hung from the exit stile and entered it into the receptacle. The monitor flashed: "Cleared to Exit."

Still walking leisurely, he passed through the automatic doors to the covered portico just as Squint drove up. He placed the bag in the back and climbed in the seat beside Squint. While the van slowly pulled away from the hospital entrance, Becky quickly unzipped the bag and recovered the infant.

"How does he look?" asked Gator.

"Pretty and pink," said Becky as she cuddled the child and rocked him back and forth. "First time I ever held a baby. Can I keep him, Gator?"

"You'll never have that much money, Becky," said Gator, grinning. "Just go make one of your own."

"I wouldn't want one made by you."

"Could be worse."

"Stop your bickering! Where from here?" asked Squint.

"Just as we rehearsed—drive down the freeway while I call Tate."

# 8

As soon as the last of the five babies assigned to her for the night had been delivered to their mothers, Barbara busied herself putting the nursery in order and making entries in each baby's chart. She wanted to spend more time with Leanne, so she would return each of the other babies to the nursery first and save Leanne's baby for last. So far she had managed to avoid Wilda, but she knew her luck wouldn't last. Wilda enjoyed reprimanding her too much to miss this opportunity.

Barbara wondered how she would explain the discrepancy between her swipe-in and swipe-out times when Wilda confronted her. She glanced at the clock, checked out to one of the other nurses, and after assuring herself that Wilda wasn't around she headed for Leanne's suite. Leanne appeared to be napping when she entered but opened her eyes the moment Barbara brushed against the bed.

"You didn't bring him back?" she said, her brow furrowed. "Anything wrong?"

"What do you mean?" Barbara asked. With a quizzical look on her face, she looked about the room for the bassinet and baby. "Where is he, Leanne? Where is the baby?"

"Barbara …! You came back and took him out!" she cried. "You said his pediatrician needed to check him."

"I haven't been in here since I delivered him to you. Who picked him up?"

"Don't you remember … you were wearing a mask and you sounded like you had a cold. You were so hoarse, I could hardly understand you."

"Leanne, believe me, I have *not* been back in this room. Something's not right here." She turned and raced out the door.

She searched each nursery unit and asked everyone she saw if they had picked up Leanne's baby. Panic stricken, she pounded on Wilda's door. Wilda, her face contorted in a frown, opened the door.

"I told you to come here an hour ago. I need to talk to—"

"Wilda, a baby is missing! I can't find Mrs. Joberst's baby. I left him in her room … the baby and bassinet are missing … no one has seen the baby. What has happened, Wilda? Mrs. Joberst says I came in the room and took him back to the nursery. I didn't! I haven't been back in her room until now."

"What do you mean? I saw you wheeling the crib back toward the nursery. I passed you in the hall and told you to come to my office as soon as you could."

"You did not! This is the first time I have seen you tonight."

"Where is that baby, Miss Goldeyer?"

"I don't know. All I know is that it is not in the any one of the nurseries, and it is not in Mrs. Joberst's room."

"My God! Could this be an abduction?

Barbara reached for the phone on Wilda's desk. "I'm calling a Code Pink," she said.

Wilda grabbed Barbara's hand. "Not until I've verified your story, young lady. You're not going to embarrass me with a false alarm."

"Then you'll assume the responsibility for the delay."

"I think not, Nurse Goldeyer," she said. "You will be held accountable for this fiasco. You are trying to embarrass me, aren't you?"

"I am not! Go do your own checking! If I were you, I'd signal the Code Pink now and check later."

"All right! But if you are misleading me, your nursing days in this hospital are over. They may be over anyway. I have a feeling you know more about the Joberst woman than you're letting on. You spend far too much time in her room."

"I'm out of here, you bitch! And the next thing I'm going to do is resign and look for another job. I don't have to put up with your harassment. You have a problem, you witch!" Barbara slammed the door as she exited. She needed to get back to Leanne.

Ignoring Barbara's last comments, Wilda picked up the phone and dialed the emergency number for Code Pink. The loudspeakers throughout the hospital blared, "Code Pink! Abduction! Code Pink! Abduction!" at thirty-second intervals for a full five minutes. Since no "All Clear" message had been forthcoming, every hospital employee was struck with a stark realization: This is not a drill!

The entire medical center faced an immediate lockdown. No one was allowed to enter or exit. Security guards scrambled to assume their pre-assigned positions at each exit. Department directors and administrators on the Disaster Team were notified to gather immediately in the administrative conference room, designated by policy as Operations Central. Within seconds, screaming sirens from police cars and SWAT team vehicles, their red and blue lights flashing, broke the usual nighttime quietness across the entire medical campus.

* * * *

Detective Blake Bartlett struggled to retrieve his cell phone from his jacket pocket. Earlier, he had toyed with the thought of turning it off while he watched his seventeen-year-old son play in a Roever High School basketball game. Now he wished he had done just that. Couldn't he have just one night with his family without interruption? What could it possibly be this time? It had better be important, or he'd blister the dispatcher tomorrow.

"Blake here," he answered, straining to hear with the background cheering noise from the bleachers.

"Blake, you're needed at Trinitus Hospital immediately. A baby has been kidnapped. It's Federal Judge Joberst's son. The chief said you'd better hurry. The FBI has already been notified."

After saying a few choice expletives under his breath, Blake whispered in his wife's ear and hurriedly made his way to the nearest aisle, stepping on a few toes as he went. He stood outside the gymnasium entrance while he waited for the squad car to arrive.

An off-duty policeman, moonlighting as a gymnasium guard, recognized him. "Hi, Detective! You're Will Bartlet's father, aren't you?"

"Yeah, how'd you know?"

"You look alike. Now I know where Will gets his height. He's quite a player. You ever play basketball?"

"Some ... in high school." He laughed. "Never as good as Will, though."

"With your build I bet that you—"

The patrol car, red light flashing and siren blaring, screeched to a halt before the guard could finish his sentence.

Blake jumped inside the car. He barely had time to fasten his seatbelt before the driver whirled the patrol car around and took off toward the hospital. On the way, Blake called to verify that the city's kidnapping protocol had been activated. Patrols had been dispatched to all public transportation terminals and freeway tollgates. *A futile effort,* he thought, *but it made a good impression on the media.*

Blake still held out hope that this was a false alarm and he could come back to the game. Never in all his years on the force had he dealt with baby abduction from a hospital, and it had to be tonight. It was a crucial game for Will's team, and he had looked forward to being there. He didn't look forward, however, to dealing with the complexities of a kidnapping investigation—it would drag on into the night. He would do the preliminaries, but then he would turn his file over to the FBI. *Maybe this is just a drill,* he thought hopefully.

At the hospital entrance foyer, Blake was met by Donna Kinnison, the administrative representative on call. Her attire suggested that she'd been yanked from some semi-formal affair. Her facial expression told Blake that this was not a drill. Donna hustled him down a back corridor to the administrative conference room. They had to fight their way through the throng of disgruntled visitors who had been denied exit, all with the same questions: "When can we leave? Why are we being held here like prisoners?"

Once they were seated around the conference table, Donna, wide eyed in panic and halting in her speech, tried to brief Blake as thoroughly as possible on the abduction. With pad and pen in hand, Blake jotted down the details along with the many questions that came to his mind. He listened intently to Donna's narration, wondering how much of it was truly objective and how much was colored by her own perspective. He didn't interrupt her but waited for a pause in her story to speak.

"I will need to talk to these individuals that I have listed here—the ones from your story," said Blake. He pulled the page out of his pad and handed it to her. "Of course, you do understand that the FBI will do a thorough investigation after I am through."

"I understand," she answered, her lower lip trembling and her hand shaking while she held the list. "We have never faced anything like this. I don't know what to do. How do I tell Mrs. Joberst? Her husband is on the way here. He's a judge."

"So I've heard," Blake replied in a hurried tone that reflected his impatience. He drummed his fingers on the table top. "Look … first, let me interview these people as soon as possible. About the mother … let her husband tell her. He likely will not be very happy with your hospital security if this is indeed a kidnapping—and I won't be happy with your hospital if this turns out to be a false alarm. I was pulled away from watching my son's high school basketball game."

"I'm so sorry," she said, her head hanging low. "I just don't see how it could happen. What are we going to do? We have taken such extreme measures to ensure security."

"Please *assemble* these people!" he snapped. "Time is of essence here. This isn't the time to speculate on whether your security system is adequate. Obviously it isn't."

Donna jumped to attention, startled by Blake's abrasiveness. "Whom do you wish to see first?"

"They are listed in the order in which I want them brought in here. Don't let any of them leave the building until I tell you."

\*     \*     \*     \*

Still seething from her words with Wilda, Barbara returned to her assigned nursery unit to complete her paperwork for the hours that she had been on duty. All the nursery nurses were still in a state of shock and disbelief when she returned. She wandered through the other units carrying the Joberst infant's chart with her, hoping one of the nursing staff would say they had picked up the baby by mistake. In less than thirty minutes, she gave up hope. The baby had been kidnapped! What would happen now?

She had to see Leanne and tell her again that she had not returned to the room for the infant, that it was someone else. She stepped out into the hall, still with the baby's chart in hand, and started toward Leanne's room. The usual security guard was no longer present, but instead two uniformed Dallas police officers guarded the access to the suite. They were so involved in their dialogue—punctuated by frequent outbursts of laughter—that they hadn't noticed that the door had been left partially ajar.

"I need to see Mrs. Joberst," she said as she flashed her badge.

"Sorry, miss," one of the policemen answered. "Her husband is in the room. He is breaking the news to her about the—"

Loud voices from inside the room interrupted the officer. No attempt had been made to completely close the door and seal off the obvious dispute between Leanne and her husband. The policeman turned back to talk to his partner. Barbara stood away from the door, still within earshot of the conversation inside, and pretended to study the hospital chart.

"How did this happen, Leanne?" Judge Joberst yelled. "Weren't you the least bit suspicious when the nurse returned so soon for the baby? I'm sure there'll be demands for ransom, and now we'll have to face the media." Glancing through the crack in the door, Barbara could see Anthony pacing around the room.

"I just want my baby back, Anthony, whatever the cost," said Leanne, seated in a chair with her hands covering her wet face as she sobbed.

"The demands will come and the FBI will try to negotiate, but they are rarely successful finding children—not until they find the dead body."

Leanne leaped to her feet, her eyes showering daggers. "You son of a bitch! How can you be so cruel? How can you talk about my baby being dead? Your only concern is the money and your goddamn image. You bastard, get out! Get out of my room! You hope the baby's dead, don't you? You know it's not yours. You can't stand to be beat, can you, Anthony? But you've lost this time, Anthony. I'm leaving you as soon as I can get out of here."

"Sure, and you'll run right after that Marchesa bastard again, won't you?" he screamed. "You're not going to humiliate me in public again, Leanne. Stay away from him, do you hear me! Make one attempt to contact Marchesa, and I'll kill you!"

"I might just take my chances!" she replied, pointing her index finger at Anthony in a jabbing motion. "You're evil, Anthony. You're a disgrace to your profession. You're a despicable fraud. Get out of my room!"

"You want the baby back, you whore? You goddamn well will pay the price. As soon as the ransom demands come in, it's going to be your responsibility to pay it. You want the kid back, you pay!"

"Get out! Get out of here!"

Barbara peeked around the edge of the open chart in time to see Leanne crawl into her bed and hide her head in the pillow. Her entire body convulsed from her sobbing. *Maybe I can go in now, after her husband leaves*, she thought. She dropped her head as if studying the chart just as Anthony stormed out of the room and slammed the door behind him.

Barbara glanced up as Anthony raced by her and realized for the first time that she had never before seen him. His appearance didn't match the picture she had carried in her mind's eye. His professionally styled graying hair and the wrinkling of his clean-shaven face and neck told her that he was much older than Leanne. His well-groomed attire was a bit of a surprise: The cream-colored jacket over lighter colored pleated slacks, the pink tie, and the scent of fragrant cologne when he passed by certainly didn't give Barbara the impression of a strong masculine figure, such as she had seen in Mark.

When Anthony saw Barbara, he slowed his pace momentarily and stared at her with a haughty yet fiery look before moving on. A chill swept through her body and her heart skipped a beat. Did he know that she had heard his outburst when he threatened Leanne? There was no question about it: she had heard him threaten to kill Leanne! Mark's words, *I have a plan*, flashed through her mind. *I must talk to Leanne*, she resolved. *She may think that I had something to do with the disappearance of the baby.*

As soon as Anthony was out of sight, Barbara approached the policemen. "I really need to see Mrs. Joberst. Is it all right if I go in now?"

"I'm sorry, miss," one of the officers said. "We've been instructed to forbid anyone from entering except her husband and the OB-GYN unit nurse. Right now, no one else is allowed in the room."

"Could you ask her if she wants to see me?"

"I'm sorry. You will have to ask Detective Bartlett."

Barbara took a few steps down the corridor toward the nursery. She spotted Josie Trevino from dietary pushing a cart with food trays for mothers who were up late nursing their babies. Josie had taken a liking to Barbara and often at midnight she brought surprise dessert to the nursery. Seeing Josie triggered an idea.

"Hi, Josie," said Barbara. "Busy delivering snacks as usual, I see."

"We've got to keep 'em happy. I'll be by to see you after I deliver the last tray."

"Josie, I need to send a message to Mrs. Joberst. Would you take it for me?"

"Sure," she said. "I'll put it under the napkin. She'll be sure and see it. I can't go in her room, but the floor nurse will deliver the tray."

"Thanks, Josie. Don't tell the nurse what we've done. I'll explain later," said Barbara as she scribbled a note that said, *Leanne, I had nothing to do with taking the baby. Please call me. Barbara.* She wrote her cell number on the note and handed it to Josie.

As she turned to walk away, she heard steps behind her and turned to face Donna Kinnison.

"Oh, here you are. You are Nurse Goldeyer, aren't you?"

Barbara glanced at Donna's ID badge. "Yes, ma'am," she answered, startled by the uncommon presence of someone from administration on the nursery floor at that hour of night.

"I'm the administrator on call tonight," she said in a shaky voice after noticing Barbara's surprise. Barbara was struck by Donna's appearance—deep creases in her forehead and quivering facial muscles. "There's a detective in my office investigating the disappearance of the Joberst baby. He needs to talk with you."

The color drained from Barbara's face and her hand shook as she placed the baby's chart on one of the pull-down work desks that hung from the corridor wall.

"When? I'm on duty right now."

"He'll want to see you next—after he finishes the first interview."

"Let me complete my charting and I'll be down," she replied. She felt her throat tighten. *A policeman! What does he want from me?* she wondered. She needed to call Andy.

"Stay in the nursery and we'll call you when he's ready," said Donna. She turned to leave then stopped and turned back. "Miss Goldeyer, don't try to leave the hospital until the detective clears you to exit."

*Why did she say that?* Barbara wondered. *I hope Andy will hurry.*

## 9

Barbara returned the newborn's chart to the nursery and announced to one of the other nurses that she would be in the break room for a few minutes in case a call came for her. She retrieved her cell phone from her purse, entered the restroom, and locked the door. Andy answered the phone promptly, which told her that he had been studying late.

She struggled to find her voice. "Andy ... Andy," she said haltingly, in a muffled tone. "Are you awake?"

"Barbara, what's the matter! Where are you? I can barely hear you."

"Andy, I need you to come to the hospital—now, Andy. I am so scared." She began sobbing. "Please hurry."

"Barbara, what's wrong? What's happened?"

"Policemen are here ... someone took Leanne's baby ... they are going to interview me," she said between breathlessness crying. "I need you, Andy. I'm frightened."

"Barbara! Please calm down. Who is Leanne, and why are you being questioned?"

"I didn't get to tell you the story this morning. You were still asleep when I got home. I didn't want to bother you. I'll explain later. Please get a taxi and come help me," she pleaded. "There's some money for the taxi in the bottom drawer of my dresser—hidden under my jewelry box.

"I'll be there as soon as I can. Now stop worrying. We'll talk about it."

"The hospital is sealed off from anyone coming in. I'll try to get someone from administration to let you in. Please hurry, Andy."

"I will. Now, don't talk to anyone or answer questions until I'm by your side."

\*     \*     \*     \*

The call from Donna Kinnison came, and with trepidation Barbara entered the dimly-lit, empty, and eerily quiet reception area of the administrative suite of offices and took a seat in the corner. She had never been in an administrator's office before. She felt as if she were a student being sent to the principal's office. She could hear voices through the closed door to the inner offices. Her heart pounded inside her chest. Why was she so nervous? She had nothing to hide. She wished Andy would hurry. Soon, Donna appeared.

"Detective Bartlett will be ready for you soon," she said in a stern, authoritative voice. She had no sooner uttered those words than Wilda waddled through the door to the inner offices faster than Barbara had ever seen her move. She paused for a moment, scowled at Barbara, stuck her nose in the air, and marched out without saying a word.

"I am so frightened, Miss Kinnison. I want my husband to be here with me."

"I'm afraid that's impossible, miss," she answered. "The hospital is locked down. No one enters or leaves."

"Could you just ask the policeman? Please?"

Donna studied the pale, frightened nurse for a half-minute. "He said no one was to leave or enter."

"Please. I just don't think I could say anything … I am so scared," she pleaded, tears forming in her eyes. "I need to talk to Andy."

"Andy is your husband, I presume. Wait here while I ask Detective Bartlett."

Donna quickly returned. "He will arrange for him to be brought in. The detective said he needs to talk to him anyway."

"Why? Why does he need to talk to Andy?"

"He didn't say. You may go into the conference room now."

"Not until I talk to Andy," she retorted, her demeanor suddenly changing. Her eyes flashed with fiery resolve. *Why do they want to bother Andy?* she wondered, groping with her anger at the insinuation that Andy was involved in some way. *I haven't even had a chance to tell him what this is all about.*

Blake Bartlett walked in just in time to hear Barbara's response to Donna. He frowned, glanced at his watch, and shook his head slowly with an expression of constrained annoyance. He looked at Barbara. "I'll wait five minutes," he said. "You will talk to me here or I'll take you in. Where are the restrooms, Miss Kinnison?"

Donna jumped to attention and motioned for Blake to follow her toward the outside corridor. Simultaneously, Andy, escorted by two uniformed policemen, appeared at the door. Barbara leaped to her feet and ran to Andy's outstretched arms. Andy held her close for a second and turned to Blake.

"What's going on here?" he demanded.

Blake ignored Andy and glanced at Barbara again before leaving the room. "You have five minutes."

Alone in the reception room, Andy and Barbara huddled in a corner while Barbara, speaking in a near whisper, narrated the story of her attempt to help Leanne, her encounter with Mark Marchesa, the disappearance of the baby, and her accidentally hearing Judge Joberst's threats toward Leanne. Andy remained silent while Barbara spoke, the look on his face a mix of astonishment, curiosity, and irritation.

"Don't the babies wear those electronic security bracelets?" Andy finally asked.

"Someone gave the order to discontinue their use."

"I wish you had told me about all this earlier," he said. "You've been dealing with this alone for two days."

"I thought I was just helping a patient in need," she said. "The baby was abducted tonight, soon after I started my shift, and now they act as though I know something about what happened."

"I know. Now quit worrying. You've nothing to fear. We'll get through this fine. I'll stay with you while the detective questions you."

Blake returned and motioned for Barbara and Andy to follow him into the conference room. Just as Donna attempted to enter, he closed the door in her face. They took seats, with Blake on one side of the large conference table and Barbara and Andy on the other. Blake opened his yellow pad to a clean sheet and silently began scribbling notes. After an agonizing five minutes or so, he looked first squarely into Barbara's eyes and then into Andy's.

"I'm ready for your explanations—both of you."

"I'm not sure what you expect from us," said Andy in a bristling tone. "You ask the questions and we will answer."

"Mr. Goldeyer, a baby has been kidnapped. Your wife was seen taking the baby from the mother's room and the baby hasn't been seen since. We have strong suspicions that she had an accomplice, and right now you are the number-one suspect. As we speak, FBI agents are searching your home and are here in the hospital interviewing employees. I'm not asking questions, Mr. and Mrs. Goldeyer. I'm waiting for you two to give a statement before I turn you over to the FBI."

"Then we can end this promptly," said Andy, while Barbara clung to Andy and blotted her tears. "My wife has told her story to me and I believe her. We have no statement to give. We've done nothing wrong." Andy stood and helped Barbara out of her chair. "Right now, I am going to take my wife home, as soon as she turns in her resignation from this goddamn place. And whoever is in our home better have a warrant. We have nothing further to say to you without an attorney present. So the ball is in your court. We are leaving now. If you are going to hold us, you had best start now."

"Mr. Goldeyer ... please! Don't make me have to book and hold both of you," said Blake, his demeanor softer. "I apologize for my abruptness. I don't know you, but I have a feeling you are telling the truth. Please sit down for a few minutes. If you are innocent, then you are in a position to help us."

"Of course we want to help," Andy answered, as they both sat back down. "My wife is a dedicated nurse-caregiver. She has worked in several Dallas hospitals and has an exemplary performance record. I am scheduled to begin work at Trinitus Westlake as an administrative resident in a few weeks. Neither of us has anything to hide."

"There are likely explanations here, so let's begin at the beginning. First, Mrs. Goldeyer, would you mind taking off your shoe covers for me."

"Of course," she answered with a quizzical look on her face as she removed the throwaway shoe covers, showing her freshly polished, clean white shoes.

"Are those the same shoes you have been wearing all night?"

"Yes, sir," she answered.

"Nurse Witcher states that your shoes had no covers and that they were 'filthy-dirty.' I believe those were the words she used. You must have changed your shoes."

"No," said Barbara, "I clean and polish my shoes almost every day, and I always wear covers when I'm in the hospital."

"What about facemasks? Nurse Witcher said you were wearing a mask."

"We never wear masks unless we think we are coming down with a cold or unless we have a cough. Neither applies to me right now."

"May I call you Barbara?"

"Certainly," she answered.

"Barbara, Wilda Witcher seems to think that you spent far more time in Mrs. Joberst's room than would be expected of a nursery nurse. Would you mind narrating in detail your visits with Mrs. Joberst—what she said, impressions that you formed, and why you stayed in her room longer than you usually do when you deliver a newborn to its mother?"

Barbara glanced at Andy, who now had his arm around her shoulders. Her chin quivered as she cleared her throat and tried to speak. After a few moments, she faced Blake.

"When I went into her room with her baby, I could see that she was emotionally distraught. She was crying. I asked her if she wanted me to bring the baby in later. She asked me to stay. She was so upset that I stayed with her for a while to try to comfort her."

"Did she say why she was upset?"

Barbara looked at Andy again. He nodded his head and patted her back in encouragement. "Yes, sir," she said.

"So, why was she so distressed?"

"I'm sorry, sir," she replied. "We are not allowed to discuss anything about a patient's condition without their consent. We have to respect their confidentiality."

Blake jerked his head up and his mouth dropped in an astonished expression. He stopped his note taking and slammed his pen down on the table with a bang.

"Mr. and Mrs. Goldeyer, we are dealing with a serious crime here. I remind you that neither of you are beyond suspicion in this case. Now, you can either answer my questions or I'm taking you to headquarters."

"I will not betray a patient's confidence, sir," said Barbara. "I answered your question about why I stayed longer in Mrs. Joberst's room. I stayed because I was needed. It was my obligation and responsibility as a nurse, but I will not discuss the patient's condition further."

Blake threw his note pad on the table, stood, and paced around the room. He pulled his cell phone from his shirt pocket and headed for the exit door as he dialed a number and placed the phone to his ear. As the door closed behind him, Andy and Barbara could hear him say, "Blake Bartlett here. Please put me through to Agent …"

A full fifteen minutes passed, during which time Andy and Barbara exchanged only a few words. Barbara checked her cell phone. No missed calls, but she expected none. Finally, Blake re-entered the conference room.

"You are both confined to this room. I have policemen outside the door, so you should not try to go out except to go to the bathroom. I'm not sure how long it will be before the FBI agents will be with you. I am leaving now to find some place where I can write my report. I'll be back later to help the agents if they need me. Good luck … you seem like nice kids. Oh, I have one more question, Barbara. Do you know why the security tags were left off the baby's ankle?"

"No, sir. I was told someone in administration gave the order."

"Thank you, Barbara. Nurse Witcher thought you might know why the tag on the Joberst baby was missing."

# 10

FBI agent Ralph Walton clicked the off button on his speaker phone and turned to his associate.

"You heard the message, Wes. We've got our work cut out for us. Let's get moving."

Both Wes and Ralph jumped to their feet and grabbed their coats and cell phones, ready to rush to the crime scene. Ralph, surprisingly agile and athletic for his fifty-nine years, surged ahead. Wes Perkins, in spite of being at least twenty years younger than Ralph, struggled to haul himself and his fifty surplus pounds at the same pace.

They scrambled down the corridor to the express elevators to the basement parking garage in the multi-storied Dallas Division FBI building, Ralph on a high from the anticipation of working on a kidnapping case. He was sad that a child was missing, but it would be a pleasure to work on something other than mundane Medicare fraud cases. He had had his fill of those. They were all the same. No matter how thoroughly they had prepared their case, convictions were rare—especially if a Trinitus Healthcare System hospital was the accused. If the case went to Judge Joberst's court, which it nearly always did, the case would be dismissed on a technical ruling in favor of the Trinitus hospital every time.

Now that same judge's baby had been abducted—and from a Trinitus hospital—Ralph pitied the CEO of the hospital. Judge Joberst was known for his explosive personality when he faced adverse circumstances. The judge would demand not only explanations but also prompt action by the CEO. This alleged kidnapping sounded like a cut-and-dried case, according to the Dallas detective who first reported it to the FBI. Based on the detective's call, agents had been dispatched to the suspects' house and had started interrogating hospital employees.

*Probably someone was hoping to tap the Blanton fortune for a nice ransom*, thought Ralph. He was confident they would solve the mystery in a matter of days, negotiate the suspect into a trap and score a capture. It would make a good story for the media. Hopefully they could save the baby. The story of the Lindberg baby kidnapping ages ago came to mind. The alleged kidnapper was convicted, but the baby was never found. Ralph reassured himself that modern criminal investigative technology, which wasn't available in those days, would make a great difference in this case.

With red and blue lights flashing, Wes Perkins raced their vehicle down the freeway toward the hospital. "What's the status of the detective's investigation?" asked Wes.

"The DPD detective—I think his name's Bartlett—is holding two suspects at the hospital, but he has reached an impasse with his interrogation. He thinks our presence will help break the block."

Ralph and Wes presented their identification to the police officers and were passed through the front entrance of the hospital. They were met in the lobby by Donna Kinnison and Blake Bartlett and escorted to a private office in the administrative suite, separate from the conference room. Wes extracted a tape recorder from his bulky briefcase and clicked the "on" button. After formal introductions, Blake flipped through the pages of his notepad and briefed the agents on his findings to date.

"Your problem, then, seems to be the reluctance of the nurse to reveal the details of her visit with the mother of the baby. Am I right?" asked Ralph.

"She says she is not allowed to discuss anything about the patient's condition—that it violates confidentially," Blake replied.

"She probably doesn't know that the privacy law doesn't apply when a crime like this is being investigated," said Ralph. He glanced at Blake with a look of skepticism. "Apparently, you are not familiar with that fact either."

Blake bristled but restrained his ire. "Only vaguely," he said.

"Well … is she a suspect or not?" asked Ralph with contempt as he impatiently tapped his fingers on the conference table.

"I really don't think she is. It looks like a case of mistaken identity," Blake answered, and he told the agents about the information he got from Wilda relating to the face mask, the dirty shoes, and the hoarse voice. "But she knows more than she's telling. The nurse's husband couldn't have been here at the time of the abduction. He doesn't have transportation, for one thing, and the security system shows no record of his even attempting to enter the hospital at that hour."

"Have you checked the surveillance tapes?" asked Ralph.

"Yes. No one came across that met his description."

"Did *anything* unusual happen at the time?"

Blake told Ralph about the check-in system, which showed that Barbara was already in the nursery when she tried to enter at her usual time. He also mentioned the absence of the electronic ankle tag.

"If the nurse is not a suspect, as you say, then we have a case of ID card forgery to deal with also. We need to check the surveillance film carefully and look at everyone that entered last evening. The accomplice must have had a forged ID as well. Is there any explanation for the missing security device on the infant?"

"Only that someone ordered the bracelets discontinued."

"Let me talk to Nurse Goldeyer and her husband."

"Be my guests," Blake answered in a sarcastic tone.

\*   \*   \*   \*

Blake led the agents down the corridor and stopped at the entrance to the conference room. "I'll go in first and announce your arrival," he said, his hand gripping the doorknob. "The girl's name is Barbara. She's pretty unstable at this point, as you would expect. You'll need to handle her carefully. Her husband is very protective and can get pretty defensive."

Ralph rolled his eyes sideways and upward toward the ceiling as if to say, "What's new." Wes dropped his head and grinned, waiting for Ralph's response. "I've interviewed one or two suspects before, Detective," Ralph replied with a tenor of arrogance.

"I'm sure you have," Blake answered. "Your reputation precedes you. I am well aware of your investigation of the Alberto Marchesa case."

Ralph's face paled; the pallor was quickly replaced by a faint wave of pink. Wes's grin flattened. "What do you know about the Marchesa Mafia case? That was three years ago."

"The FBI Police Academy for law enforcement officers uses that as a teaching tool," Blake replied as he turned away to hide a smile. He went into the meeting room and closed the door behind him.

Just hearing the name Alberto Marchesa caused Ralph's stomach to knot and a cold chill to race through his veins. Would his goof in that case ever be forgotten?

Now it was being used in a classroom. *How Not to Screw Up an Investigation.* How embarrassing.

Andy jumped to his feet when Blake entered. "Are we about through here? I need to take my wife home."

"I'm afraid not, Mr. Goldeyer," Blake replied. "The FBI agents are here and will question both of you further. I will stand by, but it's up to the agents now to determine what steps to take. They may have to get a subpoena to force you to answer questions if you refuse to cooperate. In the interest of time, Barbara, I really think you should go along with their requests for information."

Barbara looked at Andy. "I am so scared, Andy. What's going to happen?"

"You'll do fine," Andy replied. "Let's just see what kind of questions they ask."

"Barbara, I've told the agents there's no evidence to suggest you are guilty of wrongdoing," said Blake. "It seems to be a matter of mistaken identity. A crime has been committed, and you might have knowledge of information that will help the FBI solve the mystery."

"We have to trust Detective Bartlett, Barbara," said Andy as he seated himself next to Barbara, dabbed her wet face with a tissue, and put his arm around her shoulders. "Let's get on with it, Detective."

"You'll do all right," said Blake. "Just tell your story as accurately as possible. Try to remember every detail."

Barbara raised her head, smiled at Andy, and looked up at Blake. "I'll do my best. Thank you."

Blake invited the agents in and introduced them to Andy and Barbara, now seated at the conference table. Blake elected to stand near the door and observe. Ralph and Wes took seats across from the couple and pulled pads from their briefcases. Wes again activated the recorder. The sight of the tape deck and its whirring noise caused Barbara to stiffen. "It's okay," Andy whispered, patting her shoulder.

# 11

"Miss Goldeyer, I know you must be exhausted from all of this questioning. Detective Bartlett has been kind enough to do the preliminary inquiry here, but as you know the FBI assumes the lead role in investigating cases such as this. Kidnapping is a federal offense. The local detective has provided us with the information that he has discovered so far, and he tells me that you are reluctant to discuss details of your visits with Mrs. Joberst."

"I'm just not sure how much confidential information I can reveal. We are warned over and over again about the patient's privacy protection."

"I can appreciate that, Miss Goldeyer, but you must understand: in the investigation of a known crime, a federal offense, the privacy law does not apply. In fact, when urgency is of paramount importance, your reluctance could be interpreted as obstructing justice. You are at liberty to disclose details of any conversation you have had with Mrs. Joberst without feeling like you have violated a patient's rights."

"How could our conversations be of assistance to you?" asked Barbara, now appearing more composed.

"There might just be a fragment of information from our talks that would lead us in the right direction. I urge you to cooperate. We must act quickly if we are to recover this infant."

Ralph paused for a few moments to let Barbara contemplate his words while he shifted his note pad on the table top and uncapped his pen.

Barbara glanced at Andy, dropped her head, and stared as though she were looking at the bottom of a deep canyon. She couldn't betray Leanne. But if anything could be done to return the baby, Leanne would want her to tell everything. Finally, Barbara looked up at Blake, who quietly nodded. She turned to Andy. "What do you think?"

"It's your decision," he answered. "I think we can trust these gentlemen not to lead you astray."

"Will anything I say be made public?" she asked Ralph.

"No, the information we get from you will only be used by the FBI to track down the kidnappers. No one will have access to what you tell us."

"Let's get this over with."

"I would like for you to describe every detail of your visits to Mrs. Joberst—what she said, how she acted, anyone's name she mentioned, and anything about her personal life. Can you do that?"

"Yes, sir. I think I can," she answered. She described everything she could remember from the time she arrived at the nursery two days ago until the time of the abduction. Ralph scribbled rapidly on his yellow pad, occasionally raising his head and studying Barbara's face as if confirming in his own mind the truthfulness of her story. At the first pause in her statement, he interjected a request.

"Tell me more about this 'Mark' person. What do you know about him? What's his last name."

Barbara described Leanne's relationship with Mark and his position with the hospital company that his father founded. "His last name is Marchesa," she said. "His father is Victor Marchesa. Leanne said he founded a hospital company called CareCompHealth."

"Marchesa!" said Ralph aloud. Would that name haunt him the rest of his life? Here he was investigating a totally unrelated case, and the Marchesa name had arisen twice in the last hour. He remembered: Alberto did have a brother who had nothing to do with the Marchesa Crime Family. That had to be Victor. The FBI had tried unsuccessfully for years to link him to the Mafia. All reports showed him to be indisputably clean.

"So, Mrs. Joberst asked you to notify Mark about the baby? Why didn't she call him herself?"

"I told you!" Barbara spat back with fire in her eyes. "She was confined to her room without a telephone. She was a virtual prisoner."

"She had no way of communicating with the outside world?"

"That's correct. She said her husband had her guarded and had forbidden all incoming and outgoing calls."

"Did she make any comments about what she planned to do about her unpleasant relationship with her husband?"

"She said that she wasn't going to take ..." She stopped. Her eyes widened and her mouth dropped.

"What was she not going to do?"

"She said she didn't want to take her baby home," Barbara finally said.

"Why?"

"I don't know."

"Come on, Miss Goldeyer. Didn't you ask her out of curiosity? Why did she not want to take her baby home?"

Barbara looked at Andy. Did she have to answer the question? What was the agent trying to prove? Surely he knew from what she had said that Leanne was afraid of her husband. Barbara hesitated, as though searching her mind for the right way to answer Ralph.

"She just wasn't getting along with her husband."

"When you met with Mark, what did you talk about?"

"I just delivered the message that Leanne had had a baby boy."

"There was no other discussion between you?"

"He just said words to the effect that everything was going to be all right."

"That he planned to do something?"

"He didn't tell me what he was going to do."

"So, do you think he planned or had plans to do something?"

"I have no way of knowing."

"Did you arrange to see him again?"

"No! I just helped Leanne get the message to him?"

"Did Mrs. Joberst or Mark Marchesa pay you to help them?"

"No! I just felt sorry for her because she was so miserable."

"Miss Goldeyer, did you know that whoever took the baby had an accomplice?"

"How would I know that?"

"Look, I'll ask the questions. Did you help Mark abduct the baby? It would be worth a lot of money to you to assist Mark Marchesa, wouldn't it? Did the two of you kidnap that infant?"

"Of course not! I have told you and Detective Bartlett the truth. I want to go home, Andy."

"I think it is time to stop this harassment—all of you," said Andy, standing and flashing daggers at all three. "If you have any more questions, ask now. I'm calling a lawyer. I think we still have some rights in this country."

Ralph paused for a painful half-minute and studied the young couple carefully during the silence. "You may go—both of you. You are not to leave the city under any circumstances until we grant you the freedom to do so. We will monitor your every move, every telephone call, every visitor. We are a long way from solving this mystery, so I can't tell you how long you will be under our surveillance. If you hear anything from either Mark Marchesa or Leanne Joberst, you are to let me know immediately. Do you understand?"

"Yes, sir," Barbara and Andy both replied.

"Keep my card handy. If you dial this number and identify yourself, either Mr. Perkins or I will return your call."

"I hope I hear from Leanne. I don't want her to think I had anything to do with taking her baby."

"We will tell her that likely someone masquerading as a nursery nurse took the child. One other thing, Miss Goldeyer. Have you noticed anything unusual in or around the hospital recently? Anything out of the ordinary that stirred your suspicion?"

"No ... not that I can think of. I wondered why the security system showed me present when I checked in for work. I am certain I checked out after my last shift."

"Nurse Witcher seemed to doubt that."

"That doesn't surprise me. She doesn't like me. I don't know why. I had a hard time convincing her to call a Code Pink. She thought I was trying to embarrass her."

"Wait, now," said Ralph. He and Wes came alive, their eyebrows raising and chins dropping in obvious surprise. "She told us that you tried to stop her from sounding the alarm about a missing baby."

"That's not true. She delayed calling the code and threatened me with disciplinary action if it was a false alarm."

"Whom do we believe, Miss Goldeyer?" Ralph retorted. "Do you have a nickname for Nurse Witcher?"

"All of the nursery nurses call her the same."

"And what is that?"

Barbara face became flushed for a second before she answered. "We call her 'the Witch.'"

"So you don't like *her*, do you?" Ralph said, keeping his eyes fixed on Barbara's. "How do you explain someone else having your ID card, Miss Goldeyer?"

"No one else had my card—it never left my possession."

"One other item, Miss Goldeyer. I am told that the baby did not have an electronic security tag on his ankle. How do you explain that?"

"I don't know. When I came to work I was told that administration had discontinued their use."

"How do the security tags work to protect a newborn from being abducted?'

"There are sensors in the stairwell and in the elevators. The security tags trigger the alarm system if the babies get close enough."

"Then their presence is important, isn't it?"

"Yes, sir," she answered.

"Did you remove the ankle device from the Joberst baby, Miss Goldeyer?"

"No ... no," she said, her eyes flashing with resentment. "Of course not. Why would I do that? I didn't want that baby kidnapped." Andy bristled and started to stand. Ralph motioned for him to remain seated.

"Thank you, Miss Goldeyer. Don't forget my instructions about leaving the city," said Ralph as he stood, repacked his brief case, nodded to Wes that they were finished, and turned toward the door. Wes turned off the recorder. "Now, once again before you go: Have you noticed anything else unusual at the hospital this evening that might be crucial to our investigation?"

"I think my wife has endured enough of this torture, Agent Walton," said Andy. "She has answered every question truthfully. We are—"

"Wait," said Barbara, gazing pensively across the room. "Each evening lately when I park my car and come into the hospital, the same old gray van has been parked in the entrance driveway. Never anyone in the car, but I always had a weird feeling that someone was watching me when I entered. Then, tonight, there was an odd-looking man in the driver's seat. He didn't look at me, but I could see his eyes were fixed on his rearview mirror."

Ralph stopped and whirled toward Barbara, motioning to Wes to restart the recorder. "Every evening?" he inquired. "For how long?"

"Probably a month at least."

"Describe the vehicle, Miss Goldeyer. Try to recall every detail."

"It was a dirty gray, like it hadn't been washed or polished for a long time. One of the windows was cracked, and so was the windshield."

"What make was it, like a Ford or a Chevy or a Dodge?"

"I can't be sure—I think maybe an old Dodge."

"Anything else?"

"I do remember noticing that one of the fenders—I believe it was the left front ... no, it was the right front—was loose and the right front door was partly ajar, held partially closed by some kind of wire—I think a piece of electrical wire."

"So this last evening you saw the driver for the first time?"

"Yes, sir."

"Can you describe him?

"I just saw his head. It was large, sort of puffy looking. I could hardly see his eyes—his eyelids were so puffy—but I could tell that he was staring at his rearview mirror."

"You're sure no one else was in the front seat."

"I didn't see anyone, but as I was walking away, I heard a door slam. I didn't look back, but I heard the engine start and the van pull away from the entrance, moving fast."

"What did you think at the time?"

"I was just startled. It just didn't seem right, but I thought it was nothing to worry about that close to the security station."

"We may be on to something here," said Ralph, as he scrambled to repack. He turned to Blake. "Detective, put out an all-points alert on the van right away, please. Wes, we need to get to the office and a computer. Call in now and get somebody working on this. Start a filter process."

Blake bolted out of the room with his cell phone in hand, followed by the agent. As he passed through the door, Ralph called back, "Miss Goldeyer, please let us know if you can think of anything else. Thank you very much, both of you, for your help. We will be in touch. Don't leave town!"

# 12

A week passed without any word from Leanne. Barbara was just beginning to enjoy the housewife routine—spending time with Andy and trying recipes that her mother had given her after her wedding—when Melanie Phelps, chief nursing officer at Trinitus, called. She pleaded with Barbara to withdraw her resignation.

"We need you, Barbara," she said. "I have learned more about the circumstances surrounding your decision to quit. I'd like to talk to you about it."

"I do miss my work, Miss Phelps, and I have to work while my husband is in school."

"Then you need to come back."

"Anything new on the kidnapping?" asked Barbara. "The newspapers seem to be keeping it quiet."

"That's the FBI's instructions to everyone. We are not to discuss the abduction with anyone. Apparently it's getting more complicated than they originally predicted. From what I heard, there have been no ransom demands so far, and they have no suspects."

"Does anyone know how Mrs. Joberst is doing?"

"Not a word since she went home. No one seems to know anything about her. They say that Judge Joberst was about as antagonistic and abusive as anyone could be before Mrs. Joberst left the hospital. He blames the hospital, especially the nursing staff, saying if we had had a better security system this would never have happened. When you watch his interviews on TV, he acts like he enjoys being in the spotlight."

"I agree," said Barbara. "I saw him once. All I could think of was how miserable Mrs. Joberst must be. She was never given a chance to express her grief or plead for the baby's return."

"What do you say, Barbara?" she asked. "Can we count on you?"

"I'll talk to my husband and let you know. I would welcome a chance to return, but my husband doesn't like me working at night."

"Do you want daytime hours?"

"I'd love that. You need to know that we will be moving to Westlake shortly."

"I know. I have spoken to the administrator and he agrees that we owe you special consideration after the chaos you went through a few days ago."

"Thank you, Miss Phelps. Just let me know when to start."

"Right now, just take a few days off. You'll need to go by HR when you return. With the confusion after the abduction we are recalling all of the ID tags."

\*   \*   \*   \*

Barbara had welcomed the time off—she had had a lot to do for the move to Westlake—but now she looked forward to returning to work. Her mind wandered as she dodged in and out of the early-morning traffic. Leanne should have contacted her by now. She desperately wanted to hear from her. Something kept telling her that Leanne needed someone to talk to.

Why had Miss Phelps been so condescending? Were they really being apologetic because of the way she had been treated? Or were they worried that she might reveal something about the breakdown in the security system at the hospital on the day of the abduction—no electronic devices on the newborns' ankles. *Maybe I'm getting too suspicious*, she thought.

It seemed strange to Barbara to be cruising through the employee's parking lot looking for an empty slot at that early hour—the same time she was usually finishing her night shift and preparing to head for home. She felt guilty thinking of all the night-duty nurses dragging themselves to their cars after their night shift, hoping to get a few hours' sleep before attacking their housework. Again she reminded herself how fortunate she was that Andy helped her around the house so much.

She swiped her new ID badge and entered the nursery unit and the report room for the coordination meeting between the exiting and oncoming shifts. She scanned the group—Wilda the Witch was not present. No one volunteered why and she didn't ask. What a pleasure it would be to work day shifts without Wilda watching her every move. After report, she moved into her assigned unit. The first thing she noticed was the presence of ankle tags on every baby.

\* \* \* \*

The babies were out with their mothers, and Barbara was attending to her routine paperwork when she heard a knock on the view window. Melanie Phelps motioned to her to come out. Barbara glanced at the wall clock. *Awfully early for anyone from administration to be at the hospital,* she thought. *Must be important.*

"Welcome back, Barbara," she said. "We've missed you around here."

"Thank you, Miss Phelps. Glad to be back. I'm having a problem adjusting to a daytime shift." Barbara laughed. At the same time, her suspicion tugged at her again. Why was the chief nursing officer here at this hour, and why the patronizing tone? Miss Phelps's broad smile and musical intonation seemed anything but genuine.

"I wanted to have a few minutes with you before the day gets too far underway, Barbara," she said.

"I have a few minutes before I go back after the babies."

"Good," she answered and motioned for Barbara to sit beside her on one of the benches in the viewing corridor. "I know you will be moving to Westlake soon. I presume you will want to continue working in the nursery."

"Yes, I want to work toward certification so I can be assigned to the neonate intensive care unit."

"They have a good program at Trinitus Westlake. I encourage you to enroll there. I can assure you that you will have a good chance of being accepted."

"Thank you, Miss Phelps."

"Our administrator here has contacted the key people in Westlake. You'll have good recommendations."

"I'll send my resume right away."

"Good! I'll get the recommendation letters ready. Everyone I've talked to in administration says they hope you will stay on the Trinitus team."

"I'm looking forward to it," Barbara replied. *Where is she going with this?* she wondered. *Administration doesn't know me from the kitchen dishwashers. She'll get to the point soon, I'm sure.*

"I guess you noticed the security tags are back in use?" she asked, looking straight into Barbara's eyes. Her fake smile now transformed into a furtive smirk. "I don't know why there is so much concern about the ankle bracelets, do you?"

"I imagine someone thinks they might have prevented the abduction."

"That's another reason I wanted to talk to you, Barbara," she said, her smile and lilting tone now gone. "We don't think anyone on the Trinitus team needs to say anything more about the missing ankle tags the night of the abduction. Of course, the kidnapping is considered a sentinel event, and we have to make a full report or we could lose our accreditation."

"Neither the FBI agents nor the police detective seemed concerned about the electronic ankle tags."

"That means they don't think it important in this case," said Melanie Phelps. "But we know it is, don't we? I'll let you get back to work, Barbara. Again, we're glad to have you back, and wish you the best in your training at Trinitus Westlake. We know you won't disappoint us."

"Thank you, Miss Phelps. I'll try not to."

* * * *

Another week passed. Barbara's disappointment at not hearing from Leanne was tempered with her enjoyment of daytime duty in the nursery. Every day, Barbara thought back about her discussion with Melanie Phelps, especially her comment on the tiny electronic devices wrapped around each baby's ankle. Could that have saved Leanne's baby from being taken?

Barbara couldn't erase the thought from her mind. With the ankle bracelets in place, if a newborn was taken close to an exit door or too close to an elevator, an alarm would sound and the "Code Pink" protocol would be activated automatically. Why was their use discontinued the very day that the baby was kidnapped?

Barbara finished her day. After completing last minute entries in the babies' charts, she swiped out and exited through the employees-only passageway. In the parking lot, her faithful old VW awaited her. As she did each day, she prayed it would start. On the driver's side windshield, under the wiper, was a folded paper note. Her heart skipped a beat. Was she in some reserved parking spot? She and Andy just couldn't afford one of those fines that were so liberally assessed by the hospital for parking infractions by employees.

The note was handwritten, so no parking fine, thank goodness. Who would leave her a note? Who even knew what her car looked like? She opened the note. In very neat handwriting, the message said,

> Miss Goldeyer, Leanne sends her regards. She would like for you to meet her in the lobby of the Monique Salon, tomorrow if possible. She is there each day from 1:00 to 3:00 for massage therapy and she is eager to see you.
>
> Mark Marchesa

What a surprise! Not only had she heard from Leanne, but the message came from Mark, meaning Leanne and Mark had to be in communication with each other. She remembered passing the Monique Salon in the Prescott center. The luxurious appearance of the salon from the outside probably meant that the monthly membership dues were more than she made in six months. By good fortune, she was off duty all day the next day. If Andy approved after she told him about the note, she would go there about one-thirty.

*     *     *     *

"Barbara, I'm not sure you should go," said Andy. "We told the FBI agents we'd let them know if Leanne or Mark contacted us."

"I just feel like Leanne needs me. I've had that feeling all along. We need to go, Andy."

"You're usually right. I'm just concerned. I'll go with you and wait in the car."

"Good, or let me out in the back so I won't be embarrassed about our car. I remember what the cars in the parking area looked like when I passed by there."

"I think we should call Agent Walton, like we promised."

"Okay, we'll discuss it later, but I have to go."

"Then I will drive you there and wait for you outside."

"I wish you'd go in with me."

Andy laughed. "Good idea, a massage by a French masseuse."

*     *     *     *

The interior of the Monique Salon looked just as elegant as Barbara had imagined: shiny brass fixtures and marble everything—floors, columns, and pedestals on which sculptures rested. Tastefully placed contemporary art work decorated each ten-foot marble wall. The lobby area was as large as that of a five-star hotel. A delightful fragrance saturated the air, a mix between lilac and jasmine. No receptionist was visible, but Barbara could see objects strategically placed near the vaulted ceiling that were probably the lenses of surveillance cameras.

Within seconds after Barbara entered, a stylishly dressed young girl with heavy makeup, appearing as though she had just stepped off of a fashion magazine cover, came from behind one of the columns. She looked quizzically at first at Barbara, studying her appearance from head to foot and then smiled, now remembering that she had been told that Leanne was expecting a visitor.

"You must be Barbara Goldeyer. Mrs. Joberst is expecting you. Please follow me; she is in one of the private treatment chambers."

Leanne, dressed in a colorful silk robe, was reading a magazine, her feet soaking in a pink-colored solution in a large stainless-steel vessel. She jumped to her feet the minute she saw Barbara and held out her arms for a greeting hug.

"Barbara! You did come. Mark said he'd find you. How are you? I have so much to talk to you about."

"I've worried about you every minute of the day," said Barbara, as they released each other from a long embrace, neither girl making any attempt to conceal her tear-glazed cheeks. Barbara sat beside Leanne on the plush upholstered bench. "You did get my note?"

"Yes, it was a life-saver for me knowing someone in the world cared."

"You can't imagine how exhilarated I was when I found Mark's note. So you have been in touch with him?"

"Finally," she replied, "thanks to Monique. Mark is being followed day and night, either by Anthony's hired detective or by the FBI, or both. His driver has been able to outmaneuver the pursuers and drop him off here. How have you been? We need to bring each other up to date."

"I just can't imagine the torture you've gone through—losing a child, living under constant duress. How are you feeling? Are you taking care of yourself?"

"I'm doing fine. I'm still a little sore but getting better every day."

"Any word on the investigation? How have you survived this loss and this waiting?"

"We've had no word until last night. The ransom demand came. It was mailed to Anthony at his office. I haven't seen the demand, but I am told that it is a staggering amount. Anthony has decided not to tell the FBI that he received it—he just wants to pay it. It was accompanied by a picture of the baby." Her chin quivered. "It's heartbreaking, Barbara."

"I know it must be difficult for you. I feel so guilty, Leanne. I keep wondering if I could have done anything to prevent it."

"I knew you had nothing to do with the kidnapping, Barbara; I just knew. And then the thought of you being accused. I was devastated. Tell me how you have stood up to such a horrible accusation."

"It was a nightmare. First, I had to promise the FBI agent I would notify him if I was contacted by you or Mark in any way."

Leanne's chin dropped, she gasped, and her eyes widened with fear. "Do you think you were followed here?"

"No, I'm reasonably sure we were not. Andy dropped me off a half-block away, behind the building, and I walked in here." Barbara laughed. "Andy and I were embarrassed about our old car."

Leanne seemed to relax a bit and laughed at Barbara's comment about the car. "If we're discovered, we can always find another place," she said. "Tell me the whole story, please! Don't leave out anything. I feel so guilty getting you involved."

Barbara narrated the sequence of events from the time she discovered the baby was missing until she returned to work at Trinitus. She included accidentally overhearing the argument between Leanne and her husband, when he threatened to kill her.

"You understand what kind of person he is then," said Leanne. "He means it, Barbara. Somehow he's going to make an attempt. I know it's going to happen."

"We can't let it happen, Leanne," Barbara replied. "You've got to get away from him."

Barbara continued with her update. She described her confusion at the hospital's offer to allow her to work day shifts until she and Andy moved to Westlake. "That was so unusual. It seemed like they were trying to coerce me into doing something or saying something that I might be reluctant to do otherwise. Maybe I'm too suspicious."

"You're right to be suspicious," said Leanne. "They have some ulterior motive in mind. It probably has something to do with the security system at the hospital. Of course, the hospital knows that Anthony would never sue—Trinitus is one of Anthony's benefactors. Trinitus is probably afraid that their image will be tarnished if the public learns the ankle bracelets were not in place."

"All I can do is tell the truth if I am ever questioned."

"I don't think that holds true for most upper-level executives at Trinitus—according to bits of information I've heard from Anthony and from what Mark tells me about their tactics. According to Mark, the Trinitus non-profit status is a joke. They have as many for-profit divisions in their organization as they have so-called non-profit entities."

"How can they mislead the public year after year? Wait ... don't tell me." Barbara laughed. "They are saintly. No one would dare question the integrity of a church-owned business."

"You sound like Mark," Leanne answered with a chuckle.

"What's going on between you and Anthony? Are you still as miserable as ever?" asked Barbara.

"Of course—and it gets worse by the day," she answered. "I need to bring you up to date on my life since I saw you last. As you know, since a United States district judge is involved, the FBI took over soon after the abduction. With the investigation going on and no information about the baby, I had to go back home with Anthony. It was pure agony. I was interrogated in depth about every aspect of my personal life. They know that the DNA test was falsified and why. Therefore, with my story, they know the father of the baby is Mark."

"They didn't hear that from me."

"I know that. They played the entire tape for me so I could hear them question you and Andy. Of course, I confirmed everything you said as the truth. And by the way, the way you evaded the question about Mark's so-called plan was very tactful."

"You mean to say that Mark is a suspect?"

"Yes, he's still under suspicion. He couldn't explain to the agent's satisfaction his whereabouts on the night of the kidnapping."

"Do you know where he was?"

"I do now. He had donned a clinician's coat and ID badge from one of the CareCompHealth hospitals, put a stethoscope around his neck, and managed to get into the hospital as a doctor. He had intended to talk his way into the Women Services Unit and find me. Then the Code Pink was sounded. He was able to slip out past the guards just before the hospital was locked down, but he was seen on the surveillance tapes. He tried to deny he was here, but the agents have strong evidence that he was."

"Do they have any serious suspects?"

"None. That's what is so frustrating," Leanne replied. "Anthony says that he is sure Mark is responsible, that he hired someone to do the job. He has pressured the attorney general to file charges against Mark. Mark wouldn't put me through this agony, Barbara."

Barbara gently grasped Leanne's hand with both of hers. "I agree. "Mark cares for you, Leanne."

"Why won't Anthony let me go on TV and make an appeal for the return of my …"

She stopped and turned her head, her face wrinkled in grief as tears flowed. She turned back to Barbara and fell into her arms. "Oh, Barbara, will I ever see my baby again. Could he be dead? I am so alone. Please help me."

"Of course I will. I feel helpless, just as you do, but we can't give up hope," she replied as she held Leanne close and blotted her eyes. "What are you going to do, Leanne? What are you going to do about Anthony?"

"I can't leave Anthony with all this investigation going on. I can't go to Mark while he's a suspect. I just don't know what to do. I have no one to turn to, Barbara. I'm not a spiritual person, but I know that some force sent you to me. I always believe that everything happens for a reason. Just talking to you gives me hope."

"I'll help you, Leanne. Andy and I will help. Surely there is something we can do."

"Thank you, dear. And thank you for coming. Sometimes I don't think I can make it another day."

"Sure you can. It's going to be fine," said Barbara as she stood to leave.

"Oh, before you leave, I want to give you Mark's phone number. It's a payphone close to his office. He will be there exactly at ten o'clock in the morning every day he can get away. You can always call him and get a report on what's happening. Will you come back to see me, Barbara?"

"I promise. Can you call me?"

"I'm afraid to. The agents are probably monitoring your every call—just as they are Mark's. I can call Mark's payphone number, and so can you. That's how we'll stay in touch."

"Don't give up, Leanne. Andy and I will help you. There has to be a way. We'll find a way."

# 13

The move to Westlake was only three weeks away. Getting around in their tiny apartment meant sidestepping and jumping over boxes. Andy had done most of the packing, but Barbara had found time to wrap her fragile possessions carefully to guard against breaking. She had so many prized pieces of china that she'd gotten as wedding presents, but she had never had an occasion to use them. Some day maybe they would be able to entertain.

With her daytime work schedule, Barbara had managed to visit Leanne at least twice a week, always at the Monique Salon. The disappearance of Leanne's baby remained a mystery, and the one ransom demand had been followed by a long period of tormenting silence. Each time she had visited, Leanne seemed closer to a breaking point, appeared sleep deprived as well as malnourished. Barbara had spent hours reassuring Leanne, begging her not to give up hope, and encouraging her to notify the FBI about the first demand.

"You've got to let the FBI know what's going on, Leanne," Barbara advised. "They know how to handle situations like this."

"Anthony will not agree," Leanne said.

"What did the note say exactly?" asked Barbara.

"I haven't seen it," she replied, "but Anthony told me it warned that if we let the FBI know about the ransom offer, we would never see the baby again."

Barbara was silent for a few moments, as if contemplating Leanne's reply. "I understand how you feel," she said finally. "I don't know what I'd do in a similar situation."

"The visits you and Mark make are the only thing that keeps me alive, Barbara," Leanne said with tear-filled eyes. "You have no idea how much it means to me for you to come."

"I'll keep coming," Barbara said. "You've got to relax and take care of yourself. I have another day off this week—I will see you then. Now, get that sad look off your face. I have a feeling that good things are going to happen."

"Thank you again, Barbara."

\* \* \* \*

Barbara climbed out of the car—parked two blocks away from the alley behind the Monique. She gave Andy a kiss and started her trek toward the entrance. She paused once and glanced back. Nothing seemed irregular, and she again chastised herself for being so suspicious. But she couldn't erase the weird feeling that something was not right. She waved to Andy and continued around the corner.

She entered the front door and was met by the receptionist, a frantic look on her face.

"She's not here, Barbara. She had a phone call and then hurriedly dressed and rushed out. She knew you would be coming so she scribbled a note and left it for me to give you."

Barbara's hand trembled as she opened the envelope while the receptionist looked on. The note read,

*Barbara, a new ransom letter! Anthony wants me to meet him at the bank immediately to arrange transfer of funds to his Bahamas account. He's convinced the baby's all right. Please call Mark.*

"Is anything wrong," the attendant asked, eyebrows arched.

"Uh ... no. I don't think so. She probably had to rush for an appointment."

"She looked so frightened ... and pale."

"I'm sure she's still recovering from her surgery."

Barbara walked back to her car at a fast pace, plopped in the front seat beside Andy, and let out a deep sigh.

"What's the matter? You look like you've been chased by the FBI." Andy laughed.

"No time for jokes, Andrew," she replied sternly. She narrated her experience in the Monique and handed Andy the note. "What do you think?" she asked after he had read the message.

"Something's happened here," Andy replied. "Agent Walton should be notified."

"Do you think I should call him?"

"You have to," he said. "You can't take the responsibility for not calling in case something goes wrong."

"Let's get to a phone. It's almost ten. She asked me to call Mark too. I'll call him first."

At the first public phone they could find, Barbara dialed the payphone number but got no answer. She repeated the call every five minutes until she was assured Mark was not there. It was the first time ever that he had not been by the phone when she called. Something had to have happened to keep him away from their only means of communication.

She dialed Ralph's number, knowing there would be a delay in reaching him. Andy circled the block while she waited for the return call. When he stopped to pick her up, Barbara could see that something worried him.

"What is it, Andy? What's wrong?"

"We're being followed. Has Mr. Walton returned your call?"

"No, he hasn't. Should we wait longer?"

"We've been identified by now. Let's just go straight home and wait there for Agent Walton to return your call."

As they drove away, Barbara looked in the rearview mirror and saw a dark sedan pull away from its parking spot across the street.

At their apartment complex, Andy parked in their designated slot. Both he and Barbara hopped out of the car at the same time and headed for the stair to their second-floor apartment. They had taken no more than two or three steps when the dark sedan screeched to a halt in the street adjacent to their unit. Ralph Walton and Wes Perkins approached in a near run.

"Are we going to tell them what we found out? We need to decide in a hurry," Andy whispered.

"Let's wait and see what they want. I'm sure Mr. Walton already knows that I placed a call for him," she replied.

"I agree."

Despite their different body shapes, the two agents looked much alike with their identical attire and stern, unsmiling expressions. Andy smiled, wondering if they rehearsed those appearances in front of a mirror each morning before they left home, like actors just before going on stage.

"Good evening, gentlemen," said Andy. His demeanor couldn't have been more cheerful.

"We need a few words with you," said Ralph with a stern tenor.

"Please come in," said Barbara. She turned to climb the stairs and motioned for the two men to follow. She stood before the door with the key in place and jiggled the lock until it finally worked.

"Would anyone like coffee?" she asked as they entered the packing box—cluttered apartment.

"We don't have much time, Miss Goldeyer. An urgent situation has arisen, and we need your help, both of you."

"I can't imagine any other questions you need to ask," said Andy as he scooted some boxes aside so the agents could sit.

"I see you're close to making your move to Westlake," said Ralph.

"Yes, sir," said Barbara. "You remember, we told you we were moving."

"I remember," Ralph answered. "I hope nothing has transpired that would force us to retain you as material witnesses."

"What do you mean?" asked Andy, his arms crossed and his brow furrowed.

"We have reason to believe that the kidnappers of the Joberst baby have sent a ransom demand to Judge Joberst—to his office. Now there are indications that Judge and Mrs. Joberst are making arrangements to transfer sizable funds to an offshore bank account in Anthony Joberst's name."

Barbara stood beside Andy and avoided looking directly at the agents. She wondered where they were going with all this—why they were there?

"How does that involve us?" asked Andy.

"We know that both Miss Goldeyer and Mark Marchesa have visited Mrs. Joberst at the Monique Spa on several occasions," said Ralph, carefully observing their reaction. "Miss Goldeyer, were you aware of any ransom demands?"

Barbara squirmed, trying to hide her astonishment at the question, and looked at Andy. How should she answer? The two agents had made it clear that Barbara and Andy were to notify the FBI of any information that might be related to the abduction. Neither Andy nor Barbara spoke for several moments. Ralph and Wes kept their eyes fixed on the couple while they waited for a response. Barbara turned to the agents with an unblinking fixed expression.

"Leanne needs friendship badly," said Barbara. She paused for a few moments. "I took it on myself to fulfill that need by visiting her. I have nothing to hide. When I see a need like that, I try to do what I can to help."

"That is a noble stance, Miss Goldeyer," said Ralph, "but you should have called us."

"I apologize. I encouraged Leanne to let you know about the first ransom demand. She said it had gone to her husband's office, that she had not seen the note."

"Now, do either of you know about any further ransom demands? Remember, we can hold you as material witnesses in this case. We expect you to tell the truth."

Andy looked at Barbara without speaking for a few moments and then nodded. He turned back to the agents.

"I will answer for Barbara," he said, an authoritative tone to his voice. "Leanne Joberst told Barbara several days ago that her husband had received a demand … for ten million dollars. Mrs. Joberst indicated to Barbara that when the time came she would transfer that amount to an offshore account in the name of her husband. He had convinced her that he could negotiate terms with the abductors for the return of the baby in exchange for the ransom—without help from the FBI."

"Then the kidnappers were to be paid out of the offshore account?"

"From what Leanne told Barbara—correct me if I am wrong, Barbara—the note contained no other instructions, only a picture of the baby. Until today, there had been no new contact with the kidnappers. There has been complete silence. That in itself has been devastating to Leanne, not knowing whether the baby is even still alive. My wife has done what she can to comfort Mrs. Joberst. Also, she has emphasized to Leanne the need for the FBI to be informed about the contact."

Ralph kept his eyes fixed on Andy. "And today?" he asked. "Mrs. Joberst burst out of the Monique in a run. She had obviously been expecting Barbara to visit, because you dropped her off at the usual spot." He turned to Barbara. "Why did Mrs. Joberst leave in such a hurry?"

Barbara dropped her gaze to the floor and remained silent for a moment. Then she reached into her purse and pulled out the note and gave it to the Ralph.

"Maybe this will explain her haste," Barbara replied, her chin trembling. "As soon as I learned that there had been further contact with the kidnappers, I placed a call for you, Mr. Walton. I have advised Leanne over and over again to call you. She said that her husband was dead set against it."

"That attitude could mean that the baby is no longer alive," said Ralph, scowling as he read the note. "The crucial component in cases like this comes at the time of the exchange of money for the abducted child. If we had been told about the first request, we might have been able to turn up enough clues to apprehend the kidnappers and save the baby. Once the criminals have the money, they have no concern for the baby."

"What can you do now?" asked Barbara. "Is there a chance to recover the baby?"

"We'll continue to try," he replied. He held up the note. "This information will help. Both of you need to know this: A crime has been committed. Whether or not the Jobersts want the FBI involved, we are obligated to do everything in our power to arrest the criminals. Anyone who interferes is obstructing justice. That includes the parents and the two of you."

"We were just complying with the Leanne's request."

"By withholding information, those parents might have denied us a chance to save the baby."

Andy looked at Barbara with a look of admonishment. "We'll be moving in a few days, but in the meantime, what should Barbara do about visiting Leanne?"

"I agree that Barbara's visits help Mrs. Joberst cope with her loss," he answered. "I hope I can rely on both of you to pass on to us any information that might be helpful in bringing this complex case to a close."

"You can count on our assistance," said Andy. "We are so close to making the move, Barbara won't be able to spend much time with Leanne, but if she finds anything you need to know about, I'm sure she will call." Barbara nodded in agreement.

Agent Walton stood and paced about the room (as well as he could with all the packing boxes in the way). He was silent for a half-minute, but his wrinkled face conveyed his irritability and despair.

He spoke directly to Barbara. "I'll ask one more question. If the parents' attempt to redeem their baby without our help had been successful, as a nurse, what role would you have played in recovering and caring for the child?"

"That possibility has never been discussed," said Barbara, wide eyed with surprise at the question.

"I would not permit her to assume any role," said Andy sternly.

Agent Walton ignored Andy and kept his focus on Barbara. "If by some turn of events, we do become involved and are able to identify the location of the baby, would you assist us in a recovery operation."

Andy bristled. "Absolutely not!" he answered. "I would not agree to my wife being placed in that sort of danger."

"Miss Goldeyer?"

Barbara answered without even a pause, "Yes, I would do anything to help return that baby to its mother."

"Thank you, Barbara," said Ralph. He smiled and glanced at Andy with a look of triumph. "That's exactly what I expected you to say. I hope your new positions work out well for you. We'll be in close touch with both of you until this case is solved, no matter where you are living."

# 14

### *Westlake, Texas*

Andrew stepped out of the Yellow Cab, paid the fare, and stood for a minute at the taxi stand. He gazed across the street at the gigantic multistoried "Trinitus Westlake Medical Center" and its attached parking garage, which was almost as tall as the main hospital and almost as awe striking. A steady stream of automobiles entered and left the structure.

He climbed the marbled entrance staircase, entered a large foyer, and was met with a choice of three access-control gates, much like those found in an airport. He walked past the "Visitors" and the "Employees Only" signs, found the gate that said "Administration Guests," and, as instructed, stood in front of the turnstile while electronic equipment and cameras whirred.

Multiple laser dots showered his charcoal pinstriped suit, newly purchased at Barbara's insistence for this special occasion. After pressing his finger print in the appropriate square, an identification card inscribed with his name and his personal demographics popped up from a slot at the gate. As soon as he reinserted it, the gate opened, and the card immediately sprang back stamped with date, time, and a red letter warning him to wear the ID badge in plain sight at all times during his visit.

*Why the overkill on security?* he wondered.

Once inside the ground-floor administration wing, Andrew strolled down a long corridor past the myriad non-clinical departments. Portraits of Trinitus Healthcare System executives, dignitaries, and philanthropists lined each side of the hall. Finally, he came upon large, thick mahogany double doors, with panes of stained glass in the shape of a cross. On the wall alongside the doors, heavy polished brass letters declared this was the entrance to the Executive Suite.

Andrew checked his watch—ten minutes early for his appointment. Barbara would be proud of him. With trepidation, he slowly opened the door and entered to find an elaborately decorated waiting room. Indirect, subdued lighting bathed the rich-textured wall panels and the tasteful oil paintings of contemporary art that accented the color-coordinated decor. Immediately on his entering, at one end of the empty room, a door opened and a fashionably dressed "thirty-something" woman with a warm, captivating smile appeared.

"You must be Mr. Goldeyer," she said in a soft, lilting voice that seemed designed to calm anxiety.

"Yes," he answered, hoping the quivering in his voice was not too evident. "Am I too early?"

"Not at all, Mr. Goldeyer," she said. "Please be seated. Mr. Hensley will be with you in a few minutes. May I bring you coffee or a Coke?"

"No, thank you," he replied. He surely didn't need any caffeine, which would have made him more tremulous.

"I will let you know when Mr. Hensley can see you."

"Thank you, Miss …?"

"Oh, how rude of me! Henderson. I'm Karen Henderson. I am the administrative assistant to Mr. Hensley. Since you will be joining us, just call me Karen."

"Thank you, Karen."

Andrew picked up a copy of *Modern Healthcare* and eased into one of the several plush upholstered chairs. Within a few minutes, Karen again appeared and motioned for him to follow her. They traversed a wide inner corridor into which opened several private offices. *Must be assistants' offices,* Andy surmised. He could picture himself in one. At the very end of the hallway, Karen tapped on a door and cracked it open slightly.

"Mr. Andrew Goldeyer is here for his nine o'clock appointment, Mr. Hensley."

"Thank you, Karen," Mr. Hensley replied from across the office. "Please have him come in."

Karen opened the door wider to allow Andrew to enter. Jake Hensley's private office was a decorator's showplace. The large corner suite overlooked a courtyard so elegantly landscaped that it appeared to be a part of the office itself. Beautiful pecan-wood parquet floors were partially covered with expensive-looking oriental area rugs with muted colors that blended with both the wall covering and the tastefully chosen artwork. The same motif as in the waiting area was carried throughout.

Jake Hensley sat behind his huge oval desk with his back turned, gazing out the window, his cell phone cradled against his right ear. His low voice was barely audible. From the few words that Andy heard, he surmised that it was a personal call.

"He should be finished with this conversation a few moments," Karen whispered.

"Should I wait outside?"

"No, he signaled me to bring you in."

The waiting seemed like hours instead of moments. Andy could feel his stomach knot up and his throat tighten as he stared at Jake's head of generous, perfectly styled dark brown hair, not a single strand out of place. Recollections of stories Andy had heard about Jake Hensley sprinted through his mind. Rumors had it that Trinitus had transferred him from Amarillo to Westlake to "turn it around" like he had at Trinitus Memorial Hospital in Amarillo. Rumblings of the ruthless tactics he had used in Amarillo caused some anxiety among the physician-healthcare providers in Westlake.

Jake turned to face Andy and Karen as he finished the phone conversation. His clean-shaven face wrinkled into a broad smile, and with parting words that sounded like, "Meet you at the club," he snapped his cell phone shut, stood, and walked around the desk to greet Andrew. He was much taller than Andy thought when he'd seen him seated. A charcoal suit that appeared to be tailor-made draped his slender, athletic build.

"Welcome to Trinitus Westlake, Mr. Goldeyer."

"Thank you, Mr. Hensley. I'm looking forward to working here."

"I'm impressed with your resume, Mr. Goldeyer. Oh, by the way, how do you like to be addressed? Andrew? Andy?"

"Just call me Andy, sir."

"Good, Andy—and no 'sirs.' Everyone here calls me Jake."

"That may be a little hard for me for a while," Andy laughed and relaxed a little for the first time.

"You come to us highly recommended, Andy," said Jake as he thumbed through Andy's applications. "I have one small concern, Andy. Have you ever worked in a hospital—in any capacity?"

"No, sir … uh, Jake." Andy could feel perspiration forming around his hairline. *Where was Jake going with this?* he wondered

"So, your knowledge of hospital administrative problems comes from academic exposure."

"That's true," Andy replied. "Of course, we studied mock scenarios in our classroom work."

"The reason I ask, Andy, is this: You will encounter issues and problems in a hospital that are never discussed in any classroom," said Jake. His brow furrowed, he leaned forward on his desk, and he stared straight into Andy's eyes. "I expect you to be curious about what you encounter—ask questions, pin down any of us in administration with your questions. And along with that, when you bring problems and issues to us, I expect you to bring your own answers along with them."

"I understand. I don't have to tell you that I am in a learning mode. Some of my questions may sound foolish."

"Never doubt that we will take that into consideration, and don't be afraid to ask. All of us learn every time you inquire about the operation or organizational structure of our hospital."

"I guess I'll start with a stupid question. What will my specific duties be?"

"Nothing stupid about that question!" he answered. "First, you need to study the organizational chart, find out which department reports to whom in administration. Each associate administrator has certain departments that they are responsible for—like Laboratory, Radiology, Nursing, Dietary, and Physical Therapy. The directors of those departments report to one of the administrators. You will rotate time with each of the administrators, learn what they do, follow their budget reports, learn the problems each one faces. And most important, if you see room for improvement, speak up! I'll be grading you on your recommendations for improvement."

"Sounds exciting, Jake!" Andy said. "I'm eager to get started."

"Good," Jake replied as he leaned back in his chair, elbows on the armrests, chin resting on his hands, his fingers intertwined. "I have been told that your wife is a nurse."

"Yes, sir," said Andy. "She's worked as a nursery nurse in hospitals in Dallas—always as a pool nurse. We hope she can find an opening here at Trinitus Westlake."

Jake reached for a notepad and pen to scribble a message. "Give me her name, Andy, so I can pass this information to the director of nurses."

Andrew produced from his folder a resume that Barbara had already prepared and handed it to Jake.

"I hope you don't think I'm being presumptuous by giving this to you. She hopes to complete her training in NICU nursing."

"Good idea!" he replied. "We have just such a program in place. We work with the university here so the student can work while studying for a master's degree in nursing, training specifically for NICU certification."

"She'll be pleased, Jake. I must say, she is a very good nursery nurse. I hear this from the people she works with."

Jake rotated his chair slightly, looked away from Andy for a few moments, and glanced out the window at the courtyard below.

"How did she handle the allegations against her in the Judge Joberst case?" he asked as he turned back to face Andy.

Andy hoped that Jake hadn't seen his startled reaction. He quickly zipped his gaping mouth but was speechless from the tightness in his throat. Minutes ago, Jake had asked for Barbara's name. Now he dropped this bombshell, which said he knew all along about the FBI's interrogation of Barbara and their investigation of the Joberst baby's abduction case in Dallas.

How did Jake know? The FBI file was supposed to be confidential, and Barbara had been assured it would not be available to any potential employer until it became public. Andy regained his composure and looked at Jake with an unblinking, fiery stare before he spoke.

"That is confidential information, *sir*."

Jake leaned back in his chair as he scrutinized Andy, his mouth twisted into a smirk. "Just curious."

"Are you implying that unverified charges might interfere with my wife's chances at Trinitus?"

"Cool it, Andrew!" he said, returning Andy's unblinking stare. "You're entering the realm of hospital administration, Andy. In the Trinitus system, we play by our own rules. In school, you've had your head crammed with health legislation, an acronym for each statutory law—Stark I and II, HIPPA, ERISA, EMTALA. We know how to circumvent bothersome government regulations here at Trinitus. You had better learn that right now. Furthermore, we make it our business to know what's going on in other Trinitus hospitals."

"You haven't answered my question, *sir*," he retorted.

"Let me put it this way, Mr. Goldeyer: I make the decisions around here. I decide whether or not a person, guilty or innocent, is employed or fired. And anyone who works for me conforms to *my* standards, not some fuckin' textbook idealism."

Andy relaxed a bit and stared out the window with a contemplative look on his face. What a shock to hear Jake's remarks! To witness such a change in his demeanor. Andy had looked forward to working in an organization that stood as a symbol for exemplary professional conduct. Now, minutes after stepping into the hospital, that illusion had crumbled."

"I guess I am being defensive, Jake. Let me say this: there is absolutely no foundation for charges against my wife. I am disappointed that any information about this unfortunate incident has come up at this time. Barbara and I would like to work in the same hospital, but—"

"Are you saying if your wife is not hired you are not interested in a position with us?"

Jake had set the bait. Andy wanted this job desperately, but if he fell into this trap, he would never gain respect in the hospital administration field anywhere. He would stand firm. He glanced at the courtyard for a moment, lifted his eyes, leaned forward, and looked straight at Jake.

"Let me put it another way, Jake. If you deny her a job based on invalid evidence, I have no interest in working for you."

"What if I showed you *valid* evidence that your wife was involved in some way—by commission or by negligence."

"You would have a hard time convincing me."

"Who's supposed to be doing the convincing here, Andy? You or me?"

Andy stood, slowly sorted his and Barbara's resumes in their proper order, and placed the loose pages in a manila folder without looking at Jake. He picked up the packet and turned to Jake, who watched every move in silence.

"I apologize for taking your time, Mr. Hensley. I don't think I am the person for you. I don't want to work in a place where my superiors treat me as untrustworthy before I even begin."

Andy left without looking back. He glanced at Karen and paused for a moment. "Thank you, Karen," he said as he started toward the entrance doors.

"How did it go, Mr. Goldeyer?"

"Not very well, Karen," he replied. "I won't be coming back."

"I'm so sorry. Is there anything I can do?"

"I think not. Good day, Karen," he responded.

As he grasped the door handle, he heard the door to Jake's office slam shut. "Andy, come back in here! I was just testing you. I wanted to see what you're made of. I think I found out."

Andy stopped but didn't release his hold on the door handle and kept his back to Jake. He hesitated before he responded. What kind of guy would play tricks like this? Was he sincere? Andy dropped his hand and turned to face Jake, not sure what he would say.

"I know all about your wife's experience in Dallas," said Jake. "And I know about her work record. I told human resources to place her in line for a position in the nursery even before you got here. You have strong commitments to principle, Andy—I like that."

"Thank you, sir,"

"Again, Andy, leave off the 'sir.' Come on in. We need to talk about what you're going to be doing."

\* \* \* \*

Andy made his way through the maze of corridors to the exit lobby, passing other executive offices, conference rooms, one door labeled "Medical Staff," and another marked "Quality Assurance." Sooner or later these departments would not be so unfamiliar. He nodded to most everyone he met in the halls but received few return smiles or acknowledgments of his friendliness.

His interview with Jake had left him with an empty, heavy feeling in his stomach. There certainly was no call for jubilance, as he had hoped. So far, every experience in Trinitus Westlake, except the warm reception from Karen, had been a disappointment. He guessed he had set his expectations too high.

The attack on Barbara's involvement in the Joberst baby abduction had been disconcerting to say the least. Jake had implied that he had *valid evidence—by commission or negligence*, that Barbara was involved. There was absolutely no evidence that Barbara was guilty of wrongdoing—certainly not by negligence. The Dallas Police Department detective and the FBI agents had exonerated her completely in their investigations. Jake must have been referring to the missing anklet bracelets. It was still a mystery who had given the order to discontinue their use. Barbara had made it clear to Agent Walton that she had not removed the ankle device, and she had fully disclosed to the FBI the details of every encounter she had had with Leanne and with Mark Marchesa.

Andy wondered why Jake had even brought up the subject. Jake had already passed the word to HR that he wanted Barbara to be employed. Was there some ulterior motive in his decision to hire her and then to make those remarks to Andy about her employment? Andy remembered Barbara's story about how cordial the chief nursing officer in Dallas had been when she called to encourage Barbara to return to the nursery at Trinitus Dallas—even offering her daytime shifts. Something just didn't add up in his mind. Would the hospital expect Barbara to give false testimony if the occasion arose? Maybe he was too skeptical?

Andy stood inside the spacious entrance foyer watching for the taxi Karen had summoned. Soon the cab appeared, stopped under the giant entrance canopy, and announced its arrival with a beep.

"Airport," Andy said, and with nagging qualms chasing through his brain he leaned back against the head rest and closed his eyes, thinking that surely everything would fall into place someday. Right then, he just wanted to get back to Dallas and to Barbara.

## 15

### *Dallas, Texas*

Barbara's last day in the nursery at Trinitus was anything but sad. She looked forward to putting behind her all of the unpleasant memories of working there—the night shifts, the harassment by Wilda, the accusations and questioning by the police and the FBI. But had she not been working there she wouldn't have met Leanne. She missed her regular visits with Leanne and wondered how she was managing the stress that she surely must be enduring.

She would not miss the "Witch" for sure. She wondered briefly what had happened to Wilda. She had just disappeared after the abduction interrogation. Probably she had been terminated after it had been discovered that the newborns were not wearing security devices on the day of the kidnapping. Had administration really given that order, as Wilda had contended? That question remained an unsolved mystery.

Barbara had been notified that she had a position in the nursery at Trinitus Westlake and that she wouldn't have to go through the interview process. She would have to go through the new employee orientation, however, as a routine procedure in order to get her ID card and parking card. Her request for a one-month delay before reporting for her first shift assignment had been granted. She would need ever bit of that time for unpacking and getting her new home in order.

The first-floor apartment they had selected during their pre-move visit to Westlake would be a substantial upgrade from their Dallas abode. With the second bedroom to furnish they would have to buy more furniture eventuality, but not until they were both in an earning position. They each had their own bathroom for a welcome change. That would be sheer delight. She laughed thinking that she wouldn't have to clean the splashed water on the mirror and countertop every time she followed Andy's shaving routine. And she especially looked forward to being able, for the first time since their wedding, to unpack all of their stored wedding presents.

She was worried about Andy. He had seemed so tense about his position with Trinitus in Westlake—probably just the anxiety that went along with starting a new job. Barbara reassured him every chance she had; but something during his interview with the hospital administrator had disturbed him. He didn't want to talk about it, but they had been together long enough that when he woke up at four o'clock every morning and stayed awake for an hour or so, she knew that he was upset about something.

They had heard nothing from the FBI agents about the kidnapping or about the ransom demands, and there were no updated news stories that hinted that the baby might be alive or near recovery. Barbara wanted desperately to talk to Leanne again ever since she had last talked to Agent Walton. But with packing, the many last-minute details of making the move, and Andy's final exam schedule, she was forced to miss her visits with Leanne.

Barbara had become so close to Leanne that the thought of no longer being able to see her had triggered a nauseating lump in the pit of her stomach. She wondered how Leanne would get along without someone around who showed concern. Barbara also worried that Leanne might have resented her giving information to the FBI. If only she could talk to Leanne, surely she would understand. Barbara was hesitant to call Mark again, but she longed to communicate with Leanne in some way before they left Dallas.

Barbara had just finished packing the last box and placing clothes that they would need for the next two or three days in suitcases. She glanced at her watch. *Andy should be home any minute*, she thought. *He should be finished with his last exam about now.* The thought no sooner crossed her mind than she heard Andy bounce up the stairs. She laughed. Must be taking them two at a time. He crashed through the door with an ear-to-ear grin on his face. He grabbed Barbara and danced around the room.

"Finished!" he said. "And I passed every one with a good grade."

"Great!" she said. "I never doubted you could do it. Now you have just one more year and you'll be a degreed hospital administrator. Ready for the next stage?"

"Let's go to Westlake! I'm ready to take on anything that comes along."

"We're ready. We're all packed."

"Good. Tonight we celebrate. Pick a restaurant. We'll order a bottle of wine."

"Andy! We can't afford that. We'll pick up a sandwich, and you can have a beer."

"We're going out. Part of our moving expense," he insisted. He picked up a kitchen chair and with one chair leg in the palm of his hand and attempted to balance it in the air while he staggered about the room. The chair fell, but he caught it before any damage was done.

Barbara tried to constrain her laughter. "Andrew! Calm down. You'll hurt yourself. Okay, you've earned it. We'll go out. But we'll have to go dressed as we are. Our clothes are packed."

"Let's go," he replied.

"And we have to come home early. Don't forget, you've got to pick up the U-Haul truck and hitch the VW in the morning."

"We'll make it. You worry too much, little one."

\* \* \* \*

They pulled the apartment door closed, put the key in the mailbox, and without looking back climbed into the medium-sized rental truck, the VW hooked behind. They left a little later than planned but still had time to get to Westlake before dark. Andy noticed that Barbara had seemed unusually dismal. It seemed that she had even looked for last-minute things to do that would delay their departure. She was unusually quiet as they drove away.

"Goodbye, Dallas!" yelled Andy as he manipulated his vehicle onto the Interstate. He grinned and glanced at Barbara—no response. *I think I know what's bothering her,* he said to himself. He took the very next exit and turned back north at the Prescott Street intersection.

"What are you doing, Andy?" she said. "You don't need gasoline. Is there something wrong?"

"I know you want to try to see Leanne one more time," he replied. "We'll see if she's at the Monique Salon."

"How do you read my mind? I didn't dare mention it since we were late leaving."

"I'll stop at the Quick-Stop for coffee. It's just a short walk to the Monique. It doesn't take a mind reader to know what you're thinking and why you kept waiting around for the phone to ring a while ago."

She laughed. "You could tell what was whirling through my mind, couldn't you?"

"Of course I could. Now be careful, and don't feel rushed. And one other thing: tell Leanne that we'll see to it that you make regular trips to Dallas to see her."

"I love you, Andy," she said as she jumped down from the truck.

*   *   *   *

Barbara entered the Monique and was met by the same receptionist. The welcome smile on her face told Barbara that Leanne was there.

"She has prayed every day that you would come by. I am glad you're here. She is so lonely. She always seems so much better after your visits."

Leanne ran to Barbara's outstretched arms when she entered the treatment room. Barbara wondered how Leanne could change so drastically in such a short time. Her sallow, drawn face was accented by the dark circles under her eyes, which were sadder than Barbara had ever seen them. She must have lost twenty pounds in the last two weeks. Barbara struggled to keep from showing surprise at Leanne's appearance.

"Oh, you did come to see me," she said after they embraced for almost a minute. Her sunken cheeks glistened from tears. "I hoped you would. When do you leave?"

"We're packed and leaving Dallas right now. I just had to check with you one more time."

"You don't know how much this means to me," she replied while blotting her eyes and face. "Will I ever see you again?"

"Of course," said Barbara. "We're only going to Westlake—not all that far away. And Andy just told me that he would see to it that I come back regularly to Dallas to visit."

"I think I'll just go with you." Leanne's laugh was followed by a chuckle from Barbara.

"Fine," said Barbara. "At least you've found something to laugh about. How are you doing?"

"I'm fast losing any hope of ever recovering the baby. I'm not accepting that very well. Our attempt to transfer funds for the ransom was scuttled by the FBI as soon as they found out. Anthony said that he received another 'last warning' call at his office. He's waiting on instructions now. The money is still in the bank—in Anthony's name. He's ready to comply with the ransom demands. It's just this waiting that's killing me."

"It's obvious that it's pulling you down," Barbara replied. "What can I do? What can Andy and I do?"

"Something's just not right, Barbara."

"What do you mean?"

"It's Anthony. I get the feeling that he is not doing all he can do to help find my baby—not being honest with me. I feel like he would be just as happy if we never found out what happened."

"Surely not. From what you say, he has a public image to uphold."

"That's the only reason he's making any effort at all. He doesn't care anything about the baby. Also he knows that I will leave him soon. If we're still working to recover the baby, he knows I'll have to stay. I'm about fed up with the whole scheme."

"You can't give up, Leanne."

"How do I even know that the baby's still alive?"

"You are working with the FBI now, aren't you?"

"Anthony says he is. He tells the agents that I am too distraught to cooperate; he keeps me away from the news media. I find out more about what's happening by reading the newspapers and watching TV than I do from Anthony. He continues to make accusations to Agent Walton that Mark is responsible in some way."

"Maybe you should get more aggressive, Leanne. Ask to see Mr. Walton. Ask him if he can provide you with some proof that the baby is still alive and see what it will take to get him back."

"Anthony would hit the ceiling."

"What do you care? If I heard you correctly, you're putting up the money out of your inheritance. You need to find another way to contact the kidnappers. Tell Mr. Walton that you would like to make a public appeal for the baby—on television or by a press interview. He'll help you. Ask for proof that the baby is all right, and then arrange your own negotiations in exchanging the money for the baby."

"Can you imagine Anthony's reaction? He would be furious." She stared past Barbara for a few moments and remained silent as if contemplating Barbara's suggestion. She looked back at Barbara, her eyes filled with tears. "What can I do, Barbara?" said Leanne. "You are the only person who understands what I'm going through, and now you will be miles away."

Barbara walked around the room, silent and keeping her back to Leanne for what seemed like a lifetime. She finally turned and sat beside Leanne.

"Look, why don't you do this: just disappear. What would happen if you did that? You could still stay in touch with Agent Walton without telling Anthony where you were. I can talk to Mr. Walton if you want me to and explain your dilemma. Andy and I can help you. If you decide to negotiate with the kidnappers on your own—hopefully with the FBI's help—you will take control of the situation. We laughed about your coming to Westlake with me, but you could do it. Find an apartment or a suite in some remote hotel under an assumed name. We'll help you, Leanne. You don't have to put up with this torture. Think about it."

"Barbara! Do you know what you're saying? Remember, you heard Anthony threaten to kill me. He would for sure if I leave now."

"He wouldn't be able to find you. Think it over. You want to find your baby if at all possible. This will work. We will help you."

"What will Andy say?"

"I'll explain it to him. He's a good person, Leanne. He might hesitate, but he'll understand that you need some help. Leave that to me." Barbara rummaged through her purse and found a pen and pad. "Here's my new address. I'll call here and leave my number as soon as we get settled. Call my cell phone; the FBI agents know we communicate anyway."

"I don't know …"

"If you decide to make your break, let me know some way. I need to leave now. I'm sure Andy is getting anxious to go."

"I'll let you know. Barbara, thank you. Just talking to you gives me hope—maybe it will give strength."

"You can do it, Leanne," said Barbara as they embraced each other in a farewell hug. She turned to leave, thinking, *Now the hard part—telling Andy.*

# 16

## JFK International Airport, New York

Deo Carminagni deplaned from the first-class section of Flight 84 from Naples, Italy, to New York and dutifully stepped in line, pulling his carry-on bag through customs. He knew ahead of time what the questions would be and that as soon as immigrations officials recognized him, they would ask him to step aside while others went ahead. He could have ducked into the familiar conference room before being told to do so—he'd been there so many times before—but instead he stood by and continued to read the short fiction story in the *United Airlines Magazine* that he had started on the plane.

He wasn't sure what he was in for on this expedition, only that Alberto had said to go to Nashville and talk to his brother Victor. That in itself was a mystery. Out of respect for Victor's image in the Wall Street securities community, Alberto had always stayed clear of Victor. As far as Deo knew, they had never been seen together socially and had never communicated in any way. For some reason, Victor had summoned Alberto's assistance for something.

Deo sat at the table in the small conference room in the detention center. Immigration, CIA, and FBI agents milled in and out. Some of the people constantly pounded computer keyboards. The monitors faced away from Deo, of course, but he was aware of what they were checking. He had been through this routine every six months—every time he made his routine return visits to the United States to implement Alberto's newest orders.

"You're two months earlier than usual, Mr. Carminagni. Is there some special reason you are here this time?" asked one of the agents.

"No, it's just a visit for pleasure."

"How long will you be here this time?"

"I have no definite plans at the present."

"Where will you be staying? I presume you will be staying with friends in Las Vegas and staying at the same hotel you list every time you visit."

"That's right. I have friends in Las Vegas, and of course the Frontagio is like a home for me."

"Yes, we have a record of that. Then that will be your address while you are in this country?"

"I suppose so. Why do I need to say where I will be or how long I'll stay? I'm a citizen of the United States, you guys."

"Mr. Carminagni, you work for Alberto Marchesa. You're probably here under orders from Alberto. Mr. Marchesa is wanted in this country for more crimes than I have time to list right now," said a new face in the room. "You will be under surveillance during your entire visit—just as you have been each time you return. I have one question for you: do you know where Mr. Marchesa is living at the present time?"

"I'm sorry. I can't answer that."

"Can't or won't?" the agent asked, his mouth twisted in a smirk. "Have you talked to Mr. Marchesa recently?"

"I can't remember the last time I talked to Al."

"That's the same answer you gave the last time we interrogated you. Have you seen or talked to Mr. Marchesa since your last visit to the United States?"

"I don't think so."

"You show your residence as Corsica. Is that correct?"

"Yes, sir," said Deo. "I live there with my family."

"Is that where Alberto lives also."

"Not that I am aware of."

"Is Alberto Marchesa currently managing the activities of the Marchesa organization?"

"It's been quite some time since I have heard from Alberto."

"Come on, Mr. Carminagni. You're here to carry out orders from Alberto, aren't you?"

"I've been given no specific assignment from anyone. I am just here visiting. Is that a crime?"

"I think we're through here, sir. I warn you, however, that because of your past relationship with the Marchesa Family, you are looked upon with suspicion. Your every move will be observed closely for any suggestion that Alberto Marchesa is in the process of reviving his criminal organization."

"I am at your mercy—as always. If you will excuse me, I have a plane to catch. You know where to find me."

Under the watchful eyes of the interrogators, Deo repacked the contents of his suitcase, now strewn halfway across the conference table, brushed back his recently styled graying hair, and straightened his tie. "Good day, gentlemen. Nice to be back in America again."

\* \* \* \*

Deo checked the timetables on the monitors in the gigantic JFK International Airport. He had a little over an hour to reach the boarding gate for his connecting flight. He stopped at the first bank of public telephones he came across, pulled his PDA from his pocket, looked up the number, called to reserve his room at the Frontagio in Las Vegas.

Glancing over his shoulder, he caught a glimpse of his assigned tail, a young man pretending interest in a nearby magazine stand. His dress and demeanor spelled FBI as clearly as if he were wearing a jacket with bright yellow letters imprinted on the back. Deo amplified his voice so the man, now seated in an adjacent telephone cubicle as if making a call, could hear clearly his conversation with whomever he was calling.

Deo found the correct gate for the next flight to Las Vegas. He stood at the check-in counter, talked to the attendant for a couple of minutes while he shuffled papers around on the countertop, checked his watch twice, and then re-pocketed his ticket as though he had received a boarding pass.

He glanced up and down the terminal concourse, avoided looking at his follower, and began walking toward a close-by gift shop. He browsed through the shop, keeping the racks between himself and the FBI agent. At his first chance, he maneuvered behind a group of entering shoppers and eased into the open area without being seen. Once clear of the shop entrance, he streaked down the walkway opposite his boarding gate before "Agent Novice" realized he had left.

He went to the lower level, found the American Airlines ticketing counter, and, using false ID, booked his flight to Nashville. He would have a one-hour wait. Next, he took the airport monorail to an entirely different terminal and booked an alternative flight on Continental to Dallas, using still a different ID. He smiled, thinking how confused the young agent would be trying to determine which direction his quarry had taken.

\* \* \* \*

## Nashville, Tennessee

Once in the Nashville airport, Deo called to reserve a suite at the Marriott Hotel near the CareCompHealth headquarters building. At the same time, he put in a call for Marcello Liscano to check in at the Frontagio in Deo's name. Deo had no idea where Marcello was at that hour—likely in bed with some bimbo as usual—but he knew he could depend on him to carry out the instructions without asking questions. He arranged to have a rental car delivered to the hotel the next morning, even though he probably would have little use for a vehicle, since the CareCompHealth office was within walking distance. However, he had no idea what his encounter with Victor might entail.

As he climbed into the cab for the trip to the hotel, he looked forward to a few hours of sleep before contacting Victor Marchesa. Deo laughed thinking of the FBI questioning him at the airport about his assignment. He wouldn't even know himself what his mission would be until he talked to Victor. By the time the FBI unraveled the confusion of where he was and what he was doing, he would likely be finished with whatever Victor Marchesa needed and on a plane back to his home in Corsica.

\* \* \* \*

Deo slowly opened one eye and then the other, keeping them open long enough to notice daylight rays filtering through the semi-opaque curtains. After a couple of seconds, he realized where he was. He glanced at the clock on the bedside table—eight o'clock; he hadn't slept this late in ages. Maybe it was jetlag. He would call Victor at 9:00, so he needed to hurry and dress in case Victor wanted to meet right away. After placing an order for coffee, juice, and bagels, he shaved, showered, and dressed.

He searched his billfold and found the saved portion of Alberto's note with Victor's phone number—scrambled digits to confuse curious customs people but easily decoded using the trick that he and Alberto had devised years ago. Deo recalled, with some bit of nostalgia, days past when he and Alberto communicated openly instead of passing messages through the priest in a confessional booth. He took a deep breath and dialed Victor's correct number. While he waited for an answer, he wondered what the day would bring—surely an answer to the mystery of why he had been sent to help Victor.

## 17

*Westlake, Texas*

The half-day orientation session at Trinitus Westlake left Andy's head spinning. Would he ever remember the location and the function of every single department in the hospital? And the department directors—they were just faces. It would take time for him to link each person to his or her name and work area.

It had taken far less time than he had predicted to receive his photo ID card, so he could spend the rest of the afternoon with Barbara, shopping for the new apartment. They might even have time to look for furniture for the second bedroom. After they had unpacked the truck and moved their belongings into the apartment, the one vacant room looked so empty.

Every quiet moment since they left Dallas was filled with thoughts of the bombshell Barbara had dropped. She had tried to convince Leanne to steal away from Dallas and hide in Westlake, and she had offered their assistance in negotiating the return of the kidnapped baby. What else would she turn up with? He was starting a new job that required his deepest concentration. He couldn't just break away at any time to play detective. Barbara's charitable deeds were going to get both of them in deep trouble someday, if they hadn't already. But what could he do? *Just accept it,* he told himself. *You'll go along with anything Barbara wants.*

\* \* \* \*

"How did it go?" Barbara asked as she climbed into the car.

"Fine. No problems. I have my ID card and I start work tomorrow. I didn't get to talk to Mr. Hensley. Karen, his administrative assistant, said he would spend an hour or so with me in the morning."

"Are you nervous about starting?"

"Yeah, a little." He threw a glance at Barbara but avoided eye contact. "It's all so complex. I have already seen oceans of data that I have got to learn. It's going to take every minute of my time for a while."

"You're trying to tell me we won't have time to help Leanne if she calls, aren't you?"

"No ... no," he replied, looking away sheepishly. "I'll find time."

"I know you're not sold on this idea."

"I'm sure you have your reasons for getting involved—it's just that I don't see how we can be of help."

"Leanne is so pitiful, Andy," she said. "She doesn't have anybody to turn to."

"I just hope you're not getting yourself into a situation where you'd be in danger," he said. "Apparently her husband will stop at nothing to keep a status quo at home. From what Leanne says, he's some kind unscrupulous demon who wants to portray just the opposite image."

"Leanne doesn't think he cares whether the baby is recovered or not."

"These periods of silence *are* strange," Andy answered. "You'd think he would make appeals on television, let the public know how they are suffering and how they're doing everything possible to apprehend the kidnappers and recover their baby. But there's almost no news about the crime."

"I agree. It's just not right. I think Leanne feels the same way. If she could just talk to the FBI agents and work out some plan of her own. She doesn't mind surrendering the money. She just wants to get on with it. That's why I suggested she come and let us help her."

"I suppose if we're working under the FBI we'll be protected."

Barbara was silent, gazing out window as the shops in the strip malls flashed by—names that she had never heard of and wouldn't remember. Finally, she turned to Andy, who was busily weaving his way along the crowded street. "I don't know, Andy," she said. "I can't explain it. Something just tells me we are going to get involved, whether we want to or not. And we can't walk away. What's wrong with me, Andy?"

"I know what you're thinking: the safest and easiest thing would be to turn our backs and forget that you ever met Leanne Joberst," Andy replied. He brought their VW to a halt alongside one of several self-serve gasoline pumps near the giant shopping complex. He sat glued to the steering wheel for a few moments, and then he pulled Barbara to his side. "But we're not going to do that. We're in the race—we just have to deal with it."

"It's scary, Andy."

Andy grinned as he climbed out to fill the gas tank. "I don't think that's ever stopped you."

The breeze was just strong and erratic enough to send gasoline fumes into his nose and chest. When he turned his head to protect his breathing he saw a dark four-door Malibu sedan pull into the parking lot. Something about it looked familiar. He then remembered Agent Walton following them in a similar looking car just before they left for Westlake. Andy could make out the silhouettes of two people in the vehicle. Could they be FBI agents trailing them again here in Westlake? Surely Agent Walton wouldn't come here all the way from Dallas. *Maybe I'm being overly suspicious*, he thought. *Lots of black Malibu sedans around*. He decided not to mention it to Barbara.

"Do you have your shopping list ready?"

"It's pretty long. I left so many household items behind when we moved. But it shouldn't take too long."

Within the hour, they were ready to load the VW and head for home. Andy could make out the same dark sedan, now parked alongside their own car, as they walked across the lot. Andy's suspicions were confirmed. Agent Ralph Walton and his partner, Wes, stood beside their vehicle awaiting Andy and Barbara.

"What a coincidence," said Andy. "We were just talking about you, Mr. Walton."

"I see you made the move with no hitches," Ralph answered. "Just wanted to touch base with you. A new development has arisen."

"You've found the baby?" asked Barbara, her face glowing with excitement.

"I wish I could say that. No, we haven't found the infant and we have no proof that the baby's alive. All communications have come to a halt. I must admit, I've never seen such a complex case."

"Leanne must be so distraught," said a wistful Barbara with tears forming in her eyes. "I feel so sorry for her."

"I'm sure you do, Barbara," said Agent Walton, in a rare moment of compassion. "You've been very supportive and helpful ... We need you again, Barbara, now."

"How can *she* help?" asked Andy, his irritation surfacing. "What can she possibly do now?"

"We'll need cooperation from both of you," said Ralph. "We have located the old van that was used during the abduction. It was abandoned in a remote canyon in west Texas, near Del Rio. It has been moved to Dallas and is impounded in a secure location. We need you to ID it, Barbara. We have already searched and scrutinized the interior and found some interesting things. There is enough concern here that we are assigning top security to this case."

"Does that mean we will have to go back to Dallas?" asked Andy.

"Barbara will," Ralph replied, "just to identify the vehicle." He waited a few moments for Andy and to absorb his statement. "And Andy, you must not reveal her location or reason for returning to Dallas. We'll see that she is protected while she's there."

"What does that mean? Why such extreme measures?"

"We have our reasons, Andy. Here's where we stand in this case. I think you'll understand. We're fairly certain that we have fit together almost all of the pieces of this puzzle …"

Ralph recited the sequence of events that the FBI had reproduced from evidence and supposition: A young woman had masqueraded as Barbara after Barbara's ID card had been photographed while she was walking to work. They surmised that her ID badge had been reproduced from the photographs. They were reasonably sure that they knew how the so-called grandfather who had visited the nursery viewing window managed to pass through security with the baby after the "nurse" had taken the infant from its mother.

"I remember the 'grandfather' that day," said Barbara.

"I hope you will be able to identify him when we find him," Ralph replied.

"I'm sure I could," she said.

"The picture is almost complete," said Ralph. The look of abstraction on his face betrayed the fact that the answer to the riddle was far from complete. "We still have some questions, though. The scheme had to have been hatched weeks or months ahead of time. The perpetrators somehow had to know approximately when the baby would be born. That's one thing. Another: why were the anklet tags discontinued just at the right time? And the big mystery: who conceived this plan, who was behind implementing the scheme, and who paid for it?"

"Then you have no idea who could be behind this?" asked Andy.

"We have some leads," Ralph answered as he dropped his head and stared silently at the ground for a few seconds. "Here's where you two come in," he added. "Andy, you are not to reveal to anyone the confidential information I have talked about here, and Barbara, you will be under protective custody for a while."

"What are you saying?" yelled Andy. "Why is that necessary?"

"I told you: this is a high-priority case. Barbara can identify the vehicle, and she might be able to identify the so-called grandfather. As a material witness, she could be in jeopardy, and we cannot afford to lose her."

"*You* can't afford what?" said Andy, now red with fury. "*You* don't want to lose her? I don't want to lose her! Are you thinking of her testimony or are you thinking of her? I always thought the FBI could solve any crime, and now you tell me you are going to have to hold my wife in custody?"

"Calm down, Andy," Ralph said, placing his arm across Andy's shoulders. "I understand how you feel. She will not be held, but she will have an FBI agent close by at all times—day and night—even when she starts her work at the hospital. She likely will not be able to identify the agent. We believe these people will stop at nothing to protect their identity, but we will protect her—and you. This is not a run-of-the-mill kidnapping, Andy. We have never seen this pattern perpetrated before."

Barbara remained quiet, mulling over what Ralph had just said. The FBI didn't know who had conceived, paid for, or implemented the plan. With that thought, Mark Marchesa's words flashed through her mind: *"I have a plan."*

"When will she go to Dallas? How will she get there? She has her hands full right now making our apartment livable, getting ready to start a new job."

"We'll take care of everything, Andy. She will go by FBI plane from a private airstrip. She will be well protected and will be back the same day. Don't worry, Andy. Please, just go about your daily routine and say nothing about Barbara being gone—not to anybody."

"I'm going to worry," said Andy, his forehead creased in a frown.

"Of course you are," said Ralph as he placed his arm around Andy's shoulders. "I would expect you to worry, but everything's going to be fine."

## 18

His first day at work! Whatever lay ahead, he was now employed and his brain was like a sponge—ready to absorb every tiny morsel of knowledge of hospital administration. He was ready to move forward. But the threat of danger to Barbara would never totally leave his thoughts.

As soon as he entered Jake Hensley's office, Karen came out to greet him. She couldn't have been more hospitable. Andy couldn't help but notice her fashionable, business attire and her professionally styled hairdo.

"Good morning, Mr. Goldeyer," she said, "Welcome to Trinitus Westlake."

"Thank you, Karen," he replied. "I'm excited to be here. Of course, I'm a bit nervous."

"No reason to be," she said. "We are pleased to have you join us."

"Could you just call me Andy, Karen? I think I would feel more at ease if you would."

"Certainly," she answered. "Andy, Mr. Hensley will be a little late this morning, but we have a few orientation items that I need to go over with you. And it will give me a chance to visit with you."

"Fine." Andy replied.

"First, let's go to your office so I can walk you through a few protocols. Then I will give you a few documents to study so you can get to know more about the organization and the administrative team."

She handed him a loose-leaf packet that was neatly assembled and indexed. "Good," said Andy.

"Your office will be down the hall from Mr. Hensley's," she said as they walked down the corridor. She pointed out the other administrators' offices as they walked along. "I will do all of your secretarial work until the volume justifies another secretary." Karen held the door open for Andy to enter. "I think I have everything in here that you will need," she added.

"It certainly looks complete. Nice view," he said, looking through the floor-to-ceiling windows at the outside landscaped courtyard.

"Your desk is stocked with the usual. On the desktop, I left instructions on how to gain access to our internal intranet program. You'll have access to patient information and to performance data of the medical staff."

"Then I will have access to patient care data."

"Yes, but for a while you won't have access to financial data. You won't need that right now," she replied. "Now, you will be attending A-team meetings every Monday morning. You'll hear a lot of numbers presented and talked about. It will probably take several weeks before you're able to make sense of what you hear."

"I can already see I have a lot to learn."

"In this stack of folders," she said, pointing to an in-and-out box, "you'll find a leadership organizational chart. You'll need to study that so you'll know which member of the Senior Leadership Team each of the department director reports to. Also you can learn the names of the team members and the directors. In the same stack is a calendar of committee meetings that Mr. Hensley wants you to attend."

"I'm a bit overwhelmed."

"You'll catch on fast. It will seem complex at first, but you'll learn."

"Thanks, Karen," said Andy. "I appreciate your help here."

"We're glad to have you, Andy," she replied. "It's always a pleasure to see young graduates come in—they seem so baffled at first, but in no time they act like veteran administrators. Oh, one more thing. In the desk drawer you'll find a zippered leather folder that contains the basic material you need for meetings. You should always carry that with you when you go to meetings."

"I'll do that," he replied "Have you been working here very long, Karen?"

"Quite a while," she said. "I started here as an assistant secretary ten years ago. About five years ago I was raised to the level of administrative assistant."

"That must carry added responsibility. You know much more about what's going on in the hospital now, I'm sure."

Karen chuckled. "Sometimes I think I know too much," she said. A faint crimson flush swept over her face. "Oh ... I'm sorry. Don't get the wrong idea. I love my work here, Andy. You will too."

"What's it like working for Mr. Hensley?"

"I know you had an unpleasant experience when you were here for your interview, Andy. But you'll learn a lot from Mr. Hensley. He'll expect you to be precise, direct, and truthful when you report to him ... just as he expects from me."

"I can handle that."

"I've heard that your wife will be joining us also."

"Barbara will be working in the nursery as soon as she gets settled in our apartment."

"That will be nice ... both of you working in the same hospital. Do you have children?"

"Not yet, but we are hoping to start a family soon. And you? Do you have children?"

"I have never married, Andy. Lots of nieces and nephews." She laughed. "I'm becoming known as the obsessive-compulsive spinster aunt in the family."

"I can't believe that ... that you don't have guys clamoring to date you."

"You're nice to say that, Andy." Karen chuckled. "I've dated a few times, but no one wants to get serious with anyone who demands perfection."

"Nothing wrong with that," said Andy. "You are a lot like my wife in that regard."

"Well, that speaks well for you, Andy. She must consider you to be perfect."

Andy laughed. "I'll tell her you said that. "And thanks again for your thorough orientation."

"Mr. Hensley should be here any minute. He'll outline your work schedule for you. And don't hesitate to call on me if you have questions. I'll be close by."

\* \* \* \*

The tap on the door jolted Andy from his reading materials. He opened the door to face Karen again.

"Mr. Hensley is here now, Andy, and would like for you to join him in his office," she said. "Good luck."

"Thanks, Karen."

Andy eagerly leaped from his chair and scrambled for the leather folder in preparation to meet with Jake. He looked forward to this session with Jake—hopefully he'd get some specifics on what Jake expected of him. Their last meeting had left him somewhat confused over his role in the organization and even uncertain that he had made the right decision to join the Trinitus system. He vowed to avoid another explosive reaction.

Jake's office door was open and Jake was shuffling through papers on his desk when Andy entered. To Andy's surprise, he was dressed in gym clothes, and from the moisture at his hairline he seemed to have just come from a workout. He dropped the papers in his hand and came from behind the desk to greet Andy.

"Hi, young executive! Glad to see you," he said, a broad smile creasing his face. "How are you, Andy?"

"Fine, sir," Andy replied.

"You've already forgotten your first instruction." He laughed. "Drop the 'sir.'"

"Sorry, Jake."

"I see you're startled at how I'm dressed," he replied, still grinning.

"I'll admit it was a bit of a surprise."

"Lesson number one, Andy," he said. "Learn to hide your reactions. I exercise early in the morning and dress after I arrive here." He chuckled, grabbed the towel draped over his shoulder, and wiped his face and neck. "I don't advise your doing that."

Andy matched his laughter. "I get the message."

"Sit down, Andy," he said, motioning to a nearby bench while he plopped in his desk chair. "Hey! Your first day in the world of hospital administration! We have a few things to talk about. I see you have your pad so you can take notes."

"I'm overwhelmed by everything I have to learn. Karen has been very helpful. I can already see I only learned in school a fragment of what the real world is like here."

"You're right. In a year from now, you will look back and be surprised at all you've been exposed to working for Trinitus. The opportunity to learn is here; whether or not you grasp it depends on how hard you work and how well you listen—especially to what I tell you," Jake said, firm in both his tone and expression. "The path to success starts right here; it's up to you to follow it."

"I'll do my best, sir ... uh, Jake," said Andy

"Good!" he said, leaning back in his reclining desk chair, holding his clasped hands against his chin and fixing his eyes with Andy's. "The first thing I want to tell you about running a hospital system, Andy—and don't ever forget this—the three 'P's of successful hospital administration: people, physicians, politics."

"I'm not sure I understand."

"It will become obvious to you as you go along," he replied. "You've got to surround yourself with good, loyal people; you've got to give your doctors on the medical staff what they want; you've got to play politics—local community as well as medical community. If you keep that in mind, you won't fail in this business. You'll think I'm a bit ruthless at times, Andy, but there is a reason for everything I do, and it always falls into one of the 'P' categories."

"What about the other 'P,' the patient?"

"Good question, Andy," he answered, his upper lip flattened in a smirk. "If you always keep in mind the three 'P's I listed, the patient-care element will fall into place. You'll see, Andy. Your first concern has to be your hospital." Jake then leaned back and nonchalantly locked his fingers behind his head. "Besides, if you put the system first, your bonuses will be greater."

Andy looked away; he remained silent and appeared deep in thought. He glanced at Jake, who by then had assumed a look of arrogance as though he had made his point with this naïve student-intern. *This is not a time to argue*, Andy told himself, remembering the vow he had made. *I'll try to get Jake onto another subject.*

"What will my first assignment be, Jake?"

"I have sent Karen a calendar of areas that you will work in, beginning today," he replied. "Your first will be a month's duty with the physicians relations coordinator. You'll learn what we do to keep our doctors happy and you'll learn about the recruitment incentives we use to get them to use our hospitals."

Andy hurriedly scanned his organizational chart for the physicians relations coordinator—Jonathan Mastin. "Is his office in this part of the hospital?" he asked.

"Karen will show you. It's close by. Again, welcome to Trinitus Westlake, Andy," he said as he stood, took Andy by the arm, and escorted him toward the door. "Come by any time you have a question. And don't forget: when you bring a question, bring a recommendation for an answer. Good Luck, Andy."

"Thank you," Andy replied. Jake pulled Andy to a halt.

"Oh, I almost forgot," he said. "How is Barbara? I'm told she will begin work within the month."

"She's looking forward to going back to work. Right now she's busy getting our apartment up to her standards," Andy said with a laugh.

"I heard there's a breakthrough on the Joberst kidnapping case."

Andy struggled to suppress his surprise that Jake knew anything about the new development in the case. How should he answer? Jake's tone suggested that he was fishing for information. Andy decided to play it cool.

"I haven't seen anything about it in the papers or on television. What has developed? Are they closer to finding the baby?"

"I don't know," he said as he turned back to his desk. "I'm not sure where I heard it, but I think the FBI has news to announce."

"I'm sure the mother and father are quite anxious and frustrated by now," Andy replied as he grasped the door handle. "I'll be around if you think of anything I need to know."

"Check with Karen every morning, Andy."

"I'll do that." Andy walked away once again with a feeling about Jake that he couldn't explain. Why had he asked about the abduction? If Agent Walton had knowledge of any breaking news, he surely would have shared it with him and Barbara.

# 19

## *Nashville*

Deo checked the departure times to Dallas. Using one of his assumed names, he reserved a one-way first-class ticket on American Airlines, leaving at 2:30 pm. His meeting with Victor had been much shorter than he expected, but Victor's problem was loaded with challenges as well as complexities. Deo had his work cut out for him. He would need Marcello and a few others in the family from the old days to help.

He could make the flight if he hurried, but he had to make a few calls first—cancel his car rental, have a taxi waiting in front, and call Marcello to get to Dallas as quickly as possible. After checking the flight schedule from Las Vegas to Dallas, Deo figured they both would arrive at DFW at about the same time; they would meet in the Admirals Club to plot their strategy. Deo smiled as he hastily threw his belongings together. Marcello never questioned anything: if told to get to Dallas now, he wouldn't ask why. Exhilaration, like an intravenous shot of adrenalin, rushed through Deo's brain at the thought of being back in action with Marcello at his side. Just like the old days.

\* \* \* \*

## *Dallas DFW*

Deo was reasonably sure he had evaded his FBI pursuer. However, wherever he went, he constantly looked over his shoulder for any sign of a person who resembled a stereotype FBI agent. No one even looked up from their reading except to grasp their newly mixed drink from the bar in the plush DFW Admirals Club.

Shortly after Deo ordered his first drink, Marcello arrived. Deo saw him enter and cast his eyes around the room, looking for a familiar face.

He stood so Marcello could see him. Marcello showed no sign of recognition but instead took a seat where he had full view of anyone coming or going. He watched as Deo walked to the complimentary coffee bar, poured a fresh cup, and then proceeded down the passageway toward the conference room that he had reserved. After a full five-minute wait, Marcello duplicated Deo's trip to the bar and his casual stroll to the private room.

"Marcello!" said Deo as he jumped to his feet and greeted Marcello with an *abrazo*—an embrace that always reminded him of Marcello's size and muscularity. Deo felt as if he were being lifted from the floor. "How have you been?"

"Fine, Deo," he answered "How is Al?"

"Doing well. He wishes we were all together again."

"Will he come back?" Marcello asked.

"Maybe some day. In the meantime, he depends on us," Deo answered. "You're doing a great job, Marcello. Alberto wanted you to know."

"Thanks," he replied, responding with a rare smile that was distorted from the deep scar that extended from his mouth to his ear. Deo had wondered for years but had never asked out of respect for Marcello's preference for privacy how he had gotten it.

Deo reflected on the days three years ago when they had all worked together. Marcello had proven his loyalty during that chaotic period when Alberto had to flee the country—and he was still doing his part in implementing Al's strategic business plan in the States.

"The numbers from the last report look good, Marcello, said Deo. "Al also told me to tell you how pleased he is with the business volume."

"He still wants to stay out of crack and heroin, I hope," said Marcello.

"Absolutely! Look at the reports—we're doing fine, and the risk of trafficking, compared to our casino and betting operations, would be tremendous."

"Our men know that ... less chance of doing time."

"Alberto doesn't ever want to have to pay off the law again. It eats into the profits."

"You came early. I thought maybe something was wrong."

"We have work to do, Marcello."

"I guessed that. I have Reyes Dinardo standing by."

"Reyes is in charge of Dallas now?"

"Yeah, he does a good job."

"Who took over all of Al's narcotics business?" Deo asked.

"Several tried as soon as Al crashed—Baronelli on the west coast, Chacon in Florida, and a few others. Then Paretto moved in. Nobody challenges Paretto."

"Does Paretto bother us?"

"Nah, he thinks Al is through, but he is scared shitless that he might come back. He has no idea of our casino and off-track volume."

"And we don't have to fight for our territory," said Deo.

"Right. It's peaceful everywhere now, but occasionally we gotta remind everyone not to mess with us."

"Here's the pitch, Marcello," said Deo after ordering in drinks and snacks.

Deo marveled to think they had been conversing for over thirty minutes and Marcello had never once questioned why he, Marcello, was called to travel half-way across the country to meet with Deo, sent half-way around the globe for a meeting.

"There's been a kidnapping. A newborn baby was lifted out of the hospital. The child's mother is a federal judge's wife, so the FBI is handling the case. The investigation apparently hasn't followed the usual sequence of events for snatched kids—no negotiations, no arrangements for exchanging money for baby, only two ransom demands. Something odd about the whole fuckin' deal. The family is frantic. The strangest thing is this: you know no one would pull a job like this unless they expected a quick reward from the family or a sizable roll from somebody else."

"The FBI got no clues?"

"They've told the judge they don't. The mother is an heiress to a fortune. The ten million dollars the kidnappers have demanded would hardly make a dent in her share of the family trust. She's ready to pay it to get the baby back, but there's been no contact for several days."

"Then we're going after the ten mil?"

"What do you think?"

"I think there's more to the story."

"You are right. This abduction was a job. Victor said that the FBI thinks the kidnappers were probably from the street, but someone else planned it and backed it."

"And what else, Deo?" asked Marcello, swishing down the last drop of his neat bourbon. He leaned back in his chair, with no hint of a smile, and waited for the punch.

"The baby is not the judge's. His wife's lover is a prime suspect. If there is a link between the lover and anyone capable of putting this together, we need to find it. If there isn't, we have got to uncover who is involved. And most important, if that baby is alive, we have to find it. We have to dig deep into this mess and come up with some answers *and* with the baby."

"What's Al's interest?" asked Marcello. "Wait. I don't need to ask. The father is Mark Marchesa, Al's nephew. The affair has been in all the tabloids."

"Right! Victor turned to Al for help. It's family—the only thing that would bring Victor to Al."

"I've been thinking ever since you started talking," said Marcello. "When some punk comes into a lot of money like that, they never keep their mouth shut. Shouldn't be too hard to find who fits that picture.

"I'm staying in Dallas until we do."

"Another thing, Deo: this has to be Paretto's action. Since Al has backed off, everything goes through Paretto."

"Any contacts?"

"Sure," he said. "Inside. We still have our FBI plant. Haven't used him for a while, but he's available."

"Could all of this be a reprisal against the judge?"

"I haven't heard any rumors," said Marcello. "Paretto's people are always under suspicion, and some have been arrested. It would have to be a Capo, and no one big has been indicted or sentenced to time that I know of. I'll find out."

"You think Paretto might be behind all this?" asked Deo.

"Most likely, even though we don't know the motive. Somebody's paying a good price to get this done."

"That's for sure," said Deo. "Marcello, first thing's first. We need to find out if Mark Marchesa has had anything to do with the kidnapping. I doubt it, but somebody hired Paretto to do this. Have Reyes mobilize everyone he can. Come up with some names."

"We likely will be facing some pretty tight situations, Deo. Think you're ready for this?"

"Come on, Marcello. We've been there, man. Can you get me a piece?"

"Already arranged. Reyes has one for both of us and will deliver when requested."

"I should have known. Let's have another drink."

"Fine with me. As you say, we have work to do. Where can I find you?"

"I'll be at the Doubletree Campbell Center. Let me know when we're ready to move."

# 20

***Westlake, Texas***

After checking with Karen, Andy searched for Jonathan Mastin's office, the second down the hall from Jake's. Jake had said it would be close by. He entered and was greeted by a stocky, matronly lady behind a desk in the waiting area. He glanced at his watch: 8:45. He was sure he was too early. He introduced himself. Her ivory-textured face broke into a sparkling smile.

"You must be our new resident. I heard you would be joining us. Welcome to Trinitus Westlake, Mr. Goldeyer. Mr. Mastin will be in shortly. Can I get you coffee or a Coke?"

"No, thank you, ma'am," he answered as he reached for a magazine on the table. "I'll just sit here and read."

"My name is Claire ... Claire Wellborn. I'll be ready to help you while you're assigned to this department, Mr. Goldeyer."

"Thank you, Claire. Please just call me Andy."

Only minutes passed before Claire motioned to Andy to follow her to the door to Jonathan Mastin's private office. Jonathan jumped to his feet when Andy came in. Andy suppressed his surprise at Jonathan's appearance. At school, he had been drilled on the importance of following the expected dress code of a hospital executive. Jonathan wore athletic shoes, baggy trousers and a casual pullover sweatshirt. With his fingers he repeatedly brushed back the fine-textured locks of tousled, blonde hair that hung almost to his shoulders.

"Welcome to Trinitus Westlake, Andrew. Jake has told me a few things about you. Looks like I'm going to be your first mentor."

"I'm glad to be here, Mr. Mastin. I can already see I have a lot to learn."

"Call me Jonathan. I see you've met Claire. What questions do you have about this department, Andrew?"

"Maybe you could tell me something about its function."

"Sure, that will be a starter. We get involved any time an issue comes up about our doctors. Any complaints they have, any special needs. You'll see. They bring quite an assortment of concerns in here—most of the time it is concerns about patient care or about equipment. We look at all of their complaints and try to resolve them."

"I would imagine that isn't always easy."

"You're right there," he replied. "Andy, you're going to see how we treat our doctors on the medical staff. We go all out to please them. Some say we go to extremes. You'll see that at the quarterly staff meetings and holiday parties. And twice a year we charter 747 jets and take a couple of hundred of the docs that qualify on elaborate trips—with their wives—to some resort in the summer and a ski trip in the winter."

"How do they qualify?"

"It's based on their support of the hospital—how many patients they admit, how many procedures they perform at Trinitus, how many diagnostic tests they perform."

*What am I hearing?* Andy wondered. *How can they justify that kind of expenditure? Isn't that against the law? They're buying the doctors' business.*

"Now, Andy, I can tell you're wondering about this policy. They don't teach in school the strategy we use here at Trinitus." Jonathan's eyebrows raised and he grinned. "On these trips we arrange for medical education sessions. That makes it legal. We are providing our physicians a chance to upgrade their education."

"And I suppose you require mandatory attendance at all of the education sessions."

Jonathan winked. "Of course ... and we keep accurate attendance records."

Jonathan's cell phone sounded a series of musical notes. He glanced at the number on the screen and walked to the other side of the office while he talked. When he finished, Jonathan turned his attention back to Andy.

"Are you ready to face the ire of a medical staff physician for the first time?"

"Should I step out?"

"No, you need to hear this."

"I hope it's nothing serious."

The door was ajar, and the irate physician could be heard speaking with Claire.

"I need to see him now, Claire," he said. "He told me to come right down."

"He'll be with you in just a few minutes, Dr. Jenkins," she said. "He's in his office. Please be seated. Can I bring you some coffee or something else to drink?"

"No, thank you, Claire. I need to see Jonathan now," he screamed and stormed through the door to Jonathan's office.

"Hi, Jay," said Jonathan, all smiles. "I want you to meet Andy ... Andrew Goldeyer. He's our new administrative resident. He'll be working with me for a month or so."

"Shouldn't we talk in private?"

"No, not necessary," said Jonathan. "I know you have a problem that we need to resolve, Jay, and I want Andy to be here. He may have some suggestion for a way to resolve it."

"Jonathan, how can you do this to me?" the doctor said as he paced, his arms swinging, and his fists clenched.

"Calm down, Jay," said Jonathan as he sat in his plush leather chair, placed his athletic shoe—clad feet on his desk, and motioned for the doctor to pull up a chair. "Sit down and cool it, Jay. Andy, will you close the door please?"

"You told me I had a three-year lease," he said, his eyes on fire. He threw down a blue paper—covered document that slid across the desktop, almost falling in Jonathan's lap. "Now I get this notice, which says I have thirty days to get out."

"I can't do anything about it, Jay," he said. "Look, you're a nice guy. I tried to help you. I did all I could. I guess you just didn't comply with the provisions of the lease."

"What do you mean," Jay answered. "I paid my rent on time every month—never even a day late."

"But, Jay, look, we gave you a break when we let you move in. You do remember that, don't you?"

"Yeah, but I've only been in my office a little over a year. I have a three-year lease. Where will I go? You can't do this to me. I can't afford to pay more."

"They're not asking for more, Jay. They've rented your space to someone else already, and they have given you adequate notice. I'm sorry, Jay. I don't make the rules. It's a legal agreement."

"I'll get a lawyer," he said. "You can't just kick me out."

"Jay, a lawyer is just going cost you a lot of money, and you don't have a case. We managed to get this space for you, a premium location, but there were certain restrictions. You are aware of that, aren't you?"

"Can't we negotiate a new lease, Jonathan? Do you realize what this will do to me?"

"I'm sorry, Jay. I wish I could do something."

Jonathan was silent for a few moments. His brow furrowed as he pulled out a manila folder from a lower desk drawer, extracted a document, and tossed it to Jay. He fixed a fierce stare on the other man.

Jay paled at first and then reddened. His hand trembled as he thumbed through the pages of the report. "Have you pressured any of these other doctors? Why aren't you after them also? And who is this Joseph Waterman?" he asked, pointing to his office lease and to the lease termination notice. "I didn't lease from anyone named Waterman. I leased from the hospital."

"I'm sorry you don't remember, Jay. The hospital doesn't lease office space. We build the office building and then lease the entire building to others. They sublease to the doctors. We can't control what they do."

Jay shoved the papers back to Jonathan. He stood and slapped the surface of the desk. His eyes glared with anger as he whirled to walk away. At the door, he turned back toward Jonathan.

"You haven't heard the last of this, Jonathan. You can't run roughshod over people like this and get away with it." He slammed the door to Jonathan's office as he left, and seconds later the walls shook when he slammed the door to the outside corridor.

Andy looked for some explanation from Jonathan, who was reassembling the folder. He filed it back in the desk drawer, and an eerie half-minute silence followed. Finally, Jonathan faced Andy with a sober look on his face.

"I knew this was going to happen, Andy. Let me explain how this all evolved: Jay was an eager internist with a wealthy father when we recruited him. Well trained but naïve. We thought he would build a practice quickly and admit his patients to this hospital. After a year, we find out that not only is he working as a hospitalist at another hospital, our competitor, but that he's admitting all of his patients there. And his father has not come through with contributions to the Trinitus Foundation Fund, as he promised. We had to get Jay out and put someone in his place that would support Trinitus."

Andy shuddered. "You mentioned you had someone else lined up for the space."

"We have recruited a well-known cardiologist with a large, established practice and a large following of referring physicians. He'll bring in heart patients, which means heart surgery, which means high income procedures for the hospital."

"How did you get him to come here?"

"We gave him a sizable rent reduction—plus a few more incentives," said Jonathan. A sly smile creased his face.

"Then he will be paying less rent than Dr. Jenkins for the same space."

"Yeah, but that's only one thing that brought him into our building."

"But didn't I hear you say that a Mr. Waterman did the leasing?"

"I see why it's confusing to you. Here's the story: As you know, hospitals can't give rebates to attract doctors their facilities. That's the law. So we lease the office building to an investor group, like Joseph Waterman and Associates, and guarantee them a good return on their investment. But we maintain final approval on all of the subleasing. The lease agreement is legally between the investors and the doctor, so the doctor is not leasing from the hospital. We simply control the leasing."

"So you can determine the amount of the rent even though the doctor is renting from someone else."

"That's it, Andy. We control which doctors we allow in the building—and those are the ones that can help the hospital the most. You're thinking of the Stark law, aren't you?" asked Jonathan, noticing the frown on Andy's face. "It's strategy, Andy. It's part of the Three 'P' strategy that I'm sure Jake mentioned to you—people, physicians, politics. Mr. Waterman is a member of our board of trustees. He's a community leader and a political kingmaker behind the scenes."

Andy laughed. "I sure didn't learn anything like this in school."

"Of course not."

"What if information like that became public?"

"Now who do you think the public would believe, some greedy doctor or the Trinitus Healthcare System? We are a religious organization with a religious mission. Nobody would dare challenge Trinitus."

"I guess it's just a shock to me, Jonathan."

"You'll get used to it."

\* \* \* \*

The long day, filled with skepticism of the integrity of the Trinitus system, left Andy's brain whirling in bewilderment. He remembered the anti-kickback laws from his classroom days. From what Jonathan had said—and what he had seen with is own eyes—the incident he had just witnessed was grossly illegal. *How do they get away with it?* he wondered. *What else will I uncover in this so-called non-profit hospital system? Nothing I can do but stick through this year—one month at a time.*

## 21

Andy glanced at his watch—almost six o'clock as he dragged himself through the front door to their apartment. He had hoped Barbara would be back from Dallas by now. He was certain she would be safe, surrounded by FBI agents and traveling in an FBI plane. She likely hadn't called because Agent Walton was worried the call could be traced. But his new cell phone was registered as hospital property; the call couldn't be traced to him. The thought no sooner crossed his mind than his phone vibrated in his pocket.

"Andy," Barbara said, sounding faint and tired, "are you home yet?"

"Just got in."

"How was your day?"

"I have a lot to tell you. Where are you?"

"Still in Dallas. I'm on a pay phone. I should be home in a couple of hours."

"Are you all right?"

"I'm fine, just very tired. It's been a long, trying day," she replied. "We'll discuss it when I get home."

"Good. I'm worried about all of this."

"I know you are. Any word from Leanne?"

"I haven't had time to check the answering machine. I see it's blinking."

"It wasn't my call. Maybe it's Leanne."

"I'll check. Be careful, Barbara."

Barbara laughed. "How could I be any safer? I love you, Andy."

"I love you too. I just want you to come home."

Andy clicked on the "play" button on the answer machine. There was no question of the caller's identity. It was Leanne's voice.

"Barbara, I am on my way to Westlake. Left Dallas at about two. I should be there by eight or nine. Call me on the OnStar number I gave you as soon as you can. I'm worried that I am being followed."

*Oh, my God! She's left her husband and coming here*, Andy thought. Andy rummaged through Barbara's dresser drawers looking for Leanne's mobile number, but it was nowhere to be found. He did find Agent Walton's number. Had Barbara told him of their offer to assist Leanne? He had to take a chance. If she had planned to tell him, she should have by now. He dialed Ralph Walton's number. His voicemail kicked in with the first ring.

*"Please identify yourself and your location. Someone will return your call as soon as possible."* Andy followed the instructions, and within seconds, Ralph called.

"Andy, you called?"

"Yes, sir," he said. "I apologize for bothering you. I need to talk to Barbara."

"She's aboard the plane and ready to leave, Andy. Is it urgent?"

"Yes it is."

"I can arrange for her to call you back from the plane. The call can't be traced from the satellite phone on the aircraft. Is there anything that I should be made aware of before we take off?"

Andy was silent for a few moments while he contemplated his answer.

"Yes, I think there is, but I want Barbara to tell you if she hasn't already."

"I think I already know. Barbara will call you right away. Oh, Andy, you and Barbara are two brave people, and I'm grateful for what you're doing. We won't let anything happen to either of you."

"Thank you, sir." Andy chuckled. "I appreciate that."

"We'll be in close touch, Andy."

Within a few minutes, Barbara called and Andy gave her the news.

"Leanne's on the way there, to Westlake?" asked Barbara. "What did she say? Where will she stay?"

"She wants us to call her on her mobile phone," Andy replied. "She said you had her number, and she said she thinks she is being followed. Have you told Agent Walton that you encouraged Leanne to do this?"

"He knows," she answered. "He's aware of the trouble she has had with Anthony. I have her OnStar number. Will you call her, Andy?"

"I think she wants to talk to you."

"But she suspects that she is being followed. Andy, we can't wait that long to contact her. You have to meet her somewhere. I'm sure she must be terrified."

"I'll talk to her. Call me back in an hour or so. You have my new cell phone number."

"Thank you, Andy. I love you for this. Be careful."

"Don't worry, little one. Just get home so we can dig our way out of this quagmire of complexities."

"Andy, are you disappointed in me?"

"We'll deal with it. I love you."

"I love you too."

\*　　\*　　\*　　\*

Andy noted the time and tried to calculate where Leanne would be. If she left Dallas at 2:00, she should be no more that two hours away, assuming that she hadn't stopped on the way. That was unlikely if she thought someone was following her. He punched in her OnStar number. Within seconds, she answered. Even though her voice was muffled by the roar of the highway, Andy could detect a quiver in it.

"Leanne, this is Andy. Barbara's in Dallas and she won't be back for a while. She asked me to call. Are you all right?"

"Yes ... I think so," she replied. "Andy, thank you for calling. In all honesty, I'm frightened."

"What's wrong?"

"Ever since I left Dallas, there's been a car following me, a dark sedan. I took some side roads in San Antonio, but I couldn't lose it. It's always there and it turns when I turn. I'm scared, Andy. I don't know what to do."

"Tell me exactly where you are and what car you are in."

"I saw a mileage marker, number 120, a minute ago. I'm driving a white Jaguar sedan."

"Give me a few minutes to think this through. I'll call you back."

Andy remembered stopping for gasoline about sixty miles before they had reached Westlake during their move from Dallas. He had been amused at the sign on the gas station and convenience store. What was it called? *M. T. TANKS—FUEL AND FOOD.* He recalled seeing the parking lot behind the store filled with eighteen wheelers and thinking it had to be a favorite stop for truckers. Leanne couldn't find a safer place to be until he could get there.

He called Leanne again, and after reassuring her that he was on the way to meet her, he gave her instructions to park as close as possible to one of the large trucks and stay put until he arrived.

"Just stay in your car. I should be there in an hour and a half."

"Andy, I am so grateful to you and Barbara for helping me. All I know right now is that I am getting away from Anthony—I don't have any idea where I'm going."

"Don't worry about it. We'll get through this somehow."

"Thank you, Andy. I feel better already."

Andy raced outside the apartment and to the carport. Once again he would have to rely on their old VW to make the trip—and at a fast rate. He had no idea what he would face when he reached Leanne. Who could be following her? It was not the FBI. Agent Walton would have been aware and would have warned him. Probably some private detective that Leanne's husband had hired.

A cold chill swept over him as he remembered that Barbara had heard the judge threaten Leanne. If the judge is so jealous that he is having her watched, he might think she is running away to meet Mark. *I might be mistaken for Mark*, he thought. *My God! What a predicament. But there's no turning back. I have to deal with it.*

A faint tint of dusk lingered in the western sky as Andy approached *M. T. TANKS—FUEL AND FOOD*. He saw that it was just as he had remembered: bright neon lights and at least six or seven large trucks parked behind the store. He circled slowly and did not see the dark sedan that Leanne had described, but he did see Leanne's Jaguar, barely visible between two eighteen wheelers.

"Good girl!" he said aloud. As he circled the lot again, thinking through his next move, he spotted a black sedan with two occupants rapidly approaching along the interstate frontage road. The vehicle slowed and then pulled into the front parking area. Neither individuals exited. Andy had to move fast now.

He called Leanne. "We've got to hurry. They are here. I'll park behind you, so don't be frightened."

"I want you to drive, Andy," she answered.

With Andy at the wheel, they shot out from between the trucks and raced down the frontage road toward the interstate. Leanne's followers must have predicted their move, as they had entered the road ahead of them. Just before the pursuers had reached the access ramp, they had turned their car sideways, blocking Andy and Leanne's entrance to the main highway. Each of the men had gotten out of their vehicle, and each held a handgun pointed straight toward Andy and Leanne.

"We can't get past!" Leanne yelled. "They have guns, Andy. What can we do?"

"Hold on!" said Andy. "Get down!" Pushing down the accelerator, he swerved into the median ditch. The car bounced and skidded as it jumped the ditch, but Andy managed to keep control as he maneuvered the Jag up the other side of the ditch toward the interstate highway. As they passed the gunmen, both opened fire, but the fast-moving, weaving target eluded their aim. Only one bullet shattered through the window on the passenger side, passing millimeters from Leanne's face before grazing Andy's forehead and exiting through the left front window.

Before the surprised gunmen could turn their car to go after their quarry, Andy and Leanne had put a fair amount of distance between them. As the speedometer neared 110 miles per hour, the distance gradually increased. Andy figured the men's car was a Lincoln or Mercury, no match for the Jaguar at high speed.

Andy and Leanne, both pallid and tremulous, were silent for a half-minute. Leanne turned to Andy. "You've been hit!" She pulled a tissue from the glove compartment and dabbed at the blood oozing from his forehead. "Are you all right?"

"Just a scratch. I get clammy thinking how bad it could have been. Oh, I'm Andy Goldeyer, incidentally," he said with a laugh.

Leanne joined his laughter. "At least we can still laugh. Not a very pleasant way to meet."

"Am I making you nervous, driving so fast?"

"Not at all. You seem like you can handle the speed. I couldn't. That's why we're in this mess. I couldn't escape them."

"There's no question that they mean business," Andy replied.

"Andy, can you ever forgive me for getting you and Barbara into this mess?"

"Look, Barbara is always right about people. She is determined to help you with or without my assistance. I discouraged her from getting this involved, but after seeing what those goons tried to do to you today, I'm glad I'm in the middle of it."

"Thank you for being honest, Andy. What do you think we should do now? I know I have to make some long-range plans but this not the time for that."

"The first thing we need to do is notify the FBI ... notify Mr. Walton," said Andy. "Who do you think is after you—after us, now?"

"It has to be—"

Before she could answer, her OnStar rang. She pushed the dot for a two-way conversation.

"Where are you? I told you what I'd do to you if you tried to leave. Where are you now?" Anthony demanded in a gruff voice.

"I've left you, Anthony. I won't be back."

"You bitch! Don't you see what that will do? You're on the way to meet that Marchesa bastard again, aren't you? You're not going to do that to me, you whore. You get your ass back home—now."

"I'm not coming back, Anthony."

"I'll kill you before I let you run off with that son of a bitch. You're with him now, aren't you? I'll kill you both!"

"I'm turning you off, Anthony. Don't call me again."

"Leanne, Leanne, wait...."

Leanne pressed the dot again. "I'm sorry you had to hear that, Andy."

"Barbara has told me about your relationship with your husband," said Andy. "Hearing him now confirms Barbara's impression. We need to contact Barbara and Agent Walton?"

Andy had no sooner uttered those words than the OnStar system sounded again. "It's Anthony again," said Leanne. "I'm not going to answer it."

"It might be Barbara. If it is Anthony, you can cut him off."

She pressed the dot again. It was Barbara.

"Are you all right? I haven't been able to reach you. We're home. Mr. Walton is here in the apartment with me."

Andy narrated the harrowing events. "We've evaded the pursuers so far. I'm worried about ever having to slow down."

"Andy, are you hurt? How is Leanne?"

"We're fine right now."

"Let me talk to Mr. Walton, Andy," said Barbara, her voice cracking. "I'll call you back. Be careful."

The next call was from Agent Walton. "Andy, come straight to your apartment. Mrs. Joberst needs to stay here with you until we can find a more suitable place. I'll arrange to have your car brought back, and we'll need to take custody of Leanne's car. Come straight here. We'll scour the area later for evidence. I'll get a more detailed report from you when you arrive."

"We're both pretty shaken right now."

"I'm sure you are. I'm asking for a highway patrol car to escort you into Westlake. As soon as you see the patrol car, you can slow to a safe speed. Are you sure you're not injured?"

"Yeah, I'm fine. The bullet barely scratched my forehead. Leanne's not hurt. Just glass fragments everywhere."

"We now have another piece to the puzzle. I'll tell Barbara you're on the way."

## 22

Andy followed the highway trooper onto the street that led to his apartment complex. As they came to a stop, two agents—Agent Walton and another Andy recognized as his partner, Wes—stepped out of a car and approached. Each held his badge in clear view. The two agents kept their eyes glued to the entrance street while Andy and Leanne walked to the front door of apartment.

Barbara rushed into Andy's arms when they entered. She held him tight for a few moments, tears forming in her eyes as she kissed him.

"I have been so worried," said Barbara. "Let me see your forehead." She pulled his head down to her level and carefully touched the area around the wound. "That could have killed you."

"I haven't had time to even think about that."

Agent Walton looked over Barbara's shoulder at the wound. "Does he need to go to the emergency room?" asked Barbara.

"It is not deep. The bullet barely broke the skin. Wash the wound and cover it with a Band-Aid. You're a lucky young man."

Barbara turned to Leanne. After a long embrace, her forehead creased into a frown. "Leanne, you mustn't subject yourself to danger like this—never again."

"I had to leave, Barbara," she replied as she blotted the tears on her face. "I think you know why. I just couldn't take it anymore. I tried to find Mark without success. He must be frantic by now."

"You did the right thing," said Barbara. "You'll be safe here. We'll let Mark know that you're safe. Mr. Walton has placed twenty-four security watches around our apartment. He has some ideas on how we can move forward and find the baby."

"We *are* going to find him, aren't we, Barbara?"

"Absolutely! You and Andy try to relax for a few minutes," Barbara replied. Leanne seated herself on the couch while Andy paced the floor and intermittently peered out the window blinds while Barbara comforted Leanne.

"You're safe now, Andy," said Agent Walton. "There's no one out there now."

"I guess it's just now hitting me—the close call, I mean."

"You might experience some post-traumatic stress for a while," he replied. "I agree with Barbara: you both need to try to relax. As soon as you feel up to it, I'm going to need you both to narrate everything that transpired from the time Mrs. Joberst left home."

"It's going to work out, Leanne," said Barbara as she gently massaged her tense neck and shoulder muscles. "Let me get you and Andy a glass of wine. Maybe it'll help you relax."

"I'd love that," she replied. "What am I going to do, Barbara? Anthony's ruthless. I think you can see that now. He's capable of doing anything to get his way. I am so relieved to get out of that house."

Barbara returned with glasses of Chardonnay for Andy and Leanne. "You will stay with us as long as you need to, Leanne. Mr. Walton wants you to be under constant protection." She turned to Andy. "I'm glad we went ahead and furnished the extra bedroom ahead of time."

Andy grinned as he sipped his wine. "You must have had some sort of premonition."

"I hate to impose on you two, but I am glad you're doing this," said Leanne. "I have never been so scared. And I've never been as thankful in all my life as I was when I saw Andy. I thought this was the end."

Leanne held her head in her hands, her sobbing barely audible. "I have made such a mess of my life."

"Enough of that," said Barbara as she patted her shoulder and pulled her to her feet. "Let me show you where you will be staying. Bring your wine with you. You'll even have your own bathroom. We were lucky to get this first-floor unit with two baths. Now, dry those eyes. Everything's going to be fine."

"I can't think of anything else, Barbara. I'm a deplorable wretch, the typical 'poor little rich girl,' and all I want is to have my baby back and to have Mark. Is that asking too much?"

"It's going to happen, Leanne," said Barbara. "Just keep telling yourself the baby's alive and well. You and Mark eventually will be together. This is no time to be pessimistic. We're going to make it happen."

"How could I be so fortunate to have had you come into my life?" said Leanne, wobbly on her feet and needing Barbara's support. Her speech had become thick and garbled. "I must have drunk that wine too fast. You are a remarkable person, Barbara. You are the person that I've always wanted to be, and you have everything I've ever wanted in life."

"It'll happen, Leanne," Barbara replied. "Sometimes I think everything like this happens for a reason—obstacles are placed in our way just to test our strength. But you can't curl up in the corner and do nothing. You have to get up and fight. If it's worth having it's worth fighting for."

Leanne looked at Barbara in wonderment for several seconds without speaking. Her face blossomed in a sparkling smile.

"You're my psychotherapist!" She broke into an almost uncontrollable hearty laughter with tears flowing simultaneously.

Barbara joined her in laughter, followed by a hug. Their revelry was interrupted by a tap on the door. Andy was standing outside the room. "Mr. Walton wants to update us on the status of his investigation. I just finished giving him details of the chase."

\*     \*     \*     \*

Agent Walton, with Wes now indoors and at his side, sat before Andy, Barbara, and Leanne as he gave his presentation.

"Here's where we stand: Your first questions, I'm sure, are, 'Is the baby all right and do we have any clue who is responsible for this crime?' The answer to both questions is no, we don't at this time."

Leanne grasped Barbara's hand. Tears welled in her eyes. She stiffened, her knuckles white as she squeezed Barbara's hand, but she remained quiet.

"Here's what we do have," Agent Walton continued. "We are piecing together the evidence to determine how this was perpetrated. All of you know firsthand what happened at the hospital that night, so I won't repeat those details. This entire scheme was masterminded by individuals who had access to high-level computer technology, underworld counterfeiters, and small-time street gangsters to execute their plan."

"How can you deduct that much information from what you have?"

"Bits of evidence here and there, the mode of operation, the smooth transition of events. We know, for example, that someone gave the order to discontinue the sensor anklets on babies the very day of the kidnapping. No one in the hospital administration admits to giving that order. We have interrogated Ms. Witcher extensively. She's terrified, but we're not through questioning her. We think she was forced to give the order to stop the bracelet process, but we can't determine who coerced her or why."

"That explains why she acted so strange when I tried to call a Code Pink," said Barbara, a blank stare on her face.

"Exactly!" said Walton. "We hope to get some idea from her who was responsible for the order. She keeps saying that it came from administration, but no one concurs." Agent Walton continued, "We think the baby was placed in a modified travel bag with an oxygen apparatus that kept the baby alive during the abduction. We found evidence in the old van that Barbara identified that the baby had been fed a bottle after it was removed from the bag."

"Then my baby was all right at that point."

"Yes, we know that. And from past cases, based on the usual sequence of events, we believe the baby is still alive—somewhere. But the path stops there. The unexplainable element in this case is why there have been no more ransom demands. Our staff criminal psychologists think our inability to communicate effectively with the criminals is a part of their scheme to increase Mrs. Joberst's anxiety—wear her down to the point that she'll comply with any dollar amount that they demand. None of this is consistent with the usual kidnapper's pattern."

"So maybe my baby is alive somewhere," said Leanne, her chin trembling as she spoke. "And they know I would pay anything to recover him."

"Right. We also believe they may be waiting so they can silence any secondary characters—the three individuals who pulled this off—so there is no link to those responsible for the abduction. In short, this entire plan appears to have been perpetrated by a major underworld organization. The mystery remains: why would any such group waste time on a kidnapping? The risk is too great. Someone else is behind this crime."

Agent Walton paused to let his words soak in. The room was eerily quiet. The awestruck threesome—Leanne, Barbara, and Andy—each with dropped chins, stared into the distance as if contemplating the FBI agent's report. Mark Marchesa's words, from Barbara's very first encounter with him, flashed through her mind: *"I have a plan." Surely Mark had not been responsible for causing Leanne this grief,* she thought.

"Then you think the attack on Leanne and me came from the same individuals—the Mafia?" asked Andy.

"That's the way it appears to our crime lab analyzers. But everyone agrees this sort of crime is not consistent with the pattern of underworld organizations. We don't think that a criminal organization would take a risk like this unless they had more to gain than ransom. Some of our analyzers believe this was an act of revenge. The attack on Mrs. Joberst substantiates that theory. For example, it could be retribution for an adverse verdict by Judge Joberst."

"My God!" said Andy. "What can we do?"

"We wait, and try to be patient. Secrecy is essential. Andy, you should go on about your work as usual. Leanne and Barbara will be well protected. Anytime they go out, which I hope will be infrequently, our agents will be close by.

"Mrs. Joberst, this is something I think you will be glad to hear: we have arranged for the major television networks in Dallas to run a taped appeal by you and your husband pleading for information about the baby and giving phone numbers where you can be reached. Of course, all calls will be directed to operators in our office."

"What do I do about my husband?"

"As you know, he has not been in favor of any public appeal. However, we'll plead with him to join you during the filming. We need some emotional scenes. This will be done in Dallas—in one of the TV studios."

"I'm not going back to that house," said Leanne, a panic-stricken expression on her face.

"You'll be fine, Mrs. Joberst. We'll fly you to Dallas in the FBI plane and after the taping we'll whisk you away so fast no one will know what happened. Your husband won't know where you are staying. There will be no interviews with reporters."

"My husband has ways of getting information, Mr. Walton," said Leanne. "Don't be surprised at what he might attempt to do to me."

"We'll be alert to any possibility. For now, all of you need to get rest."

"When do you think we will do the taping?" asked Leanne. "I'm anxious for the opportunity to make an appeal to the public. Someone might come up with a clue."

"That's what we're hoping for. Hopefully in the next day or so. Please be ready anytime I call."

## 23

*Dallas*

Lieutenant Blake Bartlett looked forward to a restful weekend after a week packed with various robberies, misdemeanors, and domestic disturbances that stretched his duty into ten- and twelve-hour days. Finally, he'd have some time with his wife and children. His two youngest had been put to bed most every night even before he had arrived home. Were they growing up without knowing they had a father? He had to change that. And now maybe he'd have time to shoot a few hoops with his teenage son.

He shoved one arm through his blazer and was poised to repeat the process with the other when he glanced at a new report that flashed on his monitor. He froze. Something caught his eye and held his attention. A twenty-six-year-old white female was found dead in a flophouse in the 2400 block of Harry Hines Blvd. Cause of death, based on statements from bystanders and pending report from the forensic medicine department, drug overdose. Unconfirmed identification reported as that of Barbara Goldeyer, a nurse formerly employed by Christus Healthcare System in Dallas.

"What the hell?" he said aloud as he removed his coat, sat in front of his computer, and started pounding the keyboard. "Something's not right here." He had heard nothing further about the Joberst kidnapping since the FBI had taken over. In fact he had planned just recently to contact Agent Walton to chastise him for not keeping him apprised of the progress of the case. Barbara Goldeyer was the nurse that had been involved in the abduction.

His scorching note to forensics left no doubt that he wanted confirmation on the identification and cause of death immediately. Blake called his wife and once again had to tell her that an incident would keep him from coming home early.

He had no sooner placed the call than the investigating officer on the scene called.

"Blake, this is Jim Donavan. I think you had better get over here quick."

"I'm on the way, Jim. Anything I need to know."

"I'll tell you when you get here."

Blake sped down Central Expressway, red lights flashing. He exited on Mockingbird and turned down Harry Hines.

*What would Barbara Goldeyer be doing in this part of town?* he wondered. He was usually right about his impressions of the individuals he interviewed. She seemed to be a high-class lady, with a nice husband. There had to be a mistake. He thought about Jim Donavan's message. The urgency in his voice was worrisome. Jim was a lead officer in homicide and was known for his integrity and good judgment in cases like this.

Ahead, Blake could see the revolving red and blue lights atop the two patrol cars. A crowd surrounded the vehicles, people whose dress and demeanor indicated their lives revolved around prostitution, drugs, or both. In front of the Ecstasy Bar, its name spelled in red neon light followed by two more signs that declared "Rooms for Rent" and "Ladies Drink Free," two patrolmen stood beside the door preventing anyone from entering or exiting. An ambulance, also with blinking lights, was parked close by.

Blake parked, nodded to the guards, took a deep breath, and entered the Ecstasy Bar. Through the smoke, he could barely distinguish the few glassy-eyed patrons still seated with drinks in hand as if it were business as usual. He was met by Jim Donavan, who escorted him up one flight of stairs, down a narrow, dimly lit corridor, and into a small bedroom.

"What do you have, Jim?"

"Strange case, Blake," he replied, motioning toward the bed where the victim lay—a petite young girl, head turned to the side with blood-tinged foam draining from her partially open mouth and covering much of her cyanotic face. Other than the bed, the room was furnished with one chair and a dresser of sorts, over which hung a mirror. A duffle bag, apparently filled with clothing, had been thrown in one corner.

"Forensics have done their thing?" asked Blake as he scanned the scene.

"Preliminary DNA. No report yet," replied Jim. The slightly detectable tremble in his chin and the hesitancy in his voice betrayed his emotionally shaken state.

"It's all right, Jim. Being a tough cop doesn't keep you from showing emotion. We all feel this way at times. Go on with the story."

"According to her acquaintances, although she's been living in the area for the last month or so, she's shown no interest in working the street.. As far as they know, she has no enemies. Stays to herself most of the time. They know her as Becky. At one time, she told someone her last name was Coward."

"The report out of Communications Central said she had been identified as Barbara Goldeyer," said Blake.

"When I got here, I looked through the dresser drawers and found this," he said as he handed Blake an ID badge with the girl's picture. It's for the nursery at Trinitus Hospital. That's why I reported the identification."

Blake looked closely at the body and back at the photograph on the badge. "Close resemblance," he said, "even the hairstyle."

"What do you mean?" asked Jim.

"Do you remember the baby abduction at Trinitus Hospital about two months ago—the judge's baby?"

"Yeah, I heard the FBI took over the investigation."

"Right. I was first on the scene. Barbara was the nurse we interrogated. I was shocked when I read the identity of this victim."

"You're sure this is not Barbara?"

"Yeah, she's been groomed to look like Barbara. This is the girl who lifted the baby from the hospital. Barbara was cleared as a suspect."

"I'm glad I called you. Nothing about this case makes sense. The story I got from her friends, if you can call them friends, is that she entered her room with some guy early in the evening. Shortly afterward, he came running out, stuffing in his shirttail, and stopped by the bar just long enough to tell the bartender that something had happened to Becky. Then he made a quick exit."

"Probably didn't want to be identified. Did you see any sign of a scuffle?"

"None," he said. "Of course, in this room who'd notice?"

"Forensics should be here soon. We'll have to wait. Find any drug paraphernalia?"

"Just the usual. It appears she was into coke," he replied. "One of the girls said she was using more heavily recently. Also she bragged about coming into a lot of money, that she was going to some fancy treatment center and then apply for nursing school. When the girls told me, they laughed about it. The word was out that if anyone on the street needed emergency cash, she was available to assist them."

"I'm sure you've searched the room."

"I was waiting for you and for the crime lab. I didn't want to disturb anything that might be evidence. You probably want to ID the last person to see her."

"Yeah, and I've got to let the FBI know what we're into here. This does not appear to be a homicide, but there might be a link to the kidnapping case that Agent Walton has been working on."

"You want me to go through that duffle bag."

"Yeah, very carefully so you don't disturb anything that might prove useful to the crime lab."

\* \* \* \*

Blake stepped out of the room into the corridor, searched his PDA, dialed the FBI number, and asked for Agent Ralph Walton, knowing that there would be a short delay before Ralph returned his call—if indeed he did return it on the first try. Within minutes, Agent Walton was on the line.

"Detective Bartlett, nice hearing from you! I hope you don't have another complex problem like the last one you called me about."

"Part of the same case, I believe," said Blake, straining to keep the tenor of his voice cordial. "Our police officers have uncovered some interesting information that I think you might—"

Jim Donavan's yell interrupted his sentence. He kept Agent Walton on the line while he re-entered the room, cell phone in hand.

"Hold just a minute, Ralph. The police officer at the scene has just found something. What is it, Jim? Agent Walton is on the line."

"Blake, look at this, hidden in the bottom of the duffle bag: a canvass case containing stacks of $100 bills and a generous number of $1000 bills."

Blake turned back to his cell phone. "Ralph, the dead girl had a large amount of cash in her possession."

"Are your forensic people doing their thing?" Agent Walton asked.

"They are on the way—in fact, just arrived. Do you want your own people to take over here?"

"Nothing wrong with two labs working on the same thing," said Ralph.

"Right. We'll correlate our findings with yours."

"Wes and I will be there as soon as we can. We are in Westlake right now; it will take a couple of hours to get there by plane. Where will I find you?"

"We'll be through here by then. Come to my office." said Blake. We should have a full report for you by then."

"Good. I'm sure you are thinking the same thing that I am: the girl was one of accomplices to the kidnapping," Ralph replied. "But why was she living in that neighborhood. She didn't need money. She was probably there just for access to drugs. If only we had had a chance to talk to her before this. I knew she'd show up somewhere. The mystery here is where did the money come from? A ransom hasn't been paid yet."

"I'll be waiting for you at headquarters, anxious for an update."

"One other thing: try to keep the media out of this. Ask your officers to say only that the cause of death is suspected to be drug overdose."

"No problem," Blake replied as he closed the flap on his cell phone. He turned back to Jim Donavan.

"Jim, find out which hookers were closest to the girl and bring them in. The FBI agents may want to interrogate them. And see if you can find out if anyone else has contacted her or asked about her."

"I know what you want. I'll be in touch."

"Thanks, Jim."

Blake turned further management of the police investigation over to Jim Donavan, made another call to his wife, and headed back to his office to await the arrival of FBI Agent Ralph Walton.

\* \* \* \*

Ralph studied the police photographer's pictures at length with Blake looking over his shoulder. Then he turned his attention to the report regarding the cash found in Becky's duffle bag—a little over ninety thousand dollars in hundred- and thousand-dollar bills. Where did it come from? She wouldn't have hidden it with her clothes and left it in the room while she was gone. If she had left it in a safe somewhere, why was it in her room now? The identity of the last person to see her alive was crucial to answering these questions.

"Do you have any idea who her visitor was?" asked Ralph.

"We have conflicting descriptions from the other girls and from the clerk at the front desk. According to most of the witnesses, he didn't look like a typical John. He wasn't seen in a car. One girl said she'd seen him before—came asking for Becky earlier today. She thinks Becky might have known him. She saw him come in tonight carrying a canvass tote-bag; we didn't find it in the room."

"Anybody hear any conversation or sounds of a struggle?"

"None."

"What did the desk clerk say?"

"His is our best description. He confirmed hat the guy was carrying a bag and looked different than most customers. Couldn't explain why except that the man's clothes looked tailored. Said he was tall and heavy-set, that he had slicked-down black hair and a small moustache, no beard. He didn't stop to ask directions but went straight up the stairs toward Becky's room."

"I'm sure you searched the room thoroughly."

"Jim Donavan's one of my best. Jim thinks the witness who saw the man stuffing in his shirt when he left the room was wrong, that he was actually fastening his belt and tying the bag around his waist. He probably delivered drugs to Becky, got her stoned, and then smothered her."

"What makes him think she was smothered?" asked Ralph.

"Look at the pictures. You can see the tiny ruptured blood vessels in the skin of her face."

"That is reasonable to expect. Still, why all the money hidden in her room?"

"The only thing I can think of is that she was getting ready to cut out. Earlier today, another witness heard her screaming at someone over the phone, saying she knew where he was and that she was coming after him. For some reason, the girls think she had been talking to someone in Miami the last day or so."

"That would give somebody time to send in a hit man," said Ralph, still staring at the pictures. "The bag probably contained weapons. We'll need to check plane reservations. Becky was probably talking to one of her accomplices. We'll need to track it down."

"We'll have the pathologist's report in a couple of days. I'll let you know," said Blake.

"I'm going on the probability that Becky was murdered," Ralph replied. "That means the other two kidnappers will be next, so we'll start looking for the others in Miami right away. We have to find one if we're ever going to find out what happened to the baby."

"Good luck. Please keep me informed. If this was homicide, I'll need to know what you uncover."

"Sure, I'll do that, Blake. Sorry I haven't updated you on this case, but progress has been unbelievably slow. I'm catching flack from my director. He's catching the political pressure."

"Yeah, a federal judge's baby," Blake replied, a smirk on his face. "I don't hear many comments coming from the judge. You'd think he'd be screaming at everybody in the bureau."

"That's one thing that's had me wondering from the beginning—his attitude. It just doesn't fit," said Ralph, frowning and shaking his head. "I have national TV lined up to interview the parents, an emotional appeal for information about the baby. Looks like this has torn the judge and his wife apart; they're not living together right now. I'm anxious to see how they interact during the upcoming TV interview."

"Where do you think Becky got all that money?"

"I'm pretty sure I know, Blake, but I have to find out for sure."

# 24

*Dallas*

Deo's restlessness was beginning to erode his patience. Eight hours into the second day—a whole package of cigarettes gone up in smoke, three calls made to room service for ice and snacks, and every line in the *Dallas Morning News*, including the want-ads, read twice—and still no word from Marcello. It was not like him to wait so long to report in.

Deo resisted the impulse to call Marcello. He knew that Marcello was working day and night tracking down rumors and, along with Reyes Dinardo, rounding up underworld characters to be interviewed. He grinned, thinking of the FBI searching for him in Las Vegas after discovering that he had not stayed one single night in his hotel room at the Frontagio.

He poured himself another scotch on the rocks and sat down to watch more television when the phone rang.

"Marcello!" said Deo. "What's going on?"

"We need to talk. A driver will pick you up in an hour. Wait outside the hotel entrance. Wear your piece but don't put on a coat and tie. You'll see why when you get here."

\*     \*     \*     \*

The limousine driver didn't volunteer any information on where they were going and Deo elected not to question him. Conversation was limited to casual remarks about the traffic and the long waits for light changes at intersections. Deo, seated in the front passenger seat, watched through the side window as the street turned into a row of establishments with bright, flashing neon lights of all designs, bars with eye-catching names, porno parlors, and a liberal selection of scantily-clad street walkers of all descriptions. Near each block corner, a bejeweled, colorfully dressed man—usually in bright pink, purple, and yellow attire—leaned against the building as though keeping a watchful eye on his "girls." Deo laughed at Marcello's remark about wearing a coat and tie. He could also see why Marcello wanted him to carry his gun.

"Marcello said to let you off a couple of blocks from the Ecstasy Bar," said the driver. "He said not to worry, you could take care of yourself."

"I'll try. Thanks." Deo laughed as he hopped out of the limo and started walking at a casual pace, stopping occasionally to gaze into a window. This usually brought out a hustler with remarks like, "Looking for action, pal? This ain't the place. Follow me." Ahead he could see the sign for the Ecstasy Bar standing out bigger and brighter than most of the others.

What disturbed Deo was the yellow barrier tape around the bar's entrance. He spotted Reyes standing behind the tape conferring with one of the police officers. When Deo approached, Reyes raised the tape and motioned for Deo to enter. Reyes led Deo inside and through the bar, past a handful of glassy-eyed patrons slumped over a table, past the two stinking restrooms without doors, and before a door at the end of the hall. He tapped lightly on the door. Deo could hear Marcello's voice beckoning them to enter.

The objects and occupants inside the dimly-lit, smoke-filled room were barely visible. In one corner sat a frail, pallid, tremulous middle-aged man staring at Marcello, who leaned back leisurely in a comfortable upholstered desk chair. A faint glimmer of light revealed the man's bloodshot eyes with dilated pupils and the incessant twitching of his facial muscles. Intermittently, he licked his lips and blotted the saliva with the back of his hand.

Marcello stood when Deo entered.

"Glad you could make it. Any trouble?"

"None," said Deo. "Glad to see you."

"A few items to report."

"Good."

"This is Squeak Letz," said Marcello. "He's made some interesting observations. He lives here at the Ecstasy and helps the girls—and they help him."

"And he's been helping you and Reyes?"

"Yeah, he's an old friend of Ray's."

"He knows how to keep his mouth shut?"

"Depends on who he's talking to. Yeah, he's reliable, and he's our friend."

Squeak shook more vigorously while Marcello talked. Deo figured he needed a fix badly and Marcello knew it. Marcello kept his eyes fixed on Squeak without saying a word for a few seconds.

"Reyes, I think Squeak needs a drink. You want to take him outside."

"I ain't talking to nobody, Marcello, please," he pleaded. "Don't take me out, Ray. I ain't no canary."

"Stop it, Squeak. Ray is just gonna to help you. You're not going anywhere. I know that you know better than to talk, Squeak."

"Yeah, I know. I know."

"And what happens if you do, Squeak?"

"I know, I know," he stammered. "I need a drink, Ray."

"Come with me, Squeak, while these two guys talk."

"Yeah, Yeah. While they talk."

"Who is that man that I brought in here just now, Squeak?" asked Reyes.

"I don't know … I don't know … I didn't see you bring any man in here."

"That's right. That's the way to stay healthy, isn't it, Squeak."

"Yeah … yeah. Can you get me a fix, Ray?"

"Sure. Come on with me," said Reyes as he led the poor, terrified wretch—now shaking and swaying from side to side—out the door. Marcello poured Deo a fresh drink of scotch on ice, placed it on a side table between them, and motioned for Deo to drag up a chair.

"Some good leads, some bad news. Looks like we'll need more time," said Marcello.

"Take all the time you need, Marcello," said Deo. "Just get it done. Any feel for where you are?"

"Yeah. No question that Paretto is paying the tab. We're making progress."

"What do you have so far?"

"Here's what we know: the word from street rats and from our plant in the agency is that the FBI is baffled. The abduction of the baby was slick, well planned, orchestrated by top professionals. Had to be the Paretto organization. They used two small-time characters that Paretto has used as gophers before. One fits the description of a blob called 'Squint.' They call him that because he's so fat-faced that his eyes are swollen shut. You could spot him a block away."

"Why would they use someone that easily identified?"

"He's an expert with a camera. And he has connections with every counterfeiter and every identity thief in town. The other guy is John (Gator) Dunbar. He's another small-time wannabe with a gambling habit. Poker, horse racing, numbers—anytime he gets a buck it's gone overnight. Has spent most of his life looking for a winner. He'll do anything to support his habit. He's an ex-Broadway actor from New York. He and Squint have pulled capers for Paretto before."

"How did they pull it off?"

"They recruited a young hooker, new on the street, looking for money to keep her drug habit going. It seems she was a loner and a mystery to the other girls, but we found enough of her casual acquaintances who were eager to talk, in exchange for a couple of twenties, and we put together a picture of sorts. She went by the name of Becky. Fancy looking kid, well dressed compared to what you'd expect. She would have been the key to learning more—"

"What do you mean 'would have been'?"

"Ray and I were going to talk to her this morning. When we got here, she had been found dead in bed. Looked like an overdose, but our agency guy reports a strong suspicion of homicide. The FBI already knows about the murder. They think she was high on coke before someone smothered her with a pillow."

"Damn, damn!" said Deo. "You know what that means."

"Yeah, if Paretto is involved here, he's out to wipe out any link to his organization."

"Sure. Our only chance is to find the other two guys before Paretto does. Let's hope they are still alive."

"We have a lead. Here's the rest of the story, Deo. When Becky moved into this place, she wasn't interested in working—just drugs. She let it slip that she had come into some money. Didn't say how much. A couple of the girls and Squeak overheard her phone conversation with someone, probably Gator. The phone is at the end of the hall, so she had no privacy."

"How do you know who she was talking to?"

"They heard her yelling over the phone. Things like, 'You and Squint cheated me. We were supposed to divide the money three ways.' She apparently had Gator's cell phone number. Becky's friends keep saying the guy she was talking to was in Florida. The FBI traced her call, and according to our plant, Gator was in Miami."

"We've got to move fast, Marcello. Gator and Squint will be next on Paretto's list."

"I'm afraid you're right. Wherever we find Gator, he'll be gambling his new money away. He's probably smart enough to stay away from casinos or poker parlors—too much close contact with strangers. That means racetracks."

"What are you thinking?" asked Deo.

"He'll go for the biggest, get lost in the crowd. Ray has called our man in Miami to check for any rumors of a high roller recently coming on the scene."

"Good. We need to get to Miami."

"We already have plane reservations to Miami tomorrow; too late tonight. Ray will stay here and keep looking for Squint. We need to move before Paretto does."

"Marcello, I should have known. You think ahead of me. If we find Gator, can you get him to talk?"

"What would you do if you knew Paretto was after you and I was your only hope of staying alive?"

# 25

*Westlake*

Andy surprised himself that he was able to concentrate at all on his work at the hospital. Every minute of the day he worried about Barbara and Leanne's safety at home. The two agents guarding them, hand picked by Mr. Walton, surely would keep them safe from attack. Barbara was now a target for silencing, but why Leanne? Was her husband as vicious as Leanne had described? Would he go to such extremes to get rid of her, or was the threat aimed at Leanne another act of revenge against Judge Joberst? There was no question that the attackers were serious; their wild chase was evidence enough of that.

Although he fought to constrain his irritability about the quandary in which they found themselves, Andy had accepted the fact that Barbara was determined to help Leanne through this entire ordeal. Barbara certainly seemed happier now that Leanne was with them in Westlake. Without giving an excuse other than "personal reasons," she had delayed the start of her new job another month. At Agent Walton's request, and to Barbara's delight, she spent her time at home with Leanne.

Of course, keeping both Barbara and Leanne in one location made the chore of protecting them much easier. Also, Leanne badly needed the support and comfort that Barbara could provide since there had been no assurance that the kidnapped baby was alive and no recent demands by the abductors. Being with Barbara kept Leanne from total emotional decompensation. And Andy knew that keeping Barbara "confined to quarters" alone would have been devastating for her as well. So there was mutual benefit for the two of them to be together.

\* \* \* \*

Having Todd Langley, the hospital's chief operating officer, as his new mentor for the month was a welcome relief. His month with Jonathan Mastin in Physician Relations had been rewarding, but he was ready for a change. Andy felt comfortable around Todd. He seemed knowledgeable about the many operational issues related to managing the hospital—not only those of his own department but those in every administrative field. He seemed to enjoy educating Andy on the innermost structure and activity in hospital management. Sometimes he would begin a narration about some problem and then stop himself, saying, "I guess I better not tell you everything."

Andy sensed that Todd knew more about the irregularities that he had uncovered but was cautious about discussing them with a naïve administrative intern. Andy decided to wait, watch, and listen. Opportunities would arise to learn more.

\* \* \* \*

The first glimmer of light sneaking around the closed blinds started Barbara awake. She reached for Andy. His side of the bed was empty. *Of course. He had had to leave early to make his early-morning breakfast meeting*, she remembered. She bounced out of bed, and while she made herself ready for the day, she reminisced over the events of the past few days and tried to imagine what lay ahead. She peeked around the edge of the front blinds and was relieved to see the two agents still parked outside. For a minute she wondered if she should take them coffee and a Danish or something. *Perhaps I should ask Agent Walton first*, she decided.

There was no sound from Leanne's room. *The poor girl probably has had the first good night's sleep in ages*, thought Barbara. *How miserable she must be: alienated from her husband, worried sick about her baby. The world must seem so bleak to her.*

By the time Barbara made coffee and set the table for breakfast, she heard Leanne's door close. Wearing baggy pajamas, no makeup, uncombed hair, and a smile that creased her entire tranquil face, Leanne came into the kitchen.

"Good morning," she said. "I must have overslept."

"You look fresh and ready to take on the day," said Barbara. "Did you sleep all right?"

"Just heavenly. I had forgotten what it was like to feel safe. I feel stress free, Barbara, optimistic for the first time in ages."

"You needed that sleep. You have a lot ahead of you today. I'll put breakfast together. I imagine Mr. Walton will be calling soon."

"I'm not even nervous about being around Anthony for the televising."

"Do you think he'll show?"

"Oh, yes. He wouldn't miss this chance to be seen as a 'distressed parent' standing next to his 'beloved wife,' making an appeal for help in recovering their child."

"What will you say to him?"

"Nothing more than I have to. He'll try to get me to say where I am living. I hope Mr. Walton will not betray my whereabouts."

"You don't need to worry about that. I think he knows what's going on between the two of you."

"What can I do to help?"

"Not a thing. Just sit down at the table with a cup of coffee."

"I wouldn't be much help anyway. I never learned to cook—or do any housework for that matter. You should have seen me trying to make the bed I slept in." Leanne laughed. "You need to teach me a few things, Barbara."

"I'll do that," she replied with a chuckle. "How do you like your eggs?" said Barbara as she poured orange juice for both of them.

"However you do," she replied. "We had a cook once that insisted I have a poached egg every morning. By the time I left home, I couldn't stand poached eggs."

Barbara laughed. "Good to know—no poached eggs."

Other than Leanne's complimentary remarks about Barbara's housekeeping, they said little while Barbara prepared breakfast. They both appeared contemplative. Leanne finally spoke. "Barbara, in the bedroom where I slept there was an open box of photographs on the side table. I hope you don't mind … I looked at a couple."

"Oh, those are just family photos. I haven't had time to organize them into albums yet. Sure, go ahead and look. You'll see how bratty I looked when I was a child."

"On the contrary. You looked adorable. I loved the family group photo—I guess it was your parents, brother, and sister."

"Yeah, I know the one you're talking about. That's my favorite from those years."

"You are so fortunate, Barbara. I can't ever remember a picture being taken of my family."

"I'm sure you have some pleasant memories."

"Nothing like yours. My sister and I were left with a nanny most of the time. My mother and father were much older than yours when we were born. They traveled a lot. The most vivid memory I have is that of my sister and I scrambling to see what they had brought back to us and most of the time being disappointed that they brought nothing."

"I'm so sorry, Leanne. The memory of the lack of closeness in your family probably intensifies your need to recover and raise your own child."

Leanne chuckled and blotted tears from her face at the same time. "There you go, again, 'Dr. Goldeyer.' You're a psychoanalyst in hiding."

"Am I right?"

"Absolutely! If I get him back, I'm going to be the best parent ever. And I can say the same for Mark if we are ever fortunate enough to be together."

"There's no 'if' about it, Leanne. You and Mark will be together, and I am optimistic there will be three of you."

"Thanks, Barbara. I just need to hear you say that every once in a while."

"You know, Mr. Walton doesn't think you should contact each other right now—for the safety of both of you."

"What if the same attackers go after Mark? Shouldn't he be warned and protected also?"

"I imagine Mr. Walton has thought of that," said Barbara as she placed the egg casserole on the table and poured orange juice for both of them. "I hope you like cinnamon toast."

"It smells delectable, Barbara," said Leanne. "You put all of this together in just a few minutes. How do you do it?"

"You can do it too," she replied. "Try it one morning while you're here."

"Only with your coaching." Leanne laughed. "It wouldn't be edible otherwise."

Few words were exchanged during breakfast. Leanne poured a second cup of coffee and glanced out the window toward the front street for a second before sitting back down. She seemed deep in thought, momentarily detached, and then jerked her head to look straight at Barbara.

"Tell me again how all of this is going to end," she said, her eyes becoming misty, her voice barely audible.

"You're going to have waves of despondency, Leanne. This is not a time to be pessimistic. We're going to win this fight and we will do it by overcoming every single adversity we face—real or imaginary."

"It's worth the risk, isn't it, Barbara?"

"Sure it is. Anything worth having is worth fighting for."

"It's just—I've never had to fight for anything."

"Look, you've already shown you've got what it takes. Sit here and sip on your coffee. I'll straighten up the kitchen."

"No, I'll help. It's time I learned," she said with determination. "Barbara, when all of this is over, please consider going back to school and studying psychology. It's incredible. You can make me feel better with one sentence."

"I'll think about it," Barbara replied, laughing. "We should be hearing from Mr. Walton before too long."

"I hope so. I want to get the TV appeal appearance done as soon as possible. I didn't see the FBI agents out front when I looked out awhile ago. Maybe Mr. Walton is on the way to relieve them for a break."

"What are you saying?" cried Barbara. "They're not in the car out front? They were there just a minute ago."

"Oh, my God!" yelled Leanne. "Come here. There are two guys I've never seen before coming this way. Looks like one is going around to the back."

"We've got to get out of here," said Barbara as she grabbed her cell phone. "Out the back, onto the patio, and over the back fence. Hurry! He'll have trouble getting that side gate open."

"I'm right behind you."

The front doorbell rang as they raced through sliding glass door to the patio. As Barbara climbed to the top of the fence that separated their patio from their rear neighbor, she could hear their pursuer struggling to open the gate at the side of the building. She reached down to pull Leanne over the top just as the gunman managed to get the gate open. When he saw the two girls, he raised the silenced muzzle and fired, but the shot went wild as Barbara and Leanne slid to the other side of the fence.

They searched for a way to exit the neighbor's patio. Leanne tried to open the gate at the side of the house, but it would not budge. In the meantime, the attacker was attempting to climb over the fence and had his hands over the ridge trying to pull himself over the top. Barbara spotted a loose brick, picked it up, and smashed the man's fingers with all the force she could muster. A loud cry, followed by expletives, told her that she had hit her target. She joined Leanne, and with their combined effort they were able to pull the gate open.

Once outside the enclosure, they both began running and shouting for help at the same time. Barbara dialed Agent Walton while she ran, hoping he was in Westlake and could return her call promptly. Fortunately, a resident in a home a half-block away heard their cries and came to their rescue. The two breathless girls collapsed on the front porch of the Good Samaritan, who was too shocked to speak. Their newfound friend was in the process of dialing 911 when the musical tone on Barbara's cell phone signaled Agent Walton's return call.

"Barbara, where are you? I've been trying to call you. Are you and Leanne all right?"

"Just barely," she said between gasps of hyperventilation. Leanne sat speechless, as if in shock, while Barbara narrated the incident to Agent Walton.

"We knew something had happened when we couldn't contact our men. A SWAT team and an ambulance are on the way. Stay where you are. Let me talk to the man who lives there. I'll ask him to allow you to wait inside. We'll be there in seconds. What's the address?"

"What can we do?" asked Barbara. Barely able to speak, she rattled off the house number on the wall beside the door. "We are not even safe in our own home with guards."

"I know what you're thinking. We have to change plans. We will need to move all of you to a different site. You need to call Andy home right away. Let me talk to the man." Her hands still shaking, she handed the phone to their pallid, tremulous neighbor-friend.

"Sir, this is FBI Agent Ralph Walton speaking. Please allow the girls to stay inside until we get there."

"Ye … ye … ye … yes, sir," he answered. "They'll be inside."

Barbara dialed Andy's cell phone number, praying he would answer. Where was he? No answer after four rings, after which his voicemail kicked in to announce that he was not available at the time and to leave a number.

"Andy, call me immediately. An emergency has come up. Andy … I need you at home now."

Inside the house, Leanne sat bent over on a couch, sobbing softly, her head cradled in the palms of her hands. "I've brought all of this on you, Barbara. How can I ever make it up to you?"

"We're in this together, dear. Let's just muster enough strength to get us out," she answered.

She had no sooner uttered those words than the sound of emergency vehicle sirens pierced the air. Agent Walton's car came to a halt in front of the house. He and Wes, both with guns drawn, sprang out of the vehicle simultaneously and came to the girls' side. The awestricken neighbor and his wife stood by silently while Ralph and Wes escorted the girls to their vehicle.

"We'll take you back to your home; then you can tell us what happened."

Once back in the apartment, Ralph stood beside the frightened pair and patted their shoulders. "You're safe now. It may be hard for you to do, but it's important that you try to describe the attackers."

"I don't think I can," said Leanne, her chin quivering. Barbara, her arm around Leanne's back, pulled her close for a few moments while she prepared to report to Agent Walton.

"Just by accident, Leanne looked out the window to see the two guys we'd never seen before approaching our front door. One turned to go around to the back. That's when we decided to run. Fortunately, the back gate stuck long enough so we could scamper over the back neighbor's fence and scream for help. We hid in his home until you arrived. I called you while we were running. One of the attackers actually fired at Leanne."

"The two agents assigned to protect you apparently left for a couple of minutes—probably to get breakfast. They'll be severally reprimanded and replaced. Only one was supposed to leave at a time. Your pursuers must have been waiting for an opportunity to hit the house. They know where you live now. We'll have to make other—"

Barbara's phone sounded. "It must be Andy," she said.

"Barbara, what's going on? Are you all right?" he asked franticly.

"We're all right—shaken but all right. Mr. Walton is here—"

Agent Walton intervened, taking the phone from Barbara, and talked to Andy briefly.

"The bottom line, Andy: we're going to have to move the girls to a safer place."

"*Safer* place? What the hell? Two FBI agents can't keep my wife—and Leanne—from being attacked in our own home? What is a safe place? I'm pissed, Mr. Walton. We've been chased, we've been shot at, we've exposed ourselves to danger. We haven't had a normal day's existence since all this started. I'm coming home. Be there in a minute."

"Andy, I know how you feel. Please calm down. We need your help now more than ever," said Ralph.

## 26

By the time Andy reached home, patrol cars—at least four or five with red and blue lights flashing—were parked on the street where he lived. He braked to a halt, leaped from his old VW, and raced to the front door. He passed the scattering of neighbors, all gawking inquisitively at the bedlam before them. A uniformed policeman stood in front of the open doorway and stopped Andy from entering. Another person in a CSI jacket was busily lifting fingerprints from the door.

"I live here," shouted Andy in the officer's face. "I'm going in. I need to find my wife."

"Do you have some identity, sir?" the cop politely asked.

"You goddamn right! I have 'rights' identity," Andy yelled. "The Constitution of the United States. Now get the hell out of my way."

The policeman held his ground, shoved Andy gently aside, and placed his hand on the butt of his gun. "Don't take another step toward the door, sir. There has been an attack on the occupants of this house, and I am to let no one through that door. Those are my—"

Agent Walton stepped out and tapped the officer on the shoulder. "It's all right. Mr. Goldeyer lives here. Andy, please remain calm. Barbara is fine; she and Leanne are inside packing. You need to come in and do the same."

"What the shit are you talking about, packing?" asked Andy as Ralph escorted him into the house.

"Andy, you and the girls are moving out for a while."

"Don't we have anything to say about it?"

"I'm afraid not, son. All of you are in danger. You are material witnesses in a federal crime investigation, and we must keep you in protective custody. The attackers now know where you live."

"What about my work, Mr. Walton? I have to go to work. I can't move out of town or stay at home."

"An agent will be watching you wherever you go. You won't even know the identity or description of the agent."

"When do we make this move?"

"Right now, Andy, as soon as possible. Two agents will stay behind and see to it that your belongings are protected. Someone will bring you anything that you leave behind if you need it later. You must hurry, before too many people realize what's going on, before the news media gets here."

Andy took a deep breath. Ralph gave him a few moments to contemplate the reality of the situation. "The girls are in the bedroom throwing a few things together. You need to join them."

"Just give me a second," Andy said, turning back to the doorway to find the policeman guarding the entrance. "I want to apologize, officer. I was out of line."

"That's all right, Mr. Goldeyer. I understand," he replied as he extended his hand.

Agent Walton watched while Andy rushed to the bedroom to find Barbara. She ran into his arms and held him tightly for a half-minute without speaking. Her chest heaved rhythmically as she tried to muffle her sobbing. She released Andy, gazed into his eyes, and smiled. Andy held her at arm's length for a few moments with an expression of affection on his face. *She has to be the bravest person ever*, he thought.

"Are you all right?" he asked.

"We're fine, Andy," she answered. Barbara quickly narrated the recent events. "But we're fine now. We have got to hurry. I've packed most of the things that you will need."

"Do you know where we are going?"

"Mr. Walton's office has made all of the arrangements. I'm not sure myself where we'll be. He'll tell us in a minute."

"I don't like this, Barbara. You and Leanne were almost killed right here in our own home. How do we know it will be any safer where we are going?"

"I know you are upset, but we have to trust the FBI to protect us, Andy."

Leanne came into the room in time to hear their last remarks. "Andy, it's entirely my fault. I'd give anything if I could turn back the clock to the time before I turned your lives upside down."

"You are not to blame, Leanne," said Andy. He put his arms around her for a reassuring hug. "It's all right. We just have to show the world that we can deal with it."

"Thank you, Andy. I am forever grateful that both of you have come into my miserable life."

Barbara blotted the tear moisture from her face. "All right you guys, we've got work to do."

Andy, Barbara, and Leanne scurried about gathering clothes and essentials for their move. Agent Walton in the meantime talked non-stop on his cell phone. Within thirty minutes, all was in readiness to make the change in residence.

\* \* \* \*

The fifteen-mile trip across Westlake, winding through the manicured, landscaped parkway along the periphery of the clear water lagoon, took less than thirty minutes. The agents driving kept up a brisk pace and kept a lookout for pursuers. Even though they spotted none, each driver took a circuitous route, careful not to appear to be following one of the other vehicles.

By the time they reached the secured destination, Agent Walton was standing in front of the automatic door of the four-story parking garage. The agents designated to guard the elevators and stairwell accesses to the condo had already taken their positions. Each agent had combined headpieces in place already tuned to each other and to Agent Walton.

Once in the penthouse, Andy, Barbara, and Leanne roamed about, exploring their spacious, luxurious suite. The entire outside wall of the large, elegantly furnished living area, as well as that of the two bedrooms, was made up of tall plate-glass windows giving a magnificent view of the lake. Sailboats with colorful mainsails and spinnakers dotted the rippling surface of the lagoon. A wide balcony outside the glass windows extended across the living room and the bedrooms.

Andy walked out onto the balcony and inspected the wood-slatted covering that reached far out over the balcony's safety rail. He assured himself that no one could drop onto the balcony from the roof above without risking a twelve-story fall to the ground below. Still, he would suggest to Agent Walton that an agent be assigned to the roof.

## 27

*Miami*

Deo put his seat in an upright position as the plane began its descent to the runway of the Miami International Airport. His half-empty glass of scotch and water was right where he had left it when he fell asleep. Marcello, wide awake, had been studying some report on his laptop before the flight attendant informed him that it was time to shut down all electronic equipment.

"What did you find of interest?" asked Deo, pointing at the notebook while Marcello snapped the lid closed.

"Just checking on Trini Esparza's current performance report."

"He's our lead man in Miami?"

"Yeah," Marcello replied. "Does an outstanding job. Comes from Ecuador. He's assembled an impressive work force from his people. He'll meet us."

"How does his record look?"

"Outstanding," said Marcello. "I worry about him sometimes. He wants to get back into drug marketing."

"Why, is he unhappy with his cash flow or just bored?"

"He just gets pressure from his men. He says they don't worry about the risk. Most of them are illegal aliens with nothing to lose, anxious for more action."

"You know what Al would say."

"I do, but that's not an option right now. We don't want any fights with Chacon."

"Chacon has control of the market here now?"

"Yeah, along with Paretto, but it wouldn't be hard to crack,"

"Have any of Trini's men jumped ship?"

"Only two." Marcello chortled. "They didn't jump. They were lowered slowly over the side of the ship wearing their concrete boots. No one has tried since."

"That would discourage rebellion," laughed Deo. "What will be our first step here?"

"We'll see what Trini has to report. Most likely, Gator headed straight for the heavy action. That would mean Gulfstream Park—crowded, a lot of betting, loaded with celebrities. Gator would get lost in the throng. If he's there, he's worked his way into the private club by now."

"Where else would he be?"

"Maybe Hialeah. Trini will know."

Deo and Marcello deplaned and climbed the ramp to the half-mile-long concourse that led to the baggage claim and the exit. Out of habit, Deo scanned the crowd ahead, knowing it was unlikely that any FBI agent assigned to Miami International would be looking for him.

As Marcello predicted, Trini had parked his black Mercedes-Benz S600 Sedan at the passenger pickup gate and was standing along side the front door. When Deo and Marcello approached, Trini opened the doors and met them both with a typical South American *abrazo*. Within seconds, they were racing down the freeway.

"What do you have, Trini?" ask Marcello.

"Reyes called. Said to tell you Squint's body was found at bottom of Devil's Canyon in west Texas, whoever Squint is. Ray said he had been a target for a hit by Paretto."

"Not unexpected," said Marcello. "Gator will be next, Trini. Have to find him before he's wasted."

"He's at Gulfstream. Didn't take long to find him. He's throwing C-notes around like confetti and stays wired with speed and alcohol most of the time."

"Let's go there first, Trini," said Deo. "Hope we're not too late."

"We are watching his every move. Don't worry. Right now, he's never been safer from Paretto."

"Where are we staying?"

"Hyatt Regency. They have a good golf course if you want to lounge a few days. You want to check in first?"

"No time, Trini," said Deo. "Thanks anyway. Let's get on with the business at hand."

"Don't let me forget to give you confirmation information. It will show your assumed names. The rooms are already paid for."

Trini pulled into the driveway that headed toward the entrance to the massive Gulfstream Park. Deo hadn't been there for a few years ago and was surprised at the sweeping changes. The main building had been remodeled, with new surrounding amenities and updated landscaping.

Trini dropped his keys off with the valet and then, along with Deo and Marcello, approached the main entrance.

"We'll go straight to the Jockey Club on the third floor first. I'll find our men who have this guy under surveillance."

Trini flashed his club membership ID and they were promptly seated at a dining room table next to the twelve-foot floor-to-ceiling plate-glass windows overlooking the track. Carpeted stairways led to the betting windows on the balcony tier above.

"Wait here while I round up our crew."

Trini skipped off, taking his small frame up the stairs two steps at a time. Deo and Marcello relaxed with scotch and water and snacks at their table on the lower tier. The loudspeakers blared, announcing the next race, jockey changes, horses scratched from the lineup, and calls for various individuals to report to the office. Of interest to Deo were the changing odds that flashed on the giant billboard near the finish line.

"Think we should go up and place a bet?" he asked Marcello.

Marcello laughed. "Wait and get a tip from Gator."

"Let's see how much he's won before we take his advice." Deo chuckled. "How are we going to handle this?"

"Just let me handle it, Deo," he answered with a grin that almost hid the ugly scar on his face. "You've been out of touch too long."

"Have a go at it."

Trini soon returned, accompanied by two large men roughly escorting a pallid, grim-faced John "Gator" Dunbar. Gator, wearing white shoes, was dressed in a cream-colored linen suit, underneath which was an open-necked bright yellow shirt and a heavy gold chain around his neck. He glanced at Deo and Marcello with a look of recognition and paled even more. When he reached for the handkerchief in the pocket of his coat to wipe his sweaty brow, the four diamond rings that adorned fingers of both hands sparkled like fireflies on a dark night. Quite visible below his left coat sleeve was a diamond-studded Rolex watch.

Trini motioned for Gator to be seated. "You know these gentlemen, Gator?"

"Uh ... uh ... I ... I ... I think I do."

"Know why they want to talk to you?"

"No ... no ... I don't want no trouble, Trini. I ain't done nothin' ... I'm just here for the races."

"Gator, the three of us are gonna sit at that table across the room so you can feel free to talk to Deo and Marcello. Quit shaking so much. I'm sure you have nothing to worry about. Now, when they finish with you, we'll be ready to help you out, whichever way you decide you want to go out."

"Sure ... sure, Trini," Gator said as he wiped his face again. "I just want to do what's right."

"That's the way to talk," Trini replied. Trini patted Gator on the back and beckoned the two guards to follow him to a nearby table.

Gator sat motionless, his head drooping and his eyes glued to the tabletop, avoiding eye contact with Deo or Marcello. Marcello let an agonizing minute or two pass before speaking, but he didn't take his eyes off Gator. Gator started to speak.

"Whaa ... what do you ..." He couldn't finish the sentence.

Marcello finally spoke. "You look great, Gator. Hitting the numbers regularly, aren't you?" he said pointing to the rings and the Rolex. "You wanna know what we want from you, don't you, Gator?"

Gator lifted his head and turned to Marcello. "Yeah ... yeah," he said, nodding his head, a tone of apprehension to his voice.

"Gator, I know you have things to do," said Marcello. "We'll make this quick. Where is the baby?"

Gator jumped so violently that the table shook. Blood drained from his face as he grabbed the arms of his chair. "Whaddya mean? What baby? I don't know nothin' about no baby, Marcello."

"That wasn't a very smart answer, Gator," said Marcello. "Wanna try again?"

"God ... what can I say?"

Gator looked at Deo, then back at Marcello, and then across the room at Trini and his two companions. No way out. The conversation stopped abruptly and there was silence for another painful half-minute.

"Please ... I can't tell you anything, Marcello," Gator pleaded. "They'll kill me for sure."

"Who'll kill you, Gator?" asked Deo.

"You know who," he replied. He suddenly changed his demeanor—appeared arrogant, held his head high, a smirking smile on his face. He looked first at Deo and then at Marcello. "Now I know what you're doing: you're trying to cut Paretto out of the ransom money, ain't you? Somehow you found out the ten mil was out there, and you think you can jerk me around and grab the baby. All I have to do is tell Tate what you've done; then we'll see who's sweating in the hot seat. No thanks, big shits. Tate will take care of me. Go fuck yourselves."

Gator stood, dusted off his clothes, shot a finger at Trini, straightened his coat and shirt, and folded and replaced his handkerchief in his coat. He grabbed the *Daily Racing Form* he had left on the tabletop, and turned to walk away. Marcello and Deo both remained quiet during his outburst and his elaborate exit.

After he had taken his first step, Marcello said, "Becky was killed a couple of days ago; Squint's body was found half-eaten by buzzards a few days before that. Who do you think is next, Gator? I agree, I think Tate will take care of you, just the way he took care of Becky and Squint. Your only hope to stay alive is to let us help you."

Gator froze in his steps; his eyes swept across the club lounge area as if looking for some familiar face. He kept his back turned to Marcello and Deo for a few seconds; then he stood straight and slowly turned to Marcello.

"How do I know you're not lying?"

"Know anybody on Harry Hines in Dallas? Or better still, call the Dallas PD; they'll tell you. In the meantime, keep a close lookout every minute, Gator. Never know when they'll hit, do ya?"

Gator hesitated several seconds before answering, his down-turned eyes reflecting melancholy pensiveness. "Did you get to talk to Becky?"

"She was gone before we got there. We conned a police photographer for a picture. Wanna see it?" Marcello pulled a photograph out of his pocket. Gator winced and turned his head away.

"How'd you find me?"

"Easy, Gator—for us. Will be for Tate and the FBI too. You *know* you kidnapped a federal judge's baby. The FBI doesn't like that. But we won't tell the FBI either—if you cooperate."

"What's in it for me, Marcello? What will you do for me?"

"Let's start with this: we'll keep you from getting blown away. First, you tell us the complete story—start from the beginning. Next, prove your story is the truth, and then we'll talk about money and getting you out of the country."

"Tate will find me ... wherever I go."

"We have ways to deal with Paretto."

"I know about you, Marcello. Who is this other dude?"

"Deo Carminagni, Alberto Marchesa's *consigliere*—the same as Tate is for Paretto."

"What's Al Marchesa's interest in the baby?"

Marcello pushed his chair back as though he were ready to stand. "Gator, we've told you enough already. No more questions. Either start talking or we're outta here."

"All right, all right. Gimme some slack. If Tate finds out, I'm a goner."

"You are anyway, Gator." Marcello stood and glanced first at Trini then back at Gator. "Start singing, Gator. I see Trini's men are getting impatient."

Gator squirmed in his chair. He looked at Trini and the two men. All three were sitting erect in their chairs as though they were about to go into action. Their eyes were fixed on Gator in a penetrating stare.

"Okay, okay," said Gator. He glanced again toward Trini. "Is there somewhere else we can go?"

"The only other place we will go with you, Gator, is to wherever you left the baby."

"I don't even know if the baby's still there, or if it is alive."

"Was it alive the last time you saw it?"

"Yeah … yeah, Marcello. We didn't hurt that baby."

"You're running out of time, Gator."

"All right," he replied as he turned his back to the club entrance foyer—as if he were hiding from anyone coming through the door.

Gator narrated the entire scheme: his first contact with Paretto's *consigliere*, Nicolas Tatum, the details of the plan, Becky's makeover, and the abduction itself.

"You've done work for Tatum before?"

Gator whirled and glanced around the club again. "Yeah, Squint and I have both done jobs, but we're not in the books."

"So, what about the electronic bracelets?"

"My God, you found out about that, too?"

Marcello glanced at Gator and smiled without answering. "Keep going, Gator."

"Paretto's computer guys couldn't break the code to disable the ankle bracelets, so it couldn't be cut off. Tate found out about a son of one of the nurses at the hospital who was upside down to Paretto. He forced his mother to stop using the device that day to save her son."

"Good story, Gator. Now take us to the baby."

"If I go back to Dallas, I'm dead. Can't I just tell you?"

"No. You're going back to Dallas with us."

# 28

## *Dallas*

The setting sun dipped behind the horizon. The twilight quickly thickened into darkness as the Southwest Airlines Flight 38 plane circled over the downtown Dallas skyscrapers and made its approach to the Love Field north-south runway. Deo looked out the window in time to see the lights below come alive and sparkle—like a giant jeweled blanket covering the city.

Gator insisted on sitting in the very back seat. "I don't want anyone to know I am with you," he had said earlier. Deo glanced back toward the rear of the plane, turned to Marcello, and chuckled. "Well, he's still there. Thought maybe he'd bailed out. What do we do with him, Marcello?"

"We'll let Reyes worry about watching him until we're finished with him. I think he's convinced he has to cooperate with us."

"I guess the critical time will be when we go through the airport," said Deo.

"Yeah, I imagine by now everyone knows Gator's been in Miami. Both Paretto and the FBI will be watching the airports," Marcello replied. "We just need to be sure he stays close to us when we deplane. If Ray has picked up the scent of FBI agents or Paretto's men, he will warn us."

"Surely Gator's smart enough not to make a run for it."

"He wouldn't get far with Reyes waiting for us."

Reyes and one companion met them in the baggage area. A second assistant had their limousine waiting at the passenger pickup gate. No signs of the Paretto mob or anyone from the FBI. They climbed into the vehicle. Reyes had scotch and water ready in the miniature bar in the rear compartment.

"Gator, give the driver directions to the place where you left the baby," commanded Marcello as they all sipped their drinks.

"But it will be dark, Marcello."

"So what? It was dark when you took the baby there before."

"Can't we wait until daylight?" asked Gator.

"Hell no!" said Marcello. "You might not be alive in the morning. You take us there now, so if Paretto burns you tonight, we'll know where to go tomorrow."

"Goddamn, Marcello," said Gator. "Stop that shit. I'm scared enough just being in Dallas."

"You'll be okay, Gator, as long as you listen to us."

"All right," Gator replied. "Get on the LBJ Freeway and head for Garland. I'll tell you where to get off when we get there. God, I'll be glad to get this over with. I have a feeling someone's watching us every minute." His upper body and arms shook uncontrollably. He twisted his neck to look out the side and the rear windows. Finally, he slumped down in his seat, closed his eyes, and remained silent for the next several minutes.

Deo saw the Garland exit sign and nudged Gator. "Look where we are, Gator. Do we exit here?"

"Take the third exit and follow the highway marker until we cross town, then look for a big white mansion-like house on the right," said Gator without looking up. "Damn it, why am I doing this?"

"Cause you want to stay alive, Gator," said Marcello.

Within minutes, the traffic thinned and the usual city suburban subdivisions along the way were left behind. It their place, five to ten acre fence-enclosed tracts of land cropped up on both sides of the highway.

"We've gone trough the town, Gator. We're in the country."

Gator sat upright in his seat and scanned the landscape.

"It's a large house with a sign in front and a driveway that leads up to the front door."

The sign close to the road read, *St. Jude Children's Home.* There was no sign of activity as they slowed almost to a complete stop.

"That's it," said Gator. "Becky took the baby up to the front door, rang the bell, left the baby wrapped in blankets, and ran back to the car. Squint gunned the engine of his van and we took off. No one saw us."

"So you don't know if anyone came to the door or not, do you?" asked Marcello.

"We did just what Tatum told us to do."

"How do we know you are telling the truth?" asked Deo.

"Guess you'll have to take my word."

"We'll find out, Gator," said Marcello. They slowed to a creeping pace in front of the large, white two-story plantation-type house with tall pillars in front, surrounded by large elm trees. "We're gonna keep you close to us until we do. And you know what comes next if we find out you're lying."

Hardly before he had finished the sentence, two guards appeared from the shadows on each side of the house, stood motionless with their hands in their jacket pockets, and stared at the limousine.

"I told you!" yelled Gator. "Damn it! Now Paretto will know I led you here. I'm the only one alive who knows where the baby was left. Damn! Marcello. I'm just as dead as if you had shot me."

"Calm down, Gator," said Marcello. "They can't tell who we are. They're just security guards. Maybe this proves you are telling the truth."

"Let's get out of here," said Gator as he again slumped down even lower in his seat. "Those are Paretto's men. They mean business."

"You're just being paranoid."

"No, no. Those are Paretto's hit men. I can tell."

"Ray, drop us off," said Marcello as they drove away. "We'll see you tomorrow, Gator. Deo and I need to do some planning. Don't try anything you'll regret."

\* \* \* \*

Once in their hotel, instead of going to the restaurant, Deo and Marcello found the dark piano bar, flopped in the overstuffed chairs in a remote corner, and ordered drinks and heavy snacks. They needed to explore their strategy options. They knew where Becky had left the baby, but they didn't know whether the baby was still there or not—or even if the baby was still alive.

The mysteries still hovered over them: Why had Paretto orchestrated the kidnapping? Who paid him to do so? Why had no serious ransom demands been made or met? Becky, Gator, and probably Squint had been handsomely rewarded. Paretto must have paid them to do the job, but who was behind the arrangement? Who had paid Paretto? There was no obvious reason why Paretto was even in the picture. None of the Paretto Gang members had been indicted or had come to trial, so why the vendetta against Judge Joberst?

"We need some answers, Marcello," said Deo.

"Any suggestions?" asked Marcello. He logged into his computer while he listened for Deo's reply.

Deo stared pensively at his glass. "I think it's time we pay Paretto and Tatum a courtesy visit."

"Good idea. You're probably thinking the same thing that I am."

"How do we arrange it?"

"I'll take care of it. I've always gotten along with Tate. He and Paretto both will be less than thrilled that you are in the States. The word I hear is that they cringe every time they hear rumors that Al is cranking up again."

"Let's try to pull this off without a fight," said Deo, "but we have to move fast. If Paretto suspects we're on to something, there won't be any baby left to find."

"I agree. We were lucky to get to Gator before Tatum found him."

Deo glanced at Marcello's notebook. "Do you have any news from our FBI contact?" he asked. "Surely the FBI team is not far behind us in discovering what we have."

"Let me finish this cryptanalysis of our man's message."

After a minute or so, Marcello looked up from his computer. "My God!" he uttered. "If the FBI ever breaks this code, our man's dead."

"They would have to suspect something first, wouldn't they?"

"Yeah, and the code changes so often it would be almost impossible for them to make sense of these texts."

Marcello kept tapping on the keyboard and kept his eyes glued to the screen. After a couple of minutes, he closed it. "They know about Becky—know she was murdered. They know about the other guy, too, the one called Squint." Marcello chortled. "They were closing in on Gator when he disappeared."

"We *were* lucky," said Deo. "And we've got to be cautious now. Did you learn anything else?"

"Yeah, the nurse on duty when the baby was lifted, her husband, and the judge's wife have been attacked. The FBI has them sequestered somewhere for their safety."

"Looks like Paretto *is* on the move. Still the same question hangs out there: why is he doing this?"

"And here is one bit of news that will grab you," said Marcello, again focused on the computer monitor, and with a glint of a smile on his face. "The FBI agent in charge of the investigation is our old friend Ralph Walton."

"Jesus Christ! How did he get in the act?" said Deo.

"Bet he wishes he had been assigned to some other case."

"He will when and if he ever finds out we're involved. Of course, we might want to arrange for a back-alley conference with Agent Walton before we're through. That could give us another card to play against Paretto."

"Good thinking, Deo," said Marcello. "Sleep late in the morning. I'm going after Tatum."

"Hell, you know I won't sleep. I'll be waiting for your call."

# 29

### *Westlake*

Andy shut down his computer and glanced at his watch—six o'clock. Whatever happened to the nine-to-five workday? With the additional traveling distance to their new home, he would be late enough that Barbara would worry. He would call her on the way. He headed for the door when his cell phone rang. *Probably Barbara*, he thought. Instead, it was Todd Langley, his administrative mentor for this month. What could he want at this time of day? He checked the administration on-call list under the glass on his desk. Todd was on call.

"Hi, Todd, it's me."

"Andy, where are you?"

"Still in my office, just leaving."

"Don't leave. I'll be right over," he replied urgently. Within seconds, he was at the door.

"You might be interested in staying around for a while—big-time happenings."

"What's going on?"

"Here's the story: some high-level members of the President's White House staff and a group of their Texas cronies were participating in an all-day pigeon shoot and retreat on the Abercrombie Ranch in south Texas. After lunch three of the guys, including a staunch Republican supporter, a lawyer from Dallas named Richard Weatherford, go on a Jeep ride around the ranch in a Jeep Wrangler. The Jeep flips over and throws the occupants out. The lawyer is the only one injured. They're bringing him here to Westlake, to our ER."

"My God! Do you mean *the* White House staff?"

"Yeah, *the* President's White House staff."

"Jeez, how bad is it?"

"From what I have heard he is not critically injured, maybe a couple of fractured ribs."

"The media will be all over the place."

"We'll try to keep it quiet. The secret service is already here. They're bringing the patient by helicopter. Our ER people are on alert."

"Fat chance of keeping it quiet."

"You're probably right. I'd better call Jake." Todd laughed. "You can bet he'll want to be here if the media is swarming."

Todd and Andy raced out the door and down the corridors toward the emergency room, arriving just in time. Like a flurry of marines gaining a military beachhead, a half-dozen stone-faced men in black pushed authoritatively alongside the EMS attendants, trying desperately to guide the victim-laden stretcher through the throng of curious onlookers. With less-than-gentle encouragement by Todd and Andy, the bystanders peeled back to let the entourage pass.

"Andy, I'm going to the nursing station. Go check our ER security. Make sure they call in enough people to control this fracas." As Andy took off in a run, Todd shouted after him, "Come back here when you're finished. And keep your ID badge visible."

Andy returned from his mission, weaved his way through the mass of people, and joined Todd, who now had his cell phone to his ear. Andy heard only one side of the conversation: "Yes, sir," Todd said. "We've done that, Jake. The ER medical director is on his way … Yeah, all over the place, cameras and mikes everywhere … Our security is handling it … He's some lawyer from Dallas, a known powerful GOP supporter; he was on a pigeon shoot with a bunch of the President's White House staff, No, the president wasn't with them. We'll stay right here, Jake, until you get here."

* * * *

Within minutes, Jake Hensley appeared and joined Todd and Andy. He was dressed as if he had just come from a cocktail party. The faint scent of alcohol followed him as he paced the nurses' station. Andy wondered how Jake would handle this. *As the CEO of the hospital, he would have to take charge*, thought Andy. One of the men in black, apparently the leader of the secret service group, strutted around giving orders to everyone he encountered. Jake approached him.

"Excuse me," said Jake in a polite but firm tone. "I think it would be well for you and your group to wait outside so my people here can take care of our patients."

"I'm afraid you don't understand, sir. My orders are to take charge here. If you have any authority over these people, I would like everyone cleared except the essential caregivers."

"Look, I'm the CEO of this hospital. That includes this department. Now either you people leave or I will have to call for law enforcement to move you out."

"What is your name?" he asked, stiffening.

"Hensley, Jake Hensley. And yours?"

"Commander Howard Woodman. I am in charge of this secret service unit. We operate under the jurisdiction of the executive branch of the government. The President has declared this an emergency military zone—much like a disaster zone. I have broad authority in situations like this. I will need your help, of course, while we work our way through this emergency situation."

Jake hesitated for several seconds, as if mulling over his options.

"All of my people are ready to cooperate, Commander."

"Good," Commander Woodman replied. "Now, first, I would like for you to designate one person to communicate with the media. This is very important. Have your person prepare his statement and then present it to me and to you. Once it is cleared by both of us, then your person may address the media."

Jake turned to Todd. "Can you handle this, Todd?"

"I think so," he answered.

"Then we have an agreement?" asked Jake, speaking to the commander. "This is Todd Langley, one of my administrative associates. Todd will be on site to follow the progress of this case. He will collaborate with our ER medical director, prepare a report at regular intervals for us to approve, and then present that to the reporters."

Commander Woodman scrutinized Todd for a few prolonged moments. "You pulled duty at the White House once, didn't you, young man?"

Todd's blank expression reflected his lack of surprise at the question. He kept his eyes glued to those of the commander for a few seconds before he answered.

"No, sir," he finally said. "You have mistaken me for someone else."

"Yes, I must have," he said, breaking eye contact and turning back to speak to Jake. "Your plan sounds fine to me, Mr. Hensley. We have found in the past that when public figures are involved in any way, stories have a way of getting distorted."

"I understand. The hospital representative will be Todd. Of course, he will report to you and to me regularly on the patient's condition. And before he delivers any report to the news media he will get our approval of the content of his message."

"Absolutely," said the commander, as he turned to walk away. "We must be very careful of any information that is made public."

Todd turned to Jake and out of earshot of the commander said: "The reporters will want to hear something direct from one of our doctors. Who do you think?"

"Of course, right now we don't know how serious the injuries are or how many doctors will be involved. Let me know when you find out. Ideally, we should use only Dr. Grayson to report on the medical status."

"Good idea," Todd replied. "He will say whatever we tell him. Can't say that for many of the others."

"I still want to see a word-for-word text of what he's going to report—*before* he is interviewed," Jake said. "We've got to be careful, Todd. We're going to be in the spotlight for a while."

"I know what you mean, Jake."

"Call me if you have any trouble with the secret service people or with the White House staff," said Jake. "I'm leaving now, but my cell phone is on."

✳ ✳ ✳ ✳

Andy had his back turned, dialing Barbara to explain his whereabouts, when he realized someone had joined them. It was Ken Striker, director of the Emergency Medicine and Critical Care Services department.

"Oh, hey, Todd," said Ken. "I didn't know you were here. Hi, Andy. Just the people I need to see."

"And we were looking for you," Todd replied. "I thought that somebody would have called you by now."

"Have you seen that throng of media out there? How did they get here so fast?" asked Ken.

"They smell it, like ants going after honey."

"What's the plan? How is the guy?"

"From what I hear, he's doing all right," Todd replied. "Jake was here; he wants us to handle the media inquiries. Andy is staying here to help. We need to camp in your office. Keep in touch with your staff and let us know every few minutes what's going on—especially if there is any change in the patient's condition. Every few hours, we'll gather the press outside and give a report. Jake wants only me and Dr. Grayson to talk when we give reports, and he wants to edit what we say before we say it."

"Why Dr. Grayson and not one of our regular ER doctors?" asked Ken.

"Are you kidding?" said Todd. "Jake wants someone to repeat exactly what he tells him to say."

"Grayson's the one, then," said Ken, chuckling. "He has to have somebody telling him what to say during his every waking hour."

"How long before we'll be able to give some sort of a report?" asked Todd.

"Average time for evaluation, testing, and interpretations—two to three hours. On this case I imagine it will be much less."

"Good," said Todd, looking at his watch. "Let's put the word out that the first press conference will be at 9:30 PM. That will give them plenty of time to hit the airways."

"I'll take care of it. I'll keep you updated. First, I need to find food and drink for you."

"Thanks, Ken. If the report on the injuries doesn't look too bad, we'll leave after the nine-thirty session."

"Who's the guy with the buzz cut prancing around giving orders like a marine drill sergeant?" asked Ken.

"You'll find out soon enough, like when it's time to conduct our first news release. He's the secret service commander in charge. In case you didn't know, we've been declared a military combat zone by the White House."

"Oh my God!" said Ken. "Who is the victim, some foreign country's prime minister?"

"They're acting like it. Nah, he's just a wealthy contributor to the Republican Party."

"No wonder everyone's scurrying about," said Ken, his face creased with a smirking grin as he exited.

*   *   *   *

The sandwiches from the cafeteria and the hot coffee helped Andy and Todd tolerate the wait. The minutes dragged by like hours until Ken tapped on the door.

"All right, you guys. Here's the word: looks like minor wounds only. He has three fractured ribs, but no puncture of the lung. Painful, but no serious internal effects. Dr. Grayson has prepared the speech he's gonna give before the mikes and cameras. You need to talk to him. He's shaking like a first-grader going on stage."

"Thanks, Ken. Bring him on. We need to get the text of his statement so we can call Jake."

"You guys weren't very complimentary of Dr. Grayson," said Andy as Ken left the room.

"You'll see why," replied Todd. "He got the position of medical director of emergency service some twelve years ago—to everyone's surprise, they say. There was always a question of how he got there. He's long since lost any skill in handling emergencies. He isn't even ACLS certified anymore, if he ever was."

"How *did* he get the position?"

"His father is Walter Grayson, a wealthy south Texas oilman and a strong Catholic. He's been on the Trinitus Westlake Board of Trustees for years and has been a heavy contributor to the Trinitus Foundation. Grayson's name, year after year, has been linked to the elaborate Trinitus Carondolet fundraiser. It's attended by the most prestigious citizens in south Texas. The affair always features some celebrity as the guest speaker. Receiving an invitation to attend is likened to being invited to an inauguration of the President of the United States."

"What does that have to do with being named the medical director of emergency services at Trinitus?"

"Come to the party, Andy," said Todd with a laugh. "Walter Grayson raises millions of dollars of contributions from the annual Carondolet fundraiser, and they're channeled out of the community into the coffers of the Trinitus system under the guise of supporting the hospital's charitable causes. With that kind of money, you can get anything you want from Trinitus."

"So Paul Grayson gets the position, even though he's not qualified?"

"Right! You'll see, Andy. Don't fight it."

"I'm struggling."

\* \* \* \*

An ocean of cameras, microphones, and bright lights bobbled in front of a lectern placed on the unloading dock just outside the emergency room. Andy stayed out of view of the cameras while Todd took his position before the clamoring mass of news people. Andy surmised that the stocky, balding, white coat—clad middle-age person standing next to Todd was Dr. Paul Grayson. The crowd of reporters became quiet and turned their attention to Todd as he addressed them.

"Good evening. I am Todd Langley, one of the associate administrators at Trinitus Medical Center Westlake. Thank you all for your patience this evening. We are happy to report good news here from Trinitus. Mr. Weatherford is medically stable and resting quietly. As most of you know, at Trinitus we have a complete staff of competent physicians representing every specialty, ready to provide the very best care available. I can say with no reserve that they have performed admirably during this crisis.

"At my right is Dr. Paul Grayson, our medical director of emergency services. Dr. Grayson has coordinated the medical care of Mr. Weatherford. He will give you a report on Mr. Weatherford's clinical status and will be available to answer any questions you might have regarding his condition."

Dr. Grayson stepped up to the microphone. Beads of perspiration sprouted from his forehead. He shifted toward the microphone and with bulging eyes, widened eyelids, and quivering chin he looked out at the gathering of reporters for a few painfully long moments. He turned to Todd as if pleading for support. Todd tapped on the speaker as if confirming that it was alive.

"It's all right, Paul," said Todd, smiling as he patted the doctor on the back. "It's working. Just give your report. Just say what you have written on the paper you're holding."

"The patient ... doing well ... has three fractured ribs on the left side of his chest. We have determined that he has no injury to his lungs. He's sleeping after we gave him a sedative. Thank you." He stepped back to make room for Todd.

Todd stepped up and tried to quiet the clamor among the reporters, who were now shouting questions.

"We'll take questions now," said Todd, pointing to the nearest reporter. "Yes, you, sir."

"Doctor, what tests have you done to ensure there were no serious injuries to Mr. Weatherford?"

"We're monitoring his condition closely in the ICU. We have done X-rays and found no indication of internal injuries."

"Did he have a CT scan of the abdomen?"

"No, it wasn't necessary."

"Is he in pain?" asked another.

"Fractured ribs are quite painful, but the pain is being controlled."

"You say the injury is to the left side of his chest ... has his heart been damaged?"

"No, we checked that carefully," said the doctor. "The only injury is the fractured ribs—painful, but not serious."

"We've been told that Mr. Weatherford is in the ICU. Can you tell us why? Is he that critical?" asked a reporter.

"We're keeping him there overnight so we can observe him closely. He is on telemetry monitoring. We will transfer him to a regular room in the morning."

"Do you plan to keep him in the hospital?"

"Yes, we will keep him in observation for twenty-four hours before releasing him."

"There's been a rumor that Mr. Weatherford might be transferred to a major medical center, like San Antonio or Dallas. Can you comment on that possibility?"

Todd stepped forward between Dr. Grayson and the microphone before the doctor could answer.

"There's no validity whatsoever to that rumor. Here at Trinitus Westlake we have the very finest physicians and specialists in the country. There is no reason to transfer the patient anywhere. Thanks you, ladies and gentlemen. If all goes well, we will hold another conference in the morning, at nine o'clock."

\* \* \* \*

Once back in Ken's office, Andy, Todd, and Ken had a chance to compare notes. Todd gave a sigh of relief.

"Went all right, don't you think, Ken? Andy?"

"Yeah. I thought Dr. Grayson was going to collapse a couple of times," said Ken. "I imagine he had to go change his underwear."

Todd and Andy joined him in laughter. "I think Jake could have suggested someone else to face the reporters," said Todd. "We were lucky they didn't get more inquisitive about the patient's care. Was he right, Ken? There was no CT scan done in the ER.?"

"The ER docs were surprised since he had three fractured ribs right over his liver, spleen and kidney. They told me that Grayson canceled the request."

"I still don't understand why one of the ER physicians wasn't asked to give a report on Mr. Weatherford's initial examination," said Andy.

"I guess Jake had his reasons. I imagine he wanted to edit the statements any doctor made. You know Jake. He wouldn't take a chance that some remark might incriminate the hospital. He knew he could control Grayson."

"Andy, I think we've done all we can do here. Let's go home."

"I'm with you, Todd," Andy replied. "This has been an experience I never expected to face."

"A good lesson. I'll see you here in the morning."

"Wouldn't miss it."

\* \* \* \*

The next morning, Andy managed to dress and slip out of the house without disturbing Barbara or Leanne. He left a note on the breakfast room table—a few words explaining why he was so late getting home the evening before and telling Barbara to read the front page of the morning paper.

When Andy pulled into his parking spot, he noticed that Todd's car was already there. He checked his watch—he was fifteen minutes early. Maybe something had happened that brought Todd back early. He found Todd in Ken's office thumbing through the morning edition of the newspaper.

"Good coverage and good photos," said Todd, tossing the paper to Andy. "Jake should be proud."

"Ready for the next news media conference update?"

"Yeah. Grayson wrote his statement last night. As far as I know, he hasn't changed it, and Jake has given his approval. They'll transfer Mr. Weatherford to regular floor care this morning."

"Todd, this is exciting. This news is being sent all over the country by AP News Wire," said Andy, scanning the newspaper articles.

"Most people are probably wondering, 'Where is Westlake, Texas? Never heard of it,'" replied Todd.

"They know now. What time do you face the reporters again?"

"We'll hold the conference this morning, after the patient is transferred out of—"

Ken Striker crashed through the door before Todd could finish speaking.

"Todd! Andy! You won't believe this: Weatherford was being transferred to a bed on the regular nursing floor just now when he began feeling faint and having abdominal pain. The nurses had noticed a rapid heart rate during the night and called Dr. Grayson. He said to go ahead and transfer him anyway. He's been taken back to ICU."

"Have they called a cardiologist?"

"Yeah, Dr. McAuliffe just happened to be in the building and they grabbed him. He said it doesn't appear to be his heart. He thinks the patient is bleeding internally and recommended a surgical consultation. You had better hold off on the news conference."

"What happened to the team of specialists that we said are standing by?" asked Todd.

"They all signed off the case. The patient was supposed to spend one day on regular floor and then be discharged home."

"What can I tell the media?"

"Better check with Jake."

\*　　\*　　\*　　\*

"Damn, Todd, what the hell happened?" yelled Jake.

"Looks like Mr. Weatherford has had an injury to his spleen. He started bleeding internally while he was being transferred to floor care and had to be moved back to the ICU. A surgeon has been called. Weatherford probably will need emergency abdominal surgery. What do I say at the news conference this morning?"

"Tell them Mr. Weatherford is doing fine, that the doctors have discovered complications from the injuries and that the patient will need surgery. Don't say anything more except that he will stay in the ICU. How did they miss the diagnosis?"

"They failed to do a CT scan, I'm told."

"A CT would have shown the injury?"

"Yeah, according to the ER doc."

"Why wasn't it done?"

"Dr. Grayson said it was not necessary."

\*　　\*　　\*　　\*

The same news crew had gathered, yet there seemed to be more individuals than before. Although information on any patient's condition was held in confidence, somehow word always leaked when celebrities were concerned. Todd appeared as cool and calm as a weatherman forecasting the next day's highs and lows. Dr. Grayson couldn't hide his apprehension. He was trembling more than ever and appeared as though he were facing a firing squad. Todd announced that Mr. Weatherford had suffered a minor setback but that he was faring well, was in good spirits, and was comfortable.

"Thank you for your attention," said Todd. "I will turn the mike over to Dr. Grayson, who will give you details of this unexpected and unavoidable complication that the doctors faced in providing Mr. Weatherford's care."

Dr. Grayson, his hands in the coat pockets of his white jacket, looked first at the crowd of reporters and then at Todd with a look that silently said he'd like to bolt and run. Todd, smiling all the while, practically dragged the doctor to the lectern. He then lowered the microphone to the correct level for the doctor and whispered something in Dr. Grayson's ear. Without removing his hands from his coat, the frightened doctor began to speak.

"Mr. Weatherford's condition is stable. He underwent a splenectomy this morning for a ruptured spleen that often occurs after injuries of this sort. He is doing well and will remain in the hospital for about one week."

Hands shot into the air like jumping mackerel, each reporter trying to get the doctor's attention and an answer to his or her question. Todd stepped forward and pulled the mike aside. Dr. Grayson willingly surrendered his position at the podium.

"Thank you, Dr. Grayson. I know you have been committed to ensuring the patient receives the very best care while here at Trinitus. We are fortunate to have the finest physicians in the community associated with our hospital system." He turned to Dr. Grayson. "Also I know that you are eager to get back to the ICU. In order for you to return to the unit as soon as possible, I will stay and attempt to answer any questions here—based, of course, on information that you and the other physicians have given those of us in administration."

Dr. Grayson hurriedly turned away and headed for the emergency room entrance amidst yells from the reporters. Todd raised his arms, trying to get the newsmen to direct questions to him. Finally, after Dr. Grayson stepped out of sight, Todd was inundated with inquiries regarding the delay in diagnosis and what residual damage could Mr. Weatherford look forward to?

Andy, discretely standing in the shadows while the debacle took place, wondered how Todd could hold up to this pressure. At the same time, he wondered if he himself could ever stand this sort of attack. In less than a year from now, if he landed a permanent position with a hospital somewhere, would he be exposed to this same type of treatment? He would have to be cautious choosing a hospital system after he finished his training. He would never comply with an instruction from anyone to tell an untruth.

Like a broken-field running-back on a football field, Todd did a masterful job in answering the questions, skillfully sidestepping entrapment when the issue arose regarding the delay in revealing the diagnosis. He never admitted that a CT scan would have revealed the life-threatening injury from the beginning.

\* \* \* \*

Andy wondered how Todd and Jake would handle this unexpected turn of events—the patient thought to have non-serious fractured ribs now required major abdominal surgery. At some time the media had to be told some semblance of the truth. The patient's family had to have an explanation for the complication that led to major surgery. How could this flagrant incompetence in Mr. Weatherford's care be explained—a missed diagnosis because the CT scan was not done in the ER?

Jake had announced that his first order of business for the day would be to assemble the caregivers—Ken, Dr. Grayson, and the ER physician. Todd was required to attend. He could imagine Jake's reaction to the gross deficiency in the care of a major contributor to the Republican Party. The tongue lashing he would dish out to all of them would be scalding. Andy, thankful he was excused from that meeting, would busy himself with routine chores. He needed to talk to Karen about the upcoming medical staff meeting.

\* \* \* \*

Andy tapped on the sliding glass window to Karen's private office. She was busily making copies of some document and the whirring noise of copy machine muffled Andy's knock. He decided to wait a few moments and try again. He sat in a chair close by while Karen completed her project. While waiting, he recalled some of the comments Karen had made on a few of the occasions he had been in Jake's office. There often seemed to be a furtive posture about her demeanor, as though she wanted to say something to him but was reluctant to do so. He wondered if Karen was aware of all of the irregularities that he had discovered. Surely she must know and is just ignoring them out of loyalty—or maybe out of fear. Karen was a beautiful woman and the fleeting thought crossed his mind that there might be more to her and Jake's relationship than he knew.

Andy no longer heard the grinding noise from the copy machine and tapped on the window again. Karen looked up in surprise, flashed a broad smile, and pointed to the copier. As soon as she was finished gathering her copies, she opened the window.

"Hi, Andy. I know why I haven't seen much of you lately. Looks like Todd has kept you busy." She laughed. "Come on in. Did you want to see Mr. Hensley."

"No. I just need to see the agenda for the medical staff quarterly meeting. I have some statistics that Jake wanted presented, and I need to get these on the program."

"Sure, no problem," she said as she took Andy's document. "Jake is in a meeting right now. Do you want to wait?"

"I don't need to see him. I think everything he wanted prepared is there," he answered, pointing to the papers. "How is Jake holding up with all the chaos?"

"You know Mr. Hensley. He never shows what he is thinking. He is in conference now with Todd and the others, and from what I heard through the closed door, I think he's pretty unhappy."

She had hardly finished the sentence when the door to Jake's office swung open. Andy could see Jake seated at his desk, gazing out on the courtyard with his back turned to his visitors as they exited. Todd, Dr. Grayson, Ken, and the ER physician—all with downtrodden looks on their faces—marched past without speaking a single word to either Karen or Andy.

"I guess that is your answer, Andy," Karen said with a fleeting, knowing smile. She looked at her calendar. "He has arranged for a private meeting with Mr. Weatherford's wife, Marion, and their two daughters. They should be arriving any minute."

"Which means it's time for me to disappear," said Andy with a chuckle. "I don't want to be on his interview list today."

"I have some documents Mr. Hensley wanted you to study. I'll bring them to your office as soon as I get a few things in shape here."

"Fine," said Andy. "I'll be in my office for a couple of hours unless Todd needs me for something."

"I'll find you," she said with a laugh. "Mr. Hensley wants me to update you on a few things. Maybe we'll have time."

"I will welcome that." Andy chuckled. "I think everyone is getting a little tired of having to put up with the high-level security."

"I agree. See you later."

\* \* \* \*

An hour later, on his way to the copy machine, Andy walked past Jake's office just as Mrs. Weatherford and her two daughters were exiting. Jake was standing by the door extending cordial farewells. The smiles on their faces told Andy that Jake had pulled off the impossible with a mixture of charm and a generous serving of bullshit. He had convinced them that Mr. Weatherford's complication was not only unfortunate but that it was unpredictable.

* * * *

Jake rarely communicated with Alan Shipman, the chief executive of the mammoth Trinitus Healthcare System with headquarters in Dallas, except during the quarterly administrators meetings. If an administrator was performing satisfactorily, it was Alan's policy to leave him alone. At each quarterly meeting, Trinitus Westlake led the pack in statistics and margin of profit. Alan never questioned Jake's strategy to achieve those commendable goals, but he knew, from his other contacts, that Jake was following the three-P principle—people, physician, politics—a blueprint for success.

When Karen announced that he had a call from Alan, Jake leaped to his feet and hurriedly gathered Todd's reports on Richard Weatherford's injury before he called Alan back. Jake surmised that Alan would want a first-hand report on an incident, which by now had received worldwide attention.

"Jake, Alan Shipman here. How is it going?"

"We're under control, Alan. Have you watched the news?"

"Every hour. Looks like you've handled that well."

"Thank you, sir."

"Jake, keep up the good work. Send me an e-mail on what really happened. Did we goof somewhere?"

"I'm afraid so, Alan. Richard almost bled to death before they diagnosed the ruptured spleen. But we've got it covered."

"That is all that's important. I'm sure you've smothered Richard's wife, Marion, with your usual charm."

"She's fine, Alan. I met with her and her two daughters and I think I put them at ease."

"I've already heard evidence of that here in Dallas. Here's why I've called, Jake. You know that Richard Weatherford and Anthony Joberst are close friends—and business associates of sorts, partners in Qlozd."

"Yes. I'm aware of the relationship."

"Richard has sent word to me that he wants a private conversation with Anthony as soon as possible. I have arranged for Anthony to make a trip to Westlake late today. I want you to arrange to slip Anthony into Richard's room, past security, and see to it that no one knows who he is or why he's there."

"Might be hard to do." Jake hesitated a few seconds before continuing the conversation. Then he laughed. "I guess we could disguise him as some sort of medical specialist brought here to consult."

"I see you're already thinking," said Alan, chuckling. "Just get it done, Jake. No slip-ups."

"I understand," said Jake "Shall I contact him or will he call here?"

"He'll be there about midnight tonight by our Trinitus private plane. Have someone pick him up at the usual airport and take him to the private entrance to your office. Plan your scheme from there."

"I will meet him myself. We'll get it done somehow."

"I know you will. Nice talking to you, Jake. Oh, by the way, you did hire that nurse who was taking care of Anthony's wife and baby, didn't you?"

"Yes. She hasn't started to work yet, but she's accepted the offer. She'll pose no problem, Alan. I know your concern, since an abduction is a sentinel event."

"You're right. Let me know how it goes. We don't need any more slip-ups."

\* \* \* \*

Karen knocked before entering. "May I come in, Andy?"

"Sure. I'd hoped you'd get here before I have to make rounds with Todd again."

She seemed to avoid eye contact as she placed the packet of hard copies on the edge of his desk. "These are papers from Trinitus headquarters that Mr. Hensley wants you to read. Be sure to shred these after you're finished."

"I'll do that," Andy answered. He noticed that Karen's eyelids had become a bit swollen and red since he had seen her earlier. He decided not to ask her why.

"Do you have a few minutes to talk?" she asked hesitantly. Andy looked up and saw a definite suggestion of sadness in her eyes.

"Of course. Sit down for a minute. Can I get you a Coke or a cup of coffee?"

Karen laughed. "That would be a change, wouldn't it?"

"I would feel privileged," Andy said with a chuckle.

"No thank you. Nice of you to ask, though."

"You're having a rough day?" asked Andy.

"Yeah, how can you tell?"

Andy flashed an affectionate smile. "You have a mirror?" he asked.

"It shows then. Yeah, sometimes Mr. Hensley can be cruel … that's not a good description. He can be so *abrasive* with me when he's upset about something."

"Have you worked for him for a long time?"

"Over fifteen years. And I still haven't learned how to take his remarks sometimes."

"I can't imagine Jake being short with you, Karen. You always seem so efficient."

"He probably doesn't mean anything by it. He knows I would never resign," she said. Her head slumped and she sat with her fingers intertwined and stared at the floor for a few seconds. Moisture formed on her cheeks and she dabbed at her eyes with a tissue.

"What do you mean?"

"I'm sorry, Andy. I shouldn't bother you with these petty issues."

"What can I do, Karen?" he asked. She was quiet for what seemed like forever. Finally, she stood, straightened her back, and edged toward the door.

"Are you all right?" asked Andy.

"Yeah, I'm fine," she replied. She took a couple of steps toward the door and turned back. "Andy, have you ever heard of the Qlozd Network?"

"No, what is it?"

"You seem to get along with Todd real well—I can tell—and he thinks a lot of you. Take him out of the hospital sometime for lunch or for a beer, just the two of you. I think he can explain a few things for you."

"I'll do that," said Andy. "If you intended to arouse my curiosity, you've succeeded."

Karen looked straight at Andy, her dark eyes in an unblinking, piercing stare. "Andy, be very careful while you work here. I know all about Barbara. It's not anything to laugh about."

"What do you know about—?"

In a flash, she was through the door and gone.

\* \* \* \*

A visit with Todd suddenly became top priority. What could Karen possibly have meant when she made the statement about Barbara? Andy sat at his desk without moving. Every possible answer to this new mystery bounced through his mind. Karen's recent tearful behavior suggested that she was privy to more information about Trinitus Hospital management than met the eye. What or who was Qlozd Network? Todd had to know. That's when Karen suggested that he talk to Todd—right after she asked if he had ever heard of the Qlozd Network.

Andy put his feet on his desk and leaned back. He closed his eyes for a few seconds while he tried to sort the myriad uncertainties that raced through his brain. What did Karen mean when she said she knew about Barbara? After a few seconds, he opened his eyes and glanced at the stack of loose-leaf papers that Karen had left on his desk. She had said Jake wanted him to read the reports.

Andy thought it odd that she had brought hard copies of corporate directives to his office. They always came electronically, and he was on the distribution list for those messages. They were usually mundane reports about the day-to-day administration of hospital affairs—multiple informational items such as the frequency of medication errors, infectious disease trends, and Medicare/Medicaid issues—most of which he had already seen in he own office e-mail.

Andy swung his feet off the desk and sat erect in his chair. His eyebrows raised and his mouth dropped. Karen must have been trying to tell him something. He grabbed the stack of documents and began to thumb through them. As he suspected, they were only corporate e-mail messages that had been printed, that he had seen before.

He thumbed through the papers, page by page. In the middle of the packet, he came across a sheet of handwritten notes. He held it sideways to the light. It too had been copied. It was Jake's handwriting. His first impulse was to call Karen and tell her of the mistake, but then he stopped. Karen had wanted him to see what was on the page. The sheet of paper had been folded and turned sideways. Jake had written a list of reminders to himself. The items were numbered, and Jake's handwriting was surprisingly legible. Andy's hands trembled. He felt as if he was invading another person's privacy as he read.

> *1) Call Alan re C/U*
>
> *2) Pick up Anthony at M/N*
>
> *3) Call Todd—escort Anthony inside hospital*
>
> *4) Schedule Qlozd Network mtg.*
>
> *5) Call Paretto*
>
> *6) Check on Barbara Goldeyer employment*

Andy read Jake's handwritten list carefully trying to decipher each item. The note about Barbara was especially bothersome. Maybe Todd could answer the question of why Barbara's employment was of so much interest to Jake. Could C/U stand for cover-up? Why was Anthony Joberst coming to the hospital in the late hours of night? And how did Paretto and the Qlozd Network link to the overall picture? Should he take Jake's memo to Mr. Walton? Surely the FBI would want to know about this finding. According to Mr. Walton, Dimitrio Paretto was known by the bureau as an underworld kingpin. But how could an organized crime character possibly be linked to hospitals, especially those that were a part of the giant Trinitus Healthcare System? Andy wondered if Mr. Walton might know something about the Qlozd Network.

Karen had wanted him to see Jake's note; there was no question in Andy's mind now—she was scared of something. Andy definitely needed a session with Todd as soon as possible. He could only hope that Todd would be honest with him.

# 30

*Dallas*

To most neighbors and passersby, 48 Oak Manor was nothing more than another mansion on a three-acre wooded track in fashionable Highland Park, located in the center of Dallas. A select few in the elite Dallas social circle knew that Dimitrio Paretto lived in the luxurious mansion. They had attended lavish receptions and fundraisers sponsored by Paretto. They perceived him to be an esteemed, respected local philanthropist who was on every social organization's guest list of community leaders.

However, a few urban residents in Dallas and other major metropolises in the nation knew, sometimes with fear and dread, that Dimitrio Paretto was the don of the largest criminal organization in the nation. The Paretto Mob had enjoyed fabulous success in drug trafficking, money laundering, and extortion for years, especially after the Marchesa Family reduced their operations to gambling when Alberto Marchesa went into seclusion.

Other than during social events, few vehicles ever passed through the gates of the eight-foot brick wall—capped with razor wire—that completely encircled the property. One accessed the front and rear through heavily guarded gates that opened electronically only after visitors were positively identified. Inside, state-of-the-art surveillance equipment kept a cadre of security guards informed of any activity anywhere near the estate.

On a fairly regular monthly schedule, a parade of limousines with heavily tinted windows entered the compound in the early hours of the morning, stayed for four to five hours, and exited in the same order. Those few individuals who casually knew Paretto perceived these meetings to be nothing more than business sessions attended by the regional management executives of Paretto's vast network of beer distributors.

Paretto ruled his organizations with an iron hand, but never by micromanagement. He depended on Nicholas Tatum, his confidant as well as his hit man, to scrutinize the performance and loyalty of his managers. Following Alberto Marchesa's decline and exile three years earlier, Paretto moved into control of gangland activities and had gone to extremes to protect his empire. Still, in the back of his mind—undoubtedly remembering the past—he often made comments that showed that he was constantly in fear of the return of the Marchesa Family.

\*     \*     \*     \*

Following Nicholas Tatum's instructions, Reyes let Deo and Marcello out of the limousine near the rear gate of the Paretto compound and drove off to wait for a signal to return. When Deo and Marcello approached the guardhouse, with Marcello in the lead, they could hear the whirring of motors followed by a sudden flash of bright, blinding light in their faces. It was so intense they could barely discern the voice that came from somewhere.

"Marcello, I'm sure you're not armed, but you will have to walk through the detector cage."

Marcello recognized Tatum's voice. "Turn off the fuckin' light, Tate," said Marcello. "What the fuck is that for?"

"It's automatic, Marcello. So you can't identify the face behind the voice."

"Get it turned off or we're leaving," yelled Marcello.

"Okay, okay, just come on in and it will turn off."

"Who the shit you think you are treating us like that? I ought to pinch your head off right here on the spot."

"I'm sorry, Marcello. Hey! Let's don't start off our visit gettin' mad. Haven't seen you for a while."

"You might see a hell of a lot more of us if—"

"Come on. Paretto's anxious to see you."

They climbed into a waiting golf cart and headed for the entrance to the home on 48 Manor Drive. Once inside, they were led to a large, elaborately decorated chamber with ten-foot ceiling, marble walls, and a marble floor covered with colorful Persian rugs. At one end stood a heavy, oval-shaped desk and a leather high-back chair. More leather-covered guest chairs ringed the front periphery of the desk.

The room was empty when they arrived. Tate motioned for them to be seated. "I'll let Mr. Paretto know you are here," said Tate. "His private quarters are next door."

He tapped on the door to the adjacent room and entered. He soon returned, trailing two steps behind an unsmiling Dimitrio Paretto—a rotund, balding individual of average height with a round, rather pasty face and piercing black eyes set deep behind narrowed eyelids. His expressionless face reflected distrust and dislike for any and everyone in his presence. Deo and Marcello stood. There were no handshakes. Paretto seated himself behind his desk and waved his hand as a signal for the others to be seated.

Paretto kept his beady eyes fixed on Deo and Marcello, looking away only to glance at his watch or spit a piece of wet tobacco to the floor from the unlit cigar in his mouth.

"I don't have much time. What can I do for you?" said Paretto abruptly and coldly.

"You have any idea why we're here?" said Deo.

"Get to the point. Did Al send you?"

"As a matter of fact, he did," Deo replied. "Good thinking, Dimitrio. I'll tell Al you asked about him."

"Goddamn it, Deo, what the hell do you want?"

"We hoped we could have a friendly conversation with you and Tate," said Deo. He turned to Marcello and motioned for him to stand. "But I see we were wrong. Get in touch, Dimitrio, if you want to talk."

"All right, all right," said Paretto, "settle down. What do we have to talk about?"

"Very simple, Dimitrio," said Deo. "We want the baby."

Paretto blanched, coughed, and spat a sizable chunk of tobacco, and then he turned to stare at Tatum. "What the hell is he talking about, Tate?" Tate cringed and squirmed in his chair. His chin dropped and a curtain of fright covered his face. "I ... I ... I don't know Mr. Paretto."

"Cut the shit, both of you," said Deo, piercing them with his stare. "You know what we're talking about."

Paretto looked back at Deo and Marcello and then rotated his desk chair a quarter-turn, leaned back, gazed across the room, and remained quiet a half-minute. He turned back, his facial expression showing no change.

"Assume for a minute that we don't know what you're talking about," he said. "Patronize us by describing what you mean when you refer to some mysterious baby—tell us the who, what, where."

Deo, trying to suppress a grin at Paretto's ploy, looked at Marcello. "Perhaps you could let Mr. Paretto and Mr. Tatum know something about what we have found since I have been back in the country, Marcello."

"I will be pleased to gratify such a sincere request for information," said Marcello in a tone of profound seriousness. Deo had to lower his head to suppress outright laughter at Marcello's sarcasm. In all the years he had worked with Marcello, he had never witnessed such a performance.

Marcello narrated, before his spellbound audience, Deo's trip to the United States and their attempts to learn the details of the abduction. He described how they came to learn that Gator, Squint, and Becky had been engaged by Paretto to carry out Paretto's carefully planned scheme to kidnap the judge's baby. When he finished, he looked at Deo.

"Does that cover it, Deo?"

"Well, yes, completely—to a point, Marcello. Thank you. Now I know you are very busy, Dimitrio, so let me make this quick: all we want from you is the baby. Simple. Where is the baby?"

Awestricken, Paretto and Tate were speechless for a few moments while Marcello's recounting slowly infiltrated their cerebral cortexes. Their smugness had melted into flat affects.

Paretto, again radiating an air of arrogance, ignored Marcello and looked straight at Deo. "An intriguing story that Marcello has told. Of course, there is not a word of truth in his accusations when he says I am responsible for some plan to kidnap a baby. Where in God's name is there a motive for me to kidnap a baby?" Paretto laughed. "I don't even like babies."

"We have Gator, Dimitrio. We missed Becky and Squint before Tate iced them. Sad that neither had much time to enjoy the money you dropped on them."

There was total silence in the room except the audible, rasping whisper of Paretto's breathing. Tate loosened his collar and wiped his forehead with a handkerchief. He looked at Paretto expectantly, as if waiting for some direction. Deo leaned back in the comfortable chair and picked at his fingernails as if awaiting Paretto's next move.

"Who else knows about this?" Paretto finally asked.

"The FBI are close behind us," said Deo. "Kidnapping a federal judge's child is a federal offense, you know—from the first day."

Paretto stood, motioned with a nod for Tate to follow him, and started for the door. "We need to talk."

"Before you leave, Mr. Paretto," said Marcello, "you need to know this: Ray Reyes has an explosive device set by your back gate, and he has twelve of our top marksmen, armed with scatter guns, ready to storm this place if I push this button. Just thought you should know."

"We're just going to talk," Paretto said. "I know you wouldn't come here without backup."

"We're in no hurry. But I do need to report to Al," said Deo. "He knows we're here."

Paretto and Tate retreated to the adjacent quarters, but the solid oak door didn't muffle the sound of Paretto's voice tearing into Tate. Deo was sure he could make out the phrases "I told you to take Gator out first" and "You dumb son of a bitch. You left a fuckin' trail." Interspersed were references to the FBI. Deo and Marcello perked up, trying to hear Tate's answer to Paretto's question, "Is the baby alive?" but neither could hear the answer.

A full fifteen minutes passed. The voices from the room next door could no longer be heard. Deo turned to Marcello.

"Is Reyes really on standby?" he whispered. "Where do you think they've gone?"

"I imagine Paretto sent Tate out to the gate to confirm that there's actually a bomb there," Marcello answered, also in a whisper.

"Is there?" asked Deo.

"Yeah. And Ray's men are thick in the shadows waiting for the gate to blow. They haven't had this much excitement since you and Al moved to Corsica."

Marcello's phone vibrated. It was Reyes. "Are you okay?"

"Yeah, we're fine—alone in Paretto's office. What do you have?"

"Tate came back in the cart without you. Do we need to come in?"

"No. I'm sure Tate was just checking to see if you really were on ready. I'll let you know. Stay on alert."

In a couple of minutes, Paretto and Tate came back in the room. Paretto, maintaining his haughty manner, took his place behind the desk. Deo and Marcello stared at Tate. His inability to hold eye contact reflected a hint of embarrassment—a dead giveaway that he had doubted Marcello's statement about Reyes and had gone to find out.

Paretto reached down to open a desk drawer. "Don't do that, Mr. Paretto," said Marcello, extracting the electronic signal device from his pocket. "We prefer that you keep your hands where we can see them."

"Don't be so suspicious, Marcello. I'm only reaching for a cigar," said Paretto.

"I stay alive by being suspicious, sir. If you don't mind, I'll stand while you retrieve your cigar."

Tate held both hands in the air, palms facing Marcello. "It's all right, Marcello. He knows Reyes is outside." Marcello sat but kept his device in his hand.

Paretto passed the box of cigars around. No takers. He leaned back in his chair, lit his cigar, and focused his attention to Deo.

"What's your offer?" he asked.

"Offer?" asked Deo. "Offer? There is no offer, Dimitrio, except letting you and Tate stay alive. I guess that would be considered an offer."

"Don't threaten me, Deo. I see through your little trick. Al's moving back in, isn't he?" said Paretto, his eyelids almost squinting shut as he yelled at Deo. "Al knows, and you know, that the Blanton estate is worth millions. A few million in ransom wouldn't make a ripple. Whoever holds that child can make a fortune. That's what you're doing. Somehow you found out about the baby and you think you can come in here and negotiate a deal where Al ends up with millions to help finance his re-entry. Now, don't fuck with me, Deo. We either negotiate or we go to war."

Deo had stayed composed during Paretto's tirade. Marcello looked at Deo and held up the device. "Do we need to do any more talking, Deo?"

Deo grinned, changed his position in his chair, and again made a move to stand as if he were going to leave. "I think you're right, Marcello. I don't think we're getting anywhere."

Paretto stood and turned toward the credenza behind his chair. "Wait … wait!" he said with panic as he crushed his cigar in a container of sand. "Maybe we have some common ground here."

"You like to talk about offers, Dimitrio," said Deo, both he and Marcello standing. "What kind of offer would you like to make before we leave?"

"Sit down, both of you. Let's be sensible."

"We prefer to stand."

"Give me Gator. You get the baby"

"We'll think about it and let you know. But we won't even think about it unless you tell me who hired you to do this scam."

Paretto looked stunned for a brief moment. "What makes you think someone hired us?"

"Kidnapping babies? Not your style, Dimitrio," said Deo.

"As you said, I'll think about it. Depends on whether or not Al is moving back in.

\* \* \* \*

Seconds after Deo and Marcello exited through the rear gate of 48 Manor Drive, Reyes brought the limousine to their side and Deo and Marcello climbed aboard.

"You had me worried," said Reyes, "and we have a dozen disappointed guys in the van busy cleaning black paint off their faces."

"We were glad to know you were there," said Marcello. Sorry the men didn't see any action, but it is best this way."

"How did it go?"

"I think we are on the right track," Deo answered. "We'll schedule another session with them soon. Be on the lookout—they'll be coming to us next. What do you think, Marcello?"

"Yeah, I agree," he replied. "You got Paretto's attention, and we left him sweating. Give him three days."

Deo laughed. "It's like a chess game. I thought I'd croak when you stood up and told him to keep his hands in plain sight. Neither he nor Tate expected that."

"I was serious. You did catch his question: 'Who else knows about this?'"

"Right. That's when I was glad you had arranged for a back-up play."

"Do you think he'll try to move the baby?" asked Marcello.

"He might. Do we have the place covered?"

"Yeah, but it's hard to watch—so many large trees around the house, and delivery trucks coming and going."

"I think Dimitrio is smart enough not to make a move against us right now."

"What's our next move?" asked Marcello.

"We wait. But in the meantime, we need to hurry and make plans for a session with Agent Ralph Walton."

# 31

Judge Anthony Joberst slammed the door behind him as he entered his private chambers, disrobed, and hung his long black gown in the closet adjacent to his office. His next stop was the washroom. The fifty-nine year-old face looking back at him from the mirror looked older today than he remembered from the last time he had looked closely. The streaks of gray hair seemed more noticeable and the bald spot on his crown, visible in the mirror on the wall behind him, was getting larger.

He vigorously scrubbed his face and hands with soap and water. He wasn't sure why, but he always felt dirty after hearing cases like this last one: a Mexican illegal immigrant, simply looking for food, had been shot and killed by an irate rancher. How could he be impartial in judging the accused when he probably would have responded the same way if he had had a similar encounter with a wetback?

His cell phone's voicemail indicator blinked. Who could this be? Only a few select individuals had his private cell phone number. Maybe it was Leanne, begging to return home. It would certainly simplify his plan to get rid of her if that were the case. He checked the missed call list and saw no familiar numbers. He clicked on the last one that appeared on the screen. To his surprise, Alan Shipman answered.

"Alan! Is that you? I didn't recognize the number."

"Yeah, Anthony, it's me. New number. Hope I'm not disturbing you."

"No, not at all. Just finished a hearing. What do you hear from Richard?"

"He needs to see you, Anthony. That's why I'm calling."

"Do you think that's a good idea?"

"I think you should go. I called Jake. He'll see to it that you're not recognized.

"What do you think Richard wants?"

"Anthony, how should I know? The two of you are close. All I know is that he is a member of Qlozd. That's reason enough to go see what he needs."

"You're right. When is Jake expecting me?"

"I'll call the hangar. The company jet will be ready when you are. I told Jake to pick you up at the airport in Westlake exactly at midnight. No cell phones, Anthony. Just go. Jake will be there waiting for you when you land."

"We have a Qlozd meeting scheduled soon. Richard is probably worried about making it—probably wants us to go on without him."

"Out of the question. The newspaper report on Richard's condition is favorable, but he didn't sound that way when I talked to him," said Alan.

"I'll find out for sure. Thanks, Alan."

"No problem. Check with me when you get back. Oh … Anthony, I'm sure Jake has already thought of it, but make sure there's no intercom operating from Richard's room to the nurses' station while you're there."

"Good idea. I'll confirm with Jake."

*   *   *   *

"Of course, Alan was right," said Anthony aloud as he leaned back in his heavily padded desk chair with his feet propped up on his desk and puffed on a newly lit cigar. The dense smoke disappeared almost instantaneously through the powerful exhaust fan he had installed in the ceiling over his desk. "Richard is a Qlozd Network partner." They had all worked too hard to build and promote the close camaraderie of the network for anyone to abandon a fellow member in a time of need. Richard's injury had been foremost in his mind after reading about the accident. He needed some first-hand information on Richards's condition.

Anthony wondered if there was any way the incident had been a planned attempt on Richard's life. With all the secret service men protecting the White House staff members, it would be impossible for an imposter to infiltrate the group. But who could trust the secret service anymore? For enough money, at least one of them could be bought.

Anthony closed his eyes for a few moments to relax. He wondered what the other Qlozd members would think about expanding the membership. They now had federal judges from each judicial district in Texas—judges that he had personally recruited. Why would they need any others? He needed to talk to Alan and Richard again. He had an ominous feeling about expansion. Greed could lead to their downfall.

Jake Hensley was the only hospital CEO in Qlozd. Anthony wondered why. Alan wanted him for some reason, but Anthony just didn't trust Jake, didn't feel comfortable around him. He always had the feeling that Jake was patronizing him and Richard when he was around them. Jake never seemed to appreciate the legal support Qlozd received from Richard's Dallas office. Also, it seemed to Anthony that Jake talked too much. In a covert organization like Qlozd a talkative member could be a hazard.

There was no question: it was a strong, easily managed organization—highly secretive, highly profitable—but he knew that if it became much larger, there would be a greater risk of exposure. Considering the size of the dividends declared each year for each member, they would have no trouble attracting new partners if they decided to do so. But why risk it? Other than the profit from money laundering and drug trafficking that came from Paretto, the highest yield came from lawsuits in Texas.

Anthony turned his thoughts to Leanne. What a spoiled, rich brat. Had her money made it worth living in the same house with her this long? He had gained prestige being married to an heir to the Blanton fortune, but he didn't need that now. Alan had saved his image by seeing that the DNA report was falsified. If he could prove that the Marchesa stud was the father of the baby, he could get Richard to sue for alienation of affection. Victor Marchesa would be quick to come up with a handsome settlement to protect his son, and his hospital system, from adverse publicity.

But Anthony knew that an alienation lawsuit, even if he recovered a settlement, would expose his secret-most private life to the world. If Leanne filed for divorce, public sentiment would be in his favor after that magazine article about Leanne's infidelity, but his reputation would still be tarnished.

First he needed to get this television appeal taping over with. Agent Walton had planned to bring Leanne to Dallas in a couple of days for the taping. They'd let it run for a few days. When there would be no response, he would get Paretto's help in faking a larger ransom demand, transfer the offshore funds to his account, split with Paretto, and finally get Tate to dispose of the baby somewhere. It was all falling in place.

\* \* \* \*

The hangar was dark except for a light in the small office along the hangar's plane storage area. While Anthony was driving up, someone turned on the lights along the accessory branch runway between the private hangar tarmac and one of the primary landing-takeoff strips at Love Field. Anthony parked his car and walked around the building just as the pilot and co-pilot were wheeling the Trinitus Health System's private jet plane out of the hangar. He stood back while they prepared for takeoff. Finally they motioned for him to board. He checked his watch: 10:00 PM. They would just barely get to Westlake and to the hospital by midnight.

\* \* \* \*

## Westlake

The flight was smooth; Anthony drifted off and awakened when the wheels hit the runway at Westlake. As they taxied to the private hangar, Anthony spotted Jake standing by his car, dressed in an open-necked shirt. Anthony had forgotten the warm and humid climate in Westlake, but was reminded when he stepped down from the plane and immediately wished he had worn an open-necked shirt. The co-pilot called after him.

"How much time, Judge Joberst?"

"I should be back in a couple of hours."

"We'll be ready when you are."

Jake walked toward the plane to meet him. After a handshake and an embrace, they were soon on the way to the hospital.

"Glad to see you, Anthony," said Jake.

"How is Richard?"

"He's doing fine," Jake replied. "In spite of the goofs our people at the hospital made."

"Yeah, Richard mentioned the missed diagnosis and something about the failure to get a CT scan in the emergency room."

"In spite of it all, he's stable."

"How is Marion holding up?" asked Anthony.

Jake chuckled. "You should know. I think she's a little disappointed they didn't just let him bleed out."

"I guess you're right. Jake ... uh, did Richard have an HIV test."

"A little late for you to worry about that, isn't it, Anthony?" Jake said as his mouth twisted into a smirk.

The remark reminded Anthony of one of the reasons he disliked Jake.

"I have no reason to worry, Jake."

"He had it. It was negative."

"Thanks. How are your numbers looking? Did you have a good month?"

"Excellent! We should be able to contribute handsomely to Qlozd this quarter. When is our next meeting?" asked Jake.

"In two weeks. I imagine Richard wants to talk about that. With his injuries healing, he's probably wondering if he will be able to attend."

"There has been some talk of expanding Qlozd. What do you think?"

"I don't like the idea," said Anthony. "We have a good bunch of partners right now. We shouldn't take a chance of being infiltrated by the feds."

"Is Paretto pressuring you?"

"Yeah, a little."

"My God, how much money does he want to make?"

"He's always worried about competition, says he needs to add to his crew."

"If you and I and Alan vote against growing the membership, it won't happen."

"I hope you're right."

Jake made a call as he entered the service area at the rear of the hospital. Todd Langley answered and stepped out of the shadows.

"Who is this?" asked Anthony.

"One of my assistant administrators, Todd Langley. He has been told that you are on a confidential mission from the White House. He has arranged for you to enter the nursing floor from the service elevator and go straight to Richard's room undetected. Todd will take you back to the airport when you're ready."

\* \* \* \*

Todd left Anthony in the stairwell holding the door slightly ajar while he checked out the hallway. All clear. He tapped on Richard Weatherford's door, looked in to confirm that no one else was present, and motioned for Anthony to join him. After Anthony entered the room, Todd quietly closed the door and stepped down the hall to the nurse's station. There he would identify himself, since the hour was so late, and explain to the charge nurse that Mr. Weatherford was being interviewed confidentially by a special agent of the secret service and was not to be disturbed.

* * * *

Anthony went directly to Richard's bedside. He grasped his hand, leaned over, and gently stroked his friend's face with his other hand. Richard opened his eyes and broke into a faint smile. Tears began to form in his eyes as he struggled to pull himself into a sitting position.

"I thought I was dreaming," said Richard. "Is that really you, Anthony?"

"I'm here Richard. I've been worried sick about you."

"I'm doing fine. I'll do better when I get out of this place. Thanks for coming. How are you doing?"

"Better now that I can see how you are. Jake arranged this visit. I wanted to hear the story from you. What the hell happened? In the first place, what were you doing on a pigeon shoot? Pulling the feathers out of the pigeon's wing and throwing it into the air to be shot at? Doesn't sound like your idea of fun."

"Pretty cruel, isn't it?"

"I just can't imagine you doing that. You're not a hunter."

"I was pretty much coerced into going. It was very political. You're right—I am not a hunter—but it was a nice outing. Nice parties and conversation right up until I was thrown out of the Jeep."

"What's this about wine at lunch? The paper played that up big."

"If they only knew. It was not wine, Anthony. It was two-, three-, and four-martini lunches. Everyone drank too much. That's what caused the accident." He chuckled. "It did help me stand the pain of the fractured ribs and the ruptured spleen."

"There are better ways," Anthony replied. "Why was there so much delay in reporting the accident?"

"The martinis. They didn't want any news media around while everyone was still saturated with alcohol," he answered. "And then they couldn't decide who would talk to the reporters and what would happen if the sheriff and game wardens came out and found a bunch of drunken shooters."

"Then that's why Cecelia Abercrombie did all the talking, I guess," said Anthony, slowly shaking his head as though in disbelief.

"And that's why none of the White House staff didn't have to lie about how much they had had to drink."

"God, what a cover-up." Anthony pulled up a chair close to the bed. "What were you doing all this time you were waiting to be brought in?"

"There was a paramedic along, and he put a rib belt around my chest and gave me a pain shot. I didn't think I was injured enough to be concerned, but after a while, when I had so much trouble breathing, they decided I should be taken to the hospital. Of course, it would have to be one of Alan's Trinitus hospitals. They brought me here by stretcher in a helicopter."

"And you're still here. They keep saying you're in a stable condition."

"By some miracle, not the result of modern medicine in this hospital."

"What do you mean?"

Richard described the internal bleeding from the ruptured spleen that wasn't diagnosed until the next day and the subsequent abdominal surgery. Anthony, his brow furrowed and his fists clinched and white, shook his head slowly back and forth as he listened to the sordid story. There was a painfully long silence after Richard stopped talking.

"Damn, Richard, that's a negligence suit served on a silver platter," said Anthony. "What are you going to do?"

"That's one reason I wanted to talk to you," he said. "Is it worth it? I know I could recover a nice bundle, but Qlozd would lose the Trinitus system."

"Yeah, you're right. I know what you're thinking: our pledge is to do nothing that would jeopardize the welfare of the group as a whole."

"I could never do it."

"Maybe there's a way for us to have it both ways."

"How could we do that?"

"Alan would cringe over the thought of adverse publicity for the Trinitus system. We could use the threat of a negligence suit to negotiate a better arrangement with the Trinitus system in the future."

"Hadn't thought of that. Good thinking, Anthony."

"Let me work on it. I will throw a carrot to Alan by telling him that when you're discharged, you will give glowing reports to the world on the excellent care you received at the Trinitus Hospital, that the Trinitus facilities are the best in the country."

"It will be hard to say that shit with a straight face."

Anthony looked at Richard, smirked, and chortled, "Just don't say it with a frown on your face."

Richard laughed and then winced from the pain in his incision. "I'll put on a good performance, Anthony."

"Richard, do you think anyone could have tampered with that Jeep ... did something that made it flip over?"

"I don't think so. The driver was a ranch employee. He had had too many martinis just like the rest of us. Do you think we have enemies that would try such a thing?"

"I never thought so before. I don't think anyone has reason to take us out. No one knows about Qlozd. Of course, some people have suffered losses because of Qlozd."

"Yeah, you're right there."

"What can we do?"

"I am going to arrange for a meeting with Paretto. He will be able to find out if there is any plan out there to attack us."

"What are you going to do about Leanne?"

"We've already split. I don't even know where she is. I really don't care. She's coming to Dallas in the next day or so—from wherever she is now. We are going to tape a TV appeal together. It will be an exercise in futility. It won't be easy to put on that act."

"Are we going to get flack from the others about this Qlozd expansion proposal?" asked Richard.

"We have to hold steady on that," Anthony replied. "We are already spread thin. I'm worried that some of these hospital CEOs other than Jake will wake up and realize what's happening."

"I think Alan would take care of that eventuality, Anthony."

"Yeah, but what if one of them stumbles onto something and decides to make a bundle for himself with a whistleblower scheme?"

"That's where Paretto comes into play, but I don't think any one of them is brave enough to challenge Alan."

"You're right. Let's just keep the status quo for now. You agree?" asked Anthony as he stood to leave.

"Absolutely!" said Richard. "Have a nice trip to Dallas. And thanks for coming. We need to get away together soon."

Anthony squeezed Richard's hand, bent over, and kissed his forehead. "I agree," he replied. They looked into each other's eyes longingly. "I miss you terribly. It's been a long time."

"Yes it has. I miss you too, Anthony, and thanks again for coming. Please be careful."

# 32

## Westlake

Andy enjoyed the winding early-morning ride through Lakeside Park on his way to work. He passed the usual cluster of joggers and walkers on the track that ran parallel to the street. The traffic was relatively light, so he made good time. He needed to talk to Todd, as Karen had suggested, but he had to do it at an opportune time and he had to tread cautiously. He would ask Todd to give his opinion on the report he would be giving at the next medical staff meeting. Maybe that would present an opening for him to question Todd.

Andy glanced at his watch. He guessed the girls would be up and stirring around about now, getting Leanne ready to go to Dallas for the television appeal. If he knew Barbara, she would try to find some way to accompany Leanne, but surely she would call and let him know. He felt assured that Agent Walton would go to extremes to see that Leanne, and Barbara if she went, were protected, but their being out in the open, even if only for a short interval, was fraught with danger.

He pulled into his parking slot and noticed Todd's car. Todd also had come in early for some reason. Andy stopped by Karen's office to let her know he was in the hospital. He entered the darkened administration waiting room, scribbled a note, and prepared to slip it under the door to Karen's office when he heard voices from within, loud and argumentative voices. Andy quickly retreated to the outside corridor and quietly closed the door.

He could identify Karen's voice; the other had sounded like Todd. When he had parked, he had recognized Todd's car in its parking slot but did not remember seeing Jake's car in its usual place. Karen and Todd must have been arguing about something.

As he entered his own office, his cell phone rang. It was Barbara.

"Hi, it's me. Thanks for the wake-up kiss. We didn't get to talk this morning before you left."

"I'm sorry. I'm trying to get my report ready, so I left early. How's it going there?"

"Fine, considering. Leanne's about to become panic-stricken. She's nervous about the TV interview. I asked her if she wanted me to go with her. She wants to go alone, some sort of 'gaining independence' thing. I'll see what Mr. Walton says."

"Something else for me to worry about."

"No need to. You know there'll be agents coming out of the woodwork."

"Just be careful. Don't let her husband see you, if that's possible."

"I hear you and I agree."

"I'm uneasy every time you go out. Call me if you go with her and be careful."

"I'll let you know."

After talking to Barbara he went back toward Karen's office with the intent of grabbing a cup of coffee before he attacked his morning's work. As he approached the waiting area, he noticed that the door was cracked open and the room was now brightly lit. Just as he reached out to open the door, it swung open and Andy met Todd head on. Todd's face was distorted by a deep, furrowed brow, tightly pursed lips, and unblinking eyes.

"Oh, hi, Todd. I just need a word with Karen."

Todd tried unsuccessfully to erase the look of hostility from his face.

"Sure, hope you have better luck than I did. She's made up her mind to be unreasonable today," he replied.

"I can't imagine that," said Andy. "You look distressed. Anything wrong?"

"Everything! I was up all night running errands for Jake. Now he expects me to be bright and cheerful and ready to meet the media again."

"About Mr. Weatherford?"

"Yeah, the guy is doing fine now, but at every one of these news conferences, someone brings up why it took so long to diagnose the ruptured spleen and if he was transferred out of ICU too soon."

"How is Karen involved with that?"

"I just asked her to tell Jake that I needed to go home and get some sleep and that perhaps he should appear before the media at the next conference," he answered. "She said she wouldn't do it, said it was up to me to answer the reporter's questions. Basically, it's up to me to tell the lies, to do the cover-up. I'm just tired of it all. And then last night. I shouldn't have to go through all that shit."

"What are you talking about?"

"We'll talk about it later. I need to get out of here before I explode."

"Sure you do. I'll check with you later. Maybe we can talk."

"Yeah, I'd like that, Andy. You are the only person around here that I feel comfortable talking to."

"I'll come by after a while."

"Sure. Good idea."

\*    \*    \*    \*

Andy still had not heard from Barbara about the Dallas trip. Surely she had not gone without letting him know. No sooner had the thought crossed his mind than his cell phone rang. It was Barbara.

"I still haven't talked to Mr. Walton," said Barbara. "He should be here soon. If I do go, we'll be back this evening."

"Be careful," said Andy. "I don't know exactly why—maybe all of this is just grinding me down—but I have an ominous feeling about your going today. Still, I know Mr. Walton wouldn't ask you to go with Leanne unless he had good reason."

"Don't worry, Andy. It'll be fine. I love you."

"I love you, too." Andy laughed. "I'll wait up for you."

"Glad to hear you laugh."

\*    \*    \*    \*

Almost three hours had passed since his encounter with Todd. Andy had finished his routine desktop chores for the morning and decided to seek some real time with Todd—maybe they could go out of the hospital for lunch.

Andy dialed Todd's number. No answer. He decided to wait a few minutes and try again. Todd wouldn't go home without telling someone; he had most likely turned off his phone and was asleep in his office. He made his way down the corridor, past Jake's office, to the door leading into Todd's office. Todd's secretary, Trish Patton, was seated at her desk busily working at her computer when he entered. Trish surely would know where to find Todd.

"Hi, Andy. How's it going? Are you getting as tired as Todd is of that accident case and the news media?"

"Yeah, just about. Of course, I'm not under the spotlight like Todd. How's he holding up?"

"He collapsed in his office a little while ago with instructions not to be disturbed for anything short of a four-alarm fire."

"Look, I'll come back."

"No, I think it's time to wake Todd. He would want to see you. I think Todd needs a friend right now. Can't say what makes me think so—just the way he acts. Not like him. I've worked for him so long, I can tell."

"Sure. I saw him earlier. He was really stressed out."

"Yeah, he was up all night."

"Why, for God's sake?"

"Something he was doing for Mr. Hensley. Todd won't talk about it. Maybe he'll tell you."

Trish tapped lightly before cracking the door to Todd's private office. "Hey, wake up time! You've slept almost two hours. Andy's here to see you." No answer from the office. Trish opened the door wider and glanced toward Todd's desk.

"Oh my God! Andy, come in here, quick! Something's wrong." Andy rushed into the office. Todd was slumped over his desk. He appeared lifeless, with his head lying sideways on his arms crossed over the desk pad. Andy shook him gently at first and called his name. No response. He felt for his carotid artery—a bounding pulse. Andy looked up at Trish. "At least he's alive." Todd began to stir.

Trish looked at Andy and flashed a devilish grin. "I'll leave him with you," she said. "Maybe you can get him awake."

"Thanks, Trish," replied Andy. "I won't be long."

"Still, I'm going to hold his calls for a while."

Todd finally stirred and sat upright. His eyelids were sleep-puffy. He rubbed the right side of his face, still red from being on his desk and pressed against his arm for so long. Andy grinned, thinking, *His hair still looks as well groomed as always.*

"How long have I been asleep?" he said as he glanced at the clock on his desk. "My God. I've been sleeping in that same position for over an hour."

"Just means you needed the sleep. I wasn't going to disturb you, but Trish insisted."

"Glad you did," he said, still shaking his head in disbelief.

"I wanted you to look over my report before I take it to the medical staff meeting."

"No problem," he said. "I'll have it back to you within the hour."

"Are you feeling better now?"

"Yeah, I shouldn't have sounded off to you this morning."

"That's all right. There's another reason I came. I wanted some time to talk to you privately. Do you have time for lunch? We could go out of the hospital if you'd like."

Todd stared at Andy with a look of skepticism, as though trying to remember anything he had said earlier that might have triggered Andy's visit.

"What's this about Andy?"

"Maybe it's my imagination. Do you ever have the feeling that you are under some sort of surveillance when you are in the hospital?"

Todd again was quiet, as though contemplating his answer. He nodded his head vigorously without speaking but glanced at the phone on his desk and answered, "No, I've never been suspicious of that. Where would you like to go for lunch?"

"There's a nice, quiet sandwich shop and deli about two blocks away."

"Great, maybe the walk will help me wake up. Let's go."

\* \* \* \*

Andy and Todd strolled leisurely along a tree-lined side street on the way to the deli. Only an occasional vehicle passed; the only other sound was the occasional dog barking in the distance. With his height and lengthy stride, Todd found it difficult to slow his pace to match Andy's.

"Nice to get away from air conditioning for a while," said Todd, struggling to walk slower. "And away from the hospital—a nice, clean outdoor smell."

"Yeah, I agree. I think there must be a jasmine vine somewhere close."

"That must be what I smell," he said. "What's going on, Andy? Are the media reporters bugging you as much as they are me?"

"I guess so. That plus other surprises since I've been here."

"What other surprises?"

"Surprises, disappointments, disbeliefs, fears, concerns—they are mind boggling. I thought you might help me work through it all."

"Give me an example. I know you don't buy into all the cover-up you've seen—all of the irregularities you've already uncovered," said Todd. "Anything else, other than the three P's we've talked about?"

Todd kept his eyes straight ahead as he talked. Andy pulled out the sheet of paper with Jake's notes on it and handed it to Todd. Andy watched closely for any unusual reaction. If there was anything that appeared alarming to Todd, he didn't show it.

"Karen gave this to you, didn't she?"

"Yeah, how did you know?"

"She gave me a copy also," he replied. "There's a lot going on around here, Andy. You'll stay healthier if you don't search for any answers."

Andy pointed to the item that mentioned Barbara. "That's the main reason I'm concerned with this."

"Curious about any of the other items?"

"Sure, mainly because of the comments I've heard from you and from Karen about the hazards of knowing too much," Andy answered.

They entered the deli and sat in a remote corner. Only a handful of patrons were inside, in contrast to the long line of people ordering to-go lunches. They checked their preferences for food and drink on the two individual one-page order menus and handed the slips of paper to the waiter. Todd silently gazed out the large plate glass window for a few moments. He turned to Andy with a look of seriousness that Andy had not seen before on Todd's face.

"Andy, ever since you've been here, I've been impressed by your moral dedication, your honesty, and your curiosity. I guess I'm a little envious of that. I've stayed around here for over three years, right in the middle of corrupt, illegal dealings, without doing anything about what I've seen. Now I'm trapped. If I report what I know or if I leave my employment, the consequences are the same. I'll be silenced. Sometimes it's all I can do to look at myself in the mirror."

"What do you mean you'll be 'silenced'?" asked Andy.

"Killed, Andy—I mean dead—so I won't talk."

"What!" said Andy. "It can't be that bad."

"Yeah ... every bit that bad."

"What about Karen?"

"I'm not sure," said Todd after hesitating a few moments. "She's in the same situation here that I'm in, but I don't know whether she wants out or not. Sometimes I think she's crying out for help. She knows everything—she can't leave. I've been trying to analyze why she gave you that copy of Jake's notes. Was it because she wanted you to be aware of the danger of knowing too much? I don't know, but it's worrisome. I imagine she told you to talk to me, didn't she?"

"Yes, she did. She sort of indicated you could explain some things to me. She asked me if I knew about the Qlozd Network. It's one of Jake's reminders."

"She knows but was reluctant to tell you. Wanted me to explain. I think she's worried about your safety, just as I am. Do you want to hear the whole story after what I've told you so far?"

"Yeah, I do, but for the reason I said. Jake's note mentioned my wife's name. That's the main reason why I want to know. I don't give a rat's ass about Qlozd

Network or Paretto. But if my wife is in danger in some way because of all this, I want to know the whole story. If you don't tell me, I'll find out some other way. I'm not going to worry about my own safety just because I know about a secret word that sounds like some sort of a cultist clan."

"I figured you'd say that," said Todd. "First, I don't mind telling you what I know. There's nothing you can say or do that would put me in any greater jeopardy than I already face."

"Can you tell me now?"

Todd looked at his watch. "Sure," he said. "We have an hour or so. Let's have another cup of coffee after we finish our sandwiches. I'm just now coming alive."

Andy stood and moved toward the coffee kiosk. As he filled his and Todd's cups, he thought of Barbara again. She still hadn't called to let him know definitely if she was going to Dallas with Leanne. That was not like Barbara. He checked his cell phone and then remembered: *Damn it, I turned it off so Todd and I wouldn't be disturbed while we talked, and I didn't put it on vibrate.* He checked the call log—there had been one missed call. Now he *would* worry. She probably had gone to Dallas with Leanne. But then, what could possible happen with all those FBI agents looking after them?

Andy returned to the table carrying two mugs of fresh black coffee plus a plate with two pieces of apple strudel, which he placed in front of Todd. "Best way to top off corn beef sandwiches," he said, grinning. "Guaranteed to prevent indigestion."

"Come on, Andy," said Todd with a chuckle. "I'm already suspicious of an ulcer."

"You'll feel better after you talk about it."

"Okay, cut in with questions any time during this sordid story. To begin with, you're going to doubt that this could happen."

"I'm ready. After a few weeks around this place, I have no doubts about anything that might happen."

Todd sipped on his coffee, gazed past Andy with a vacant stare, and was quiet for a few moments before speaking.

"I came here as an administrative resident almost four years ago—just as you have done," he said finally. "Also, like you, I was full of idealistic expectations about delivering health care to the sick and needy, thinking I had come to a place that epitomized excellence in patient care—with one mission in mind: the highest quality of patient care regardless of the patient's ability to pay. God! How mistaken could I have been?"

Andy laughed. "You've been eavesdropping on my innermost reticent thoughts."

"I've suspected that of you. So has Karen. That's why she slipped that note to you. She won't talk—I can assure you of that."

"How does she put up with it day after day?"

"An easy answer: to save her job and to save her life. She's afraid to speak and afraid to trust anyone."

"Keep going, Todd."

"To summarize the situation briefly, the Trinitus system has zero morals, zero integrity, zero compassion—none of the qualities you would expect in a healthcare system owned and managed by a religious organization."

"How could this happen?"

"It started years ago, actually, when hospitals and all healthcare providers faced a staggering number of negligence lawsuits and unreasonable judgment awards. That's when Alan Shipman, president and CEO of the giant Trinitus system, decided to do something about it. He teamed with his attorney friend in Dallas, Richard Weatherford—a strong supporter of Trinitus and a heavy contributor to the Republican Party—to come up with a plan to fight what they called 'lawsuit abuse.'"

"Is that our accident victim, Richard Weatherford," asked Andy.

"One and the same. Initially their ideas were valid and probably effective to some degree. They discontinued premium-heavy protective insurance and became self-insured. They assembled a team of crack lawyers and expert witnesses and told the legal community that they were not going to settle cases out of court any longer; they were taking them to jury trials. That too was effective—they had public sentiment on their side, and since they were representing a religious organization, they were winning the cases that went to juries. And then one Anthony Joberst entered the scene."

Todd's last statement jerked Andy to attention. "Not the judge whose baby was abducted?" said Andy, trying to hide the shock and remembering his instructions from the Agent Walton not to reveal any confidential information.

"Yeah, same one, Andy," he answered. Todd eyed Andy expectantly. "You seem to be bothered by that."

"Of course. With my wife's name on Jake's reminder list, I'm bothered about everything you're describing."

"I see your concern, but it's probably just a coincidence."

"Go on. I guess I'm a little too suspicious. My curiosity is piqued, however."

"You're probably wondering why Judge Joberst, a federal judge, would have anything to do with malpractice lawsuits, which go to district courts. He wasn't, initially, but the Trinitus hospitals were facing government charges of alleged fraudulent Medicare billing and RICO violations in connection with the hospital's joint-venture and kickback deals with physicians on its medical staff. Put more simply: charges that the hospital had 'bought' physician support by using certain rebates to doctors for admitting patients to a Trinitus hospital—strictly against the law, as you well know."

"Yeah, I've read about the OIG, the Office of the Inspector General, and its investigation of hospitals. But what could one federal judge like Judge Joberst do that would make a difference? There are many federal courts and judges. How did that work?"

"I'm coming to that. Joberst, Weatherford, and Alan Shipman devised a plan, using the Dallas district as a pilot program, whereby all cases involving Trinitus were assigned to Judge Joberst's court. Of course, his rulings always favored the hospital. Trinitus, in return for the favor, showered the judge liberally with bribe money. And of course, Richard Weatherford was paid top money for his legal fees."

"How could they do that without being detected? Surely someone would have suspected that sort of kickback in time?" asked Andy, shaking his head in disbelief.

"Even if someone knew, Andy, they weren't brave enough to do anything about it. Of course, Trinitus hid the 'expense' of the compensation with some creative accounting, always transferring the funds to the judge's offshore account."

"Unbelievable!"

"So, when Alan Shipman, Richard Weatherford, and Judge Joberst saw that the pilot program worked, they expanded it to all four federal districts in Texas. Joberst carefully selected judges that he knew would be cooperative. That was the beginning. At first, it was limited to the federal courts. There were relatively few cases at first, so they managed to expand the concept to include a select few district courts where the judges were elected instead of appointed. They compensated those judges by contributing heavily, illegally as you know, to the individual judge's campaign funds."

"I don't understand how they could manipulate a judge's docket by assigning him certain cases."

"I'll explain that. Look on Jake's list. Do you see the note 'Call Paretto'?"

"Yeah, who is Paretto? I wondered about that. That name keeps coming up."

"Paretto is the don of the largest, most powerful Mafia organization in the country. He is into every illegal operation you can imagine—drug trafficking, gambling, extortion, money laundering. He is the FBI's number-one enigma. Judge Joberst became acquainted with Paretto when members of his gang were charged with some criminal activity, drug related. They came before the judge in federal court. Of course, all of those cases were dismissed, usually based on insufficient evidence, and Paretto rewarded the judge handsomely."

"How did it come about that all those cases were assigned to the same court?"

"I'll never know why someone hasn't seen through that scam. Paretto has a team of the most astute computer hackers in the world. It is phenomenal what they can devise. If a case in question should go to a certain court, Paretto's hacker intervenes and reassigns the case to that of a cooperative judge."

"Incredible!" said Andy. "So the conspiracy has continued to grow undetected?"

"You better believe it. It's grown by the millions," Todd answered. "But that was only the beginning. The founding group—Weatherford, Shipman, and Joberst—decided that they needed to expand and needed further protection from government audits. So they organized themselves into a paper entity and named it the Qlozd Network. It's pronounced 'closed.' I have no idea why they picked the name except I think it might mean that it is a closed membership. They included themselves and the handful of select federal judges from each district in Texas, but they didn't show any of the judges as original investors, only Joberst, Weatherford, and Shipman.

"On the surface, Qlozd is an exclusive real estate holding company with luxury resorts all over the world. The accounting matrixes of the company are so complex that it is impossible for anyone to unravel them and see the company for what it really is. It's an ingenuous accounting product."

"How did they come up with such intricate accounting system? Don't tell me. It was Paretto again?"

"Right! He has used cover-up accounting for years to hide his cash flow by channeling it through his beer distributing company. So it was a perfect match. Now we have Paretto providing the computer technology *and* the accounting skills. So what comes next? He uses the accounting program with which his accountants are familiar and, for a healthy fee to Qlozd, uses the hospital system as a conduit to launder excess cash straight to offshore banking facilities."

"My God, Todd!" said Andy. "I suppose each partner in the Qlozd Network receives fabulous dividends each year."

"Seven-figure numbers," said Todd. "I saw a report once by accident. Jake is a member, I think because he knows about the Judge Joberst and Weatherford relationship. They made him a partner to keep him quiet."

"What kind of relationship?"

"They're both gay—'companions,' I believe, is the word they use. You asked why I was up all night? Judge Joberst secretly came to visit Richard Weatherford at midnight last night. Jake assigned me the duty of meeting him at the hospital and secretly escorting him to Weatherford's room for a clandestine meeting. Jake even tried to make me believe that Judge Joberst was some sort of secret service investigator from the President's staff."

"So that explains why you're washed out today. How do you know they are gay? Are you just guessing? Both guys are married, and Weatherford has two daughters."

"Jake let it slip."

"Todd, what would happen if an administrator in one of the hospitals really got curious and started some sort of an inquiry into Qlozd Network activities?"

"He would disappear. No one would ever know what happened to him. So now you know what will happen to me and to Karen if we slip up. If you get too curious it will happen to you."

Andy stared straight at Todd without blinking. "Tell me this, Todd," said Andy. "Why is Barbara's name on that list?"

Todd avoided eye contact with Andy, focused his vision on the plate, and picked at the remaining strudel crumbs. A half-minute passed without his saying a word. Andy squirmed in his chair. "Damn it, Todd, tell me if you know."

"I am not sure, but here's what I think. You know what constitutes a sentinel event in a hospital, don't you?"

"God, yes, we had that pounded into our brains in school," Andy replied. "It's an occurrence in the hospital that results in an unanticipated death or major permanent loss of function. We had to memorize that definition."

"And what are some examples?"

"Such things as medication error, blood transfusion reactions, surgery on the wrong patient or wrong body part, suicide, and ... oh, of course, the abduction of a newborn. I see where you're going."

"Here's the pitch, Andy. Several Trinitus Hospitals, including Trinitus Dallas, have had more than their share of sentinel events. By JCAHO standards, the occurrences were supposed to have been analyzed and corrected with action plans. Trinitus has been negligent in doing that. About a year ago, all Trinitus Hospitals were placed on accreditation watch. They have to respond to requirements of the joint commission within a certain time, or they are in danger of losing their accreditation. No JCAHO accreditation, no Medicare accreditation, and tremendous losses in income."

"So the abduction could be a major blow to Trinitus."

"Absolutely!" said Todd. "They are required to have a security system in place and they didn't. An abduction charge could be devastating to Trinitus. They are going to have to pull a rabbit from their hat."

"And that's why Barbara's testimony is important to Trinitus," said Andy. "And they know that Barbara would never lie about the security tags."

"Right!" said Todd. "That's my opinion, Andy, on why they are so concerned about Barbara's welfare. Keep in mind they would probably rather just see Barbara disappear. That's what's worrisome."

Andy slammed the palm of his hand on the table so hard that the dishes and silverware rattled. "Damn ... damn those people, Todd," said Andy with fire in his eyes. "We need to get out of this trap, Todd. You need to get out. You can't just keep living with this guilt, living a lie. Talk to a lawyer. Arrange to tell your story."

"I've thought about it a thousand times, Andy. I don't know how. Thank God I don't have a wife and kids. They would be in constant danger if I even hinted that I was going to divulge these guys' secret. I've thought of getting a lawyer to help me file a whistleblower suit. But I know these people, Andy. They are ruthless. Besides, filing a suit means four or five years before it's settled, and I would be in constant danger the entire time. If you are smart, Andy, you will act dumb for the rest of the year and then steal quietly away from here without revealing that you've ever seen anything irregular."

"I can't do that, Todd. I guess that's where we're different. I can't ignore it all. I'm going to search for hard evidence and do something about it. I don't know what or how, but I will not betray your confidence, Todd. Trust me."

"I do. I just worry that something will happen to you and Barbara if you cross the Qlozd Network. You're determined to dig further, aren't you?"

"Yeah, something just keeps bugging me about what I have seen."

"Now I feel guilty now that I've told you the story."

"Put that out of your mind. Before you opened up to me, I knew there was illegal activity. I just didn't realize the extent. If you decide to help me accumulate the evidence, feel free to join me."

"I'll think about it. I don't think I'm that brave. Be careful, Andy."

After Todd and Andy parted, Andy's concerns about Barbara again surfaced. Where was Barbara that very minute? Why hadn't she called? Had she decided to go with Leanne? *Damn it,* he thought. *I don't want her to go to Dallas with Leanne. I don't know why exactly, but I can't shake the feeling that something is going to happen.*

# 33

Leanne, dressed in a lightweight robe, quietly slipped out onto the balcony of the tenth-story condo, hoping she had not disturbed anyone. She glanced at her watch—seven-fifteen in the morning. The sun, against a bright blue sky, blazed just enough to take the chill out of the early-morning air. She was sure Andy had already left for work, and she had heard no sound to indicate that Barbara was up yet. She sat in one of the cushioned chairs near the edge of the terrace and enjoyed the view of the verdant park that bordered the expansive lake, already peppered with the many sailboats carrying white sails fluffed by the gentle breeze. *A perfect setting to meditate and plan*, she told herself as she leaned back in the chair and basked in the warm sunrays.

She knew the call from Agent Walton would be coming soon, but knowing didn't lessen her anxiety. The thought of any encounter with Anthony sent chills up her spine. The comfortable feeling of being with Barbara and Andy these last few days had introduced her to whole new world. Now, during the TV taping, she would have to stand beside Anthony and pretend. But she had to go through with it, had to make an appeal to the public if there was a chance that she would see her baby again.

She could only hope someone would hear her message and provide a clue to help them find the baby—*if he was still alive.* The sound of those silent words brought tears to her eyes. She didn't bother to blot them and allowed her cheeks to become glazed with moisture.

The opening and closing of the door jarred her from her reverie. She sat upright and quickly swiped her robe sleeve across her face. Maybe Barbara wouldn't notice the tears.

"Good morning!" said Barbara. "What a beautiful day. What a beautiful view."

"Did I awaken you?" said Leanne. "I tried to be quiet."

"No, no," Barbara replied, laughing. "There's no sleep after Andy is up and getting ready to leave for work. He always misplaces something—his nametag or his cell phone. I have to get up and help him search." Barbara reached over and gently stroked Leanne's wet cheek. She looked into Leanne's eyes for a few moments without speaking and then said, "Let me bring you some coffee."

"Thanks," she said. Then she hopped to her feet. "Sit here. I'll bring coffee to you."

"How are you feeling? All ready for the big day?"

"I think so," Leanne answered. "I'll be right back."

She returned, placed the coffee mugs on the side table, and sat in an adjacent chair. After a half-minute of silence, Leanne turned toward Barbara. "I am so nervous about today. I've never been able to speak before a crowd."

"It'll go fine," said Barbara. "Just stay calm and say what you feel."

"What if I start crying?"

"It's all right to show emotion. It will get the attention that you need. Would you like me to go with you?"

"No, I've got to do it alone. I've got to build a life for myself, Barbara, and I have got to take control of it. I just wish Mark would be standing alongside me."

"He'll know what you're going through. We'll let him know as soon as it is over."

Leanne became silent and gazed out over the horizon, almost as if she were in a trance. Barbara sipped on her coffee and remained silent. Finally Leanne, with a terrified look on her face, reached out and took Barbara's hand in hers. "I have a weird feeling about today."

"Don't think that way. You'll be safe. Mr. Walton will see to it that you are protected."

Leanne kept her eyes fixed on Barbara. "If something should happen to me, will you keep trying to find my baby?"

"Of course I will. Now get those thoughts out of your head. Everything is going to be fine. We should be hearing from Mr. Walton soon. You need to be ready to go when he calls."

"Of course. As always, you are right," she answered as she retired to her bedroom to dress. "Barbara, if you have time, would you help me pick out my clothes for the taping."

"Sure. Be glad to."

\* \* \* \*

The phone rang. The security officer announced that Agent Walton was on his way up. Moments later, the musical doorbell sounded his arrival.

"I know you must be tense," Ralph said to Leanne after they had gathered for a briefing. "I want to go over a few items with you both before we leave."

"Barbara's not going with me," said Leanne.

"She won't appear on TV with you, but I think it might be a good idea for her to go. This is going to be an emotional event for you. You may need her support."

"I don't mind going," said Barbara.

"Will there be any danger to her?" asked Leanne.

"Both of you will be watched every second from the time we leave here until we return. Here's the way it will go: We will land at Love Field and be whisked to the studio by a heavily guarded limousine. We'll enter the studio through the back entrance. There will be more agents and law enforcement officials around you than you have ever seen. Make sure neither of you wanders off. If you need to go to the restroom, there will be several female agents that you can ask to go with you."

"I'm not sure I like that idea," said Leanne.

"It's a safety measure. There have been two attempts at your life. We don't want another. I don't mean to frighten you, but there is the possibility of danger. So far, it seems as though someone has anticipated our every move."

"I don't want anything to happen to Barbara," said Leanne, "and I don't want to be around Anthony any longer than necessary."

"I understand, and we will deal with that. How do you feel about going, Barbara?"

"I think I should stay close to Leanne. She is afraid it's too dangerous, but this is going to be difficult for her and I want to be there for her."

"Good," he replied. "You are both very brave. Leanne, we'll keep Judge Joberst in a separate room until it's time for you to appear in front of the microphone."

"Thank you," she said. "I don't want to be in the same room with him one minute longer than necessary."

"Before the taping, the makeup people will do a few things to make you look like a distressed parent."

"That won't be difficult," said Leanne, a faint smile crossing her face.

"The studio writers have prepared a script for you to follow, and you will have a few minutes to familiarize yourself with what they suggest that you say," Agent Walton continued. "But you should feel free to say anything you feel. Don't hold back your emotions. Cry if you want to."

"What about clothing?" asked Barbara. "We were just trying to decide what she should wear."

"The main thing is not to wear a lot of jewelry. Too much glitter is distracting. As far as a dress, wear something that is easily identified, like bright pink."

"I have just the dress," said Leanne.

"Fine," Agent Walton replied. "Now, here is how it will go: The interview will be aired live on morning shows today throughout the country. Then the taping portion will be broadcast every hour for two days. This will be viewed by hundreds of thousands of people. The contact phone number will appear on the screen, and we have operators ready to take calls. We are hoping for some results here even though we have delayed getting the message to the public."

"The possible response is what's keeping me going," said Leanne.

"What do we do after the taping?" asked Barbara.

"We're out of there as quickly as possible," Agent Walton replied. "The first segment is a live appeal, and the station will announce it ahead of time to encourage viewers to tune in. That will trigger the media's interest. The reporters have been hungry for days for some news of the kidnapping. We'll try to escape as fast as we can through the rear exit of the studio and then race to the airport, but we will likely run into the news media people at the studio. We must guard against your getting surrounded and out of our protective range at that time—that holds for both of you."

"What should I do, Mr. Walton?" asked Barbara.

"Stay in the shadows as much as you can until we are ready to exit the studio; then, stay close to Leanne to help her get through the crowd. And both of you, don't answer any questions."

"I'll just be glad when it's over," said Leanne.

"Of course you will. We'll be ready to dash to the airport as soon as you're dressed. You have to be at the studio by 11:45."

"I need to let Andy know I'm going," said Barbara. "I hope he's not in a meeting."

"Good idea to let him know," replied Ralph. "It might be after dark before we get back to Westlake. If you can't reach him, you can try again while we're in flight. Are we all ready?" asked Ralph.

\* \* \* \*

## *Dallas*

They had exchanged few words on the flight to Dallas. Leanne stayed close to Barbara, either clutching her hand or huddling close, much like a frightened child whose parent had taken him to a doctor's office. Once in the studio, they were ushered into a private waiting area. The only sound came from the giant wall-mounted plasma TV. The 11:30 news and talk show was underway when they arrived.

"How do I look?" Leanne asked Barbara. "As scared as I feel?"

"Once you're on the air you'll be fine. It's normal to be a little frightened at a time like this."

"Thank you, Dr. Goldeyer." Leanne laughed. "First time I have laughed all day."

"Now that's more like it. I think the makeup person is here. Don't ask me how you look after she gets through with you." Barbara joined Leanne in laughter.

Just before the *Noon News with Crystal Sommers* broke for a commercial, Crystal announced,

*"Our next guest will be award-winning author James Torrance, who will tell us about his latest novel, just released; and after that we have Judge and Mrs. Anthony Joberst, parents of the baby recently abducted from a hospital right here in Dallas ... stay tuned."*

"Almost time," said Barbara. "Just relax and speak from your heart. The words will come—believe me. You look fine."

A smiling, uniformed attendant entered the waiting room. Her hurried conduct signaled that it was time to move. "I'm here to escort you to the filming stage. We need to hurry so Crystal can speak with you for a couple of minutes before you go live."

"Where is Anthony?" Leanne asked.

"The judge will meet you there," she answered as she hastily took Leanne by the arm and guided her toward the door. "After the broadcast you'll return to this room. Your friends will watch the interview from here. Make sure you have tissue handy to blot your eyes."

"Good luck!" said Barbara. "I'll be right here when you finish."

Soon after Leanne was seated, Judge Joberst climbed up on the stage and took his place beside her. Studio technicians busily adjusted their microphones and the high-intensity light fixtures next to the cameras.

"Crystal will be here in a few moments," said one technician. "Don't forget to look straight into the cameras when you speak."

A few seconds lapsed with Anthony and Leanne seated side by side. Anthony flashed a broad smile and leaned close to Leanne as he whispered, "This is futile, and you know it. You'll never get your baby back. I'll see that you don't. If he is even alive, that Marchesa creep has him hidden somewhere. We're wasting time here."

Leanne matched Anthony's false smile. "Why'd you come? Always worried about image, aren't you. You're cruel, despicable scum. You just hope he's dead so the public won't find out that you're not the father."

"You bitch," said Anthony, maintaining his façade. "I'm sure you're sleeping with that bastard somewhere right now, aren't you?"

Crystal bounced onto the stage and took her place in front of her guests. Lights, camera, and microphones were hastily readjusted. She had only a couple of minutes to introduce herself and explain the procedure to be followed, but the casual, soft, reassuring tone of her voice helped Leanne relax a bit in spite of Anthony's caustic remarks. "Five seconds," said the camera man.

The interview went smoothly. Although it lasted only a short time, the message was profoundly effective. Leanne presented the tear-jerking, emotional appeal of a distraught mother who had lost her first and only child. Anthony managed to profess an opinion that the perpetrators had probably acted out of bitterness toward the parents because of some courtroom decision he had handed down. In so doing, he painted himself as a man dedicated to justice in spite of the risks and sacrifices he had to endure.

Leanne returned to the waiting arms of Barbara, both girls still dabbing at their eyes with tissue. At Agent Walton's insistence, they quickly moved toward the rear exit. As Walton had predicted, a mob of reporters, photographers, and cameramen had gathered. The reporters all screamed questions at Leanne and Agent Walton at the same time:

"Do you have any suspects?"

"Why is Mrs. Joberst in hiding?"

"What about ransom demands?"

"Do you think the baby is still alive?"

Ralph said to the two women, "This is the most critical time. Stay close to me and to the other agents. Don't stop to answer questions, no matter what. Move fast!"

A phalanx of a dozen or more FBI agents and Dallas police officers assigned to assist the agents parted the ocean of reporters and formed a path to the waiting cars. The street behind the studio was packed with a caravan of curious passersby in vehicles that crept along slowly. All eyes were on the exiting assemblage. The agents scrutinized every face among the crowd and watched for any unusual motion.

No one, however, paid particular attention to the armored car in the line of vehicles—a commonplace site in downtown Dallas on a busy day—or to the flash that come from one of its diminutive side windows. The one loud gunshot echoed off the surrounding skyscrapers and could have easily have been mistaken for two or three shots. The armored car suddenly cut out of the line of vehicles, jumped the curb to the adjacent sidewalk, and raced away.

"Hit the deck. Down everybody, down!" cried Agent Walton as he drew his gun and raced to the street, his agents following close behind. The loud screams from the scattering crowd muffled his commands. Leanne stood motionless, staring into space. Barbara reached out and grabbed Leanne's left upper arm to pull her to the ground. Barbara's hand and arm immediately became slick with a gush of bright red blood. Leanne appeared dazed and speechless, her eyes glassy. Her limp body folded to the ground into Barbara's arms.

"Help, someone! She's been shot. Help!" cried Barbara. Within seconds, the upper half of Leanne's pink dress became saturated with blood. Three FBI agents surrounded the girls and crouched over them.

Barbara freed herself from the hovering agents to check on Leanne. "Leanne! Leanne!" she cried frantically, cradling Leanne's head in her arms. "Speak to me, Leanne!" When Barbara tried to loosen the dress and locate the site of the wound, the blood poured even more profusely, seeping through the dress and pooling on the walkway. Barbara clenched her hand into a fist and forcefully applied pressure over the area from which the flow of blood seemed to be the greatest.

"Somebody get me a towel, quick! Help, help!" Barbara yelled as loud as she could to rise above the clamor of mass panic. "We need an ambulance here, fast!"

Barbara turned her attention to Leanne. Her level of consciousness was waxing and waning; beads of perspiration sprouted from her pallid face. "Leanne, listen to me. You're gonna be all right. Just stay with me. Do you hear me?"

Leanne opened her eyes briefly, smiled, and said, "Take care of my ..."

"I promise, Leanne. We'll find your baby, and when you're well, you'll have him. Can you hear me? You and Mark will have him."

When Barbara mentioned Mark's name, Leanne opened her eyes again and smiled faintly. "I'm dying, Barbara. Thank you for every …"

"You're not going to die. Listen to me!" pleaded Barbara.

Leanne closed her eyes and lapsed into unconsciousness just as the EMS arrived and took over her care. Barbara, sobbing uncontrollably, had to be pried loose so the techs could seal the bubbling, gushing gap in Leanne's upper chest with a pressure dressing. Barbara held on to Leanne's hand as long as she could, but an EMS tech forced her aside, attached an oxygen mask to Leanne, and began trying to start an IV line.

The other EMS tech shouted, "Wait 'til we get her in the ambulance. This is a scoop and run. Hurry!" They carefully rolled a stretcher under Leanne and quickly loaded her into the ambulance. Barbara followed close alongside the gurney and began climbing into the vehicle as they loaded Leanne. The EMS tech put his hand out and said, "Okay, we'll take it from here."

Barbara stared at him with a determined look on her face. "I'm not leaving her," she said. The techs paused and looked at each other for a second without answering. Finally, one spoke. "It's against the rules but climb aboard. Try to stay out of our way."

They strapped down the stretcher and one tech turned on the two-way radio.

"Parkland ER, Number 16 reporting in. Scoop and run case; gunshot; long-range rifle; twenty-eight- to thirty-year-old female; open chest wound; left-upper chest; blood loss over a 1000; pressure and seal over wound; B/P dropping; respiratory rate increasing; pulse rate 120; patient unconscious; zero sounds left chest; getting central line in place; thoracotomy tray ready. Advise."

The voice on the other end responded, "Dr. Searle here. Start Dextran as soon as line open; tap chest; if blood, insert chest tube stat. Get at least two more peripheral lines open. Elevate and wrap legs with pressure bandage. Use morphine if needed and bag if you need to. Move fast. OR and surgeon will be waiting. Does she need to be intubated?"

"Not yet," was the reply, "but we're ready if we have to."

Barbara's hands were put to work—holding syringes, pumping the Ambu bag when asked, and helping wrap Leanne's legs with elastic bandages.

The tech in the back finally asked, "You're a nurse, aren't you?"

"Yes, but I work in a nursery. Not used to this."

"You saved her life, you know."

"What do you mean?"

"The pressure to the wound to stop the blood. She must have lost a major artery in the chest or neck to lose that much blood."

"You think she'll make it?"

"Maybe. We'll be there in seconds, then straight to the OR. They'll patch the artery and close the chest. Are you related to her?"

"No, just friends."

The winding down of the sirens and the abrupt turn told Barbara they had arrived at Parkland Hospital Emergency room.

\* \* \* \*

At the rear entrance of the studio the pandemonium finally settled down. Agent Walton had heard the EMS tech say Parkland Hospital and shouted orders to his agents to go to there and be prepared to stand guard. He searched for Barbara and found her just as she was climbing into the ambulance with Leanne.

Across the street, a dark limousine with heavily tinted windows had parked in the best location possible to witness the catastrophe. The rear window was slightly lowered, and occasional plumes of thick gray smoke—cigar smoke—rose out of it and into the air.

# 34

## Dallas, Parkland Hospital

At the emergency room unloading dock, the ambulance doors swung open and they were met by an already alerted crew of doctors, nurses and technicians. Barbara was shoved aside. The ER personnel grabbed the stretcher and raced through the emergency entrance—shouting terms with which Barbara, a nursery nurse, was unfamiliar. She stood by and watched as the gurney was pushed rapidly toward a pair of double swinging doors over which a sign read "Operating Room—Authorized Personnel Only."

Barbara never remembered feeling so alone and helpless. She was covered with blood from head to foot, her hair disheveled, her face distorted from the distress she had endured. When the doors to the OR swung shut, she struggled to suppress tears at the realization that she might not ever see Leanne alive again.

Soon a mature Afro-American woman carrying a clipboard and wearing scrubs approached her. Barbara welcomed the kind, caring look on her smiling face.

"I'm Calista Williams, the emergency department nurse coordinator," she said, "Just call me Callie, honey. You look like you need some help."

"Thank you, Miss Williams. I need to call my husband in Westlake, but I've lost my cell phone *and* my purse. I guess it got lost when Leanne was shot."

"Are you a family member?" Callie asked as she guided Barbara to a chair, applied a blood pressure cuff to her arm, and checked her pulse rate.

"No ma'am," Barbara answered. She could feel moisture forming in her eyes. "She's a friend. Is she going to be all right?"

"She has a serious wound to the chest, my dear, and I can tell from the looks of you that she's lost a lot of blood. But she's young and strong and the doctors are working with her right now. I just imagine she'll do fine. Now, let's see what we can do about you. Were you injured in any way?"

"No ma'am. Just scared. I'm a nursery nurse, Miss Williams. I've never gone through anything like this. Can I give blood for my friend?"

"Sure you can, but I don't think you're in any shape for that right now."

"I feel terrible. I don't know what to do ... I can't even think straight."

"Post-traumatic shock, sweetie. You learned about that in school, but you've forgotten all about it working in a nursery. We need to get that blood off you and get you out of those clothes. Follow me," she snapped with the tenor of a drill sergeant. "We're going into the nurse's lounge. You can make your call from there after you get cleaned up a bit."

"When will we know about Leanne?" asked Barbara.

"In due time, honey. I'll let you know as soon as we hear something."

They entered the dressing room. Barbara looked at herself in the mirror as she began undressing. "My God," she cried, wiping the blood from her face and hair.

"Now, just you get in that shower," Callie said. "There are clean scrubs on this shelf. I'm going to find you a cold drink. After you bathe, use that phone over there and call your husband. I'm going to call the police and tell them to find your phone and purse. I'll be back in a few minutes." She headed out the door.

Barbara called after her before the door closed. "Callie, how can I ever thank you. You've been a nurse a long time haven't you?"

"A long time, honey. Gets in your blood. You can't live without doing something for others."

"That's the kind of nurse I want to be."

"You already are, dear. I bet you stayed right by your friend while she come near bleedin' out."

Barbara cupped both hands over her face and shook her head from side to side. "I couldn't do anything to help her, Callie. She was unconscious ... she was dying."

"I've already heard, sweetie. You put pressure against that hole in her chest. Saved her life," said Callie as she slowly closed the door.

*  *  *  *

Callie returned just as Barbara finished dressing after her shower. The clean, dry scrubs felt delightful. She crammed her blood-soaked clothes in the plastic sack that Callie had laid out for her, placed her stained shoes on top, and donned a pair of disposable covers to take the place of shoes.

"You look much better, sweetie," said Callie. "Now, sip on this Coke while you call. I wrote down the code number you'll need for a long-distance call. You want me to get you a small dose of Valium or Xanax?"

"No, thanks, Callie," she replied as she dialed Andy's number. "I can handle it."

"Oh, I forgot. Your purse will be delivered here in a few minutes. And there is a police officer out there. Said he knows you; his name is Lieutenant Blake somebody. He wants to get your story as soon as you finish talking to your man. Want me to leave while you talk to him?"

"No, stay if you have time. He'll probably want to talk to you about Leanne's condition. Any word from the operating room?"

"Now you quit fretting, little gal. She must be doing all right or they would have let us know by now. You're probably looking at five or six hours. Make your call."

Andy answered on the first ring. "Barbara, are you all right?"

"I'm fine, Andy. Shaken but uninjured. You won't believe what happened …"

She narrated the tragic event in detail.

"And you were standing right next to her when she was shot? You could have been hit," he yelled.

"But I wasn't, Andy."

"I'll be there as quickly as I can."

"I'm all right, Andy. Just take care of your work."

"Are any of the agents there guarding you?"

"I haven't talked to Mr. Walton, but I'm sure we're—"

"She's fine, Andy," yelled Callie. "FBI all over the place."

"Who was that, Barbara?"

"That was Callie. She's the charge nurse in the emergency department."

"How is Leanne now?"

"She's still in the operating room. Callie says the surgery will last five or six hours. It's a miracle she's alive, Andy."

"What does Mr. Walton say? Do you want me to come there?"

"I'm fine, Andy. I need some clothes. Everything I had on is soaked in—"

Callie waved her hand at Barbara. "Don't you worry, honey. We'll take care of getting you spruced up again."

"Did you hear that, Andy? That was Callie. She has been an angel for me."

"Do you have your credit card?"

"It's in my purse, Andy. They're bringing it to me."

"I think I'd better come to Dallas."

"It's all right, Andy. Don't worry."

"How can I not worry? Damn it, Barbara. "I want you here. I'm going to tell Mr. Walton to send you home."

"I can't leave her, Andy. She doesn't have anyone else. I'll be all right here. Please understand, Andy."

Callie grabbed the phone out of Barbara's hand. "My name is Calista Williams, Mr...."

She stopped and looked at Barbara inquisitively. "Goldeyer, Andy Goldeyer, Callie," said Barbara.

"I'm a nurse here in this ER, Mr. Goldeyer. Now you listen good, young man. Your wife is a nurse, a brave nurse, dedicated to her profession. She knows what she has to do. You should be proud of her."

There was total silence on the line, except for the muffled, halting sound of Andy's breathing, as if he were suppressing sobs. "Please take care of her, Miss Williams," said Andy finally, his voice barely audible.

"I'll do that. Now you tell her you love her," said Callie. "And in a few days—as soon as you can get away from your work—get yourself up here to Dallas." She handed the phone to Barbara and quickly turned her back as she swiped a tear from her face with the back of her hand.

Callie's cell phone rang. She checked the calling number and hurriedly headed for the door. She stopped for a moment and turned to Barbara.

"Now you lie down over there, close your eyes and relax for a few minutes. I'll be back as soon as I can."

"Than you, Callie."

She had been gone only a few minutes when there was a knock on the door. Barbara panicked for a second. She had to get over this fear—fear of being terrified at every sound and every person. She hesitated before opening.

"It's Agent Walton, Barbara."

Barbara recognized his voice, finally and opened the door. Agent Walton stood before her. Barbara felt a wave of relief overcome her. She fell into Ralph's arms and broke down into sobs. Ralph held her close for a few moments until she could compose herself.

"Have you heard how Leanne is doing?" Barbara asked, seating herself at the table in the center of the lounge.

"I'm told she is stable. They are about halfway through with the surgery," he replied as he sat on a bench across the table from her.

"Do they have enough blood for her?"

Ralph grinned. "More than enough. Every agent I have on this assignment wants to replace blood they used from the bank."

"What happened, Mr. Walton?" she asked.

"We had all the coverage needed when you came out of the studio. We even checked each car passing by, but the armored car deceived us. Two guys hijacked the vehicle, tossed the driver out onto the street, and managed to get in the traffic line of curious passersby. They abandoned the car a couple of blocks away and vanished. We might be able to I.D. the men from fingerprints and possibly through witnesses who saw them run away."

"What else can happen, Mr. Walton?"

"It's hard to stay focused when we've had this many setbacks. We just have to keep going and hope for a break. The nurse outside said you want to stay with Leanne."

"She is so alone, Mr. Walton."

"We'll protect you, Barbara. I know you and Andy are skeptical of that, but trust me: we are determined to work our way through this quagmire, and your help with Leanne is invaluable." Ralph took a few steps around the room, his hands clasped tightly together, his voice near cracking. "I dread the thought of not finding the baby alive—the impact it will have on Leanne, as well as all of us. We need you around to the very end."

"I know what you mean," said Barbara, a wistful look in her eyes. "I'm not sure I could take what Leanne is going through."

"Just stay with her, Barbara. Do I need to talk to Andy?"

"I think he's all right. Callie talked to him. She is so kind to help me."

"I talked to the hospital people about your staying with Leanne and about finding a place for you in the hospital while you're here. Wherever you and Leanne are, you'll be guarded."

"We're getting used to that, but I cringe every time anyone opens that door."

"I understand, Barbara. Believe me ... an agent is guarding that door every minute."

"Keep looking for the baby, Mr. Walton. Do you think you'll get some response from the broadcast?"

"We're hoping. Barbara, if we should get a lead, do you think you could positively identify the baby? I have nightmares thinking of someone turning in a different baby just for the ransom. We can get positive identification, but the emotional trauma to Leanne would be devastating."

"No problem," she answered. "I'd know that birthmark anywhere."

"Good," said Ralph. "Does anyone else know about it?"

"I don't think so," she replied. "I made a note of it in the chart before I left the morning of the abduction, and I didn't see a comment by any of the other nurses about the birthmark."

"That's going to be important when we find the baby," he said. "You noticed I said 'when' and not 'if?'"

"Yes, and I am so glad."

"We'll find it—just keep telling Leanne," Ralph said. "Barbara, an agent will be assigned to you. We've secured the hospital, so you mustn't go outside. You can wait here until you hear from the surgeons. The hospital administration has made this room available for your exclusive use. However, I'd like you to avoid roaming around the hospital as much as possible."

"I'll be careful," she said. "Thank you, Mr. Walton, for letting me cry on your shoulder."

Ralph's face blossomed crimson. "We're all proud of the cooperation you and Andy have given us, Barbara, and we don't want anything to happen to either or you."

"I think Mark should get a report about her condition."

"I'm going to leave that up to you. There's no reason to restrict him. It might get tense if he and the judge both show up at the same time."

"I understand, but I feel obligated to let him know what's going on." Barbara slumped in her chair and gazed at the floor with a wistful look in her eyes.

"You want me to call him, don't you?"

"Would you?" she answered, suddenly coming alive. "It would be far more effective if you called. Then he would know that he wouldn't be stopped if he came here. Think what that would mean to Leanne."

"Yeah, I think she deserves a break. But my calling doesn't take him off the suspect list."

Barbara looked at Ralph and with a twinkle in her eyes.

"Thank you, Mr. Walton."

\* \* \* \*

The waiting time crept by with agonizing slowness. Barbara, lying on the couch, closed her eyes a few times thinking she could steal a few minutes of sleep, although that was impossible with Callie bouncing in and out to give her reports. Agent Walton dropped by a few times, but his cell phone calls kept him from staying still for more than a few minutes at a time. Each time there was a knock on the door, Barbara jumped, thinking the surgeon might be standing outside ready to give a report.

A full two hours had passed when Agent Walton tapped on the door and stuck his head in. "You have a visitor, Barbara." He held the door open and motioned for Mark Marchesa to enter. Barbara leaped to her feet

"Mark, you did come," she said running to him with outstretched arms. After a prolonged embrace, Barbara backed away from Mark and studied his saddened, drawn face. The usual sparkle in his eyes that she remembered was now replaced by dimness from the moisture of tears.

"Thank you for arranging this, Barbara," he said, glancing toward Agent Walton. "I have been like a caged animal ever since I heard what happened. How is she?"

"The reports we are getting are good. They are making good progress in repairing the damage."

"Is she going to make it, Barbara? Is she going to live? I've got to know." He clinched his fists until his knuckles blanched. The muscles in his jaw became so tight that his facial skin rippled.

"She's going to be all right, Mark. I just know she will," said Barbara.

"She's got to ... she's got to." His chin quivered. He swiped his shirt sleeve across his face to dry his cheeks and turned toward Ralph. "Do you have any idea who did this?"

"Not yet, Mark, but we have some leads,' Ralph answered. Try to stay calm. I can imagine how you feel. We'll find the perpetrators."

"Someone keeps trying to take her out. Is this all a part of a scheme to lash back at Judge Joberst for some decision he handed down?"

"We are working on that premise."

"May I sit down, Barbara?"

"Sure you can."

Mark collapsed on the couch. His shoulders slumped and his head dropped into his cupped hands. He stared at the floor for a few seconds. "I feel so helpless," he said finally.

Barbara sat beside him and took his hand in hers. "Of course you do. We all do, but just being here for her right now is all we can do.

Mark raised his head and looked at Barbara. "Thank you, Barbara. And you also, Mr. Walton. I'm sorry I got carried away."

"It's all right, Mark," said Barbara. "We understand." Ralph nodded in agreement.

Ralph's cell sounded. He stood and with the phone to his ear rushed out of the room. Within seconds he returned, with Callie at his side—both appearing elated.

"Leanne's fine," said Ralph. "They are finished with the surgery and the surgeon's are on the way here to talk to you. The report is good."

# 35

## Dallas

The knock on the door jarred Deo's attention away from the thick financial report Marcello had left for him to review. The morning had passed into midday without a word from Marcello. Deo had no idea how Marcello would be able to arrange a meeting with Agent Walton. Somehow he always produced. *Just leave it to me*, he had said with a chuckle. *I know how to bait an FBI fish.*

Deo leaped to his feet, confident that Marcello was at the door. He stopped short of opening it, remembering their session with Paretto. He peeked through the security eye and confirmed that Marcello was standing in the corridor, alone.

Marcello's face blossomed into a grin—as much as the facial scar allowed—as he entered. "You weren't sure it was me, were you?"

"How did you know?"

"The peek-hole darkened."

"All right, smart-ass. It could have been Paretto's hit man, you know."

"Not Tate." Marcello laughed. "He values his balls too much—wouldn't want to lose them."

"What about Walton?"

"He's here in Dallas now, still seething over the ambush yesterday on the judge's wife. We have a private conference room reserved right here in the hotel, exactly one hour from now," he said as he glanced at his watch.

"Is he coming alone?"

"Yeah, as part of the deal. He has to be alone."

"What did you promise him, Alberto's head on a platter?"

"I just told him that we had information that he would be interested in. Now that we have him, how are you gonna deal with him? You can't let the FBI know everything we've found out."

"Won't do that," Deo replied. "After the attack on the judge's wife, he's gonna be cagey with us. But at the same time he's afraid not to hear us out."

"You think Paretto was behind it?"

"Probably. Walton still has some unanswered questions. Like, why?" Deo poured himself a half-glass of scotch and added a couple of ice cubes. He pushed the bottle toward Marcello. "Have a shot."

"No thanks. I'll wait 'til later," said Marcello. He stared out the window for a few seconds as though in deep thought. "Agent Walton is under a lot of pressure right now, according to reports from our plant in the agency. The unsolved kidnapping of a federal judge's baby was burden enough. Now he has the assassination attempt on the judge's wife to deal with."

"What else does our man in the agency tell you?"

"He's pretty sure the FBI is getting close to linking Paretto to the kidnapping, but they can't fit all the pieces of the puzzle together. Like, why the assassination attempt? Also, they think they have uncovered clues to some sort of racketeering violation that involves Paretto and a secretive investor group. He said the name 'Qlozd Network' keeps coming up. He thinks Agent Walton might know something about it."

"I'm sure Agent Walton has figured out that we are after something; now he's wondering what we want from him in return for any information we might have," said Deo, sipping his drink. "This new talk about some secretive illegal dealings might give us an ace-in-the-hole when we talk to Walton."

Marcello chuckled. "It's more like a chess game you're playing with Walton."

\* \* \* \*

Marcello met Ralph Walton outside the hotel entrance. He watched the FBI agent approach and glanced about to confirm that he didn't have an army of agents trailing him. Agent Walton's furrowed brow and pursed lips, framing his aquiline nose, sent a message that he was not at all happy about being there. He was escorted by Marcello to the small private meeting room on the mezzanine floor.

Deo sat at the large cherry-wood conference table, his back to the door. He drummed his fingers on the surface and glanced at his watch repeatedly. He knew his feigned impatience had had its desired effect when Ralph entered the room and apologetically said, "Heavy traffic this close to noon."

Deo, with unblinking, piercing eyes and an unsmiling, expressionless face, slowly swiveled his chair until he faced the FBI agent. Deo decided to hit Ralph broadside.

"How is the investigation going, Ralph?" he said. Ralph showed no reaction. He remained silent for almost a full minute.

"Why am I here, Deo?" asked Ralph, casting a blank look at Deo. "And why are you here? I knew you were in the country. My desk is inundated with all-points inquiries from headquarters as to your whereabouts, but I didn't expect to see you in Texas."

"I'm touring the country, Ralph, sightseeing. Is there anything wrong with a United States citizen visiting points of interest in his own country?"

"I suppose you were in Nashville to visit the Parthenon and the Grand Ole Opry. Of course, and you came here to see a Dallas Mavericks basketball game, didn't you? Cut the shit, Deo. What do you want from me?"

"We have some information that you could use."

"So, out of the goodness of your heart you want to share it with me. What do you want in return, Deo?"

"Well for a starter, how about dropping all charges against Alberto Marchesa?"

"Come down to earth, Deo. Let me ask *you* a question. Where is Al Marchesa?"

"I answer that question every six months when I go through customs—every time I return to the United States."

"And you answer it the same way—you say you don't know where he is," said Ralph with a smirk. "We have enough charges against Al to sink him in the depths for the rest of his natural life. And you're right on the edge, Deo. I've argued with the director for years that you were guilty of impeding a federal crime investigation."

"If you had managed to get me indicted, then you wouldn't have a chance at the vital information we're prepared to give you now."

"How would your so-called vital information help me? How would it help the bureau?"

"You never answered my question about your investigation. Working on anything you're having a problem with?"

Ralph stood erect beside the chair. "Fuck you, Deo!" he yelled. "If you know anything about *any* FBI case and you don't make it available to the government, you are violating the law. You are obstructing justice, and I'll see that you are nailed. I think I'm wasting time here."

He turned toward the exit door and took a couple of steps before Deo called out to him. "Maybe the government would like to know something about the Qlozd Network. What do you think, Ralph?"

Agent Walton halted midway to the door and whirled to face Deo and Marcello. He couldn't conceal the startled expression on his face. What did you say?" he screamed as he returned to the table. "Damn you, Deo. What do you know about Qlozd? How did you know?"

"Sit down, Ralph." commanded Deo, fire in his eyes. "You want answers. Are you prepared to pay a price for answers?"

"I'm out of here, Deo," said Ralph as he turned again to leave. "If you're serious, I'll get a United States attorney to join me and we will have some serious discussions. But for now, no more cat and mouse conversation. I have Marcello's cell number."

Ralph stalked out and slammed the door so hard the wall-hung artwork shook. Marcello and Deo looked at each other and laughed.

"I'm ready for that scotch on the rocks," said Marcello.

"Let's go to the bar," Deo replied.

"What do you think he'll do?"

"I don't think he'll try any tricks, like arresting us for interfering in an FBI investigation of a federal offense by withholding information," said Deo.

"He's as angry as a disturbed mama wildcat."

"Yeah, but now he's convinced we have some critical information that he needs. I predict you'll hear from him within the hour."

"Deo, you don't know shit about Qlozd. Why did you say that?"

"Let him worry. That's what will bring him back."

"Should we change hotels, just to be safe?"

"Maybe so. Let's wait a couple of hours."

\* \* \* \*

Deo had resumed studying the financial reports that Marcello had left. By mid-afternoon, after a couple of hours, his eyelids became heavy. He leaned back in his chair, propped his feet up on the desk, and closed his eyes. He had just dropped off asleep when the phone rang. It was Marcello.

"He wants to come back with the attorney. He'll be here in about an hour."

"That's fine. Can you get the same room?"

"Yeah, already arranged."

"Check for any other agents when he arrives."

"I'll do that. I checked with our man in D.C."

"What did you find?"

"We're on target. I am sure the U.S. attorney knows the status of the FBI's investigations."

\* \* \* \*

Ralph had left his bored, arrogant demeanor behind when he entered the conference room. Accompanying him was the United States attorney. *Probably from Dallas*, Deo thought. His appearance was striking—reddish-brown, fine-textured hair, bold-sculptured facial features, and a tall, lean body that could have belonged to a triathlete. Deo and Marcello both stood and greeted their visitors with handshakes. The attorney introduced himself as Justin Haroldson.

Justin immediately chose the chair at the head of the conference table, seated himself, and extracted a large yellow legal pad from his briefcase. He sat quietly for a half-minute while he adjusted other documents in his case. He made no overtures to let anyone else assume control of the meeting. After a few moments, he looked up and studied each person present, as though he were preparing to speak to a jury. He addressed Deo and Marcello.

"I understand you have offered Agent Walton some information relative to his current investigations in exchange for which you demand that the government waive certain statutory charges against one …"

He paused and turned to Ralph. "Alberto Marchesa," said Ralph.

"Ah, yes. I remember from the file," said Justin. We are talking about Alberto Marchesa, who is wanted on multiple charges of racketeering from a few years ago. Am I correct so far?"

"To some extent," said Deo. "That was one of the conditions. I don't think we got much further than that when Agent Walton bolted and ran for help."

"And what were your other demands?"

"Let me put this bluntly, Justin. I know Ralph is not authorized to confirm deals for the Justice Department unilaterally. I certainly understand that he needs legal advice, and I appreciate your taking time to meet with us today. But our wishes, demands if you want to call them that, should be addressed with some dispatch. Time is of essence here, as you will learn later. Now we have to start somewhere. So that's why you are here. But you must convince us now that you have the authority to take this issue to the highest decision maker and comply with our requests in a timely manner."

Justin showed no sign of being taken aback. Deo looked closely at Justin as though assessing his response. *Probably his legal training is responsible for his stoicism*, thought Deo.

"I think the government can better judge the merit of your request, Mr. Carminagni, if we have some idea what information you have to offer."

"Let me confer with Marcello for a moment," said Deo as he stood and motioned for Marcello to follow him into the remote corner of the room.

Deo stood with his back to the others and winked. "You do have your sensors in place, do you not?" Deo asked in a tone just loud enough for the attorney to hear. Marcello leaned close to Deo, grinned, and responded on cue. "Of course," he said. They both moved back to the table.

"Justin, I can see your point. You wanta know, generally, what sort of information we have to offer before you consider our requests. Am I right here?"

"Yes, Mr. Carminagni. You are exactly right."

"Now, if you decide that our information is useful to you, how *exactly* are you going to help us get what we need?"

"We would prepare documents of agreement stating that you will provide the government with facts regarding specific cases in return for full exoneration for Mr. Marchesa. This is provided, of course, with the understanding that the information you provide helps Mr. Walton close those cases. Now, there would likely be another contingency: Mr. Marchesa would be expected to sign a compliance agreement that would prohibit him from engaging in illegal activities."

"I see no problem there."

"First, you have to give us some idea what you have that we be beneficial to the government."

"Let me speak to Marcello in private again."

"No problem."

Deo and Marcello again retreated to the corner of the room. "What do you think, Marcello."

"Can you commit for Al?"

"Yeah, he wants nothing more than to operate casinos and resorts—no trafficking, no laundering, all legal."

"Some of the guys will be disappointed."

"Don't forget why he sent me here. Anybody that doesn't like it can haul ass."

"I agree, Deo. I sure don't want to get back into that high-risk shit."

"Will anyone leave?"

"I think not. They know what comes next if they do."

They returned to the table. Justin and Ralph seemed eager to get on with the next phase.

"Justin, Ralph, you both need to know this. If either of you have recording devices on your person or in your briefcases, and if they are activated, Marcello will be able to tell and our meeting is over."

"We understand," said Justin. He took his pen out of his shirt pocket in readiness to begin writing.

"Here's what we have. First, we know where the Joberst baby is being held."

"What?" screamed Ralph. He jumped to his feet. "You're saying you know where the Joberst baby is, and we're sitting idly by when we could be doing something about it?"

"Just cool it, Ralph," said Justin. "He said there was of an element of time in this case."

"Is the baby alive?" asked Ralph.

"We have every reason to believe so. Next, we are holding and protecting the one surviving perpetrator of the abduction—John 'Gator' Dunbar. We also know who killed the other two. They were murdered in order to conceal the fact that the Paretto gang is behind the kidnapping plot. We don't know why."

Ralph and Justin stared at Deo with dropped chins and wide eyes. Ralph shook his head in disbelief. "And what else?" asked Justin.

"We have good reason to believe that the Paretto gang is involved in illegal operations in alliance with a phony business entity called Qlozd Network."

Justin shoved his chair back and looked at Deo with a smirk. "So, you expect that we will believe all you've told us and start the paperwork to drop all charges against Alberto Marchesa?"

"That can evolve once you determine that we are telling you the truth. The urgent request is this: We want the baby, as soon as it is recovered."

Justin and Ralph were speechless. They looked at each other, neither responding to Deo's bombshell. Finally Justin, with a deeper sneer on his face, spoke.

"You're quite a negotiator, Mr. Carminagni. Let me see if I have this right: You tell us where the baby is, Agent Walton recovers the baby and hands it over to you, you tap the Blanton trust fund for millions of dollars in return for the baby going back to its mother, we arrange for charges to be dropped against Mr. Marchesa, he returns to the United States and rekindles his organization, and we prosecute the Paretto gang, thus removing Mr. Marchesa's chief underworld competition. As far as Qlozd Network is concerned, you haven't told us anything we don't already know. Some deal you're trying to pull here, Mr. Carminagni."

"I'm sorry you have missed the point here, Justin," said Deo. "In the first place, we want no part of the ransom money. And you've insulted us by accusing us of such a despicable crime as kidnapping. Furthermore, you've accused us of the very thing Paretto is doing: holding on to the baby and trying to get the ransom upgraded. I guess we have no trust here, Justin. So there's no deal."

"Out of curiosity, Mr. Carminagni, why do you want the baby?"

"The baby's father is Mr. Marchesa's nephew. We will take the baby whether you help us or not. It will mean bloodshed to get past Paretto's guards, but we can do it. We hoped Ralph could help us. We will return the baby to its rightful mother. I'm sorry we can't come to an agreement, gentlemen," said Deo as he stood and motioned for Marcello to do the same. "Have fun with Qlozd."

"You know that with one phone call I can have you both thrown in jail and held as material witnesses. And I can get a court order before the sun sets today forcing you to surrender John Dunbar to the FBI."

Deo laughed. "I know you won't do that. Good luck on your search, Ralph. If you decide you want Gator, let me know. He'll trade with you in return for the witness protection program. I can't let you have him now. Your track record guarding people has not been too good lately." Deo chortled and walked away with Marcello following alongside.

# 36

*Westlake*

Long before the alarm sounded, Andy waked after a restless night without Barbara at his side. Barbara's call the night before—to report that Leanne had survived the surgery and that the prognosis was favorable—helped ease some of his disappointment that she had stayed in Dallas. He knew Leanne needed her, and he felt some assurance that Barbara was safe as long as she stayed at the hospital. After showering and dressing, he downed a quick bowl of cereal, grabbed a can of juice, filled his travel mug with coffee, and headed for the parking garage.

The morning air was crisp and smelled clean. He lowered the car windows to let the freshness flow through his nostrils and into his lungs. The early morning trip along Lakeside Drive to the hospital was his favorite time of day. It was his time to think. Ever since they had moved into the condo, he used this thirty- to forty-minute trip to attempt to unravel the complexities of the predicament in which he and Barbara had become embroiled.

His thoughts shifted to the note that Karen had passed to him about Jake's self-reminder memo. Was it accidental that it was left where he could see it or did she plant it in the packet on purpose? If the latter, what was she trying to tell him? Todd warned him to stay clear and play dumb. Would he be able to ignore the irregularities that he had seen as well as the many others that he suspected? He just couldn't do that. He needed to think through this quagmire and come up with a plan.

Todd's explanation about the sentinel event was the answer to why the ankle tag issue was so important to the hospital. Trinitus couldn't afford another charge related to patient safety in one of its hospitals. They couldn't take a chance on losing accreditation. But nothing they could do or threaten to do would pressure Barbara to tell an untruth about the occurrence.

Todd's explanation of how the Paretto gang was linked to the Qlozd Network seemed so implausible. How could the underworld be involved with any activity in a hospital system—as Todd had implied—without being detected on an audit by some government agency? It looked as though a discrepancy in the accounting system was beyond detection by outside auditors.

The traffic blended, through a complex traffic-control light system, into the wide Medical Parkway, the boulevard that led to Trinitus Westlake Hospital and the multiple other healthcare related facilities. He glanced in the mirror again, trying to see if he was being followed, held his glance a bit longer than he needed to, and looked up just in time to see the red light. He slammed on his brakes and skidded partway into the intersection—amid horns blaring and other cars' tires screeching. He dropped his head as if trying to hide his face, waited a minute for the adrenalin-stimulated pounding in his heart to calm down and then backed his car out of the way. "My God," he said aloud. "My greatest hazard is my own stupidity—not Qlozd or Paretto."

By the time Andy reached the hospital he had made two decisions. One, he was not going to rest until he got some answers about the wrongdoings at Trinitus. Two, he would attempt to get Agent Walton to hear his suspicions of illegal activity by the Trinitus Hospital System. He had learned enough in classes about healthcare law to be able to identity infractions, and he believed that everything Todd had told him to be true: Trinitus was knee-deep in racketeering—RICO violations—and Medicare fraud.

\* \* \* \*

Once at the hospital, still shaking from his near-accident, Andy went straight to Karen's office to check for any messages she might have for him. She was not present when he entered so he seated himself in the main administrative reception area to wait for return. He thought he could hear faintly audible voices coming from behind the door to Jake's private office. The voices grew louder:

"How did he get it? Did Todd give it to him?"

The frantic answer sounded as if it came from Karen:

"No, no ... it was a mistake. It accidentally got mixed up with the other papers."

The other voice, which belonged to Jake, then shouted, "Damn it, Karen, do you know what you've done?"

Karen answered, "It was a mistake, Mr. Hensley. I'm sorry."

"If he asks about the memo, just pretend you don't know."

Karen, her voice weaker now, replied, "I'll be careful, Mr. Hensley."

Andy felt embarrassed that he had heard parts of the conversation. When he realized that Jake was angry, he slowly rose from his chair to leave quietly, hoping that his presence would not be known. He was at the door when Karen, unable to hide her tears, came out of Jake's office. She looked inquisitively at Andy for a few seconds.

"Andy," she said. "I didn't hear you come in."

"I just got here, Karen. I wanted to make sure Jake gave the go-ahead on the report I gave you earlier. Are you all right?"

"Yeah, just more of the same," she said as she blotted her eyes. "Do you need to talk to Mr. Hensley?"

"You can find out for me. If I need to make any changes, just let me know. Otherwise, tell him I'll see him tonight."

"Sure," she answered. She then busied herself with straightening her desk.

\* \* \* \*

Andy put the finishing touches on the report, forwarded it to Todd, and awaited his response. Soon afterward, Karen sent an e-mail stating that both Todd and Jake approved of Andy's data. Andy tended to other menial tasks as the day dragged by. He called Barbara three times during the day to find that the news from Dallas was still favorable.

He tried to stay busy, but conversation he had overheard between Karen and Jake was a worry. He was sure he had heard Jake ask if Todd had given "it" to him. They obviously were talking about the reminder list that Karen had given him. Jake must have known that Todd had a copy of the memo. Andy's brain ached. He was sure that the answers he needed about Qlozd and Paretto were ensconced deep in the bowels of Jake's computer—and could only be accessed with a correct password.

\* \* \* \*

The medical staff meeting proceeded as planned. The large cafeteria had been closed to make room for the two hundred physician-staff members who attended. Andy's report seemed to be received well by most of the doctors. He walked them through his report on the core measures study on heart attacks, pneumonia, heart failure, and postoperative infections. Andy looked for Todd and wondered why he hadn't attended. He started to ask Jake but decided against asking him.

The meeting closed with Jake giving glowing reports about the hospital's role in the community. He played heavily on the notoriety Trinitus had received when dealing with Mr. Weatherford's injuries. He especially emphasized how thorough and competent the hospital had been in caring for the victim injuries. Andy looked around to see all of the doctors either nodding and absorbing Jake's BS or ignoring it completely in favor of their after-dinner liqueurs.

The meeting broke up with most of the doctors hurrying out, leaving behind their handouts that Andy had so meticulously prepared. Jake and a handful of faithful admirers lingered behind for an extra one or two cordials. Andy retreated to his office after gathering the loose packets that would be tossed into the shredding device. He found Karen still working at completing the minutes of the meeting. He stopped by to chat.

"You did an admirable job with your presentation, Andy," she said. "I marveled at the way you came across. You have some papers to shred?"

"Thanks, Karen. Yeah, I was looking for a shredder," he replied.

"Use this one," she said pointing to the slotted box used for depositing confidential data to be destroyed.

"Karen, do you think any of the doctors grasped what I was saying?"

"Yeah, some did. I didn't see anyone fall asleep tonight for a change." Karen laughed.

"You're just saying that for my benefit," Andy replied. "This core measure thing is important, don't you think?

"Sure, you know that it is and I know that it is," she answered, "but it's a hard sell when it comes to the medical staff. Look, I'm winding down here," she added as she gathered the pages on her desk to file them away. "I'll leave the office open if you need to stay in here for a while."

"Thanks. I need to shred these extra copies."

"Be sure and close and lock the door when you leave. See you tomorrow."

"Good night, Karen."

\* \* \* \*

Now alone in the executive suite, Alan quickly finished feeding the copies of confidential information into the shredder. The administration offices, remote from the rest of the hospital, were eerily quiet. He reached for the light switch and flipped off the overhead lights. The only remaining light came from the rays of the outside security lights filtering through the partially closed blinds. The flashing green lights from the computer and printer cast an eerie glow throughout Karen's office.

Andy started to open the door to the outside corridor when he glanced across the room toward Jake's private office. The door was partially ajar. He stopped and stared at the door for a few seconds. *Maybe this is my chance*, he said to himself. He checked the doorway for any entry detectors, found none, entered, and cautiously closed the door, hoping he wouldn't hear a blast of sirens. He wondered if it was time for housekeeping to clean. If it was, he could always make up a story to explain his presence.

His heart pounded and his hands shook as he sat in front of Jake's computer. *God, what if I am caught doing this*, he thought. *I'm one dead resident if Jake happens to come in.* Thinking of that very possibility, after his eyes adjusted to the subdued light, Andy looked around the massive office. What would he do if he did hear someone enter? Where could he hide? He spotted a closet close to Jake's private entrance from the outside and checked it for access and space. It appeared to be used as a coat closet—plenty of room to hide if he needed to.

A gyrating pattern of colors on the black monitor told him that Jake's computer had been left on. A click of the mouse brought up the bright desktop. He double clicked the My Documents icon and studied the multiple choices available. There it was! The letters Q-L-O-Z-D stood out like bright lights. He clicked on the item and was immediately asked for a user ID and a password. A wave of nausea accompanied his disappointment. He had no idea what the password was. He looked at the usual hiding places for passwords—under the keyboard, in a desk drawer, behind the monitor screen—with no yield.

Nothing for him to do but get out of there before he got caught. He rummaged through a few documents in the desk drawers hoping to find a clue to the right password. He found nothing that resembled anything tied to Qlozd, but he came across a loose key ring with two keys dangling. *Could these be keys to the rear door?* he wondered. He hoped Jake wouldn't notice that the keys were missing. Andy tried both keys. One key locked and unlocked the desk drawers and the other the rear door. A stroke of luck! Andy pocketed the ring and cautiously eased out the door, leaving it slightly ajar, as before. Once in the main corridor, he took a deep breath and walked away, trying to keep his pace casual while he planned his next move.

Andy retreated to his own office and was about to turn out the light but decided against it. There was no way he would take a chance on falling asleep. He sat in his desk chair, leaned back, and propped his feet on the desk. He checked his carotid pulse to find a slower rate, but the thought that he could have been caught triggered the quivering again in his chest and the tremor in his hands. He had to get control and concentrate.

According to Todd, knowing too much about Qlozd, could lead to disaster. But the answers he was looking for were buried in that Qlozd file in Jake's computer. He had to find them. How could he ever come up with the right password? The user ID was probably the same one they all used in administration, but he had nothing to start with, not even a hint of what the password was.

Andy shut his eyes for a few moments hoping to clear his mind. How could he find the password? He was looking specifically for the Qlozd file. He was sure there were numerous encryption experts who, in time, could come up with the password. But he didn't have the time for one thing, and besides, he couldn't reveal to anyone what he was doing. There was no question that his actions were against company policy and were probably illegal. If he were discovered breaking into a confidential file, it would lead to his immediate dismissal from Trinitus.

In spite of the risks, he was determined to make a few attempts before seeking assistance. Most personal files only allowed three attempts before locking the user out. He needed to devise three options before he tried again. Whenever he did go back into Jake's office, he wanted to get in and out as quickly as possible. What would he do if he failed? He was afraid to talk to Todd again after overhearing Jake's remarks to Karen. As soon as he assembled all of the relative data he could, Andy planned to discuss with Agent Walton the information that he had discovered so far. If he wasn't able to break the code, Agent Walton might call in one of the FBI's experts. Right now, he needed to start calculating.

Andy was jolted from his concentration by a knock on the door. A brief panic wave washed over him. *Who could it be at this hour?* he wondered. Before he opened the door, another knock followed, along with someone calling out, "Security." Andy opened the door to face a uniformed security guard with a broad smile on his face.

"Working late, Mr. Goldeyer? Just making rounds and saw the light under your door. Are you all right?"

"Yeah, fine," Andy answered. He waved off the guard and sat at his desk again. "I'll be leaving in a few minutes."

"Just checking."

"Thanks."

Andy swung his feet off the desk and sat upright. He grabbed a couple of sheets of paper from his printer and began his amateurish decryption plan. He first wrote down every letter in the alphabet, A to Z. Below the numbers, he wrote numbers corresponding to their order in the alphabet. The numbers that spelled out Q-L-O-Z-D were 17-12-15-26-4. He studied the numbers to see if there was any meaningfulness to the sequence and found none. Could that sequence itself be the access code? *That would be the essence of simplicity*, he decided. *That was not a likely password option.*

He placed the paper with his scribbling aside and began thinking of an alternate code, possibly still using the number-letter chart he had developed. "Q-L-O-Z-D is not a word," he said aloud after pondering a full minute. "It's not in the dictionary, and there are no matches on the Internet. It is just five separate letters." His brain ached as he searched its deepest crypts trying to come up with an answer.

He checked his watch—almost ten. Was it too late to call Barbara? Probably not, but he shouldn't wait any longer. She would be worrying why she had not heard from him. Using his desk phone, he dialed her cell number.

She answered on the first ring. "I was beginning to worry," she said. "Are you all right? How did your presentation go?"

"Fine, everything's fine here. How is Leanne?"

"Remarkably well. She's still in ICU, of course, but is improving by the hour. She's off the ventilator and is breathing on her own."

"Sounds encouraging! Are you getting any rest?"

"No problem. I'm just here to help and to be around when she opens her eyes. She always smiles when she sees me and then drops back asleep again. They treat both of us like special guests. Where are you? Are you sure you're all right. You don't sound like yourself."

"I'm fine," he replied. "I'm still at the office, catching up on some paperwork. I didn't realize how late it was."

"Go home a get some sleep," she admonished in a commanding voice.

"I'll do just that," he answered. "I miss you."

"And I miss you, too, and I love you."

"I love you. I'll talk to you tomorrow."

As he cradled the telephone hand piece, he glanced at the punch keys. Like a shock wave, the small printed letters on each of the keys jumped back at him. Could those letters and their matching numbers be the key he was looking for? When he matched the letters Q-L-O-Z-D with the numbers on the telephone, the number he came up with was 75693. A five-digit number! It had to be a Zip code. Now to find out where. The location of the Zip code might be another key to the puzzle. For the first time since he had undertaken the task to solve this riddle, Andy felt optimistic. He searched his desk drawers for a Zip code directory.

His search through the directory quickly revealed that the number was one of several postal Zip codes in the Dallas area. This was probably the password used when Qlozd was first founded by Joberst, Weatherford, and Shipman. Andy gazed at the number. Most passwords had a combination of numbers and letters. What letters could he add to 75693 to create a valid password?

Each Qlozd partner probably had a different password—different letters to add to the numbers, either before or after. On the other hand, maybe they all used the same password, like the first letter for each name of the founders (JWS, for Joberst, Weatherford, and Shipman). Andy settled on three options: Jake's initials before and after the 75693 and the letters JWS before the number. It was worth a try.

Andy checked his watch again. It was now nine-thirty. The housekeeping crew had surely finished cleaning the administrative wing of the hospital. He would wait a few minutes more and then enter Jake's office again, this time from the back entrance. He pocketed a USB flash drive that he found in one of the desk drawers. If he did discover the data he was after, he needed to be prepared to download it.

Andy cautiously eased out of his office into the outside corridor. All was quiet. He walked past the main entrance doorway of the administration offices, past Karen's office, and down the dark narrow hallway that ran adjacent to Jake's private office. The only light came from the red exit sign over the door to the outside. Near the end of the hall, Andy stopped in front of the door that bore the notice, "No Admission, Staff Only." It had to be Jake's private entrance.

Andy tried the key and it opened the door. He faced a still narrower passageway that led to Jake's suite. The same key opened that door, and he was inside Jake's office again. The room was dark except for the gyrating pattern of the monitor's current screensaver. Andy felt the tightness in his throat again. He took a deep breath and wiped the beads of perspiration from his forehead with his arm sleeve. He had to stay calm and work fast, even though it was unlikely that Jake was still in the building. Todd had mentioned that they usually went to some bar after medical staff meetings, so it was possible that he could return to pick up something that he had left there.

Andy sat before the monitor and placed on the keyboard tray the page on which he had written the three options he intended to try. First he tried the 75693 number with the JWS initials before the number. "Password Invalid" flashed on the monitor. He admonished himself for wasting one of his attempts on that combination. It was unlikely that everyone in the network would use the same password.

Logically, each user would need to add his key letters to the number. He tried placing Jake's initials, JH, before the number. His heart sank when, once again, "Password Invalid" jumped back at him. Now what? Should his final attempt be to place the JH letters *after* the numbers? He started doing just that when he glanced at the business card holder on Jake's desk. Jake's full initials were JRH. He resigned himself to making his last try and getting it over with. If he failed, he would try a new approach later. He entered JRH75693 in the password box and waited. Instead of the "invalid" message popping up immediately, there was a full-minute delay. The next image he saw was the QLOZD menu on the screen.

"My God! I'm in!" he said, almost screaming. "I'm in!"

He quickly scanned the menu—everything he had hoped for was there: membership, minutes, organizational structure, agreements, and financial data, including distribution amounts and dates. Nothing was left out, not even the oldest information on the organization. Andy's hands shook and his heart pounded in his chest as he inserted his disc into the port. In spite of the size of the file, within seconds it was all downloaded onto the tiny disc.

His moment of exhilaration was brief. Just as he had finished downloading the Qlozd file, he heard voices in the access corridor and then heard the outer door close. He didn't have time to shut down the computer by the usual protocol, so he hit the power button and scampered to the coat closet. No sooner was he inside, with the door still slightly ajar, than Jake and Todd entered. Andy could distinguish the silhouettes of the two through the crack in the door. While searching for the light switch to the floor lamp, Jake stumbled over a chair and knocked the telephone off of the desk. Jake bent over to retrieve it, lost his balance, and fell to the floor. Todd assisted him to a chair.

"Damn, Todd, what was in those drinks?" asked Jake, shaking his head back and forth.

Todd, seemingly steady on *his* feet, laughed. "Maybe you had too many, Jake."

"You sure know how to find exciting places, Todd," he said. He chuckled. "And they seemed to know you pretty well in there. Those girls put on quite a show, didn't they?"

"How much did that lap dance cost you?"

"I don't know. What difference does it make? You won't tell my wife, will you? Let me grab my briefcase before we leave."

"Can you drive home okay?"

"Yeah, I can make it," Jake answered. "You said earlier that you wanted to talk to me about something."

"Maybe this is not a good time," said Todd.

"Sure it is. I can tell by the look in your eyes, you're worried about something. What's going on, Todd?" he asked. "I wondered why you didn't make it to the medical staff meeting."

Todd avoided eye contact with Jake and hesitated before answering. "I'm turning in my resignation, Jake."

"You're what?"

"I'm quitting. I just can't take it any longer."

"Are you leaving for a position elsewhere?"

"No, it's not that—and it isn't my salary."

"Todd, you know that quitting this position is unwise, don't you?"

"You've warned me before, but I trust you to believe me when I say I will not reveal anything that I know about Qlozd."

"Sure, Todd, I'll protect you. Is there anything I can do to make you change your mind? Did I do anything to make you decide to quit?"

"No to both questions, Jake. Sure you don't need me to get you home?"

"No, no, you go on. I'll be all right."

Todd turned to walk out. Jake called after him. "Don't do it, Todd. Think it over. Come talk to me in the morning."

"I'll do that," he said, still walking.

Jake called again, "Todd, how much does Andy know?"

"Just what I told you. He found that note you sent me and asked me about Qlozd. He knows it exists, but he doesn't know its function."

"Knowing anything about Qlozd can be unhealthy, you know," said Jake. "Does Andy know that?"

"I just told him to be careful."

"Why did you tell him that?"

"He kept asking me questions."

Jake stared hard at Todd for several seconds. Todd seemed to squirm, clearly uncomfortable facing Jake's fixed stare.

"Get out of here, Todd," Jake finally said with abrasiveness. He swiveled his chair to face away from Todd.

Andy remained motionless as he watched the scene. Through the crack in the door he could see Jake, sitting at his desk, his shoulders slumped, elbow on the desk, holding his forehead in the palm of his hand. After a while it appeared that Jake was asleep. If he dropped into a deep slumber, Andy thought he might be able to leave the closet and ease out the door without being detected. Then Jake roused again, reached into his coat pocket to retrieve his PDA, and searched for a number. He then reached for his phone and dialed a number. Andy, hearing only one side of the conversation, shuddered at the words he heard.

"Tate," said Jake. There was a brief pause. "Todd has to go." Again there was silence. "As soon as possible. He just left the hospital to go home. Take him out."

*My God!* Andy whispered inaudibly. *He just ordered someone named Tate to kill Todd.*

Jake stood and held onto his chair for a few seconds as if trying to regain his balance. He rummaged through his desk drawers but apparently did not find whatever he was searching for. He slammed the drawers shut, turned out the lamp light, and headed for the door, still staggering slightly. Andy held his breath, hoping Jake wouldn't stop and open the closet door. If he did, Andy had already decided to bolt out past Jake, thinking that the surprise and the darkness might shield him from detection.

Jake paused in front of the door to the closet and grasped the door handle. *This is it,* Andy thought as he made ready to push his way past Jake and race for the corridor before Jake could recover from the surprise. Jake held onto the door handle for a few seconds and then let go. He turned back to his desk and rummaged through papers on the desk top. He picked up some document and headed back toward the closet. Andy still was prepared to break away if Jake opened the door. As he passed the door he again grasped the door handle, but instead of opening the door he slammed it shut.

# 37

*Dallas*

Agent Ralph Walton glanced at the clock on the bedside table—5:00 AM. He had been awake almost an hour turning over in his mind the events that had transpired over the last few weeks. Nothing was going right for him, and his self-confidence was wearing thin. Every move he had made seemed to have backfired. Al Marchesa's pair of underworld characters, Deo and Marcello, had undercut him by finding John Gator Dunbar before he could be interrogated. Ralph had no valid evidence that linked Paretto to the kidnapping without a statement from Gator. And now Deo and Marcello were trying to negotiate a protection commitment for Gator before they would give him up. To top it all, Leanne had been attacked and nearly killed while his agents had been guarding her.

So far there had been zero response to Leanne's appeal on television. If he could only find one fragment of valid information, perhaps he could be lifted out of his despair. Every time he thought he might be able to connect just a few of the dots, something managed to jerk the rug from under him. Were Deo and Marcello sincere when they said they only wanted to see the kidnapped baby returned to its mother? That would justify dealing with Deo if that were true. What would the director say about his negotiating with the Marchesa mob? Ralph needed to win for a change. He hadn't had a lot of failures on his record until now. The Marchesa fiasco three years earlier had been the worst—he had had nightmares over not being able to complete the arrest of Alberto Marchesa.

Now, failing to solve the kidnapping of Federal Judge Joberst's baby, in addition to allowing two attempts on his wife's life, could be devastating to his career. *I'm surprised the director hasn't called me in about my performance*, he thought. *I'm sure he's caught a lot of political flack in Washington.* If there was any validity to Deo's statement that he wasn't interested in ransom money, perhaps he and Justin should reevaluate their position in any further discussions with Deo and Marcello.

Ransom! The word stuck in his mind. Why hadn't Paretto demanded more ransom? Or had he made any demands at all? Someone had contacted the judge, but only token efforts had been made to collect money. From the beginning, the lack of a ransom demand had been a mystery. Paretto wouldn't plan a kidnapping—not his modus. Who had engaged him to pull this off? Paretto wouldn't take this risk simply for ransom. He must have done it under pressure. But who was strong enough to pressure the don of the largest criminal organization in the country?

Could Al Marchesa have manipulated Paretto, maybe by some threat? Ralph wondered if Deo Carminagni was manipulating him, throwing him off the path of the truth. The dismay of failure hung over Ralph like a black cloud. He had only one chance to recover the baby—he had to deal with Deo. He fumbled with his PDA looking for Marcello's number. Perhaps he should wait for a while before calling. He needed to talk to the U.S. attorney first.

The most tempting "bait" that Deo had thrown out had been the mention of the Qlozd Network. Ralph knew just enough about the suspicious activity of Qlozd to know that bringing down the sub-rosa organization guilty of a RICO violation would eliminate anyone's doubt of his competency. He could certainly use a boost like that right now.

Deo hadn't said what he knew about Qlozd, but where would he have heard the name? Ralph had used every means possible to find hard data on Qlozd, but he had been unsuccessful at every turn. Their own FBI plant in Trinitus Westlake, Jake Hensley's hospital, had been their only source of information on Qlozd Network activity, but he had been unable to produce any specific data. They only knew Paretto was involved in some way, but could never find a definite link.

The ring on his cell phone jerked Ralph back to reality. He threw off the covers, jumped out of bed, and groped for the light switch. He flipped open his cell. It was Andy! Had there been another crisis? He answered.

"Andy, are you all right?"

"Yeah, I'm fine, Mr. Walton … well, as fine as possible with our life in such upheaval," he answered, making no attempt to hide his irritation.

"I can imagine how you feel, Andy," said Ralph, "but Leanne is doing remarkably well—and thanks to Barbara she has an amazingly cheerful attitude. I was just thinking of calling you. I think Barbara could take a couple of days away from Leanne. We can fly her to Westlake if she agrees."

"I doubt she would want to leave. Perhaps I could come there instead for a weekend."

"Sure, sure. We can arrange that," Ralph replied.

"Thanks. I know I must sound impatient and irritable, but Barbara and I can deal with it. That's not why I called. I need to talk to you about some information that I have come across at the hospital. I believe that you would be interested in what I've found. It has to do with the Qlozd Network."

Ralph gasped, and full half-minute lapsed before he could speak. He removed the phone from his ear and confirmed that he was speaking to someone at the same number that he knew to be Andy's.

"Andy, what do you know about Qlozd?"

"I can't tell you how I got the information—so please don't ask. All I can say is that it is complete—names, history, locations, financials, meeting minutes, agreements. It's lengthy and complete," Andy said, followed by another long period during which only the sound of Ralph's heavy breathing was audible.

"Andy, in what format do you have this data?"

"In a small flash disc."

"Andy, are you in any danger right now—as far as you know."

"No, sir," he answered. "Not that I am aware of."

"Look, Andy, hide somewhere until I get there," said Ralph. He rattled off instructions so fast that he ran his words together. "Go to a library or a museum—any public place. Stay away from work, don't talk to anyone, and don't tell anyone where you are going. As soon as you can, leave me a message telling me where you are and an agent will pick you up and bring you to the airport. I'll be there in less than two hours. We can talk on the way to the hospital. Are you reading me?"

"Yeah, I'm cool, Mr. Walton. What do I tell the hospital?"

"We'll handle that later. Call your secretary and tell her you are ill, that your doctor wants you to stay at home for a couple of days, that you might be contagious. Call me immediately whenever you are in a public facility."

Ralph's rapid-fire commands reflected his exhilaration over this new development. Could this be the break that he was hoping for? With renewed energy and optimism, he raced first to the bathroom, dressed, and prepared for his trip. He paused only long enough to alert the standby pilots to ready the FBI jet plane for an emergency flight to Westlake.

\* \* \* \*

## Westlake

Andy had to let Todd know what he had heard. Doing so would raise question of why he had been hiding there in the first place, but he had to warn Todd some way. Todd had said more than once that his knowledge of the Qlozd Network placed him in danger. There was no question that Andy had heard Jake tell someone named "Tate" that Todd needed to be "taken out." Could "Tate" be Paretto's hit man? He had to be. Todd had been targeted for a hit.

Andy called the hospital and asked to be transferred to Todd's office. No answer. He then asked the operator to connect him with Todd's cell phone. Again, no answer. Instead of leaving a message, he decided to ask Karen to tell Todd to call him. He dialed the direct line to Karen's office to report his illness and his excuse for not coming into the office. He knew it was early, but Karen often came to work earlier than the usual eight o'clock.

"Karen," said Andy when she answered. He faked hoarseness, sounding like a bullfrog in a swamp, "good morning."

"Andy, you sound horrible. What's wrong?"

"I feel horrible, Karen. I didn't sleep all night and I have a high fever. I'm afraid that I will spread this if I come in. These coughing spells just tear me apart."

"Don't you even think about coming in. I'll tell Mr. Hensley. Are you going to a doctor?"

"Yeah, there's one close by. I'll go in later."

"Take care of yourself."

"Thanks, Karen. Oh, Karen, would you ask Todd to call me when he comes in? I need to talk to him about some items I left pending."

Karen delayed replying to Andy for a painfully long half-minute.

"I see you haven't heard. Of course, you'd have no way of knowing. Todd won't be coming in." Andy cringed to hear those words. "He has resigned effective immediately."

Andy relaxed. Todd knew after seeing Jake's response last night that he would have to take cover. Andy wondered if he would ever see Todd again.

\* \* \* \*

Andy checked the Yellow Pages for museums and chose the Museum of Natural History for his "hideout." He called Ralph's number as instructed and left the location on his voicemail. He browsed through the exhibits for a full hour, which crept by at a snail's pace. He was concentrating on a wall-sized oil painting of an Indian attack on early Texas settlers when he felt a tap on his shoulder. His senses already keyed high from preoccupation with the mural as well as apprehension over the day ahead, Andy jumped and let out the beginning of a yell as he turned to face a tall, smooth-shaven young man dressed in the archetypical attire of an FBI agent. The man flashed his ID badge and pressed his finger to his lips to signal silence.

"Are you ready to go, Mr. Goldeyer?"

"Sure," Andy answered, shaking his head as though clearing the cobwebs from his brain. "And you are …?"

"Caleb, sir," he answered, without giving his last name, motioning for Andy to follow his rapid gait toward the exit door.

No words were exchanged on the way to the airport. Andy spotted the large jet parked on the tarmac at the private airport. Agent Walton was standing beside the stairway when Caleb pulled up beside the plane. No sooner had the cabin's exterior door closed than the plane, its engines still alive from the trip from Dallas, began to taxi toward the runway. Ralph motioned for Andy to follow and led him to a private compartment.

"How are you doing, Andy?"

"Holding up fairly well," he replied. "I'm sure I look fatigued from being up all night. Here's the disc."

"I feel like I'm receiving stolen merchandize," said Ralph. "How did you get this, and what's more important, why?"

"Mr. Walton, Barbara and I have struggled and sacrificed for months while I have been in school working toward a degree in healthcare management. You can't imagine the disillusionment that I have experienced from the very first day that I came to Trinitus. I have witnessed fraudulent acts by the hospital.—violations of RICO, Stark I and II, and Emtala. I'm fed up with it. I was determined that I'd do something about it—so this is what I found. I really don't care if I am guilty of breaking and entering. I only hope you can take that information and stop all the abuse."

"So you illegally accessed confidential data on someone's computer, and now you are giving it to me," said Ralph. "Of course, this makes me an accessory and disqualifies the info on the tape."

"You mean you can't use it—knowing it would bring criminals to justice?"

"I have to acquire evidence legally—by warrant."

"Look, Mr. Walton, what I've observed is criminal. It's racketeering, and it's a federal offense. I believe when and if you dig into it further you will find that it dovetails in some way with another federal offense that you are investigating. I think I am obligated to pass on this data regardless of how I acquired it."

Ralph went into another of his mute modes. He sat in his chair, elbows on the arm rests, his chin resting on clasped hands, and stared into space for a full minute. He turned to Andy finally.

"Does anyone else know you have this disc—or how you acquired it?"

"No, sir, no one," said Andy.

"Whatever is on this disc—if it is as powerful as you say—must have come from a confidential file."

"That's true."

"And likely you had to have a password to get there?"

"That's correct," Andy answered, holding his head high with pride.

"Did someone give you the password?"

"No, sir."

"Andy, let's quit playing games. Tell me how you did it."

Andy stood and walked around the small compartment contemplating how he could get through to Ralph and convince him that the information he offered was valid. Ralph waited for Andy to speak. He tried to hide his impatience, but the drumming of his fingers on the tabletop betrayed his eagerness to learn more of what Andy had found.

"One of the associate administrators warned me that something sinister existed. He told me to stay quiet for my year at Trinitus, say nothing, complete my internship, and leave quietly without letting anyone know what I had observed. He said that to do otherwise would be 'harmful to my health.' I can't accept that. Here's my story …"

Andy related to Ralph the process he followed to find the right password. He described how he found Jake's office open and the computer left on, his first unsuccessful attempts at accessing the Qlozd file, and his final success at unraveling the meaning of the word "Qlozd." Ralph listened with a gaping mouth and with his eyes widened in a fixed stare.

"Once again, Andy," said Ralph. "Let me ask you: does anyone else have these documents?"

"Only Qlozd Network members. Their names are in the file. The associate administrator at the hospital, Todd Langley, whom I told you about, is aware of the dealings of Qlozd, but I don't think he has any idea of the magnitude of it all. I think his knowledge comes from bits of information that Jake has dropped unintentionally."

Ralph became pensive, gazing out the plane's small porthole window for a minute without speaking. Finally he stood, stretched his arms and legs, and rubbed the back of his neck and his shoulder muscles. The vacant look on Ralph's face told Andy that he was in deep thought. He sat back down across the small, round conference table and stared straight into Andy's eyes.

"Andy," he said, blinking his eyes and shaking his head as if in disbelief, "I don't know what to say right now. I'm going to take the disc into another compartment and scan through it while we are traveling. I'm not sure what my next move will be. You've convinced me that it is information that I can use. If I find that you are right, I need to find some way to show that I have acquired it legally. Do you understand?"

"I think so," said Andy. "I'm willing to take my chances just to see that these injustices are resolved."

"I'll see that you are protected, Andy. I know you have some skepticism about that, but I'll see that you will be protected. Go ahead and call Barbara; tell her you're on the way. I'll be back in a little while and we'll talk."

A few minutes before the plane landed in Dallas, Ralph returned. Looking at Ralph's face, Andy could tell that he had not shed the mask of worry. What would be his opinion now that he had browsed through the contents of the disc? Ralph sat directly in front of Andy and looked straight at his eyes.

"Andy, you've probably uncovered the key to this Qlozd mystery," he said. Deep creases coursed across his forehead. "You have no idea how long the bureau has searched for this information. This disc is so hot I can hardly hold it. I need to make you aware of a couple of recent happenings."

Ralph told of his and Justin's meetings with Deo and Marcello. He narrated Deo's offer to provide information on the location of Leanne's baby and on Paretto's role in the abduction of the infant and in the murders of two of the kidnappers in exchange for amnesty for Alberto Marchesa for criminal charges dating three years back.

"Are you telling me that this 'Deo' knows where Leanne's baby is?"

"He says he does. You have to understand, Andy. We don't negotiate with criminals. When I heard Deo's proposal, I suspected two ulterior motives: One, he wanted to take possession of the baby and then raise the amount of ransom. Leanne would pay a fortune for the return of the baby. Two, he would like to see Paretto put away, which would give the Marchesa mob free rein in underworld activities in this country."

"Couldn't you arrest him and force him to tell you where the child is being kept?"

"Taking action like that might be detrimental to the baby. He could destroy the baby. As you can see, I have been totally enveloped in a dilemma. If we don't move fast, we have no chance of recovering a live baby."

"Are you reasonably sure that Paretto planned the abduction and then arranged for the murder of two of the kidnappers?"

"Yes, I am," Ralph replied. "I think someone hired or pressured Paretto to plan and implement the abduction. Paretto, in turn, hired the hoodlums to do the dirty work. Then he had to do away with them to protect himself. The description of the murderer fits Paretto's hit man, Nicholas Tatum, also known as 'Tate.' Of course, they are now after the last guy—a man named John Dunbar, who goes by the name of 'Gator.' Getting rid of Gator would destroy the only remaining link between Paretto and the crime. Deo and Marcello say they are holding Gator. They are using Gator's statement as a part of their so-called negotiations."

Andy perked up when he heard the name of Paretto's hit man—"Tate." That was the name he remembered hearing when Jake called someone about getting rid of Todd. Yes, definitely, Jake had called this Tate to go after Todd.

Ralph sensed the change in Andy's demeanor.

"What is it, Andy? "I haven't had a chance to tell you this part of the story...."

Andy related the scene between Jake and Todd, and Jake's subsequent phone call. To Andy's surprise, Ralph showed little response to the news about Todd. "Can you do anything to protect Todd, knowing that Paretto is after him?"

"We'll certainly look into it," said Ralph, displaying a rather nonchalant attitude.

"I tried to call him before we left Westlake and couldn't get through to him," said Andy.

"Perhaps he knows that he is in danger since he knows so much about the Qlozd Network."

Andy was silent for a few seconds. *Why does Agent Walton not seem concerned about a threat on Todd's life?* Andy wondered. *He appears not to even care. Maybe he knows more that he's saying.*

"So, what are your plans now?" asked Andy almost scornfully. He was still concerned about Ralph's casual concern for Todd's safety.

"I can't tell you right now, Andy. This information you have given me sheds a whole new light on this case. I can tell you this: I am going to contact the United States attorney and plan another meeting with Deo and Marcello. Our first priority is to find that baby. If indeed they do know where it is, we need to move fast to recover it. Then we will deal with Paretto."

"Can I tell Barbara or Leanne any of this?"

"You must not utter a word that would give them the least hope, he said. "I've arranged for you and Barbara to stay in one of our remotely located apartments for now. I'll be in touch with you on the progress we're making, but please don't mention anything to Barbara or anyone. If I can activate my plan, I will need you both when we go after the baby. You need to be ready to move on a minute's notice."

"You know you can depend on both of us. Aren't you going to have to move fast?"

"Absolutely! After, and if, we find the baby I will have to arrange for a warrant so I can legally acquire my own copy of the Qlozd file—using your password, of course." Any action we take will likely prompt every member of the Qlozd Network to delete the file. Of greater concern is Paretto. As soon as he learns we are onto the crime, he will destroy all the evidence—including the baby."

A message flashed on the computer monitor in the compartment where they sat: "Five Minutes to Touchdown."

"Andy, did you call Barbara?"

"No, sir," he answered. "I decided to surprise her."

"That's good. You and Barbara needed some quality time together. You'll be heavily guarded while you're here. I guess I don't have to tell you."

Andy laughed for the first time this day. "We're getting used to it."

\* \* \* \*

## Dallas, Parkland Hospital

Barbara helped Leanne back in bed after her one hour of being up in a chair. One by one, tubes, drains, and IV lines had been removed. Her bulky dressing over her chest wound had been reduced to a giant Band-Aid, and she was improving by the hour. She required much less pain medicine and took only a small dose of sleeping medicine at bedtime. She begged daily for permission to bathe in the shower and to wash her hair.

"Now, why do you think you can do a better job of shampooing your hair than I can?" Barbara chided.

Leanne laughed. "How I'd love just to feel pure water and shampoo on my head. My scalp feels like one big upside-down bowl of heavy crust."

"I know you must be tired of this dry shampoo, but it keeps your hair looking fresh and clean," said Barbara. "You're doing great, and you'll be out of here before you know it."

"It only hurts now if I take a deep breath or if I laugh," said Leanne grinning broadly. "Every time Callie comes in here, I laugh so much that I feel like my stitches are breaking loose."

"She is an angel. I wish we could take her home with us."

The mention of home triggered a wistful expression on Leanne's face. "Barbara, what am I going to do now? Where can I go? I don't have a home. I've never felt so lonely, so scared," Leanne said. Her eyes became misty. She dabbed at her wet face with a tissue.

"Now, look here, lady. You've fought too hard to get well to talk like that," Barbara said with a sly chuckle while she straightened the bed cover. "Come out of that slump or I'll call Callie in."

"If you heard any news about the baby—good or bad—you'd let me know, wouldn't you?"

"Sure I would," Barbara replied as she brushed Leanne's hair.

"Sometimes I feel like it's all over and no one has told me."

"If you have to hear bad news or good news, we'll work our way through it together. We all feel the pain you're going through right now, but I am still optimistic everything will be fine." Barbara checked her watch. "It's about the time Mark comes for his daily visit. He's a remarkable person, Leanne."

"He is so attentive when he's here. You should stay and watch him, Barbara. He fluffs my pillow, tries to straighten the bed sheets, and gets ice and fresh water. He hovers over me like a mother over a newborn."

"What does Mark say about your plans when you leave the hospital?"

"We avoid talking about it too much," she answered as she stared at the ceiling a few seconds. "He does want me to start divorce proceedings now. I'm afraid Anthony will go after Mark as soon as I do. We will never be safe together."

"Does Anthony make any attempt to come in, Barbara?"

"Not any longer," Barbara replied. Mr. Walton has given strict orders that no one is allowed to visit without an agent present. Anthony doesn't know this, but the order doesn't apply to Mark for his one-hour daily visits. Barbara, what angel brought you to me?"

"The same one that's going to see that you are well taken care of for the rest of your life."

"I am going to have to make some long-term plans before long. I'm going to need an attorney to help me with a divorce and to get my affairs in order."

"Right now, you stop worrying about going home. Your home for a while is with Andy and me. Mr. Walton will see that you are transported back to the condo in Westlake and that we are well protected. Now, brighten up! You don't want Mark to see that sad look when he comes in."

A knock on the door started Barbara moving. "That must be Mark. I'll be back in an hour. Is there anything that you need me to bring?"

"No, I'm fine."

Before Barbara could open the door, Callie crashed through. "All right," she said. "What have you sisters been talking about?"

"Just the usual," Barbara replied with a grin. "Where were you yesterday, Callie?"

Callie put her clipboard down on the bedside table. "Took a day off," she said as she placed one hand on Leanne's forehead and checked her pulse with the other. "She ain't feverish; they said she had a fever." Callie laughed that deep guttural chuckle. "Yeah, I took a day off. Glad to get back to work. When you got youngins at home there ain't no rest. Glad to get back where the work's easier." She turned to Barbara with a furtive grin on her face. "Oh, I almost forgot. Some good-looking dude outside to see you. Suppose to be a surprise."

Barbara stepped outside just in time to see Andy step out of the shadows. "Andy!" she cried. "Andy, where did you come from?"

"Does it matter," he replied, holding out his arms. "I'm here!"

"Oh, Andy! How I've missed you!" she said as she melted in his arms and kissed him passionately. She stroked his cheeks and then his hair. "Have you kept your hair looking nice? Don't even try to answer. God, how I've missed you."

And I've missed you," Andy said. "Mr. Walton wanted us to have some time together. I wonder why."

"Andy, so much has happened. We need to talk."

"I wasn't thinking of talk," he said, a sly grin on his face and a twinkle in his eyes.

"All right," she said, laughing "We'll get to that also. Tell me what's going on in Westlake."

The agent that brought Andy to the hospital stepped forward. "Mr. and Mrs. Goldeyer, Agent Walton has instructed me to take you to your apartment. You'll be housed in the same building with several other agents, so you'll be safe there."

"Thanks," said Andy. "We have been apart for more time than I like to recall."

"I understand, sir," he said. "Please follow me."

# 38

***Dallas***

Once again, Marcello went to the entrance of the hotel to meet Agent Walton and Justin. He stood behind head-high plants and watched as a black Malibu delivered Ralph and Justin. The same conference room was available. Deo was seated at the table when the entourage entered. Marcello nodded his head, indicating all was clear and no phalanx of FBI agents had been seen preparing to attack the hotel. Deo smiled, thinking of his escape plans if needed. Marcello had arranged for a helicopter pickup from the hotel roof if Ralph didn't keep his word that there would be no arrests.

Cordiality was glaringly absent. The room was eerily quiet while Justin emptied his briefcase. Deo didn't remember Justin wearing glasses the last time they had met. A full minute passed before Ralph finally broke the silence.

"Justin and I have discussed the issues here, Deo," he said. "Perhaps after we talk we can come to an agreement that will be satisfactory to all."

"You called us, Ralph," said Deo. "I'm here to listen." Ralph squirmed in his seat and looked at Justin in a way that suggested he expected him to speak. Justin peered over the top of his eyeglasses, now resting over the bridge of his nose. He turned to Deo with a look of arrogance.

"Mr. Carmignani, you understand that the government does not yield to pressure when there is a blatant violation of the law, do you not?"

Deo bristled and looked at Ralph, whose facial expression was still in a grimace from Justin's remark.

"Justin, I think Deo is well aware of the risk he is taking meeting with us. Let me summarize briefly what everyone's objectives are as I see them. Our first priority is to find the baby and bring to justice everyone who is responsible for this kidnapping. Deo has indicated that his only objective in this regard is to see that the baby is safely returned to its mother. Am I right so far, Deo?"

"That's correct. Please set the record clear: we are not looking for reward or ransom. You must get that through your heads," he said as he glared first at Ralph and then at Justin."

"Noted, Deo," Ralph replied. "Now, you have said that you and Marcello know where the baby is located. Right?"

"To the best of our knowledge. Gator showed us the location, and when we drove by, two security people stepped out—apparently to show us that the place was guarded."

"So, if we assume that was where the child was taken, how do we know that it is still there?" asked Justin.

"Simple answer," Deo replied. "We have had the place under constant surveillance by our own people. The baby has not been taken out as far as we know. Reyes would have seen that happening, and he would have followed and called Marcello."

"Suppose the baby is not there," said Justin.

"Then, of course, our deal is off and we all start searching again." Deo saw Ralph cringe again.

"Now, there is substantial belief that you can provide us with information on the identity of the kidnappers as well as the individuals responsible for the act," said Ralph. "You have said that you are holding John Dunbar, known as Gator, who was one of the three involved in the abduction. Is that correct?"

"That's correct," Deo replied. "He's the only one still alive."

Justin straightened himself in his chair. "If you are holding captive someone responsible for this offense, you are obstructing justice. That also is a federal offense."

"Wait a minute, Justin," said Ralph, now irritated. "Let me continue. Right now I am summarizing the facts as we know them to date."

"To get on with it," said Deo, "Gator was hired to do the job. He can identify who was behind the kidnapping and who murdered two of the three perpetrators. In return for his testimony, he will request immunity from prosecution and enrollment in the witness protection program. We're holding him for his own safety. You haven't openly identified the person responsible for the abduction, but we know it was Paretto and, not surprisingly, Paretto wants Gator dead. We don't know, however, who engaged Paretto to pull off the kidnapping, but we know someone did."

"You completed my summary, Deo," said Ralph, grinning. Justin's face was still a flat pan. "Now, if everything we've discussed so far is correct, you want the baby returned to its mother with no strings attached. What else do you demand?"

"That all charges are dropped against Alberto Marchesa. As a part of an amnesty agreement, Alberto will agree to contain his activity in this country to legal undertakings. The only other contingency to any agreement, of course, is that you agree not to charge Marcello and me with any wrongdoing."

"You are certainly presumptuous, Mr. Carminagni," said Justin. "With one phone call, we can haul you two in immediately."

"Please, Justin," said Ralph. "I guess I haven't taken the time to discuss the full ramifications of this case with you. Briefly, we may be on the verge of breaking into major racketeering violations with this case. Let's don't scuttle it with trivial details."

"I'll have to discuss any talk of amnesty with the Attorney General's Office."

"Then discuss it, goddamn it," said Ralph with fire in his eyes as he slapped the file he was holding on the table and jumped to his feet. "If you don't move rapidly on this, we not only will lose the baby, we'll lose an opportunity to crack a case we've been working on for three years; you and your fuckin' attorney general will be to blame. If you don't get off your ass and prepare the necessary paperwork now, I'm going to call my director in Washington. We'll let him tell your boss who is obstructing justice."

Justin's face paled first and then blossomed into a deep crimson as his jaw dropped and his eyelids widened. He shook his head slightly, gathered up his papers into this briefcase and stood. "I'll have the forms prepared and ready as quickly as possible. Mr. Carminagni, do you have the authority to speak for Mr. Marchesa?" he said as he looked at Deo and avoided eye contact with Ralph.

"Yes, I do, Justin," Deo answered. "I have the affidavit in my room. I never come to America without it."

"Good," he replied. "I'll have papers ready in a couple of hours. Can I find you here?"

"I'll be waiting."

"Ralph, you can initiate whatever plan necessary to wind this up. We're both on the same side, you know," said Justin in a conciliatory tone.

"Right, Justin. But we have to move fast."

Justin grinned and started for the door. "I'm moving as fast as I can," he said. "I'll take a taxi to my office."

Ralph kept his eyes focused on Deo with an eager expression, as if waiting to learn Deo's response to their discussion so far. Deo remained silent for a few agonizingly long seconds before speaking. Could he trust this FBI agent? If he consented to Ralph's request for information, was he playing his trump card with no gain? He had to risk it. His primary reason for being in the United States was to find the baby. They still held Gator, and Ralph desperately wanted a statement from Gator that might lead to a greater personal victory. Deo looked at Marcello, who was also waiting for a response.

"Marcello, tell Mr. Walton what you found out about the home where the baby is being kept—the St. Jude Home."

"Do I need to call Reyes?" Marcello asked.

"Not yet," said Deo. "We need to hear Ralph's plan. Go ahead and describe what Reyes found."

"We checked out the St. Jude Home," said Marcello. "It is a licensed foster home. They take care of young children while waiting for adoption papers to be processed. If a baby is left there, they are required to notify Child Protective Services. The child is held for a while, since sometimes parents change their minds and return for the baby. After a period of time, the baby is put up for adoption; but still the CPS has to be notified immediately when a child is left at the home."

"Then wouldn't the CPS have a record of the infant?" asked Ralph.

"This home doesn't always follow the rules. The home has been suspected of illegal adoption practices in the past. There is no record, according to Reyes's inquiry, that CPS had ever received a referral that matches the time this baby was left at the home. Reyes thinks the home was paid by someone to delay making a report. The two security people on duty there now appeared right after our baby was left. Reyes believes they work for Paretto."

"In that case, if we move in, Paretto will be notified immediately," said Ralph. "If we find that your informant, Gator, is telling the truth and the Joberst baby is in the home, I plan to move in on Paretto before he has a chance to run."

"I'm sure Gator is telling the truth," said Marcello. "He's desperate. He knows Paretto is after him."

"We've got to get in that home without Paretto knowing what we're doing," said Ralph. "Let me think about it for a few minutes. I have to have a warrant to go after Paretto. The warrant has to be authorized as soon as we know for sure that the baby is in the home. If we find the baby, then Gator's story is validated."

"Won't you have to wait for a positive DNA to identify the baby?" asked Deo.

Ralph became pensive. He stared vacantly into space with his chin resting on his clasped hands. Suddenly his face brightened. "No, no, no! We don't have to wait. Barbara can make positive identification," he said as he reached for his cell phone. "Barbara noticed a small birthmark behind the baby's ear when he was born. She can identify the Joberst baby. I need to call Wes to get over here in a hurry."

"Then you're ready to move, right?" asked Deo. "What's your plan, Ralph?"

"We go for the baby!" said Ralph, now keyed up to a high pitch, shouting commands like a general on a battlefield. "Call your man, Marcello, and tell him that we'll be entering the home and to give us space. We'll take the two guards. If they are Paretto's men, they'll be armed, in which case we'll have them arrested and hold them in confinement as long as possible so they can't tip Paretto off to what we're doing."

Wes returned his call. "Wes, we know where the baby is hidden. Send an agent to pick up Andy and Barbara and bring them here. We're going in. Hurry! This will be a blitz. When you get here, Marcello will give you directions to the home where the baby is kept."

"What do we do while this is going on?" asked Deo.

"You and Marcello will ride with Wes and lead us to the target. I'll ride with Andy and Barbara. You'll stay in the car when we go in. I don't want Paretto's guys seeing you. For your information, Barbara was the Joberst baby's nurse at the time of the kidnapping. She has been an invaluable friend to Mrs. Joberst. She's been right by her side in the hospital ever since the shooting. You can trust her to get the baby to its mother."

"Just make sure there are no slipups, Ralph. As soon as we know the baby is with its mother, we'll deliver Gator to you. You also need to make sure Justin includes witness protection for Gator in the agreement."

Ralph flashed a crooked half-smile. "You really want Paretto out of the way, don't you, Deo? Alberto comes back, Paretto gets busted. Nice wrap up. Get the government to work for you to make the competition disappear."

"Come on, Ralph. Let's don't shit around with each other," said Deo, his eyes locked on Ralph's in a penetrating glare. "You want Paretto indicted. You need that more than Alberto needs amnesty. You'll be a hero—you'll have found the baby and brought down a powerful mob. Alberto will comply with the government's requirements—trust me,"

"Okay, let's trust each other," said Ralph, an edge to his voice that matched Deo's ferocity. "But get this straight. If you fuck with me on this deal, Deo, I'll come after you, and I'll find you." He paused for emphasis. "As soon as Barbara and Andy get here, we need to get rolling."

# 39

Andy and Barbara had been alone for no longer than one hour when there was a knock on the door. Grumbling that they had been disturbed, Andy dragged himself to the door and cracked it open enough to identify their visitor. It was the same agent who had driven them to the apartment.

"Mr. Goldeyer, Agent Walton wants both of you to come to a hotel where he is in conference about the kidnapped baby; he wants you to come to the Omni Campbell Center Hotel as soon as possible. The car will be ready outside when you come down."

\* \* \* \*

Ralph paced back and forth on the hotel entrance driveway waiting on Andy and Barbara's arrival. As soon as the black Malibu drove up, Ralph hopped into the front seat. In another black Malibu sedan, Deo and Marcello sat, with Wes at the wheel, waiting for the action to begin.

Ralph called Wes. "All secure here, Wes. Let's go!" As soon as Wes, driving the car with Deo and Marcello, pulled out, Ralph motioned their driver to follow. He turned to address Andy and Barbara.

"Barbara, Andy, I have some news for you, but I don't want you to get your hopes built high. We think we know where the baby is being held." Barbara gasped and grabbed her throat. Ralph continued, "I know you have a dozen questions. Right now, just pray that we will find the infant. I need you to identify the baby when we do. Can you do that?"

"Absolutely!" she responded. "Oh, we need to tell Leanne right away."

"Not yet," said Ralph. "We need to be sure. We think this information is valid, but we have to be sure."

Barbara fell into Andy's arms. "Andy, could it be true? Is there a chance we might find Leanne's baby?"

"Mr. Walton thinks so," Andy replied.

"We may have some trouble recovering the baby," said Ralph. "I don't think you are in danger, but stay close to me when we go into the home."

"Where is the baby, Mr. Walton?" asked Barbara.

"The baby was left at St. Jude's Home for Children," he answered. "We think it's still at the home, but we really don't know what to expect until we get there, so be ready for anything. I want you and Andy to stay in the car while Wes and I go into the home. I'll signal you when it's time for you to come in. Barbara, if we find the baby, I want you to look for the birthmark and verify that it is definitely the right baby."

"I can do that," said Barbara eagerly, scooting close to Andy. "After all this time that we've been hoping, maybe it's coming true." Andy and Barbara held each other's hands and smiled as if enveloped in an aura of anticipation.

"We all are excited," Ralph said. "Still, I must warn you, we cannot be sure what we will find. We are reasonably certain that the baby was left at this home, but we won't know until we check. Here's what we will do: There are two guards protecting the entrance. We'll deal with them first. Watch for my signal. I don't think we'll have any trouble, but if there's any chance at all of danger to you, Wes or the other agent will take you back to the car."

The procession—one black sedan following another identical automobile—entered the LBJ Freeway and headed toward Garland. Marcello, his cell phone to his ear, updated Reyes on the recent development and gave him last-minute instructions. Within minutes they pulled up in front of the St. Jude's Children's Home. Ralph and Wes exited their vehicles and approached the house. The two security guards seated on the wide front porch stood and confronted them.

One guard spoke authoritatively. "You're not allowed in here. Sorry."

Wes and Ralph both drew their weapons and flashed their FBI identification badges. "FBI," said Ralph. "Keep your hands over your shoulders, turn, and place them on the porch rail," he commanded.

Wes removed guns from both guards and frisked them for hidden firearms. "Do you have permits to carry hidden weapons?" asked Ralph. Both guards scowled and refused to answer. "Cuff them both to the porch rail, Wes, while I call for a wagon. It's the cooler for you both for a while."

Ralph and Wes didn't knock before entering the house through the unlocked front door. A startled fifty-something lady came from an adjacent small office.

"Oh, I thought you were the guards. How may I help you, gentlemen?"

"You can answer some questions, Mrs....?" said Ralph, as he held his credentials in front of her. "We are from the FBI, ma'am."

"Winstead ... Nancy Winstead," she replied. Her eyebrows arched and she stared at Ralph with a questioning look.

"Mrs. Winstead, a few weeks ago, a newborn baby was left with you. We want you to produce that infant for us to check, now," said Ralph, his voice urgent. "You have been holding a baby that was abducted from a hospital nursery."

Nancy Winstead couldn't conceal her shock. She became pallid, her cheeks blushed, her pupils dilated. She glanced briefly toward a closed door behind which echoed a murmur of energized, playful children.

"You must be mistaken," she said finally after regaining her air of haughtiness. "We would know if a baby, especially a newborn, was left with us."

"What would you do if by chance someone did indeed leave an anonymous baby with you?"

"Why, we would care for the baby and hope the mother would identify herself so we could help them both."

"And if the mother just handed you the baby and left, what would you do?"

"In that case, we would have to call Child Protective Services immediately," she replied with a tone of confidence. "The baby would be placed under their custody."

"Mrs. Winstead, you need to reconsider your answer to my inquiry," said Ralph, looking intensively into the scared lady's eyes. "First, you didn't call CPS in this case, and second, by holding this child, you have committed a federal offense by interfering with a criminal investigation."

Ralph remained silent while Nancy, her chin quivering and her eyes shining with the beginnings of tears, contemplated her answer. She glanced again at the closed door behind her before finally speaking.

"Mr. Tatum sent someone to pick up the baby last night," she said. "He said he knew the mother and that she had changed her mind and wanted her baby back."

Ralph tried to hide his despair at the story that someone had come earlier and had taken the baby away. Did this news herald another failure? How could this happen? Deo and Marcello had assured him that their men were watching the house. But with the thick foliage around the home and the presence of Paretto's guards, he could see how someone could have taken the baby unnoticed.

"Mr. Tatum paid you to take care of the baby, didn't he?" asked Ralph. "And he told you not to call the CPS, didn't he?"

Nancy eyes became tear filled and she held onto a nearby chair. "I didn't mean to break the law," she said. "I needed the money. I don't get offers like that in this business."

"We will need to search your home, Mrs. Winstead."

She stiffened, regained her composure, and fired back at Ralph. "You can't do that. You need a warrant. I will call my attorney." She whirled to return to her office. Wes blocked her way.

"I'm sorry, Mrs. Winstead," said Ralph. "I had hoped you would cooperate. In so doing, you might have been able to avoid arrest and prosecution. I don't need a warrant when I am investigating a federal offense."

Nancy dropped her head, sat in the chair, and remained silent. "What do you want from me?" she said finally, a scowl on her face.

"The truth, Nancy," Ralph replied. "Wes, call for our backup. We need to check every corner of this home. Also, call the CPS for an emergency audit and inspection."

"Our backup is already here, Mr. Walton. They came with the vehicle to pick up Paretto's men."

"Good, bring them in and motion for Barbara and Andy to come in. Let's start our search."

"I don't have to cooperate with you without a court order," said Nancy. "You're invading the privacy of a children's home. If you don't leave, I can file charges against both of you."

"Nancy, you can instruct your aides to help us or we'll have to include them also in our sweep of arrests. I want to interrogate each employee, beginning now," said Ralph. "You can save everyone a lot of trouble if you simply answer the question: Where is the baby that Mr. Tatum paid you to care for?"

"I've already told you," she screamed as she sulked in a corner and cradled her head in the palm of one hand. "He sent someone to pick up the baby last night."

"Then why did he keep the guards here?" Nancy didn't look up and didn't answer.

Andy and Barbara received the signal and entered the home, accompanied by one of the agents. Ralph's face told the story that all was not going well.

"Barbara, this is Mrs. Winstead. She is in charge here. There's bad news. She says the baby is not here," Ralph announced in a tone that conveyed his disappointment and sorrow. "Nancy, please show Barbara the nursery where you keep the infants. Barbara is a hospital nursery nurse. I would like for her to examine the babies you have in the nursery."

"Go ahead. The baby's not there. Mr. Tatum has it. I imagine he saw the mother on TV and got worried someone here might grab a chance to pick up a pile of money. That rich bitch will pay plenty to get that baby back. And what does she deserve—running around with a playboy while she's married to the father of her baby? What kind of mother would she be? Go on in. One of the girls will show you the nursery. And don't disturb the older children."

"Then you saw the clip of the parents' appeal, didn't you?" asked Ralph.

"Well, yes," she replied. "It came on every half-hour. I couldn't miss it."

With Andy at her side, Barbara found the nursery and looked at each of the babies. None had the mark that she so wanted to see. The young nursery aide stood by while Barbara inspected each infant.

"How many babies do you usually have?" she asked the aide.

"Right now we have three. Sometimes four or five."

"I'm sure you keep an accurate log of your babies—their weights, how well they nurse. You know when they arrive here and when they leave."

"Oh, yes. Mrs. Winstead says the CPS requires us to keep accurate records."

"Can we look at your log?"

"Sure," she said as she pulled out the master list of babies—each given a pet name for identification.

Andy thumbed through the log and found the baby that was admitted the day Leanne's baby was kidnapped. It was named QB. Three days later, another baby boy showed up on the log and was named RB.

"What do these initials mean?" asked Andy.

The aide laughed. "The nurse that checked both of them in is an avid football fan. QB stands for quarterback and RB for running back. She's a fantasy football freak. She gives the babies points every time they gain an ounce."

"How cute," said Barbara. "I don't see QB or RB in here. What happened?"

"Someone came and picked up RB last night while I was not on duty. Nancy said the mother wanted the baby back. I don't know what happened to QB. I asked Nancy, but she didn't say who got that baby. I guess it was an adoption agency. QB was here yesterday and gone when I came to work today."

"So both of these babies were picked up late at night?"

"Yeah, I don't know why, but seems like every adoption we do, the babies are taken out late at night."

"Do you show on the log where the babies go?"

"It's supposed to, as you can see, but the log doesn't show where these last two babies went. I guess Mrs. Winstead hasn't had time to complete the paperwork. She'll have to before the next CPS inspection."

"Thank you, Miss ... oh, I didn't get your name."

"Beatrice," she answered.

"Thank you, Beatrice. You've been very helpful."

Barbara and Andy, both appearing dejected, motioned for Ralph to join them outside. "Something's not right, Mr. Walton," said Andy. Looking downtrodden, he and Barbara narrated their findings in the nursery and in the log book—that two babies had been released during the night and that there was no address on either's destination.

Ralph gazed pensively across the expansive grounds around the home. After a moment, he seemed to come alive.

"Of course ... that's what happened!" he said aloud to no one in particular. He began calling out rapid-fire orders again.

"Wes, have your backup agents surround this house—no one comes in or leaves. Keep Nancy Winstead confined to her office. Disable the phone lines. Search and acquire all of the cell phones in the house. Find out Nancy Winstead's home address. Get six or eight other agents. We load up, go to Nancy's home address, and blitz her home as quickly as possible. Call the U.S. attorney's office. Get us a warrant to move in on Nancy's home. Just for good measure, look for dirty disposable diapers in the trash cans when we get to Nancy's house."

Ralph motioned for Andy and Barbara to follow, and they again loaded into their car. By then, four other black sedans had appeared on the scene. With portable red lights flashing, all five vehicles raced ten blocks down a side street and stopped in front of Nancy Winstead's home. The neighborhood was quiet until the blast of sirens and the flashing red lights brought a bevy of curious bystanders to the scene.

Ralph instructed Andy and Barbara to stay in the car until he summoned them. The agents crashed through the door without knocking. A young girl, about the same age as the nursing aides working at St. Jude's, met them at the door. She stepped aside as Ralph and the agents began their search of the house. Ralph opened the door to one of the small bedrooms and stopped in his tracks as if stunned at what he saw. "Thank God!" he said aloud. He called Barbara and Andy into the house and led them into the makeshift nursery. A bright eyed, cooing three-month-old baby with fine coal-black hair lay in a crib, its eyes roving as it watched a colorful overhead mobile dance with the movement of the air.

Barbara gasped. Tears flowed freely down her face. She made no effort to blot them. Andy and Agent Walton, both with wet eyes embraced each other. Barbara joined in the embrace.

"He's beautiful," said Barbara, as she confirmed the presence of the birthmark. "I'd know him even without the birthmark."

She picked up QB, sat in a rocker close by, and cuddled him close while she rocked. His eyes made contact with hers and he smiled, kicked his legs, waved his tiny clinched fists, and cooed in melodious tones while the three adults looked for ways to dry their cheeks.

\*     \*     \*     \*

On the way to the hospital, Barbara held Mr. QB in her arms. She didn't take her eyes off the infant. When he was awake she talked to him. When he was asleep she sang to him in a soft voice. Agent Walton turned toward the back seat with a look of wonderment. It was his day of victory.

"How did you know, Mr. Walton? How did you know where the baby had been hidden?" asked Andy.

Ralph smiled. "Andy, as you get older in this business, you learn to read between the lines. When Nancy began maligning Leanne as a 'rich bitch' and saying she would be a bad mother, I should have picked up on it right away. She was saying to herself, 'Here is an opportunity to take from the rich and give to the poor.' She couldn't pass up the opportunity to recover more money than she ever thought she would see in a lifetime. It's sad, but it is the nucleus of temptation in the criminal world."

"What's next?" asked Andy.

"We go to Parkland Hospital ER. I need to make arrangements for the baby to be admitted, confidentially, to the pediatric department for a routine checkup. Barbara can tell Leanne then. Later she will be able to have ... what name did they give him?"

Andy laughed. "QB," he answered. "Think he'll ever be able to drop that name?"

"I imagine his mom will change that." Ralph chuckled along with Andy. "Later, she'll be able to have QB at her bedside. We won't announce the recovery to the media until tomorrow. We storm Paretto's compound tonight. Tomorrow the media hounds will have plenty of news-meat to chew on."

\* \* \* \*

With an agent-driver at the wheel, Agent Walton in the front passenger seat—his cell phone at his ear—and Barbara, Andy, and QB in the back, a red-light run took them to the Parkland Emergency Room entrance. Ralph clicked his cell phone closed and turned to Barbara and Andy:

"Everything is arranged," he said. "Someone will meet you in the ER and take the baby to the pediatric floor for admission. I am told the infant will be examined and held in quarantine for twenty-four hours. I'll have an agent guarding the pediatric unit day and night."

"Will we be questioned?" asked Andy.

"I don't think you will, but if you are, don't comment. I am going to have my hands full for the next several hours, so I won't be going in with you. If you run into any snags, call me and I will return or send someone immediately. Find out who is in charge on the pediatric floor—get his or her name. I'm sure they will cooperate."

"When can I tell Leanne?" asked Barbara. She brushed QB's hair back as best she could and held the pacifier she had brought from the home in his mouth.

"Let her know the baby is all right," said Ralph. "She deserves to know. She can see the little one tomorrow."

As soon as Barbara entered the Emergency Room with the baby in her arms, a gloved and masked nurse from the Pediatric Pavilion—apparently alerted by Ralph Walton's call—met her at the door.

"You won't have to bother with registration. Someone will handle that later," she said as she reached for the baby. Barbara recoiled for a moment.

"I'll carry him to the nursery. He's used to me now."

"Sure," she said. "You're a nurse, aren't you?"

"Yeah, how did you know?"

"Just the way you carry the kid," she answered. "Come on, follow me. We've been told we have to keep absolute confidentiality. No one is supposed to know the baby is here."

"Can I come back and check on him?" asked Barbara.

"Sure, any time I'm here. I'll tell the next shift that you might come by. You like this kid, don't you?"

"If you knew the whole story, you'd understand."

"Tomorrow we can take him to his mother for a visit. Hope you can help there."

Barbara's grin covered her face. "I'll be glad to."

*     *     *     *

Barbara returned to Leanne's room to find her up in the chair. "How are you doing?" she asked nonchalantly, as she began cleaning the room of empty cups and strewn newspapers. "Are you ready to get back to bed?"

"I'm doing much better. The physical therapist walked me in the hall. I want to get out of here, Barbara. Any news from the outside?"

"Oh, nothing much," she answered, a cunning grin on her face. "Andy and I went with Mr. Walton to pick up a baby today. We left him down in the pediatric wing. He wants to see his mama."

"What?" she yelled. She sat up straight in the chair and attempted to stand. "Barbara, what did you say?"

"I couldn't tell you earlier," Barbara said. She bent over and pulled Leanne to her feet. The two girls clung to each other while they sobbed. "I'll explain it all to you later. He's fine, Leanne … he's beautiful," Barbara added. "Careful. Let me help you to bed. It's all over. He's back. He's fine."

"Oh, my God! I think I'm going to faint," she said as she slumped to the bed. "He's really here? He's all right?"

"He looks great. Maybe needs a haircut." Barbara laughed.

"I need to call Mark. When can I see him?"

"Tomorrow. He has to be examined and kept in isolation for a day. Then he's yours—at least until he's twenty-one."

"Am I going to be overprotective, Barbara?"

"Look, right now you have license to be any way you want to be."

"Barbara, you have got to promise me you'll help me raise him."

"I think we'll have to talk to Mark about that. He's probably going to have an opinion, you know."

"Sure, we'll all raise him. Seriously, I want him to grow up to know you and Andy. Someday I'll tell him the whole story."

"All right, enough talk," Barbara said. "Back to bed for you. I'll call Mark. Get some rest so you'll be ready for a special visitor tomorrow."

"I won't be able to sleep a wink."

"It'll be double-strength sleeping pills then. You have a busy day tomorrow."

Barbara tucked Leanne in bed. She placed a fresh pitcher of ice water on the bedside table, adjusted the bed so Leanne's head was slightly elevated, and took a tissue to her wet cheeks. Leanne lay quietly, staring at the ceiling. Her eyes closed and her lips moved as if she were mouthing words in a silent prayer. Barbara leaned over and kissed her forehead before turning to leave the room. Just as she opened the door Leanne called to her.

"Barbara, thank you."

"Good night, dear. I'll see you in the morning."

# 40

*Westlake*

Todd knew what he had to do; he had planned weeks for this very moment. He left Jake's suite through the rear door and headed for his own office, He had to move fast. His first act was to remove his shirt. He then unlocked the deep lower drawer to his desk and pulled out his gun, the shoulder holster, and the bulletproof vest that he had stashed away months ago. He examined his gun carefully to ensure that the magazine was filled. Handling the gun reminded him of the grueling daily target practice he had committed to these last few weeks. After fitting the vest snugly over his undershirt, he replaced his shirt and tie. Lastly, just before he slipped into his blue blazer, he secured the holster and gun over his shoulder.

Earlier in the day he had packed all of the essential personal items he wanted to take in the two briefcases that he had kept in readiness for that purpose. He double-checked to confirm he was leaving nothing of value behind.

Next, he seated himself in front of his computer and, with rhythmic clacking of the keyboard, began writing e-mail messages. First on the list was his letter of resignation; next a note to Karen informing her that he would not be returning; then he notified Human Resources that he would be using all of his PTO and that he didn't expect any severance pay. He smiled thinking of the confusion that would arise when e-mail sent to his current address would be returned.

He had practiced his exit so many times in his mind that within a few minutes he had completed almost everything he had set out to do—including deleting every bit of information from the hard drive of his computer. After retrieving his new passport, credit cards, and driver's license from the brief case—all showing his new name—he shredded his old documents, except for his Trinitus ID badge. He glanced about the room, his work home for almost four years. He felt no nostalgia. In fact, he looked forward to a new life—with a new name and a new assignment.

Once in the corridor he walked at a fast pace, not toward the rear entrance, which was close to his reserved parking slot, but instead toward the front of the hospital. He flashed his ID badge.

"Good night, Mr. Langley," said the guard as he opened the electronic lock on the door.

"Thanks, Sam," Todd replied as he walked past. Once outside, he waved at the surveillance camera that forever whirred overhead. He tossed his Trinitus badge into the next trash receptacle that he passed.

A short walk brought him to his new black Malibu sedan that had been delivered earlier in the day. The key was on top of the rear left wheel, as expected. When would the attack by Tate come? So far, no sign of Paretto's hit man—but it was early. Maybe Jake had fallen asleep and hadn't made the call yet. No matter when it came, he was ready. He felt sure he had prepared for any eventuality. Once inside the vehicle, he found his assignment packet in the glove compartment. What a relief to finally get away from Trinitus and Jake Hensley—forever, he hoped.

He checked his passport for his new name. Now, he would answer only to the name Tom Beatty and ignore the name Todd Langley from this day forward. How could he train himself to make his new name and social security number indelible in his memory? He remembered his surveillance class, where he was taught to say his new name one hundred times daily for a week without stopping. Next, he had had to shut out the name Todd Langley permanently.

He checked his assignment location: Dallas, Texas. That was disappointing to some degree, but wasn't surprising. It would put him closer to Tate in case Tate didn't show up at Todd's Westlake address tonight. If he didn't come tonight, Todd would leave a forwarding address to Dallas and wait for him to make his move there. Todd wondered why he felt no fear. But why worry? He could take Tatum out before he could even get off one shot. Actually, the thought of being attacked by Tate pumped adrenalin through his arteries. He even hoped Tate would try it tonight so he could go on to Dallas and find out why he was needed there.

*       *       *       *

The early dawn light filtered through the slightly parted curtains in his bedroom. He had slept fitfully for the five hours since he went to bed, the heavy bulletproof vest keeping him from fully relaxing. He bounced out of bed and headed for the bathroom. It was time to put his day-one plan into effect.

He called the assignment coordinator in Washington. "This is Tom Beatty in Westlake, Texas. My new assignment is Dallas. Can you give me the address where I will be living? It wasn't in my assignment packet."

"Sure, Mr. Beatty. Please give me your ID number, password, date of birth, and social security number."

Tom searched through his packet and read the information back to the coordinator.

"Thank you, Mr. Beatty. We show your address to be 3812 Turtle Creek Drive, number 405. You should confirm that address with our Dallas office."

"Thank you, miss. I'll do that."

He dressed, made sure his accouterments were all in place, and called Human Resources at Trinitus Westlake Hospital and gave his forwarding address. If HR wouldn't give it to Tate, Tate would get it from Jake. Tom looked forward to a leisurely drive to Dallas. He would arrive there sometime by the late afternoon. If he guessed right, Tate first would try to find him in Westlake. Once he had learned that he had moved, Tate would check for a forwarding address and make his move sometime that very day, after Tom checked into his new home. Tom checked his watch. He had plenty of time to drive to Dallas and get settled. The traffic that early was mostly made up of eight o'clock warriors. He hit Interstate 35, played the CD of his favorite rock artist, and used the travel time to reminisce about the past three years. He had wondered many times why he had put up with Trinitus and its despicable, immoral, illegal tactics for so long.

But, of course, with the bureau you just do your job and go where you are told. He had kept accurate, up-to-date logs on everything he had witnessed at Trinitus and had turned in his final report three days earlier. His report should shake someone in the upper management level of the department. On the negative side, accumulating so much data had made him conspicuous, and that was why he was being targeted by Paretto. Why did he keep referring to himself as the target? His new assignment had been only a few simple words. *Move to Dallas and assist Agent Walton when summoned.*

\* \* \* \*

## *Dallas*

By the end of the day, the sun an orange ball creeping slowly below the horizon, Tom wound through Turtle Creek Drive looking for number 3812. Almost hidden behind a cluster of giant elm trees, he spotted the multistory building with its address on a post alongside the entrance driveway. He found a slot in the visitor's parking lot and drove in. There was no visible activity around the front of the twelve-story edifice. Tom, looking closely into every shadow and behind every bit of landscaping he passed, found the leasing office, introduced himself, and received the key to his unit.

He stood in the elevator lobby waiting for one of the elevators. On the display above the elevator door he could track its progress. It stopped on the fourth floor. After a brief pause, it continued to the first. Tom stepped out of sight into a recess in the lobby near the exit door to the stairwell and watched. The elevator door opened. Tom recognized the tall, blubbery man with slicked-down black hair and a closely trimmed moustache as Tatum. He had seen enough pictures of him that there was no doubt of his identity.

Tom had already drawn his gun. He held it at his side as he stepped out of his hiding place.

"Looking for me Tate?" said Tom, a furtive smile on his face.

Tate was startled at his name being called and didn't recognize Tom at first. When he did, he went for his gun, aimed it at Tom and pulled the trigger. The bullet glanced off Tom's vest. Tom raised his gun, took careful aim, and put two bullet holes in Tate's head, not more than an inch apart. Blood mixed with cerebrospinal fluid spurted into the air like a water fountain. Tate crumpled to the floor. He gasped once. His eyes closed, but the shocked expression on his face didn't change. Tom looked around to confirm that no one had been disturbed by the muffled gunshots. He stepped into the elevator cab and pushed the button to the fourth floor. Tom put in a call to Agent Walton and waited in his new home for a return call.

# 41

## Dallas

At approximately 2:00 A.M., five carloads of armed FBI agents, led by Agent Walton, plus the Dallas Police Department SWAT team under the supervision of Detective Blake Bartlett, converged on the back gate of the walled compound at 48 Manor Drive in Highland Park. After laying a heavy, protective metal blanket over the razor-sharp barbed wire that capped the barricade, the storming attack began with the SWAT team scaling the eight-foot brick wall. Once over the barrier, the team neutralized the gate guard, who happened to be napping at the time, deactivated the alarm system link to the mansion security center, and opened the gate to allow the FBI's agents onto the grounds.

As he passed through the gate, Agent Walton placed a copy of the warrant in the guard house—in clear view of the bound-and-gagged and terrified guard, who struggled to free himself. The blitz attack, moving at incredible speed, picked up momentum when the agents crashed through the front door of the plush mansion, scattered into each room of the house, and took every person they encountered prisoner. The last room they searched was Dimitrio Paretto's private quarters.

Sleepy-eyed from being awakened suddenly, Paretto sat up in bed, his face a mask of confusion, as if he was trying to comprehend the disturbance around him. He reached toward the nightstand drawer, but one of the agents was blocking it.

"Tate! Tate!" he yelled as two agents pulled him to his feet and pulled his arms behind him for cuffing. "Where the shit are you, Tate?"

"FBI, Mr. Paretto," said Ralph, showing his FBI badge and placing a copy of the warrant on the table. "You are under arrest, Mr. Paretto." Ralph read him his Miranda rights.

"I want to call my lawyers. Where the hell is Tatum?"

"Tatum won't be of help to you now, Mr. Paretto. He's dead."

"Whaddya mean dead?" he said. "Somebody find Tatum, goddamn it. He was here just a little while ago. Can somebody tell me what the shit this is all about? Take these fuckin' cuffs off my arms. You're hurting my shoulders."

"Mr. Paretto, I will tell you again: anything you say can and will be held against you."

"I don't give a shit. I've got good lawyers. I've got connections. You're gonna be in deep trouble when your boss finds out. Hey! What are you doing?" he screamed when he saw an agent loading his computer tower onto a cart. "You can't do that."

"Let's go, Mr. Paretto. You can call your lawyers from the station. Your computer will be returned to you. We need it for our investigation. It's included in the warrant."

"Goddamn you! I'll get you for this. Nobody shits on Dimitrio Paretto and gets away with it. Goddamn Tate! Goddamn that fuckin' judge! They are both alike—greedy for more money. I told them it wouldn't work."

*   *   *   *

Three hours behind bars waiting for the arrival of his lawyers did nothing for Dimitrio Paretto's congeniality. He paced the floor, rattled the cell door and yelled repeatedly for someone to call his attorneys again. When they did arrive and were ushered into Dimitrio's cell, Paretto launched into a tirade demanding that they get him out of there, whatever it took.

"Please try to calm down, Dimitrio," said the older attorney, who seemed to have assumed the lead role.

"What the hell have I done? Why am I here?" Paretto demanded. "Probably something that fuckin' Tate has done. Can't you find out?"

"Mr. Paretto, we will try our best," the lead attorney said. "You can be held for as long as forty-eight hours without charges being filed. We will have to get a writ of *habeas corpus* in order to force the FBI to reveal why you are being held. Just be calm and let us work on it."

"Then get to hell out of here and work on it," Paretto replied. "I want out of here. I want to find Tate. Where is that son of a bitch?"

"We are told that Nicholas Tatum was killed when he attacked an FBI agent."

The news hit Paretto broadside. Stunned and quiet, he dropped his head and sat on the bench for a few moments, and then he raised his head and glared at the attorneys. "Find out if he said anything before he died."

Both attorneys, with contemptible glares in their eyes, turned and walked away. "We'll come back when we have some news to tell you."

\*    \*    \*    \*

Four carefully planned and coordinated events occurred simultaneously across the state. At exactly the same hour, two FBI agents, unannounced and carrying arrest warrants, arrived at a United States courthouse in each of the four federal judicial districts in Texas. They showed their credentials at the security desk, and from there they were escorted around the weapon-detection booth and led to a specific courtroom. Each federal district judge was arrested in his chambers and read his Miranda rights.

Without being handcuffed, the judges peacefully accompanied the agents outside the building to an awaiting vehicle. They were transferred to the nearest police station, booked, and placed in a private cell. Each of the judge's private quarters in the court house was sealed and left guarded by United States marshals. The bailiffs, secretaries, clerks, and lawyers who witnessed the events stood by aghast, looking vacantly at each other as if waiting for some explanation.

\*    \*    \*    \*

## Dallas

As he was escorted out of the courthouse Judge Anthony Joberst attempted, unsuccessfully, to use his cell phone. He yelled and screamed at his captors, who included Agent Walton.

"Do you know who I am? You can't come into a federal court house and arrest a federal judge. I have immunity from this sort of treatment. I am responsible only to the Congress of the United States. Give me my phone, you bastards, so I can call a United States attorney. I'll have your jobs, you imbeciles."

Once at the station, the agents needed to use a minimum of force to guide Anthony into his cell. The door slammed shut and locked automatically. With a look of disgust on his face, Ralph stayed outside the cell and took one last look at Judge Joberst through the bars. He looked around to confirm that no one was watching. His piercing eyes locked with Anthony's.

Knowing his remarks would be considered inappropriate and probably illegal, he still couldn't resist saying, "Shut up, you son of bitch. I hope you get the maximum sentence. You kidnapped your own wife's baby because you knew it wasn't yours, and you gave an order to have your wife killed. You're the scum of humanity."

"And who the hell are you?" Anthony asked.

"I'm the lowly public servant who has uncovered every evil deed you've ever committed. That includes organizing the Qlozd Network."

When he mentioned Qlozd, Anthony recoiled, became pallid, and sat on the nearest concrete bench. After a half-minute, Anthony appeared more composed and stood. "Don't try to bluff me, shit-ass. You know nothing about Qlozd. As soon as my lawyer gets me out of here, I'll get you demoted to a file clerk for your behavior."

"You know, I heard the same type of remark last night from your buddy, Dimitrio Paretto, when I arrested him—when he told me it was you who engaged him to plan and kidnap your own baby," Ralph said. A sinister expression creased his face. "Get your act together. It would make a great short story. Maybe we can arrange for you and Dimitrio to share cells."

"You bastard," said Anthony. "One call and I can erase your existence."

"On second thought," said Ralph. "You might luck out and get to sleep with Richard Weatherford as your cellmate."

✳ ✳ ✳ ✳

Alan Shipman, off to an early start, cruised along Central Expressway on his way to his office at a leisurely pace. The traffic was moderately heavy, which told him that he was competing with both top-echelon and mid-level managers on their way to the workplace. He tuned out the early morning radio talk show and settled on one of the oldies stations. The soft, relaxing tunes set his mind wandering to the recent performance reports that he had just read on the multiple Trinitus hospitals under his direction.

The financials of all of the hospitals looked exceedingly favorable, especially those facilities linked to the Qlozd Network. Thinking of Qlozd reminded him that he had not heard from Anthony or Richard lately. They should be planning on a Qlozd meeting soon for updating and for distribution of accumulated funds to the partners. He would have to agree with Richard and Anthony that bringing in additional participants would be risky. They had a good thing going. Why rock the boat? Why take a chance on eroding the multi-tiered risk protection strategy that they had in place? They couldn't be more secure from outside audits.

As he neared the multistoried Trinitus Healthcare System home office building and his private parking slot in the garage, the music from the radio ceased. An announcer cut in with a news breaking message:

*We interrupt this program to bring you a news update. The FBI has announced that the Joberst baby, abducted from a local hospital three months ago, has been recovered and is in good condition. At the same time, the FBI spokesperson also reported that four federal judges in Texas had been arrested for crimes linked to an ongoing investigation of RICO violations, the federal anti-racketeering law. Specifics on these arrests are not available. More will be reported later.*

The music resumed. Alan, stunned and confused, pulled into his parking space and sat motionless in the car for a few minutes trying to sift through the message that he had just heard. He reached for his cell phone and dialed Richard's number. He hadn't noticed the two FBI agents approaching his car until he stepped out. One of the agents grabbed his phone before the call went through.

"FBI, Mr. Shipman," said one of the agents. "You are under arrest, sir." Alan was read his Miranda rights, handcuffed, and led to the black Malibu parked at the entrance to the parking garage.

\*    \*    \*    \*

## Westlake

Jake Hensley arrived at his office a few minutes early. He wanted to be ready for his administrative team meeting. Tops on the day's agenda would be the discussion of Todd's replacement. He was sure there would be questions from his administrative associates regarding the reason Todd had left suddenly. How could he answer the inquiries and avoid telling the real story? He'd think of a way. Todd was the only other top-level management person who had any suspicion of the Qlozd Network—and he had heard too much. Jake felt sure there would be a message from Tate on his e-mail that the problem had been resolved.

Karen had placed a list on his desk of potential replacements, with notations after each name. Jake scanned the list. None seemed to satisfy the qualifications necessary for chief operating officer. After the meeting, he would call Alan for possibilities from one or two of the other Trinitus Hospitals. Also on his desk was the copy of the *Dallas Morning News*, which Karen brought for him every day.

He had twenty minutes before the A-Team members arrived, enough time to browse through the *Dallas Morning News*. On page three of the first section an article caught his eye. The headline read,

*Assailant Killed after Attack on FBI Agent*

The article stated that there was no apparent cause for the attack. The attacker had been identified as a member of an underworld organization. His name and that of the FBI agent had been withheld pending further investigation.

Beads of sweat erupted on Jake's forehead. He stiffened and sat up straight in his chair. He reached for his desk phone and, with trembling fingers, dialed Tate's number. He grabbed for the armrests on his chair when the voice on the other end of the line answered, "Federal Bureau of Investigation. Calls to the number you have reached are being monitored. Please state your name."

He had no sooner cradled the hand piece than Karen called. Her shaky voice confirmed what Jake suspected—the worst. "Mr. Hensley, there are two men here from the FBI to see you."

\*    \*    \*    \*

## *Dallas*

Richard Weatherford stood in the building lobby waiting for the express elevator to his office suite that occupied the entire twenty-second floor of the tallest skyscraper in downtown Dallas. He couldn't erase from his mind the profound sense of foreboding that had hovered over him since he awakened. It reminded him of his days as a trial lawyer, when he could tell when something unpleasant was going to surface in one of his cases. That clairvoyance had been a decided asset in those days, but why now? He couldn't shake the feeling and dreaded what he would face when he entered his office.

Instead of going directly to his private entrance, he decided for some reason to go through the reception room. He did that occasionally just to get a glimpse of the clientele that he and his associates would be seeing. In one corner of the room, close to the door to his own private reception area, two well-groomed young men, dressed alike in dark suits, were seated side by side but away from the other waiting visitors. Richard surmised that they had come there together for some purpose. Both were reading magazines and didn't look up when he walked through. He had not recognized either person.

As soon as he entered his office, his secretary, pallid and with a frightened look, identified the two individuals, handed Richard their business cards, and announced that they demanded that they be ushered into his office immediately on his arrival. Before Richard could take a second gasp, his phone rang. He picked up the receiver with a shaking hand. The law firm's telephone operator was on the line.

"Mr. Weatherford, some lawyer called. He wouldn't give his name, but he said to tell you as soon as possible that a Mr. Dimitrio Paretto was being held in the central Dallas police station awaiting magistrate hearing on charges. That's all he said, Mr. Weatherford."

Richard dropped the phone on the desk and turned toward his computer. Before he could reach for the button to block all access, the door opened and the two FBI agents, flashing their identity badges, surrounded Richard, pulled him to his feet, and began reading him his rights.

# 42

*Dallas, Parkland Hospital*

Barbara walked alongside the bassinet in which Mr. QB lay sleeping, undisturbed by the rocking motion of the crib, which was being pushed along the hospital corridor by the pediatric department nurse.

"Must be a special baby," said the nurse.

Barbara laughed. "You better believe it."

"Relative of yours?"

"Not blood kin, no," she replied as she held on to the bassinet to slow the pace as they rounded a corner, "but we're related."

"Must be some mystery here," she said. "On the nursing unit, all sorts of murmurs and rumors."

"Yeah, I can imagine. You'll read about it someday," said Barbara. "I'm not supposed to talk about it."

Once they arrived at Leanne's room, the nurse handed the chart over to the floor charge nurse and turned the bassinet over to Barbara. "Thanks for your help," she said. "Looking forward to learning what this is all about."

Barbara chuckled. "You'll like the story. It's got a happy ending."

Leanne, Mark, and Andy were anxiously awaiting her arrival. She knocked on the door and wheeled the baby into the room and straight to its mother's side. "The prince has arrived," Barbara announced. She lifted the now-awake baby out of the crib, placed him in Leanne's arms, and then passed around the tissue for everyone's wet eyes and cheeks.

"I have prayed for this moment for so long," said Leanne, her arms cradling QB and holding him as close to her chest as she could. Her head dropped, and even with closed eyes tear drops rolled down her face to the baby's blanket. "I can't believe that it's happening."

Mark, his arm around Leanne's shoulders, careful not to put pressure on her bandages, kept his eyes glued to the baby in an unblinking stare with a look of wonderment on his face. With his other hand, he gently stroked the baby's head and cheeks and swept his fingers through the mat of coal black hair.

He examined the baby's feet, counted each toe, and then took the infant's tiny hands in his and wrapped the baby's fingers around his index fingers. He gently pulled against QB's grip as though testing the baby's strength. His face embossed by an ear-to-ear grin of pride, he looked at the others as though expecting some congratulatory comment. When he touched the baby's chin, QB made eye contact with Mark, smiled, and started a melodious cooing.

"He's really ours, isn't he," said Mark, his voice breaking and his chin trembling as he spoke. "He's really ours." Mark pulled Leanne close and kissed her.

"He really belongs to all four of us," said Leanne, "and we are all going to see that he's well cared for, aren't we?" she added as she looked at Barbara and Andy, both nodding and blotting their eyes.

The floor nurse arrived with a bottle of formula. "We're not used to this on this floor," she said, a broad grin on her face. She handed the bottle to Barbara "I'm glad we have a nursery nurse here."

"We'll manage fine," said Barbara.

"Let me know when it is time for the baby to go back to the pediatric unit," the nurse said.

"I don't think I will ever let him out of my sight again," said Leanne with a chuckle. "And neither will his father."

After feeding, QB drifted back asleep and soon was returned to the pediatric floor.

* * * *

Agent Walton tapped on the door before entering.

"I'm glad to find you all together," said Ralph, smiling. "I know this is a solemn—but happy occasion. You all had a part in bringing this about and I want to thank you all for your bravery and fortitude during this nightmare. I'm sure you have many questions so I want to update you on what's happening."

"Are we all out of danger, Mr. Walton? Can we expect to get back to normal lives?" asked Andy.

"Andy, I know how you must feel. I wish I could say the danger is over. All I can tell you is that it is almost over," Ralph replied. He seated himself with the two couples gathered around him. "I'm going to describe the entire scenario." He paused for a second. "I think most of you have heard of the Qlozd Network. I know Andy has."

"I'm not totally clear about the Qlozd Network," said Mark, "but from what Leanne has told me, I gather it is a disreputable organization."

"That's putting it mildly," said Ralph. "The Qlozd Network was a consortium of corrupt, dishonorable individuals, and I am glad to report that it has been broken. All eight partners have been arrested. This includes Dimitrio Paretto, the don of the largest mob operating in the United States; Alan Shipman, the chief executive of the Trinitus Health Care System; Jake Hensley, the CEO of Trinitus Westlake; Richard Weatherford, the attorney for the group; and ..." He hesitated a moment and looked at Leanne. "And Judge Joberst and his three handpicked federal district judges. I'm not going into detail about the function of the Qlozd Network except to say the world is better off without it. You'll be hearing a lot from the news media for months to come about its illegal activities."

"So there *was* a link between Qlozd and the abduction and the attempts on Leanne's life," said Andy. "How did that come about?"

"Through his connection with Qlozd, Anthony Joberst developed a close relationship with the Paretto mob. Anthony knew he was not the father of Leanne's baby. Long before the baby was due to be born, he decided to get rid of it. So he engaged Paretto to pull off the abduction. He planned to extract as much ransom as possible from Leanne's trust fund, split the money with Paretto, and then get rid of the baby and Leanne. As a part of his plea bargain, Paretto has indicated that he will testify against Anthony Joberst to that effect."

"How could anyone be so evil?" asked Mark, his arm around Leanne. "He kidnapped his own wife's child and contracted with Paretto to have his wife assassinated."

"And how could I have been so naïve to get into such a miserable relationship with anyone as unscrupulous as Anthony Joberst," said Leanne.

"You can't look back, Leanne," said Mark as he stroked her glistening cheeks. "We just look forward now; we have a new life and an obligation to raise QB."

"What will happen to the Qlozd partners, Mr. Walton?" asked Andy.

"They all have been arrested and booked. They are being held while the government prosecutors prepare charges against each of the suspects. Next, they will go before a magistrate, who will hear the charges, set bonds, and decide if there is enough evidence to refer the cases to the federal grand jury. The grand jury will examine the evidence and decide if the accused should be indicted, in which case a trial date will be set."

"Anthony will get out of it somehow," said Leanne. "He prides himself on knowing 'important' people. I've heard him brag about that over and over again."

"It won't be easy for him this time," said Ralph. "I really think there's no way out for him. He is facing years of prison—maybe a lifetime."

"Are not federal judges immune from prosecution of certain crimes?" asked Mark. "I thought they could only be punished by impeachment by Congress."

"They can only be removed from office by impeachment, but if they commit a felony, they are subject to the same judicial process as any citizen. If they are found guilty, they are sentenced first, and then they would go through the impeachment process."

"In the meantime then, they could still continue serving as a judge?" Mark asked.

"Yes, they could, but they would likely resign before being impeached when guilt is so evident, as it is here," Ralph answered

"What happens next, Mr. Walton?" asked Barbara.

"Next, the prosecutors must get their act together within forty-eight hours or there conceivably could be a slipup there. It all depends on the strength of the proposed charges that the government is alleging. The attorneys for the accused could demand a writ of *habeas corpus*. In other words, they could say either charge the accused or release him. I feel sure that there is enough cause to justify charges of kidnapping, racketeering, money laundering, attempted homicide, Medicare fraud, and who knows what other healthcare regulatory statute violations."

"Then what?"

"Bail is set for the accused. As soon as bail is set, individuals like Paretto can be released, and even though Paretto's hit man has been killed, there is still danger. Also, keep in mind that the cases against these people are all complex, intertwined, and will go on for months and months."

"Mr. Walton, I've heard nothing about Todd Langley, the associate administrator at Trinitus that I worked with. He was extremely helpful to me when I worked there. He told me that he knew too much about Qlozd, that if he ever left the hospital he would be targeted by Paretto's hit man."

"His name has not come up in any of our investigations," said Ralph. He winked at Andy. "Looks like he has just disappeared."

Ralph had hardly finished the sentence when his cell phone rang. He stepped out of the room to return the call. It was from Detective Bartlett.

\* \* \* \*

"Ralph, this is Blake Bartlett. I thought you might be interested in knowing about this: A call came a couple of hours ago from Judge Joberst's bailiff at the United States Court House. Judge Joberst has been reported as missing. He resigned his position as a federal judge and now can't be located.

"Thanks for the call, Blake. I'm sure the agency has been notified."

"We've checked hospital emergency rooms and put out an all-unit alert," said Blake. "The other reason for the call is to congratulate you on your recent crime sweep."

Ralph laughed. "Maybe they'll use these cases as teaching examples in the Police Academy instead of the other case three years ago."

He clicked his cell phone closed and returned to the group.

\* \* \* \*

"Excuse me for the interruption," said Ralph. "I received a call from the Dallas Police Department that I think will be of interest to you. He kept his eyes on Leanne as he continued. Judge Joberst has resigned and has been placed on the missing persons list."

The group was silent for several moments. Finally Leanne asked, "What can we do? We are still in danger then, aren't we?"

"We should continue the same protective measures for now. As soon as we see how the prosecution is progressing, I want all of you—all five of you—to disappear. I don't think you should take any chances. We are dealing with ruthless people here. Anthony Joberst, for example, will likely seek some sort of revenge."

The room became quiet as Ralph paused to let his words reach their mark. Each person in the group likely was thinking the same thing: They were facing a drastic change in lifestyle, and the danger was still out there.

Mark stood, stepped away from the group, and stared out the window as though in deep contemplation. He finally turned to Ralph. "What will happen to the Trinitus hospitals, Mr. Walton?"

"I think you know, Mark. I can't give you a definite answer right now, but here's what is most likely to happen: They will continue to stay open but will have totally new management. Many of the top executives, in addition to Alan Shipman, will face serious felony charges. The hospitals will undergo extensive audits by the OIG and will be assessed staggering fines. They will be forced into strict compliance agreements and will be subject to in-depth audits for eight or ten years. Of course, they also will have to fight to keep their accreditation and will be surveyed regularly by the Joint Commission for Accreditation of Healthcare Organizations. Likely, some of the Trinitus hospitals will be forced to close.

Mark looked at Andy. "Andy, would you please step outside with me for a minute. We need to talk."

"Sure, but I don't withhold anything from Barbara."

"And I won't from Leanne, so I guess I'll state my proposal right now before everyone."

"Would you like for me to leave?" asked Ralph.

"No, I think you already have guessed everything that I'm going to propose, Mr. Walton. Andy, considering the present circumstances, I know you will never be comfortable working for Trinitus. I am acquainted with the SMU people and I can get you transferred to our system and arrange for Barbara's employment in the same hospital. I know, and you know, that Barbara and Leanne have become very close, and it will always be that way. We can have the best of all worlds by staying together."

Andy looked at Barbara. He knew she would never leave Leanne. Their relationship was too strong now. How could he turn down the offer? He could never go back to Trinitus. He turned to Ralph. "Do you think we can all 'disappear,' as you have put it, and still stay together?"

"I have to tell you something that all of you need to know. At one time, I thought that Mark was a suspect in the kidnapping scheme—that he had engaged some underworld group to kidnap the baby, knowing that it was his child and wanting to keep it away from Judge Joberst. When I heard that Mark had a plan and when the ransom demands were so weak, I strongly suspected he was behind the abduction. During the investigation, I crossed paths with Alberto Marchesa's *consigliere*, Deo Carminagni. It finally dawned on me that it wasn't just coincidence that he showed up on the scene at this time—after the baby was abducted."

"So how did you learn that I had no intention of kidnapping QB?"

"I had only one way to find out for sure. I knew your father kept himself and his business far removed from Alberto. But I knew Deo Carminagni, Alberto's *consigliere* had gone to Nashville for some reason, and also I had reason to believe that your family bonds were strong—that you'd risk exposing yourself, your father, and your company to danger to recover your child. How could I not admire that? I had to get confirmation of my theory from your father."

"Are you are saying that you called on my father?" said Mark. "I never intended for him to have to face an FBI interrogation."

"I understand, Mark," said Ralph. "Your father did nothing wrong. He was concerned about your interests—about his grandchild." Mark settled back and the fire left his eyes. "He handled our interview with tact and confidentiality. I got the information I needed. Again, let me say that I admire your strong family bonds and loyalty. Take my word for it: No one except those of you in this room will ever know that Victor Marchesa requested assistance in this situation from a criminal at large, his brother, Alberto."

"I appreciate those words, Mr. Walton," said Mark.

"Back to my question, Mr. Walton," said Andy. "Can we all stay together?"

"Not in this country, Andy, said Ralph. "At Mark's request, his father had already arranged Mark's reassignment to the CareCompHealth Hospital in London. That was Mark's plan. He and Leanne, with the baby when it was found, would escape to London as soon as Leanne was able to travel. It was after the abduction that Mark's father appealed to Alberto to intervene and recover the baby."

"So now, Andy, the question is will you and Barbara go with us?" asked Mark.

Andy looked at Barbara. They held eye contact for a few seconds. Without saying a word, the flat look of seriousness on their faces quickly faded into broad smiles. Andy turned to Mark, and said with a falsetto English brogue, "We will be delighted to accompany you to London, ol' chap."

\* \* \* \*

## Dallas, DFW Airport

Marcello drove Deo to the DFW Airport and dropped him off at the American Airlines check-in station. Only a few car-lengths behind him, a black Malibu sedan followed and paused while Deo exited the vehicle. Marcello parked the car and came back to join Deo in the Admirals Club for a last-minute goodbye visit.

"Nice to have you back again, Deo," said Marcello as they sat in the lounge and sipped their scotch.

"Alberto and I will return, Marcello," Deo replied. "Maybe the next time we come over it won't be for such a highly charged visit."

"Let's hope not," he said. "But we did what we set out to do, didn't we?"

"Yeah, we did. We really did," Deo said, a pensive tone to his voice. "It really was a pleasure getting back into action—even if only for a short while. Marcello, Alberto will be pleased when I tell him how you performed."

"Cut the shit, Deo," said Marcello. "Just get him back here."

"He'll be back," said Deo, pointing to the briefcase full of documents.
"You think those papers will protect Al?"
"Yeah, I'm not worried about that."
"How do you know the FBI will live up to the agreement?"
Deo laughed. "Because they wouldn't want the world to know that you and I found the baby when they couldn't."
"Will Al stay legit when he comes back?"
"Absolutely! He would never betray Victor or Mark—or Mark's kid."
"What do you think about Gator? Will he get fair treatment?"
"I hope so. Of course, we'll never know. These documents protect Al, you, me, and Gator. I don't think they'd take a chance on misleading us."
Marcello glanced at his watch. "Time to leave, Deo."
"Yeah, see you soon, Marcello. Take care of things," Deo replied. They parted with a traditional *abrazo*. Deo started walking toward the departure gates. After no more than ten steps, he looked up to face Ralph Walton and Wes. He stopped dead still in his tracks.
"Damn it, Ralph," Deo said. "We have an agreement. What is this about?"
"Cool it, Deo," said Ralph, laughing. We just came to say goodbye—nothing more."
Mark Marchesa, standing behind Wes and Ralph, out of Deo's sight, stepped around Ralph to face a startled Deo. Mark glanced furtively toward Ralph and Wes before he spoke.
"Mr. Carminagni, I want to thank you," said Mark, extending his hand. "If you are able to communicate with my uncle, please let him know that QB, Leanne, and I will be forever grateful. We will be honored to welcome him back to the United States as a member of our family when he returns."
Marcello joined the group to offer a final farewell greeting to Deo as he walked away toward the international travel gate.

The End

978-0-595-41553-3
0-595-41553-9

Printed in the United States
75275LV00002B/547-594